FREEZING REIGN

L. A. GOFF

Freezing Reign
Written by L.A. Goff

ISBN: 979-8-9862929-0-8 (eBook)
ISBN: 979-8-9862929-1-5 (Paperback)
ISBN: 979-8-9862929-2-2 (Audiobook)

This book contains references to
violence, abuse, and addictions.

PRAISE FOR FREEZING REIGN:

"A superior dystopic Sci-Fi thriller with a Texas-sized scope. (L.A. Goff) develops the premise in intriguing ways and keeps the pace brisk throughout. Compelling and refreshingly unsentimental… with nightmarish overtones."

— KIRKUS REVIEWS

"Trust, betrayal, desperation, and existential ethics blend in a patiently unfolding, thought-provoking thriller that perfectly blends social critique with suspense. The premise of Freezing Reign is entrancing and enveloping, combining a variety of post-apocalyptic themes into an original, empowering, and addictive read."

— SELF-PUBLISHING REVIEW, ★★★★½

"Just when you think you've got a handle on this story, it will surprise you. Goff showcases what people are truly capable of… and musters up a great deal of girl power in a world with nearly no girls in it. Expect sadness, friendship, survival, and a little dash of romance in this empowering Sci-Fi."

— INDEPENDENT REVIEW

A unicorn has fallen into my lap. The experience is rare, and involves a difficult-to-articulate mix of voice, style, characters, and plot. And something else, like the scent of a mysterious spice, or the faint glitter of an undertone that feels almost magical. Freezing Reign by L.A Goff is one of those unicorns. This is the first time I've ever used the U-word in a review for any book I have ever read.

As someone who was once completely under the thrall of the Hunger Games, I say without the slightest reservation that I believe this book is better."

— THE INTERNATIONAL REVIEW OF BOOKS

To Dan, who never stopped asking his wife, "Will the book be finished soon?"

And to Claire, who often asked her little girl, "Want to stop by the library today?"

The answer to both questions was always yes.

"Women are never so strong as after their defeat."

— ALEXANDRE DUMAS, QUEEN MARGOT

"What misery to be afraid of death. What wretchedness, to believe only in what can be proven."

— MARY OLIVER

RED HEADED WOMAN

12 years after the Pathogen

ROSE STOOD IN front of the examination table wearing stiletto heels and nothing else. White silk puddled around her feet like snow. She was comfortable with her nudity and the engineer knew it. She wasn't comfortable leaving her gown on the dirty tile floor. The engineer should've known this, too. He'd built her to crave cleanliness.

As his magnifying glass roamed over her body, he mumbled about polyethylene and its solubility in water. He scribbled notes on a clipboard. In her brief experience with men, she'd discovered they were prone to contradictions. This particular human was far from clean. She could smell his perspiration along with a meaty odor coming from his mouth.

Contradiction. She searched for its synonyms. *Inconsistency, antithetical, a paradox.*

"Your skin is seamless," he said. The engineer's touch was all business. His fingers were sticky—warmer than the human temperature of 98.6 degrees Fahrenheit by at least two degrees. "No scars from the bullet wounds. These repairs are excellent… if I do say so myself."

"I traveled with the queen," she said. "I have proof of her existence. My written report documents her kidnapping—"

"Come now, Rose. You're a beautiful painting held in place by a rigid, binary canvas. The Mona Lisa should never wish to forsake her gilded frame and become the artist."

She studied the man in front of her, crunching the data at billions of ticks per second. His face was round, shiny, and red, like a wet cherry. Only the hair follicles around his ears continued to produce blond fuzz. The collar of his lab coat was 19.28 inches in diameter and stained the color of iced tea.

Running the calculations, she could've whitened his collar with six tablespoons of baking soda diluted in a cup of warm water. She could've snapped his neck by applying 1,248 pounds of torque with her manicured fingers. Rose did neither one.

Her head tilted when she detected a new sound. The squeak of rubber soles was distant, but growing louder. The obese man seemed oblivious as he continued to admire his work.

"I was concerned about discoloration, especially in the areas that suffered powder burns, but your flesh is smooth," he said. "That's good news for your resale value."

When the footsteps were outside the examination room door, the engineer jumped back with surprising agility. He held his breath. Without oxygen, his face darkened from cherry to raspberry. The squeak slowed, paused, and continued down the hall. He exhaled in a low whistle as the sound retreated.

"My written report is only 827 kilobytes," she said. "I can download the document in less than three seconds."

"Get dressed."

"The queen is being held against her will. I have information that could aid in her recovery."

"What?"

"My written report. Would you like to see it now?"

"Oh, that," he said. "No thank you, Rose. Your video recordings will be more than ample."

He lifted a battered clipboard from the table behind her. Despite the electronic devices around him, he insisted on printing paper. *Inefficient, counterproductive, wasteful.* As he flipped through her file, one puffy thumb attacked the end of an ink pen with repetitive clicks.

His arrogance didn't make her angry. Although his ego was too large for such an ignorant human, the crime of underestimating his own creation didn't deserve the death penalty. She let him live.

Rose did her best work when men assumed she was an empty-headed machine. She would've been proud of the sacrifices she made for the queen, but that emotion wasn't in her programming. According to the jokes in the lab, the buying public craved a more modest creature, so instead, the engineers allowed her to experience satisfaction.

They did not install that batch of code within her as a

gift. It was a tool, like dangling a carrot in front of a horse. The engineer believed she'd work harder if she was satisfied with her achievements. The side effect of this emotion, undiagnosed by everyone but herself, was a sensation she would've called ambition if anyone had asked.

Males were attracted to women with flower names because the company also sold an Iris, Daisy, and Violet. The engineer said her name was a compliment to her beauty but she had another theory. Perhaps flowers reminded men of happier times—the "before time" when they gave bouquets to the women they loved.

Her eyes struggled to look into a mirror and describe the image reflected there. For that reason, she stored the product description from her owner's manual. The words were exaggerated, little more than advertising copy, but the buyers either didn't notice or didn't care.

"Your new Rose has long stems and just enough thorns to keep life interesting! This green-eyed redhead is passionate and prone to jealous pouts if you're caught looking at another feminal," it read below her picture. "But don't worry, gentlemen. Your lady will always forgive you with her 4.0 wish-on-demand capabilities. This model includes our domestic care package for chef-quality meals and an encyclopedia of medicinal recipes to keep you feeling fine. For even more fun, spice things up with a new blond or brunette. Visit a Martinez Motion showroom to see our full line-up of feminal companions. Financing available with approved credit."

The engineers embraced the cliché of a woman with fiery, long hair and a short fuse. She was programmed to show the outward signs of several strong emotions including anger, fear, and jealousy. When confronted with sadness, her expression of pain was a full-body experience.

She was the only feminal model that required tear fluid as a part of her maintenance plan. The men in the lab couldn't understand why buyers would "toss down piles of gold to own a weeping and wailing woman" but her sales were robust.

If her only upgrade had been a fiery temperament, Earth's young queen would've died within days of her reanimation. But Rose had nursed the girl, took more than one bullet for the girl, and in the process, was forced to wear a dirty gown for several hours in a row.

Rose wasn't programmed to experience regret, and indeed, she felt none. She'd done everything in her power to save the child. Mankind was already on the endangered species list. And without their queen, the human race was finished.

She created a reminder on her calendar. *Fill up on tear fluid. Sad days are coming.*

PART ONE

Day 763 of the Pathogen

CHAPTER ONE

LIVING ON THE EDGE OF THE WORLD

WILLIAM SHAKESPEARE CALLED death an undiscovered country from which no traveler returns. He was wrong, of course. I took that mysterious trip, booked a return flight, and came home wearing a souvenir t-shirt… so to speak. But perhaps I should back up. My death feels more like the end of this story than the beginning.

I could explain the Olympic flu—how it spread and why it was so fatal to women. Most people would start there, like this is a boring dissertation on human viruses. A global pathogen has a way of demanding attention, and believe me, that beast ravaged my life. I should have a lot to say about it. And yet, after two years of conspiracy theories and quack remedies, I wonder if I died just so I could stop talking about it.

I'm going to begin with the moon. On this particular night, I needed it to be full. One sliver remained in the shadows and I resented its shyness. If I was prone to paranoia, and maybe I was, I would've accused that cold rock of conspiring against me.

With each mile, my nose edged closer to the steering wheel and the ten fingers gripping it. I itched to turn on the headlights, but I was out past curfew. Too many of the overnight patrolmen were dudes from my high school. And too many of the dudes from my high school were assholes.

Tall mounds of whiskey grass brushed the sides of the Jeep. Their featherlight touches were a protest against my off-road invasion… a thousand tiny warnings to turn back. There was never a good time to roll a vehicle down a steep embankment. But alone and after midnight? When they found me dead in the morning, no one would believe I'd had an accident.

The edges of something solid rose in front of me. Ghost-like at first, the lump was low to the ground, motionless, and as wide as my bumper. I jerked the wheel to the right, missing the boulder, but crashing into its ugly sister. The impact snapped my head forward. I bit my tongue. Hard. As if driving by the light of a less-than-full moon wasn't reckless enough, tears clouded whatever vision I had left.

The engine shook, coughed twice, and sputtered out.

Blood filled my mouth, drowning my curses and making me gag. I spit the coppery taste into the night. A cool wind, equal parts bluebonnets and manure, tugged at my stocking cap. Its stink was comforting. If Texas had a perfume, I was inhaling it.

As my pulse began to slow, the CB radio crackled with feedback. I jumped and bit my tongue again. The static was piercing, like the squeals of an electronic pig.

"Please God, don't let it be Papa," I said, groping for the volume knob.

If he'd caught me sneaking out of the house, the punishment waiting for me would've been custom-made. Whippings and groundings and "bed without dinner" weren't manipulative enough for my papa. He'd make me memorize Ten Ways to Contract a Pathogen or give me homework from The Layman's Guide to Viruses… a current best seller. And if he was really upset, I'd get a dose of "since your mama died, you're all I have left in this world."

The shame of disappointing him could make me nauseous for days. No exaggeration. Long guilt trips gave me motion sickness. He knew that, of course, and used guilt like a scalpel in his medical bag.

"Mirari? Do you copy?"

The voice coming through the speakers was familiar but not family. Each word had an artificial growl—the sound of a boy pretending to be a man. I wasn't fooled. Unlike my papa, I could make this kid wait.

With the sleeve of my sweatshirt, I dabbed my eyes and wiped the sticky mixture of tears, blood, and snot around my mouth. The rearview mirror wasn't much help. With only the dim light from the CB radio, my brown skin was an inky gray and the contours of my face were deep and exaggerated.

"Mirari? You got your ears on? This is Lady Killer, over."

That ridiculous name got me reaching for the mic… as

he no doubt knew it would. "Ten-nine, Aaron. Please repeat. Did you say Lady Killer?"

"My handle makes Lili laugh," he said.

"Well, yeah, your sister has a morbid sense of humor." I leaned my forehead against the steering wheel and closed my eyes. "Is she awake?"

"In and out. Mostly out," he said. "I think the ventilator gives her bad dreams."

"It's gotta be helping her, right? What does the doctor say?"

"Not much. He just writes stuff down in her chart. But I'm not stupid… I can see."

Static from the radio crackled between us, giving our silence a buzz that hurt my teeth. I should've said something encouraging but I lived in a house with grief. Cliches like "remember the good times" and "going to a better place" made me choke. Maybe our stillness was better than empty words. It was a pure thing, uncontaminated by whatever pitiful attempts I would've made to console him.

"Are you?" Aaron's voice broke. He coughed and cleared his throat. "Are you still coming to the ranch? The checkpoints are out tonight. There's a big one on Highway 71 with patrols in both lanes—"

"I'm staying off the paved roads. Guess who is riding shotgun with me?"

"Whoever he is, he better have a bullet in that gun. Dad's been drunk since lunch. No way will he let your boyfriend in the house."

"My boyfriend is a four-foot-tall, stuffed rabbit," I said. "He's an Easter gift for Lili."

"What about me? I could go for some chocolate eggs."

"If I had chocolate, I'd sell it down on the drag and buy a week's worth of food." I smiled but my mouth was stiff… out of practice. "I made you an angel food cake. Try to deserve it."

"Got it, good buddy. Stay northbound with the hammer down."

"Um, sure. Ten-four." I dropped the CB mic. And with one foot on the clutch and the other on the brake, I turned the ignition key. The Jeep's engine sprang back to life. My hands shook, weak with relief.

If the patrols caught me driving through the creek bed, my plan was to babble like I had the flu. Ridiculous, of course. Even a woman with a fever of 103 wouldn't waste fuel, not with the price of gasoline at $18.27 a gallon.

I understood the risks if I got caught. And using a scoring system where the pros and cons were each assigned a number, the advantages of seeing Lili one more time outweighed the risks by six points. This gave me permission to break at least three different laws in order to say goodbye to my best friend. I'd always had a thing for math, but now I clung to its clean structure like a life raft.

It took all of my concentration to keep the Jeep moving forward. Maybe that was a blessing. On most days, I was grateful for any distraction I could find. People who didn't cut their reality into easy-to-chew bites gagged on despair.

In early January, the Austin Advertiser began counting suicides as pathogen deaths. I despised the inflation of the numbers, suspecting it was a ploy to sell more newspapers, but Papa agreed with the manipulation of the data. He called these haunted souls "collateral damage in a global battle."

After years of debating Dr. Thomas Vega across the kitchen table, there was no such thing as a taboo topic. He encouraged me to balance logic with passion and believed both had value. But if my viewpoint lacked substance, the good doctor would push his plate to the side and demolish my arguments—sometimes bouncing between English and Spanish in the middle of a sentence.

Papa was an attractive man. If tall, dark, and handsome was the standard, he had two out of three. The ladies didn't mind that he stood three inches short of six feet. I saw it in the faces of the women we met. He'd go on and on about his cryogenic projects. They'd hang on his every word, like his research wasn't as dry as, well… dry ice.

A few of the more brazen ones pulled me aside to ask, "Is your father a medical doctor or does he have his PhD?"

"Yes," I'd say and watch their eyes widen. "He has both."

Texas Governor Owen Ferguson asked Papa to join a vaccination task force seven months into the outbreak. It was quite an honor. At that time, only a few thousand women a day were contracting the virus. The world still had hope for a cure. Mama was alive.

I was tired of talking about the pathogen, but Papa always gave it a seat at our kitchen table. He'd do his best to stay positive, telling me which cousin, neighbor, or friend was still alive. Maybe his recital of survivors was better than the sound of our chewing, but not by much.

"You call this flu a battle, but our side has no ammunition,"

I said with my mouth full of pinto beans. "This isn't a war. It's an extermination and I'm sitting in this house, waiting for the firing squad."

And yes, I know what we ate for dinner… on this night and every night. Travis County gave us a twenty-pound bag of the stuff each month. Soaked and simmered, they invited themselves to all three meals like an infestation of warm, brown bugs.

Papa's fork hovered in the air. One pinto bean rolled over the side and fell back to his plate. "That's a bit of an exaggeration, don't you think?"

"It's the stages of grief," I said. "I'm at the acceptance part."

"You're eighteen years old. You're still healthy. I know kids enjoy being morbid but—"

"Aaron said Lili's on a ventilator now."

I'll admit, I enjoyed watching Papa's face fall. It felt good to see his dark eyes, the same color as mine, fill with fear. His vague promises of my survival were irritating on a good day and downright infuriating on a day when my best friend was dying.

"Good Lord, I wonder how much Billy spent to make that happen."

"Or how many people he threatened to make that happen," I said. "Billy had the ventilator delivered to the ranch."

"Have her blood oxygen levels improved?"

I shrugged. "The machine is called a Bear. Aaron says it has more buttons and dials than his stereo."

"Must be a Bourns Bear. I've seen that unit, came out about three years ago."

"Maybe I can borrow Lili's ventilator when she's finished with it. Buy a few extra weeks before my final adios. What do you think, doctor?"

I'd gone too far, like I so often did after Mama died. Shame pricked at my cheeks with hot, little needles. But I was afraid to open my mouth… afraid to make it worse.

"Don't give up, Mirari. Take some of my hope if your supply is gone." He tossed down his napkin and walked out of the kitchen. A few seconds later, the back door closed behind him with a muffled click.

"See you at breakfast," I said to the empty table.

My escape plan—version four of the plan, to be precise— went off with military precision. I waited for the telltale glow of Papa's welding torch. With all of its cracks, the shed walls couldn't contain its brightness. No doubt he was wearing his dented, black safety helmet, looking like a thrift store Darth Vader. With his earplugs pushed in tight, he wouldn't hear a bomb going off.

I buckled the stuffed animal into the passenger's seat of my Jeep. On any other night, the bunny's blank stare through the windshield would've made me smile. I hauled Papa's gas can out of the garage and filled my tank, calculating the cost with each gurgle. Round trip, this drive was a $50 adventure and that's if I didn't count the ingredients in Aaron's cake. Everything was a go at 11:50 p.m. except for me.

Men caught driving the city streets after curfew paid a fine. Women were publicly shamed as "carriers" with their faces all over the KZZI-TV, Channel 40 news. If I got stopped, the patrolman would take one look at me and jump back as if I were a rattlesnake. He'd call for medical assistance. And we'd sit by the side of the road… avoiding conversation, avoiding eye contact, and avoiding the same airspace.

When the ambulance crew arrived, the paramedics would be covered from head to toe in stiff plastic. They'd fall into their standard protocols to keep me as germ-free as possible. I'd seen pictures of them on television, breathing through oxygen tanks or cone shaped masks that gave them beaks.

Once they determined I wasn't driving around with a high fever, the paramedics would escort me back to Dr. Thomas Vega, but not without giving me a stern warning. "Listen here, young lady," they'd say at the beginning of their lecture… the four words I hated most.

A crucial part of my plan was to look like a man, or at the very least, like a teenage boy. I borrowed Papa's gray Stanford sweatshirt from the back of his closet. The fit was baggy, but the waistband hit me right where it should. My height came from my mama's side of the family, along with her barely controllable curly brown hair that became completely uncontrollable during a rainstorm.

In a hurry, I shoved the whole mess into a black stocking cap. Frizzy strands escaped every time I turned my head. Digging through Mama's old make-up case, I found a pair of rubber bands and wrapped them around my braids. The coils made my head look lumpy under the cap, but my disguise must have worked. It was good enough to fool a man who'd been drunk since lunch.

As I walked up Lili's driveway, a double click froze me where I stood.

"Whatcha doin' here, boy?"

A cigarette flickered under the front porch. The yellow tip flamed bright red as the man sucked in a drag. His eyes were half closed, but not relaxed. They watched me.

"You hear me? We shoot trespassers round these parts," he said.

"Sir, it's me… um, it's Mirari." I pulled off the stocking cap and my braids swung free. "I brought Lili a gift. I know it's late, but I can't come during the day with the patrols. It's an Easter bunny."

"How'd you get here, girl?"

Billy missed the first step as he stumbled off the porch. The shotgun bounced in his arms and I flinched as the muzzle's aim danced between my heart and the center of my forehead. The cigarette was still burning between his fingers. It should've been too hot to hold.

"I drove the Jeep with the headlights off," I said. "It's almost a full moon so I was able to follow the creek bed once my eyes adjusted."

I remember how he laughed at me. It wasn't one of those terrible laughs a man uses to scare a woman when he's feeling drunk and mean. This laugh spread through his whole body. He doubled over from the power of it and I smiled despite myself.

"You're something else, ya know that?" He flicked the cigarette into the grass, ignoring every fire warning in Travis County. "I've got men working for me, real tough guys, who wouldn't be brave enough or crazy enough to drive through that creek with no lights on."

"The checkpoints are out tonight. It was the only way I could—"

"Aaron." He lifted his chin and bellowed his son's name again. "Aaaaron." A lamp inside the house clicked on. Its light outlined the body of a tall, skinny boy. "Take Mirari up to see Lili."

"Yes, sir," Aaron called back.

"I don't trust that doctor." Billy leaned in as if he were telling me a secret. "You let out a holler if he's up there sleepin' on the job."

"I will, Mr. Martinez."

"You should call me Billy," he said and reached for one of my braids. I could smell the tobacco on his fingers as he ran them down the twisted strands. "I appreciate you stopping by, honey. It means, uh, means a lot."

"Lili is my best friend."

"Loyalty… that's good There ain't much around no more. There ain't much of nothin'—" Billy swayed. His grip on my hair tightened, like he needed a rope to stay on his feet.

I knew this man. I'd grown up playing with his kids and riding ponies through his fields. But as we stood in the dark, his alcohol-soaked grief scared me. I was going to leave those strands behind if he didn't let go. Just as the pull against my scalp became painful, the tension eased. My braid fell from his hand.

Hugging the stuffed animal, I jogged toward the house. Billy didn't follow me, and yet, his eyes had a weight. I carried that heavy stare on my back until Aaron shut the door behind us.

"Oh, I forgot. Your cake is still in the Jeep," I said. "Do you want to grab it while I take this to Lili's room?"

"The doctor won't let you in. But I put a chair in the doorway so you can see her. There's a tape player, you know, if you wanna play her some music." Aaron swallowed. "I think she likes it."

Even in the warm lamplight, his always-tan face looked pale. His amber eyes were tired, and below them, his cheekbones had a new sharpness. He'd grown since the last time I'd seen him… in height if not in pounds. I couldn't call him a shrimp anymore. This fourteen-year-old was taller than me now. His jeans were an inch too short and his shaggy, dark hair was several inches too long. It was a mess Lili would've trimmed if she'd had the strength.

"Happy Easter, Mirari," he said. And with a crooked grin, he reached out to wiggle the rabbit's ears.

I appreciated the effort, but his cheerful act was all wrong. Not fake exactly, but forced, almost desperate. The kid who lived for the next prank, the kid who followed Lili and me around the ranch like a wise-cracking puppy, was growing up. Or maybe just growing old.

"I'll go get the devil's food cake you made me with all the chocolate frosting," he said.

"This place has enough devils." I gave him my own sad excuse for a smile and pushed him toward the front door. "It's angel food cake for you."

The house felt empty after he left. A grandfather clock at the top of the stairs made the only sound. We'd been warned as kids never to open its doors or play with the chains inside.

The gears were sensitive… the pendulum easy to break. As I climbed the wooden staircase, the ticking of that old clock seemed to get slower with each step.

Winding down.

My walk toward her bedroom felt eternal. I'd rehearsed what I wanted to say. But outside her door, all of that was forgotten. I saw her body lying in the hospital bed, a ravaged body I couldn't recognize, and I snapped.

"What did you do to her hair?"

The guy with the stethoscope barked out a yelp. When he whirled around, the clipboard in his hands went flying. He looked like a kid wearing a lab coat for Halloween. Papa told me medical students were leaving before graduation because hospitals were desperate for help. Maybe even someone as rich as Billy Martinez could only get a wannabe physician for his daughter.

"We made the decision to shorten her hair. With the fever and ventilator mask, it was best," he said as he scrambled to reassemble his chart.

Lili's beautiful chestnut waves were gone. And where his scissors had cut too close, bald patches of skin dotted her scalp. Clear plastic covered most of her face. I wanted to hold the bluish-colored fingers resting on the top of her blanket and look for the birthmark on the inside of her arm… anything to remind myself that this stranger was my best friend.

Young or not, the doctor wouldn't let me touch her. I sat in the hall and listened to the whooshing sound of the ventilator. In less than a minute, I understood why Aaron told me about the tape player. The steady, mechanical rhythm of the Bourns Bear was mind-numbing.

"Can Lili understand me if I say something?"

"She's semiconscious," the doctor said.

"Does that mean yes?"

When he turned away from Lili to look at me, his gaze softened—maybe because I was a girl with braids holding a giant Easter Bunny on her lap. "Speak loud and slow," he said. "That helps."

"And you'll be like a priest and keep the secrets I'm about to say?"

"Tell you what, I could use a cup of coffee. You stay in the hall. If anything starts beeping, come get me."

I moved away from the door, giving him a clear path around my airspace. He followed the protocols and kept his distance. We both knew I'd catch this flu sooner or later, but he didn't want to be the man who pushed me into the grave. When he disappeared around the corner, I sat down in the chair.

"Um, hi. This is Mirari."

I articulated each syllable like she wore hearing aids and the batteries were dead. We could tell each other anything. From petty peeves to pinky-swear promises, nothing was off limits. But this one-way conversation was awkward as hell.

"I'm here to haul your royal butt out of bed. I think you got what it takes to be the next Miss Texas... or even the next Miss America. Come on, look at all these crowns you've won."

This wasn't the upbeat banter I'd planned, but I kept talking. "If you need moral support, I'll enter the next pageant with you... just like old times.

"I refuse to tape my boobs together. Sorry, that was too gross. But hey, I'll shave my bikini line. What's a little razor burn between friends? And maybe I'll get lucky and win fifth runner-up or best eyeshadow or something. We'll walk the stage together."

I counted twenty-seven beeps from the Bourns Bear before I could go on. "It's gotta be together because you get my weird hunches. You don't laugh when I know which contestant secretly hates you, and which pervert judge has the hots for you, and when the fix is in for another girl to win... even though she isn't half as pretty as you. I'm good at predicting your victories, you know it's true.

"Just please come back to me, okay?" My plea faded into a whisper and then into nothing but air. A sob pushed against my chest. If I'd let it out, a million more would have followed. It killed me that I couldn't touch her. I wanted to hold her hand and push my strength through her skin, like a transfusion of energy.

"I brought you a Texas-sized stuffed rabbit. He's going to sit inside your door and stand guard. He can gobble up ghosts, the Boogeyman, or El Muerto like a plate of raw vegetables. He's protected me since Mama died and now his superpowers are here for you."

The stairs creaked—the sound carrying down the hall like a warning shot. The doctor would've been pissed if he'd found me standing in Lili's room. Moving fast, I propped the stuffed rabbit against the wall and turned its button eyes toward the ventilator.

"Hey listen, your doctor might be sexy under his mask,

like Bruce Springsteen but without the arm muscles," I said from the foot of her bed. "You should check him out but, um, don't let him cut your hair again."

And that was it. My final words to Lili were as empty as cotton candy… all beauty pageants, Easter bunnies, and cute guys. We'd been friends since the first grade and this was the best I could do. Maybe it was the goodbye she would've wanted. At least, that's what I told myself as I drove home with the headlights on.

Screw the patrols. I needed to see where I was going.

CHAPTER TWO

FADE AWAY

WAS HALF ASLEEP as I cooked Papa's bacon. When I closed my eyes, the sound was comforting, like rain falling on a tin roof. Meat was a luxury item in Texas. Even with all its ranches and livestock operations, Travis County gave us two protein coupons per week. Burning that bacon would've been a sin.

"Wake up," I said and slapped my face.

Mama taught me how to cook in this kitchen. And even before I was tall enough to wear her aprons, I craved precise directions. She teased me for being too meticulous.

"You aren't performing a surgery in here. Relax," she'd say. "Behind every delicioso dish, there should be a messy kitchen."

I would arrange everything I needed before cracking a single egg. She would whisk pinches and handfuls in her bowl… with ingredients dusting every surface including her face. I'd use a measuring cup and wrap the cord around the mixer in a clockwise motion before putting it away. Mama's food always tasted better than mine, even if her measurements were never as precise.

My earliest memories are jumbled flashes of her body swaying between the living room furniture. She'd take my hand and we'd move to the tight harmony and piercing brass sounds of Banda El Recodo. Or when it was time for my nap, she'd put a Ritchie Valens record on the stereo and hum along as he sang "We Belong Together."

Other memories are clearer. At Lili's seventh birthday party, Mama kicked off her heels to rescue my friend's kite from the clutches of an oak tree. "Hold this," she said, handing me her purse. "I'm going up there."

Her beautiful legs looked a mile long as she leapt from branch to branch. I swelled with pride as I watched her climb, but the women around me puffed up with a darker emotion. They called Mama a "show off" and a "public spectacle." Their solution was to send up a ranch hand or "for heaven's sake, just buy the child another toy."

Mama received polite applause when she returned the kite into the birthday girl's hands. She also received a decade of tiny scratches from this group of mothers… a pack she named the Carpool Cats. They never declared outright war. But with a wave of their red fingernails, they'd assign her to work the dish room at the PTA carnival or iron a pile of wrinkled band uniforms before the big game.

"Empty boxes can be wrapped in shiny paper," Mama

told me once. "Don't be fooled by the outside, Mirari. Those sad women are nothing but pretty packages filled with air."

She continued to volunteer at my school, but Papa wasn't blind to their sharp claws. He didn't invite that crowd to Mama's fortieth birthday party. Instead, he let me in on the surprise he'd planned—a gift she would treasure more than the expensive clothes and jewelry so many Texas women craved.

Her eyes narrowed when she saw the blindfold in her husband's hand. Mama was a free spirit, but she liked to control which way her spirit would blow. To drag out the excitement, Papa led her out the front door, down the steps, and through the grass in winding loops. The anticipation was excruciating.

When he removed the blindfold, Mama blinked. Her mouth opened and snapped shut. She shook her head, like she didn't believe this gift was real… and really for her.

"Surprise!" My shrill cry made her jump. "Happy Birthday, Mama."

She walked and then ran toward the shiny, blue Jeep. I would have broken my ankle, but Mama's legs were graceful in her platform sandals. She did two laps around the vehicle, touched the special edition Levi's patch on the door, and sprinted back to her husband.

With the added inches of her high heels, she was taller than him, but he was stronger. The muscles in his arms strained against his t-shirt as he spun her in a circle. Mama's brown curls swirled and fell on his shoulders like a curtain.

"Thomas," she said, soft as a whisper. "Gracias, mi amor. It's, well, it's just too much."

Pretending to frown, he dropped her to her feet. "Well, if it's too much, I could take it back to the dealership."

"No way," I said before she could answer. "Come on, Mama. We're gonna make some dust fly. Can we take the top off? Ooh, look… even the seats say Levi's."

"We'll be rolling down the road in a pair of jeans." She grabbed the keys from Papa's outstretched hand. "Mirari is as excited as I am. Wanna come along?"

"No, Evelyn. The two of you should go," he said. "You'll look like sisters with your hair flowing in the wind. Mine's too short to fly anywhere."

I presented my gift to Mama once we got rolling. With the smell of Christmas on my fingers, it wasn't a big surprise. The air freshener was in the shape of a pine tree. I hung it on the rearview mirror and it swung from side to side, counting each mile.

She found a stretch of deserted highway. And when she put her foot down, the V8 engine rocketed us forward. "As soon as I get home, I'm looking under the hood," she said. "It feels like your papa's been tinkering to give me more power, probably messed around with the exhaust manifold."

We'd never had a vehicle with air conditioning and Mama said it was a shameful luxury. Whether it was a waste of gas or not, she turned it on. The Texas heat could be brutal at slow speeds. She compromised with herself, letting the vents blow cold air when we were stuck in traffic. But when the highway opened up, we put the top down so the wind and the sun could swirl around us.

That summer, she and I lived on the roads around Austin.

Her new 1975 Renegade took us from the shaded Victorian houses and bungalows of Hyde Park to the old trails near the top of Mount Bonnell. One week after her birthday, Papa replaced the factory AM radio with an AM/FM stereo and cassette tape player.

I was her trusted copilot, always there to pull a map out of the glove box, open a bottle of Coke, or change the music to fit our mood. I never complained about the heat or the bugs or the times when we got turned around. This good-natured attitude wasn't because I was a quiet, obedient child. My plan was to show her I could remain calm and make mature decisions. My plan was to get behind the wheel… and she knew it.

One July day, away from the cautious eyes of her husband, Evelyn Vega handed the keys to her fifteen-year-old daughter. We were on an empty county road forty minutes west of Austin. She picked a good spot. There were no trees, no deep ditches, and no witnesses.

"Alright, Mirari," she said. "Let's see what you can do."

I wanted to impress her. My voice cracked as I repeated every word of her instructions. She talked me through how to get the Jeep rolling—adjusting my mirrors, finding the clutch, and starting the vehicle in neutral. I memorized each step.

"Some people say to watch your speedometer, but the engine will tell you the right moment to shift gears," she said. "Just listen for it."

"My ears aren't the problem. I don't understand how only two feet can be on the gas pedal, the brake, and the clutch at the same time. It doesn't make sense."

She didn't lose her patience with me. She let me slap the steering wheel in frustration, never saying a word until I was ready to turn the key and try again. By the time school started, I could've driven myself if the state of Texas, Westlake High School, and my papa would have allowed me. All three were opposed to underage driving.

I learned something about her that summer. She had a house, a manicured lawn, and a husband who loved her. Add a frilly apron and she could've starred in her own black and white sitcom, like a Latina version of Donna Reed.

But inside that Jeep? Mama was pure technicolor… so vibrant and beautiful that my eyes stung when I watched her. Behind the steering wheel, she blazed her own path. We'd get lost, get stuck, and still get out of every scrape before dinner time.

A part of her stayed in the front seat with me even after she was gone. She didn't take on the shape of a ghost… nothing haunted or spooky. Instead, she was a golden glow I could almost see out of the corner of my eye.

Papa felt her presence most around the dinner table. I pretended not to notice the way he looked at her empty chair, the way his eyes would widen when he heard a noise at the back door. Did his heart leap to see her face again only to have his brain punish him with the truth? I was no psychiatrist, but I had a hunch as to why he spent most nights out in his shed. It was the one place she never went during the pathogen.

"I think Thomas is secretly building an ice cream machine out there," Mama had said. "Quite the production.

I'm not interested in a tour until he can make us a bowl of Rocky Road."

She felt "under the weather" a week later and locked herself in the guest room. Papa was the only person allowed inside. I read her books through the door and rehashed the plot of her favorite TV shows even though the networks aired nothing but re-runs.

Each day, the voice on the other side got weaker until I was talking to myself. I should've stopped babbling, but it hurt too much. It was as if her tired lungs were breathing my words and I had to keep going or she'd suffocate.

One Tuesday morning, I knocked on the door. "Papa, is she awake?"

The footsteps coming toward me were slow. When the door opened, he fell into my arms. I was tall enough to look over his shoulder and see the bed centered between two, small windows. The light flickered with hundreds of dust motes. They rode the sunshine down to the white sheet Papa used to cover her body.

I wasn't sure if he was shielding me from the horrors of her sunken face or from the horrors of my own impending death. My sobs were for Mama… mostly. Maybe a few had my name on them. Standing this close to her, it was hard to believe in Heaven and even harder not to.

She never saw the supposed ice cream machine in the shed. And after she was cremated, I didn't have the heart to go out there without her. I didn't have the heart to do much as I sat in the house and waited for my first symptoms to appear. Would it start with a fever or a tightness in my chest?

Papa never asked, "How are you feeling?" He'd touch my cheek or rest his fingertips on the back of my neck. His hands were doing more than giving comfort. He was checking for the telltale heat that would make me shiver despite my burning skin. Other than the natural flush of doing the dishes or boiling another batch of pinto beans, my skin stayed cool.

I can't say we relaxed as the weeks went by, but we fell into a routine. My sorrow had a manic energy. Room by room, I organized every closet, washing and pressing Mama's clothes before hanging them up. I experimented with recipes to make our meager rations go further. My refried beans with bits of wild onion were tasty. The bean pie I concocted was an inedible pile of mush and a sad waste of our flour and lard.

While cleaning the garage, I chipped away at our deep freezer and found an unopened package of bacon. Saliva flooded my mouth. I held the meat for so long that my fingers burned from the cold. And if I'm being honest, I considered gobbling up every bite and leaving Papa nothing but the smells. I'm not proud of that. After a few deep breaths, my conscience overpowered my appetite.

"A surprise," I said as I put it back. "An Easter breakfast surprise."

I fried it now on four hours of sleep. As tired as I was, Papa had to be more exhausted. The light in his shed was still blazing when I'd crept back into the house after midnight. But if he was asleep, I suspected he wouldn't stay that way for long. The aroma of bacon was too tempting

"Holy cow," he said from the kitchen doorway. "Or maybe I should say holy pig."

"Hot out of the frying pan and just for you."

The last time we'd sat at this table, I'd been a brat with my "waiting for the firing squad" speech. Bacon seemed like a good way to apologize.

I knew he was hurting. Parents should never bury their children. It puts cracks in a giant celestial hourglass somewhere, spilling sand and threating the natural order of life.

And yet, on this Easter morning, I couldn't understand the depth of his pain. I didn't recognize the panic behind his eyes for what it was… raw despair. Papa loved me. I got that. But I had no idea how far he'd go to keep me alive.

"This is pure bliss," he said with a mouthful of bacon. "What a perfect way to start the day."

"I'll need to put on a dress before we leave. It's the same one I wore to Mass last year, but nobody will remember."

"It's not safe for you to be in a crowd." He held up a hand like a traffic cop at a busy intersection. "And before the debate begins, I know you are tired of these four walls."

I dropped my face before he could see the guilt in my eyes. It was too soon for him to notice the empty gas can but it wouldn't be long. Maybe he'd blame the neighbors. We had more than a few who were unemployed now.

"You must be lonely," he said. "I know I've been gone a lot. But I've got a surprise for you, too. I'm ready to show you what's inside—"

The telephone on the kitchen wall rang, interrupting him and making both of us stare at the hateful, green box. It was a constant deliverer of bad news.

"Here, eat a few slices. I'll see who's calling us at this

ungodly hour." He pushed the plate toward me and reached for the handset as it rang again.

"Bueno," he said into the receiver. When Papa was a little boy in Mexico City, operators connected each call. He said his traditional greeting was a habit he never outgrew… a way to test the phone's sound quality.

The voice on the other end of the line wasn't low enough to be Billy Martinez or one of the other men from the lab complaining about late shipments or another failed trial. We got those calls daily. I kept a pencil and paper near the phone so I could deliver messages with more detail than just, "Tell Dr. Vega to call Ted in accounting."

Billy invited my papa to become an investor and co-owner of Advanced Cryo Technology Incorporated the day before my thirteenth birthday. Mama made a cake to celebrate both of our achievements, although mine wasn't much of an accomplishment. All I did was fall asleep, wake-up, and the calendar told me I was a teenager.

Papa worked hard for his slice of cake. He became the champion of the working man at ACTI… settling Billy's disputes with the union, lobbying for better equipment, and remembering his secretary's birthday with flowers.

"I'm sorry," he said into the telephone. "So very sorry, son. Did the doctor check for a pulse?"

This wasn't a work call. I dropped the bacon between my fingers without taking a bite. The person on the other end was talking fast. Words rained down on my papa with so much force he swayed from the impact. I was on my feet before making the decision to stand.

"You're too young to drive that truck over here by yourself. Can you put him to bed? See if he'll sleep it off?" Papa's voice was hoarse with emotion. "Wake up the ranch hands. Tell them you need help controlling Billy. Did the doctor call an ambulance?"

As he paced in front of me, the long cord wrapped around his chest, but he didn't seem to notice. "Aaron?" Papa was yelling now. "Aaron, stay with me. Is an ambulance on the way?"

I walked toward him with halting steps, impatient to know what was happening and yet dreading what he'd tell me. My stomach cramped. Acid forced its way into my mouth and sat on the back of my tongue... like a poison killing me from the inside.

I knew this call would come. I knew it the night before when I couldn't recognize the girl lying in the center of Lili's four-poster bed. Pageant crowns, silk sashes, and gold scepters had lined the shelves around her room, standing at attention in a silent vigil. They didn't mock her unconscious body with a gaudy show. Instead, their sparkle was dimmed, as if they were already mourning the death of their queen.

CHAPTER THREE

GROWIN' UP

I CARRIED AARON'S BREAKFAST, balancing the tray in one hand as I opened the guest room door. Even in the dim light, I couldn't miss the purple bruise above his left cheek or the cut on his bottom lip. The dried blood was the color of rust. He laid on the bed—awake and fully dressed right down to his socks.

"Are you hungry? I reheated six slices of bacon and added a few raisins to the oatmeal. Do you like the instant kind? Lili always did but I wasn't sure if you…"

My voice trailed off. I'd been in the room for less than a minute and I was already saying dumb ass things. The dishes rattled as I put the tray on his nightstand. To give my hands something to do, I arranged the plates and straightened his knife and fork.

His swollen mouth remained closed. Maybe this was a

"get out so I can grieve in peace" message, but I wasn't leaving until he ordered me to go.

"I promised myself, no talking about Lili until you're ready," I said. "And I can't even ask what kind of oatmeal you want without mentioning her name. You should've heard me outside her room. I didn't say half of the things I wanted to. I didn't tell her how much I missed her laugh or how, just last week, I picked up the phone to call her and then remembered that she couldn't answer."

This would've been the right moment to let him talk. But instead, I sucked in a big gulp of air and kept going. "I've had a lot of practice saying goodbye. We all have, I guess. It's just… I don't think the right words exist anymore. Not for the poor patient who is sick. And certainly not for the family she leaves behind.

"When Mama died, the phone rang nonstop and everyone said the same thing. 'I'm sorry for your loss. I'm sorry for your loss. I'm so, so sorry.' After the ninth or tenth call, I literally puked. Did I ever tell you that?"

He reached out. His long, thin fingers were warm on my skin. They curled around my wrist like he was going to lead me somewhere. "Instant oatmeal is good," he said. "Thanks for making it."

"Did you get any sleep? How are your ribs? Papa doesn't think they're broken. Do you need more aspirin?" I stood and my arm hit his water glass. "Oh, crap. I'll get a towel."

"No, just help me sit up."

I grabbed two pillows and put them behind his back. Even though the room wasn't hot, the hair on his forehead was damp. His jaw was tight, making him look older than his fourteen years.

"Should I feed you?" I asked. "I don't mind."

He coughed out a laugh and grimaced. Even that slight movement seemed to make his side ache. "I can do it. Just move the tray closer."

Eager to help, eager to give him the care Lili would've given, I arranged the dishes so his breakfast was in easy reach. I opened the napkin and placed it on his lap.

"Oh, your powdered milk is still in the kitchen," I said. "I'll be right back."

"No, don't leave. Stay here while I eat… talk to me."

I sat down on the edge of his bed. The staying part was easy but finding a safe topic of conversation was impossible. How could I comfort a boy who lost his sister and took a beating on the same day? After babbling on and on, now I had nothing to say.

He crunched into the bacon. "I'm pretty decent in the kitchen," he said as he picked up another slice. "At least, Lili always said I was."

"Then it must be true because she never lied. What's your best dish?"

"Meatloaf."

"Not carne guisada or chile verde?"

"Nope. Meatloaf with lots of ketchup and brown sugar on top." He pushed his oatmeal around with a spoon. If he was searching for sugar in that bowl, he'd be stirring for a long time. A five-pound bag would've eaten half of my monthly food coupons. I'd used honey to sweeten his angel food cake… a kitchen experiment that had actually gone right.

"What's been your best dish during the rationing?" I asked.

"Meatloaf with less ketchup and brown sugar on top."

I smiled. "Okay, rich boy. I get it. Your dad doesn't struggle like the rest of us to keep a well-stocked kitchen."

"The money he spends on whisky could buy meat for an entire neighborhood," he said. "But he's not all bad. When we butcher a cow, sometimes he gives the cheaper cuts to his men. And he brought in a doctor when our head housekeeper got sick. Didn't hesitate to reach for his wallet."

"And other times?"

"Other times he takes a swing at his son with a fireplace poker because his beautiful Lili is gone. The ambulance took her away. She was the spitting image of his dead wife and I'm not. I look too much like the face he shaves in the mirror… except younger and faster. Which is why my ribs are bruised but not broken."

He didn't cry. He didn't even raise his voice as he talked about his father, and somehow, that made the abuse even harder to hear. I wanted to be outraged with Aaron. Instead, it felt like I was outraged for him, like he didn't believe he had a right to be angry.

"Don't go home. Stay here with us." My invitation was impulsive and maybe even reckless. I had no idea if Billy would come looking for his son. All I could see was Aaron's face. The purple and green bruise was a puffy smear of ink on his skin that I needed to wipe away.

"I can't leave Dad alone," he said. "He'll kill himself."

"So your plan is to let him kill you instead?"

He shook his head. And pushing down on the mattress, he struggled to sit taller against the pillows. It might have been an unconscious move, but it forced me to look up.

"At least stay with us until the wake and the burial," I said. "Papa won't mind."

"There ain't gonna be a burial. Do you think Travis County will give us her body back? Not even the vast political influence of a sober Billy Martinez can make that happen. And no way is he sober. His drunk rants won't get him very far with the health department. Lili will be cremated when a spot opens up."

The last wake I'd attended was before the rationing began. A few of the family members were brave enough to gather in the same room with the deceased, sharing tears and stories from the past. Most paid their respects only long enough to get the free food and alcohol. Men shoved beer bottles under their suit coats. Women filled their purses with spicy meatballs and deviled eggs. It had been a twisted, drive-thru version of the long vigils I'd sat through as a little girl.

"We can celebrate Lili's life in our own way," I said. "Just you, me, and Papa… if you'll stay."

"I don't know." He rubbed his face, wincing when he touched a bruise.

"Does your dad know you're gone? He hasn't called, hasn't asked about you or the truck." Maybe it was cruel to rub salt in his wounds, but he knew I sucked at being subtle. "Listen, Papa could go by the ranch and pack a suitcase for you.

Maybe sneak into the kitchen for a few pounds of ground beef. I need to taste this meatloaf I've heard so much about."

He almost grinned. "I'm warning you. Any woman who puts my meatloaf in her mouth will fall in love with me."

"Sure thing, Lady Killer," I said and rolled my eyes. "So will you stay?"

"If your papa can get all the ingredients, including the brown sugar, I'll stay."

Aaron pulled his best dish out of our oven three days later. He wouldn't let me help, even when he had to catch his breath as he moved from the refrigerator to the stove and back again. The tangy scent of ketchup mixed with the ground beef, onion, and spices. My mouth watered. But after several warnings from the chef to "let the meatloaf rest," I kept my hands to myself and set the table.

"This is a special occasion," Papa said. "Get your mama's best dishes. We're going to eat better than any house in the neighborhood and look good doing it."

Once we were settled around our feast, I cleared my throat, held up my fork, and made a toast. "This dinner is dedicated to the memory of Liliana Raquel Martinez. She was a wonderful sister and best friend. I don't know if there is meatloaf in Heaven. But if anyone can talk God into springing for extra ketchup and brown sugar, it will be Lili."

All three of us raised our first bites into the air and made them disappear. As we told our favorite Lili stories, we piled more food on our plates... a true compliment to Aaron's cooking skills and Papa's knack for diplomacy. He'd come back from the ranch that afternoon with all of the ingredients for dinner plus a suitcase bulging with Aaron's clothes, shoes, and electric toothbrush.

"Did you see Billy today?" My voice cracked, ruining my attempt to sound casual. Everyone at the table stopped chewing. "Did he ask about Aaron?"

Papa took a long drink of water before answering. "I didn't see him. I left a note with the kitchen staff, letting Billy know that his son will be spending the next few days with us. They were very kind."

"How did you distract them long enough to steal the ground beef?"

"You mean, did I create a diversion in order to raid their refrigerator? No need. I asked for the supplies and got everything we just enjoyed. The ranch staff must appreciate this meatloaf, too. They have the recipe memorized."

Aaron tried to smile but the muscles around his mouth were tight. He was leaning at an unnatural angle, an arm braced on the table to keep himself upright. His skin had a clammy, unnatural shine.

"You pushed yourself cooking our dinner," Papa said. "Mirari, can you get the aspirin bottle under the sink?"

Aaron's water glass was empty, so I grabbed it on my way. "Thank you for the fantastic meal. I might not be head over heels in love after tasting your meatloaf, but I have a crush on you now."

Aaron sat up straighter. "The love will kick in when you crave it again tomorrow night."

"Did pick-up lines like that work with the girls at Fulmore Middle School?"

"I saved my best stuff for the teachers. I've got a thing for older women."

Papa cleared his throat, calling for a cease-fire between the two of us. "When the pain reliever hits your system, there is something out in the shed I want to show the two of you."

"Finally," I said. "He's been working out there forever. Mama thought it was an ice cream machine but after seeing the spare parts in the garage, I think Papa's building a robot."

"Maybe a robot that makes ice cream," Aaron said. "I'd walk to the shed half dead to see that."

When I sat down at the table, Papa turned in his seat and watched me without blinking. I squirmed under his gaze. Did I have ketchup around my lips? A green pepper stuck between my teeth? He examined my profile as if he were cataloging each feature.

"What's wrong?"

"Nothing," he said. "You look like your mother when we first met. Radiant… and so young."

He was stalling, using flattery to distract me, but I didn't push him to explain. I'd seen how strange Papa could act when he was on the verge of a big decision—how he could be both present and absent at the same time. Sometimes, he'd forget I was still in the room.

Aaron swallowed the aspirin without taking his eyes off the two of us. After years of living with Billy, the kid was trained to watch for sudden mood changes in grown men.

Papa rubbed his hands together. "It's too bad we don't have coffee or cigarettes anymore. I could use both right now."

"Want me to make some tea?"

"No, I'll be fine." He took a deep breath, maybe imagining the taste of tobacco and the hit of nicotine that would follow.

Papa was a proud "Marlboro Man" in graduate school until he met a pretty lady with asthma and decided to quit cold turkey. Mama knew she'd marry him when his clothes no longer smelled like smoke. After so many years, his sudden craving for a cigarette made me nervous.

He released the air in his lungs and relaxed his shoulders, rolling them in circles. When he twisted his head, the joints cracked. I'd seen this bizarre dance a thousand times. Class was in session and Papa was warming up for his lecture.

"Tell me what you know about ribonucleic acid," he said.

"Go ahead, Aaron." I nudged him with my elbow. "Take it away."

"Yeah right, I can't even spell it."

"If you don't understand how RNA works, you're not alone," Papa said. "Broadcasters dumb down the details every night on television. And that's okay. Probably for the best. Most people are carrying around as much fear as they can handle. So here's a crash course.

"The Olympic flu is a positive-strand RNA virus. I believe a recombination took place, where two viral genomes were present in the same cell and they switched strands. It's a good strategy for coping with genome damage. The resulting recombinant virus can be deadly for humans. The +ssRNA viruses were of the same species but divergent lineages."

"You've lost me," Aaron said. His face looked tired.

Papa gave him a sympathetic smile. "It's okay. The life

and times of ribonucleic acid aren't important for this conversation. Let's talk about the spread. Let's talk about what is happening inside the human body.

"Other than the equestrian sports and sailing, all of the athletes from the Montreal games were housed in the Olympic Village. It looked like one, giant structure in the pictures we saw but it was constructed with twin towers. That separation didn't slow the spread down, at least not much. Athletes, coaches, the Olympic committee, the press, and God knows who else walked through the village over the course of a few weeks… breathing the air, showering, eating, touching surfaces.

"People from ninety-two nations all in one place. People from ninety-two nations, each one with the ability to carry this new, mysterious virus back home. Some got sick while competing, but most didn't present symptoms until later— almost as if the virus was a nasty stowaway in their luggage.

"It's not a coincidence that Africa lags behind the rest of the world in flu deaths. Because of some scandal with rugby, about thirty countries boycotted the '76 Olympic games… most of them from Africa."

"The rates are climbing there now," I said, always a hopeless teacher's pet even when the lesson was at my kitchen table.

"And the fatalities will follow. Of course, you know, the mortality rate is much higher among women than men," Papa said. "But they aren't dying of the Olympic flu. Not really. Females are actually better at fighting viral infections than males. Estrogen seems to—"

"So why am I alive and Lili is dead?" Aaron wrapped an arm around his ribs, absently rubbing a spot on his back as he spoke. "We lived in the same house."

"A woman's ability to fight is her greatest weakness with this damn thing," Papa said. "The virus is activating a hyper-immunological response in females. It's triggering sepsis. And in its most severe form, which we are seeing every day now, a patient's blood pressure plummets and sepsis turns into acute septic shock. The body starves its own organs. You've seen the horrible pictures in the news… the organ failure and blackening of the extremities. And in the absence of acute shock, prolonged sepsis is causing respiratory weakness and severe muscle wasting."

"That's what happened to Lili." I swallowed but couldn't push down the emotions burning my throat. While Papa threw his technical words at us, the science felt personal to me.

"As a virus replicates itself, copy errors can occur and lead to alterations in its surface proteins or antigens," he said. "We call this drifting. It allows a virus to evade our immune system because it looks different than the original virus. So far, virologists can't keep up with the rapid RNA mutations. They are working around the clock to develop a vaccine for this variant before it evolves again."

"Dad says the scientists are trying to lasso a tornado with a piece of string," Aaron said.

"That's an interesting way to put it, but Billy is right. And meanwhile, the government keeps us distracted with promises of a cure and more meat in our monthly rations. We can blame the broken supply chains or blame the politicians. It doesn't change a thing. We get just enough food to keep from starving to death… just enough so the mobs don't storm the lawn of the White House."

Papa was more preacher now than teacher. His brown eyes were sharp, angry pinpoints of light. "There is a lot Uncle Sam isn't saying. And a lot of questions people aren't asking."

"Like what?" Aaron leaned closer to my papa.

"Like how in the hell will humans survive without women?"

CHAPTER FOUR

THE PROMISED LAND

THE SHED WAS overdue for a fresh coat of white paint. When I touched the door frame, tiny flakes fell into my hand. Anybody peeking over the hedges would've seen a tired shack, a place where a handyman might toss a broken tool or a flat tire. But if that same person noticed the solar panels on the roof? Curiosity might lead to some friendly trespassing.

"I'll lock the door behind us," Papa said. Before turning the deadbolt, he flipped a heavy switch on the wall. Lights, powerful enough to illuminate an open-heart surgery, filled every dark corner.

I winced. My eyes struggled to adjust to the brightness and make sense of what I was seeing. Aaron didn't hang back. He put his fingertips on a metal cylinder in the center of the room. It looked like an oversized keg of beer with enough storage to get the whole neighborhood tipsy. The top of the tank stopped an inch below the peaked, wooden roof of the shed.

"Is this where the ice cream is stored? The metal feels cool but not cold." He looked at the square thermostat attached to the cylinder and turned to face Papa—his eyes wide with confusion. "This can't be right. What temperature is a normal freezer?"

I studied the dial over his shoulder. "Not this cold. No way could we eat Rocky Road ice cream at -320 degrees Fahrenheit," I said. "We'd freeze our taste buds off."

"Sorry to disappoint you. That tank isn't filled with ice cream." Papa leaned against the door and watched us with a satisfied grin, clearly enjoying our exploration of his creation.

Liquid nitrogen tanks stood in a straight line down both sides of the building. Along the back wall, there was a canvas trough covered with a lid of thick glass. Inside, hundreds of brightly colored blocks filled the space, piled so high they reached the top. I followed a black cord that ran into an outlet. It was plugged in.

"Can I feel inside?" Aaron asked.

"Sure but it'll be chilly," Papa said.

Aaron lifted the lid and ran his hands through the blocks. Making a fist, he pushed down into the trough. The cold must've stung but he didn't pull his arm out. Instead, he stirred the blocks and watched them tumble around. "Now these are freezing… but not deep space frigid like that tank over there."

On a shelf above the trough, Papa had a mess of fat

electrical cords and jugs of chemicals. A foil blanket was wedged between them, sealed inside in a plastic wrapper.

"I've never seen an aluminum sleeping bag before," I said, holding it up to the light. "Very shiny."

Aaron took it out of my hands. "Looks like we could cook Jiffy Pop popcorn in this thing. We'll need a bigger stove."

"I can tell the two of you are junk food deprived," Papa said and smiled.

The bright lights made it easy to see the wrinkles in the corners of his eyes… and the clutter in all four corners of his shed. Every flat surface was stuffed with wooden boxes, tools, wires, and mysterious cans of liquid. As I wandered, I noticed his crude method of organization within the mess.

"What are all these gadgets for?" I asked.

"Do you remember the movie *Sleeper*? It's the one where Woody Allen's character dies during a routine surgery. His family decides to have him cryogenically preserved," Papa said. "When he's unfrozen, it's 200 years in the future."

"I remember. He pretended to be a robot so he wouldn't get captured." My mind grabbed at the puzzle pieces around me, trying to assemble the tank, the thermometer, the chemicals, and the liquid nitrogen into a clearer picture. "That was fiction… just a movie set with props."

"The cryopreservation of a human body isn't science fiction anymore," he said. "I know it sounds impossible. But so was the idea of a man walking on the moon and look at us now. Most human advancements are powered by imagination.

"James Bedford was a real man who lived in California.

He died in 1967 and volunteered to be the first frozen man. He is cryopreserved to this day, waiting to be revived when medical science finds a cure for cancer. And he's not the only one. In fact, there are several—"

"Is this project for ACTI?" Aaron snatched a bottle off the shelf and read its label. "Cause my dad will want to see your operation here… figure out a way to sell it. He gripes all the time about the research and development guys. He says they don't dream big enough. They'll only freeze organs for transplants."

"This is not a work project and I didn't take the equipment from ACTI," Papa said. "I mean, I didn't steal it. I bought a few pieces that were headed for the scrap heap, but most of it I constructed by hand."

"Why build it in our backyard? This shed is too small if you want to add more tanks," I said.

"The world is becoming an unstable place." He shrugged. I suspected he was lying… or at least holding something back. The one shoulder shrug gave him away.

"What are the cold blocks for?" Aaron asked before I could fire another question at Papa.

"It's an ice bath. Before a person is placed in the tank, the body must be cooled down. The trough will keep the patient at the ideal temperature as the cryoprotectants are injected."

"And you're giving us the grand tour now? Are you sick or something? Cause I'm not gonna freeze you like a creepy popsicle," I said. "Don't even ask."

Aaron let out a hoot. "He's your pop. So, he'd be a pop-sicle. That's a good one."

I gave him a big sister glare… one to make Lili proud. "Papa spends night after night out here. I think this elaborate setup is for real, even though Mama treated it like a joke. She never asked questions. She was never curious to see all this stuff. I can't understand what kept her away—"

A glint in Papa's eyes made me stop, made me rethink the final days of her life. Under the intense work lights, he must have felt like a suspect being interrogated. I took a step closer, examining his face and his body language, waiting for another one shoulder shrug.

"Mama knew about your freezer plan, didn't she? You told her. You told her you wanted to cryo-whatever her body and she hated the idea."

"She loved the idea," he said and met my glare with complete calm. "Or to be more precise, she loved me and understood my passion not to lose her. But I failed. I had two problems to solve before she died and I ran out of time."

"What kind of problems?"

"The first was with the tank itself and how to fuel it. I needed to recirculate the liquid nitrogen, create a sort of closed loop system. So, I built this." He tapped on a small metal cylinder that I hadn't noticed. It stood in the shadow of the larger tank.

"This pump takes the nitrogen gas that was once vented into the atmosphere and re-liquifies it," he said. "The system runs on solar power… a resource Texas has in abundance. I'll only need my generators as a backup."

"Why can't you just plug it into a wall?" Aaron asked.

"Who knows how long we'll have a steady supply of energy.

When our economy crashes, and that day is coming soon, electricity and liquid nitrogen will be scarce," Papa said. "For this to work, I need a constant supply of fuel to keep the temperature at -320 degrees Fahrenheit. And this gadget does the trick."

"So how come you ran out of time?" My question was more curious now than confrontational.

"If you remember, I said I had two problems. The next one was harder to solve. You've been told the body is made mostly of water, something like 70 percent water. Anatomy 101, right? Infants are 75 percent water but adult women are closer to 55 percent. And even at that percentage, the ice crystals inside Evelyn's body would've caused catastrophic damage on the cellular level.

"Water expands when it freezes. At first, the researchers at ACTI believed this expansion was the issue. But there is more going on. Water doesn't play nice with other cells. It freezes as a pure substance that excludes everything else."

"Sounds snobby," Aaron said.

"More like homicidal. Instead of remaining a solvent and allowing the other molecules to freely mix around it, water forms crystals and pushes those crystals out like swords. Its poor next door neighbor gets stabbed. And that's not good news if a body wants to breathe again someday.

"I needed, well, I needed a human antifreeze." Papa scratched his head, like he was still stumped by the problem. "I had to find a way to wrap the organs in cryoprotectants and shield them from the ice crystals around them. Each major organ demanded a slightly different cocktail of ice blocking polymers. It required a light hand.

"And the chemicals in this human antifreeze are toxic," he said. "Saving the cells from ice crystals just to destroy them with poison is a waste of time. I had the best brains at ACTI working on it. Of course, I didn't tell them about my shed project."

"Why are you telling us?" I asked.

Papa's glazed eyes looked into mine and focused. "I think I've got it… a solution for my solution, as it were. Less ethylene glycol, more ice blockers, and some other chemical alterations I won't bore you with. It's been successful with the guinea pigs I've tested. They were cryopreserved for thirty days and then brought back. One guinea pig lived for almost four hours."

"Four hours," I whispered and shook my head, pushing the image of that poor, little creature from my mind before the tears started to flow. I knew better than to cry. He used animals for medical testing and refused to sugarcoat the truth, even when I was a little girl.

"With our current technology, that's quite a victory," he said with no hesitation… no guilt. "And computers will get faster. Scientists will get smarter. We'll turn a four-hour survival rate into a forty-year survival rate or longer. I know this is an exercise in faith but aren't all of the good things in life? And for that matter, all of the good things after life?"

He wanted us to celebrate with him. I could see it in his face as he walked us through his years of research and experiments and "various chemical cocktails." Around me was a remarkable achievement. I should've been proud of my papa but all I could feel was… what? Unease, maybe? It wasn't dread, not yet. I had no psychic abilities, but I swear I shivered.

"After Mama died, you kept coming out here. And this entire cryo setup is way too complicated for anyone else to understand. You don't care about being preserved when you die. This is about me. Isn't it, Papa?" My breath hitched as I tried to pull in more air. "That tank is for me."

"Whoa… seriously? Can you freeze Lili?" Aaron paused. "Is it too late for her?"

Papa turned his back on us and walked toward a line of liquid nitrogen tanks. From behind them, he lifted a pair of orange lawn chairs. Sand clung to its woven, plastic seats—a final souvenir from our last vacation.

"Here, make yourselves comfortable," he said, handing both of us a chair.

We sat and watched Papa pace in front of us. He rolled his shoulders. Dreading the part of the ritual when he'd crack the joints in his neck, I broke his concentration.

"Let me make this easy, Papa. I'm okay with being frozen when I die. No one is getting a real burial anymore. The crematoriums are running nonstop and cold sounds better than heat because fire is too much like hell and I know I won't feel it but still—" I was rambling. "Sign me up for your tank instead."

He studied the ground between us. He put his hands in his pockets, shifted his weight from foot to foot, and still didn't speak. The man must've heard me. And just as I was about to repeat my burial instructions, like saying it once wasn't disturbing enough, he lifted his head.

"Mirari, I have no intention of cryopreserving you when you die. Not if you catch the Olympic flu and develop sepsis. Too many of your organs, including your brain, would be damaged."

"Lili got that way." Aaron's voice was low, barely discernible above the drone of the tank. "Really messed up."

"I believe in divine intervention, but I also believe God gives us intelligence. He expects us to use it," Papa said. He knelt down and wrapped his hands around mine. "If you want a life in the future, you'll need healthy organs when you get there. Do you understand what I'm telling you?"

I jerked away from his touch. "You want me to avoid catching the virus that's killing every other woman who gets it? Sure. I'll put a date on the calendar and pass away in my sleep with healthy organs and a smile on my face. Just for you, Papa."

I hated the sarcasm in my voice, despised sounding so much like the teenager I was. But how could I crawl into bed and die on command? He wasn't making any sense, unless. Unless. My eyes widened. My brain reeled, demanding a different answer than the one right in front of me.

Papa's arms were around me the instant I leapt out of the chair. I wanted out of this shed and didn't care if I hurt him doing it. I kicked at his legs. This was my life, my future. Not his. I pushed against him, out of my mind to escape, but he held me tight.

"Let... me... go." My scream bounced off the metal tanks, twisting and echoing back at me like a banshee's cry.

"Shhh, it's okay," he said against my ear. "Take it easy.

Listen to what I'm saying. I'm not going to make you, Mirari. No one is going to make you."

"That's a lie. You didn't go to all this trouble just to let me walk away."

"It will be your decision. Not mine, I swear. Breathe now. Breathe."

When I stopped struggling, he lowered his arms. I sat down in the lawn chair, drained and shaking, and put my head between my knees. Meatloaf was climbing up the back of my throat. Maybe vomiting was a perfect way to tell Papa what I thought about his idea.

"What's going on here? I don't understand," Aaron said.

He was sitting right next to me but it was hard to hear him through the roaring inside my skull. I'd wanted our house to be a peaceful place where this kid could grieve and heal. Papa blew that idea to smithereens.

"Tell him, Dr. Vega." I didn't bother to lift my head. "Tell him how you plan to freeze your daughter while she is still alive."

CHAPTER FIVE

RAISE YOUR HAND

Papa kept talking, but I only caught bits and pieces. My heartbeat pounded. And really, who could blame it? This was the time for my heart to be heard… the time for my heart to speak now or forever hold its peace.

After a quick lecture on hypothermia, Papa swore he would never put me into a liquid nitrogen tank while I was still alive. He would kill me first—as if that distinction made the entire scheme so much easier to accept. His plan was to stop my heart with a combination of potassium chloride, phenobarbital, and a few other drugs I couldn't pronounce.

"It will be painless, Mirari. You'll close your eyes. And when I reanimate your body, maybe in a year or two, the pathogen will be gone, or we'll have a vaccine. You'll survive this. You'll live again."

He was as eager as a door-to-door salesmen and Mama

never trusted those guys. Only one ever made it into our house. He threw dirt on our carpet and sucked up the mess with his shiny vacuum cleaner. "Ta-da," he'd cried, like a magician who'd just pulled a dust bunny from his hat.

Although Papa didn't force me to say yes, he did pressure me to make my decision before the sun came up. "To give you the best chance of survival, you need to be symptom free," he said. "No fever. No chest congestion. Who knows how many more days like that you'll have? Lili's death proves that we must strike while the iron is hot."

"You mean strike while the iron is freezing cold," I said, not caring anymore if my sarcasm was childish.

Papa loved me but he could also be a manipulative genius. Both of those things could be true at the same time. When I bolted from my chair, he didn't try to stop me. I slammed the shed door and white paint fell around my feet like snow.

He knew where I was going... what I needed. In my room, I could think and breathe and replace emotions with numbers. Firm, rational, glorious numbers. Reaching into the desk drawer, my fingers found a notebook and a pen in their designated spots. Much like Papa's shed, every item in my room had a precise location.

I began by drawing a table with lines as straight as I could make them. At the very top, I wrote "Freeze-No Freeze" and then created columns to list my criteria and weights. I'd give the most important factors the greatest weight. All I needed to do was name them. What did I really want?

I wrote some garbage about controlling my own destiny and put a line through it. My hand hovered over the paper...

unsure. Every option sucked. Frustrated, I snapped the pen and slammed the pieces down on the desk. I couldn't organize my way out of this.

The tears came next. As they fell on my chart, their heavy drops blurred the ink. It scared me when I couldn't stop. I never bawled like a baby. But when I tried to dry my face, the sobs got harder and louder. I pressed my palms against my eyes, like I was applying pressure to a bleeding wound.

I'd heard about people who traveled the globe on a quest to "find themselves." They'd scale Mount Everest or run with the bulls in Pamplona. I discovered the real me in my childhood bedroom and came face-to-face with a coward I didn't recognize.

Vanity begged me to lie, begged me to write "bravery no matter what the cost" on the paper in front of me. I wanted those words to be true. Most people dream of a long life, right? When it was time to take my last breath, I imagined my curly-haired children and grandchildren gathered around me. Why couldn't I fight for that? Why couldn't I be the one woman who battled the virus when it invaded her body and kicked its ass?

I picked up the broken pen. And with a shaking hand, I scrawled "avoid pain" in big letters over the entire chart. There it was. The strongest desire in my heart was to run away from the days of agony my mother had endured, run away from the torture Lili put her family through as her body and mind crumbled a little more each day.

Whatever decision I made, it had to give me the best chance of avoiding pain or causing pain in others. That was my only criteria. Death was sad. But dying? It was what my Mama called "el monstruo furioso"— the raging monster.

The men in the house left me alone until a snack arrived around midnight. In the hall, I found a tray loaded with ration crackers, peanut butter, and a glass of powdered milk. The liquid was too white, as if it'd come from a cow born in a nuclear plant. I ate and drank without tasting a thing.

At 12:55 a.m., I made my decision. I'd been tired before, cranky after a long sleepover or an all-night study session, but this was different. This was a head-to-toe weariness that numbed me. If death was an eternal slumber, its bed was already calling to me… whispering "climb under the covers, Mirari. Rest your head. Shut out the world."

Papa wasn't in the house, but it wasn't hard to find him. Light blazed between the walls of the shed. I followed it through the darkness. My teeth chattered… perhaps because the grass was wet under my feet or perhaps because ice was already wrapping itself around my bones. When I tugged on the shed door, it opened.

"I'll do it," I said in a rush.

If the mad scientist responded with an evil grin, his guinea pig didn't wait around to see it. I turned and ran back to the house. And this time, Papa was on my heels.

My decision set off a rapid chain of events that couldn't wait until sunrise. Within minutes, the three of us were sitting at the kitchen table with cups of hot tea in our hands. Aaron was still half asleep. His eyes were puffy under a wild mess of wavy hair. He slumped in his chair until Papa told him how important he'd be for the plan to work.

"We'll need Aaron to drive the Jeep." Papa put a stack of notes in the center of the table and spread them out. "Can you do it?"

"Why does he get the Jeep? I'm the one with the license," I said.

Aaron ignored me. "All of the trucks at the ranch have a manual transmission. I can drive anything, Dr. Vega. Where are we going?"

"The shed in the backyard isn't going to work. Not long term. This neighborhood is changing. Someone could break the lock, steal the solar panels, or the generators. It's too risky to keep her here."

He unfolded a map in front of Aaron and pointed to a green section of land. It was upside down… impossible for me to read.

"Hello? I'm still here, you know." I waved my hand in the air. "Maybe you can show me where I'm going."

"Sorry, Mirari." Papa flipped the map and drew a circle around our destination.

"Why San Antonio?" I asked. "It's more crowded than Austin."

"I explored this piece of property when I was in college. It's about 700 acres with the most unusual cave system I've ever seen. Remember, you're going to be in a tank, surrounded by metal. They won't be able to get near you."

"They? You mean the people who own the land?"

"They, meaning the millions of Mexican free-tailed bats who live in the largest cavern," Papa said. "Think of 'em as your private bodyguards. And there is one section in the back, blocked off from the—"

If Papa expected me to react violently to this plan, he was wrong. It was Aaron who leapt up from table. His sleepy eyes were wide awake now.

"Are you crazy? Bats have claws. And fangs." Aaron shook his head in quick, spastic jerks. "They'll drink her blood."

"Bats are insect eaters," Papa said. "We'll still want to leave them alone, of course, out of respect for their habitat. I'm remembering one of the smaller caves nearby. It's not big enough for the bats but maybe it's big enough for our equipment."

The kid didn't look convinced. He'd seen too many vampire movies, and yet, I couldn't tease him for overreacting. His concern for me was sweet in a ghoulish sort of way. I changed the subject.

"What's the plan for moving the tank? It won't exactly fit in the back of the Jeep."

Aaron sat down and looked at the map. "We could haul it in Dad's Ford 800. He'll never know."

"Please excuse the presumption on my part but I had the same idea. I did a quick search in the glove box," Papa said. "It's registered to ACTI and not the ranch. That's good news. If we get stopped by the patrols, my employee ID might keep us out of jail."

"Do you want to pack the truck now or in the morning?" Aaron asked.

This crazy plan was moving too fast. I'd given my consent, but was I ready? No way. There was no such thing as ready. Maybe it was best to take a final breath and jump into the bitter cold before I changed my mind.

"I can't, um, I mean…" I swallowed and tried again. "I don't want to wait. This needs to happen soon."

"I agree." Papa said. "So let's get going."

We loaded everything into the truck while it was still dark. I followed Aaron around like a bossy shadow and pulled the heavier items out of his arms. With sleeping neighbors all around us, we worked without speaking. He couldn't argue with me, at least not with words, but his irritated hand gestures spoke volumes as he watched us roll a Coldspot deep freezer up the ramp.

Papa struggled to put a furniture dolly under the cryogenic tank. The thing must have weighed at least 700 pounds. Aaron held the door as we steered it out of the shed. When we reached the metal ramp behind the truck, our forward progress stopped. It felt as if we were pushing a boulder up a mountain. My arms were shaking with the strain but the two of us couldn't pull the tank into the truck.

Aaron flexed his bicep, showing us what might be a big muscle someday. Papa nodded. And before I could argue, Aaron wrapped his hands around one of the metal handles. I grabbed the other while Papa pushed from the back. Inch by inch, the dolly rolled.

Aaron's ribs must've been screaming at him. His heavy breathing turned into low cries that he couldn't muffle. The weight would've crushed Papa if either one of us had let go. I counted off a whispered "one, two, three, pull." All three of us groaned.

With one painful heave, we wrestled the tank inside the truck. Aaron dropped to the ground. I didn't think I had any tears left but his pitiful wheezing made my eyes sting. I sat beside him, wanting to give comfort but not knowing how. My fingers twitched with the impulse to smooth his hair. I patted his arm instead.

Papa loaded the truck around us without any words of sympathy for Aaron. I recognized his silence for what it was… a "save face" gesture of respect between the two men. Toward the east, the sky was no longer black. We were in a race against the sun now.

I nudged Aaron and he stood. Together, the three of us loaded the generators, a box of tubing, and a green Army cot. When Papa added the final jug of chemicals, I had enough light to see the blisters on my fingers.

Did the neighbors watch us as they sipped their sugarless tea and ate their daily allotment of oatmeal? Maybe they thought Dr. Vega was a criminal, stealing and hoarding medical supplies. As we hauled our sore legs back into the house, I was too tired to worry about their suspicions.

"Get rest while you can," Papa said. He passed around the aspirin bottle and bandages for our hands. "We'll load our camping gear after dinner and be outside the Austin city limits before the 10 p.m. curfew. I want to avoid the local patrols if we can."

I was sure I'd have nightmares. But I fell asleep hard, beat-up by raw emotions and a tired body, and couldn't remember my dreams when I opened my eyes. Papa tugged me out of bed late in the afternoon. A muscle in his jaw twitched and new lines creased the corners of his bloodshot eyes. Maybe he'd had enough nightmares for the both of us.

After dinner, we packed the Jeep with last-minute supplies and waited for the sun to go down. I put nothing in my backpack other than a toothbrush and a few rubber bands for my hair. Where I was going, I wouldn't need clothes.

The men kept me hustling, an obvious ploy to distract me. As long as the pace remained hectic, maybe I wouldn't remember dancing around the stereo with Mama. Maybe I wouldn't dwell on the kitchen calendar, stuck on the month and year she died, or see the pencil marks she put on the wall to chart my height. That stopped the year Mama died, too.

Without being told, I dressed as masculine as possible. The stocking cap went back on my head. I wore faded jeans and Papa's souvenir t-shirt from our last vacation, the word "Galveston" emblazoned across the black fabric. The white letters glowed in the cab of the truck but the fit was loose, hiding my curves underneath it.

"This isn't goodbye," Papa said as we drove past our front porch. "You'll be back here soon."

Behind us, my childhood home grew smaller and then disappeared. The rhythmic hum of the truck tires was hypnotic in the dark. Papa searched for a radio station broadcasting music instead of news. I didn't close my eyes. But I let the sounds lull me... insulate me from the reality waiting for me at the end of the road.

Our little caravan didn't pass a single patrol car as we left Austin. Even though the roads were quiet, and even though it was the fastest route to San Antonio, Papa made a last-minute decision to avoid Interstate 35 and take U.S. Route 290 to Route 281 instead.

"Maybe fewer checkpoints," he said. "Or none at all if we get lucky."

There was big money in selling food during the rationing, with the highest demand for luxury items like meat and alcohol. As the shortages continued, I-35 became a black-market superhighway. Agents with the U.S. Department of Commerce could legally stop any vehicle larger than a pick-up truck and inspect its contents without probable cause or a warrant. We weren't carrying T-bone steaks, but Papa didn't want anyone to look at my face or recognize me as a "carrier."

Even after the 10 p.m. curfew, southbound 281 wasn't deserted. I positioned the rearview mirror so I could watch Aaron. He stayed on our bumper, not letting even one vehicle come between us. As we rounded a sharp curve, something behind us popped. The Jeep disappeared. I counted to five, counted to ten, and still there was nothing but darkness.

"I can't see Aaron," I said. "Should we pull over?"

Papa steered the big Ford toward the shoulder of the highway. We straddled the line between the pavement and the gravel. Beyond the reach of our headlights, the Texas night was active. Trash rolled down the highway like tumbleweed, and above us, thin clouds raced across the moon.

I jumped with every new sound. "Where is he?"

"I'm going back. Hang on."

Papa didn't wait for an intersection but made a wide U-turn in the middle of the road. The truck wasn't built to be nimble. It leaned as we veered off the shoulder, threatening to tip us into the ditch, and he punched the accelerator. We rocketed back onto the pavement in a spray of dirt and grass.

When the truck was in the northbound lane, he hit the brakes. A dim light glowed on the other side of the curve. Papa took off his gray jacket and tossed it on my lap.

"Get down. Cover yourself," he said. "This might be nothing worse than a flat tire but don't move, don't lift your head up, until I tell you it's clear."

I obeyed, taking off my seatbelt and sliding onto the floorboard of the truck. I curled into the tightest ball I could make. Under the jacket, I felt invisible in the darkness.

Papa gave the truck some gas. My body rocked to left as he took the curve, and when the ground beneath the tires turned to gravel, we slowed to a stop. He didn't turn off the engine but let it idle in neutral.

"Where's Aaron?"

"I see the Jeep… but no sign of the boy. One of the headlights is out." The temperature dropped when he opened his door. "Stay here and stay down."

"Do you have your gun?"

"Don't worry. I got it," he said and shut me inside the truck alone.

At first, I welcomed the warm air blowing out of the heater. The vent was only a few inches from my face. But as I waited, cursing the nonstop drone of the motor, I began to sweat. What was happening out there while I was cooking down here? I was worried about the kid and mad at him for making me worry.

Beneath my right ear, something struck the bottom of the truck with a metallic clink. The sound would've been no big deal if we were moving, but rocks don't fly up and hit stationery vehicles. It was too dark to read my watch. I don't know how long my patience lasted before I crawled up from the floorboard… maybe two minutes or maybe two hours. Both would've felt like an eternity.

I pulled my black stocking cap down to my eyebrows. And like a rabbit hiding from a hawk, I sniffed the air before taking a peek out the driver's side window. My peek became a stare. I couldn't look away.

They were on their knees, but it wasn't to change a flat tire. A flashlight next to Aaron's leg was pointed into the gravel. It was the Jeep's one remaining headlight that told the story and illuminated every grim detail on their faces. A thin line of blood ran from Aaron's nose. Papa's bottom lip was ripped open and swollen. They both had their hands in the air.

A man paced in front of them. He was dressed in black all the way down to his boots. A cowboy hat threw dark shadows on his profile, and if he was talking, I couldn't make out what he was saying. But the pistol in his hand? It spoke without a single stutter as he waved it toward the truck. The weapon looked identical to Papa's 9mm Beretta.

We'd been worried about a run-in with law enforcement. From my hiding place, it was impossible to see a badge on this man's chest but I had a hunch he didn't have one. He was too jumpy. As he waved the gun in the air, he rocked back and forth, twitching every time his captives moved.

Behind the Jeep, there was no squad car… just a thick lump laying halfway on the road. It looked like a roll of carpet. My eyes widened when the lump reached for the back bumper and tried to stand. In the glow of the tail-lights, the creature's face was more bear than human. His body was thick. His long hair was matted. Something sticky ran through his beard in dark clumps.

As I watched this man's lumbering rise from the ground, nothing else moved in slow motion. My brain didn't consider and toss away a thousand different rescue strategies. From where I sat, there were only three.

I could put the truck in drive and peel out in a cloud of flying gravel. Mr. Beretta would steal the Jeep, of course. Maybe he'd leave Papa and Aaron on the side of the road. But would he leave them alive? Probably not.

I could join the fight, running headfirst into the action without a weapon. And when I opened the truck's door, Mr. Beretta would send a few bullets in my direction. Call it irony or a giant cosmic joke, but I didn't want my suicide road trip to become a murder road trip.

I could create a diversion. If I gave Papa and Aaron a chance, they could take the gun from the smaller man before the bear found his legs. And I had a powerful diversion right under my fingertips.

Sliding down in my seat, I laid on the horn with both hands. The Ford 800 gave an angry blast that was impossible to ignore. It certainly got Mr. Beretta's attention. Bullets shattered the truck's windows and whizzed over my head.

I screamed a one-word prayer that was supposed to be "God," but it sounded more like "Gaaawd." The piercing noise was octaves higher than the truck's deep moan. My eyes were squeezed shut. My hands stayed glued to the steering wheel.

I didn't feel the cuts on my arm until Papa grabbed me. His touch stung. Lines of blood rolled toward my elbow… almost black in the dim light of the dashboard. When I lowered my hands, the blaring horn went quiet, but the night wasn't silent. Sirens wailed in the distance.

"Move over." He threw open the driver's side door and pushed me away from the wheel. Slivers of glass pierced my jeans as I slid across the seat. "We gotta get the hell out of here."

CHAPTER SIX

DON'T LOOK BACK

OUR GETAWAY WASN'T the stuff of Hollywood movies. Aaron jumped behind the wheel of the Jeep while Papa steered the truck through an awkward, three-point turn in the middle of the highway. As he shifted gears and stomped on the clutch, he hissed a stream of obscenities at his attackers.

His "que te folle un pez espada" was either "I hope you get screwed by a sword" or "screwed by a swordfish." I was panting too hard to ask for a translation.

When the 300-pound bear saw our headlights, he scrambled out of the way on his hands and knees. He moved fast for a big guy. I cringed, waiting to feel his body snap under our tires, but the crack of his bones never came.

Mr. Beretta's current health was harder to determine. He was either unconscious or dead. He still had his cowboy hat.

It covered his face now. His boots pointed at the moon and looked like two piles of black dirt in the ditch.

"What happened, Papa?"

"I will tell you the whole story, at least as much of it as I know, if you triage your arm first. Are there pieces of glass in the wound?"

"I don't feel anything." Wanting a first aid kit or at least a Band-Aid, I searched the glove box and found nothing but a Conoco map of Texas.

He handed me a pocketknife. "Cut a strip from the jacket and wrap it around you like a bandage. That should slow the bleeding."

I sliced off a section of fabric. And winding it tight, I used my teeth to tie a sloppy knot at the end. With my good arm, I swept tiny bits of glass onto the floor. The front windshield had no bullet holes but both side windows were shattered. Cold night air whistled through the jagged openings.

I shivered and put on what was left of the jacket. "No more stalling, Papa. Talk."

"There wasn't time to ask Aaron what happened before we pulled up. All I can do is guess." He checked the rearview mirror, confirming the Jeep's one remaining headlight was on our tail. "Those two men must've been hiding in the weeds near that bend in the road. I'm betting we were their target—specifically, whatever we were hauling in the back. I think they shot at our tires and missed. Because Aaron was following so close on our heels, a stray bullet hit the Jeep.

"When I got out of the truck, I couldn't miss the big guy stretched out on the pavement. His breathing was shallow.

To be honest, I was afraid Aaron ran over him. But if that's how it went down, where was the boy? Of course, I didn't know there was a second man. He was on the other side of the Jeep, waiting for me to round the corner, and I never saw his punch coming. It felt like my entire head exploded. My gun went off. I have no idea where the bullet went. I couldn't see, could barely stay on me feet."

"You might have a concussion or something. Are you okay to drive?"

"I think I'm alright. No one will cast me in the next Rocky movie and that's a fact. He took the gun out of my hand... easy as stealing a baby's first lollipop. It was embarrassing."

"Where was Aaron during all of this?"

"Before the cowboy could shoot me with my own weapon, I heard a whack and a grunt," he said. "I think Aaron hit him with a flashlight. It didn't take the guy down. It just flattened his cowboy hat and pissed him off. He marched us in front of the Jeep, threatening to put a bullet down the kid's throat if he didn't drop the flashlight."

"You should've seen the big man try to stand up. I was freaking out," I said. "He stumbled around like a bear... a drunk bear who was sobering up quick. I watched him grab the back bumper. It's why I honked the horn."

"Thank you for that, by the way." Papa laughed, fear and relief mixing together in its rich sounds. "You gave Aaron and me just enough time to get the gun back."

"By disobeying your orders."

He wrapped his hand around mine and stopped the trembling in my fingers. "I should've known you wouldn't keep your head down. I'm glad you didn't, Mirari. Blowing the horn was quick thinking." His praise warmed me faster than the jacket around my shoulders.

"Do you know who those guys were? What they wanted?"

"They wanted the truck," he said. "Specifically, they wanted whatever we were hauling in the truck. I'm sure they were hoping for food or alcohol—something with a street value." Papa's eyes moved from the road to the rearview mirror again. "I imagine the big guy is telling lies to the cops as we speak."

The rest of our trip was quiet. We didn't see a single patrol car. Papa concentrated on each intersection, looking for the one paved road off U.S. Route 281 that became a gravel road that became a dirt road with potholes as big as our tires.

We crept along the winding path and dodged the biggest bumps. It wasn't for our comfort. After our rough ride, he was worried about the equipment in the back.

"A broken tank will send us home," he said as put the truck in park. "Keep your fingers crossed that we got lucky."

"Oh, I don't know. A broken tank sounds pretty lucky to me." I squinted into the darkness. "Where's the cave?"

"This isn't the main entrance. We'll be looking for a side cavern, somewhere against the hill. I hope I'll recognize it in the daylight."

Aaron had my door open the moment Papa turned off the engine. Pieces of window glass scattered on the ground around his tennis shoes. "Are you okay?" we asked at the same time. I took a breath but he didn't need one.

"That man was gonna kill us," he said. "No doubt. Kill us execution style right there by the side of the road. Did you see him? He had us down on our knees with our hands in the air. And then, the horn. That wonderful, loud-ass horn.

"You should've seen him jump, Mirari." Aaron's eyes glowed in the dark, wild with adrenaline. Smeared blood ran down his nose and formed a goatee around his lips. "I'm sure he pissed his pants. I woulda laughed… but he turned the gun toward the truck and fired right at you. It gave us our chance. We took him down hard, cracked his head on the pavement like a ripe watermelon."

"That's gross," I said but couldn't hide my smile.

"We didn't kill him. At least, I don't think we did. And we got your dad's gun back."

"What happened to the big guy?"

Aaron groaned. "I should've never pulled over. Man, what a dumb move. As you guys went around the curve, something under the Jeep popped. I reckoned I had a flat tire but I didn't know which one. It took forever to find a flashlight. And when I finally got out to take a look, they were waiting.

"The first guy came up behind me… real quiet for such a big dude. I didn't know he was there until he put a meaty paw on my shoulder. Call it reflexes or a survival instinct, but I turned on him, swinging the flashlight like a baseball bat.

"The skinny dude was standing next to him. He punched me in the face, and I ain't gonna lie. It hurt like hell. When he saw your headlights, he must've dove into the ditch."

"And stayed there until he punched me in the face," Papa

said, touching his broken lip. "Come on, we need to disinfect these cuts and Aaron will need more aspirin."

As we dug through the first aid kit, the three of us took turns telling our story. My part was boring compared to their brush with death. "At first, I thought we were busted by the patrols but the whole thing felt off. The man with the gun was too twitchy," I said and shook my head. "Dear Lord, he could've shot you—"

"But he didn't. See?" Aaron turned in a full circle. "No bullet holes."

The excitement I'd felt during our escape faded into a shaky exhaustion. We'd either been damn lucky or damn blessed to get away from those men alive. And coming down from that? I was damn tired.

After doing a final search for glass, I unrolled my sleeping bag and settled into the cab of the truck. The upholstery was cloth and wide enough that I could stretch my legs. I dozed in restless spurts, waking every time the wounds on my arm brushed the seat. And just when I thought the crickets outside couldn't get any louder, they'd reach a new crescendo. I prayed for morning to come. I prayed that morning would never come.

God answered half of my prayers.

Through the front windshield, the purple horizon gave way to shades of pink and orange. I huddled with the sleeping bag around my shoulders and waited for the bats to come home. It was a bizarre beginning to my final day. I wish I could say I was numb, but Papa woke me with a bottle of peroxide in one hand and clean bandages in the other, a nasty alarm clock. The cut on my arm was now throbbing in rhythm with my strong and soon-to-be-silent heart.

Our breakfast was far from gourmet. Aaron climbed into the truck with an industrial-sized can of baked beans and held it on his lap as the three of us ate. Papa didn't say much but I caught him staring at me. He was timid in a way I'd never seen before, stiff and polite, like if he said the wrong thing, I might make a run for it. The confident vacuum cleaner salesman was gone.

I thought I'd scream if I didn't break the tension. "I'm glad it's the last day of March and not the first day of April. Imagine killing me and freezing me on April Fools' Day. What a prank, right?"

No one laughed.

Aaron took pity on me and filled the silence. "We could wake you up on April 1 next year," he said. "And when you open your eyes, we'll be in alien costumes and tell you the planet was invaded while you slept. What do you think, Dr. Vega?"

Papa gave the boy a wan smile with his bruised mouth. He lifted the binoculars around his neck and scanned the sky. Light glowed on the eastern horizon. The sunrise was impossible to stop. Was it too late to back out? Was Papa asking himself the same question? Surviving a roadside attack gave me a strong thirst to stay alive.

I was too distracted to notice the first, dark speck in the sky. But when it was joined by more flying specks, I pointed and tried to count each one. They poured in from every direction. Thousands of Mexican free-tailed bats formed swirling patterns over our heads. The wonder of it seemed to lift the tension inside the truck. And for a few precious minutes, I thought about something other than the day in front of me. Even the boy who hated bats watched in awe.

Papa kept his binoculars zoomed in on a spot through the trees. "Good news, very good news," he said. "They are using the larger opening as their entry point. When we have more light, we'll hunt for the secondary cavern."

It wasn't much of a hunt. Papa's attention to detail was sharp… even after twenty years. He found the cave's side entrance behind a twisted cluster of tree trunks.

"Aaron, get my small hatchet out of the toolbox. I believe someone planted a door. Very clever."

The cliffrose trees were taller than us—their spring buds just beginning to open. From where I stood, the rocky incline looked solid on the other side of their limbs. White petals fell as he hacked away. When Aaron lifted the chopped tree from its remaining stump, Papa moved on to the next one.

The hidden entrance grew larger with each swing of his hatchet. I expected the opening to be rounded at the top. Instead, it was an uneven rectangle with good clearance on the left side. Papa had headroom to spare as he walked into the cave.

The downed trees were in a pile around Aaron's feet. "I'm not going in," he said. "Not without a candle or a match or at least a few fireflies."

I found the flashlight rolling around in the back of the Jeep and delivered his weapon with a mock bow. "Try not to hit anyone with it."

"Only the bats," he said, turning on the light with his thumb.

He was taller than my papa. Tilting his head, he ducked under the thick slab of limestone and disappeared into the cave. I followed him inside.

The cavern looked more like a dusty, honky-tonk saloon than a geological wonder. The space was larger than Papa's shed but not by much. Once upon a time, an excited graduate painted "Mustang Pride Class of 1963" on the back wall. Instead of bat guano, the ground was littered with cigarette butts and empty cans of Pearl beer. The only thing missing was a jukebox.

"Fun place." Aaron swung his flashlight up to the ceiling. "But no blood suckers."

Picking up a discarded pop top, Papa examined the rust marks it left on his fingers. "This trash is old. Our party animals moved on about a decade ago and didn't tell their little brothers and sisters about the cave. I think we've found our spot. The ceiling is high, the entrance is large enough to get the tank in here. We'll anchor the solar panels on the west side of the incline. Looks better than I hoped for."

"Want me to pull the truck up closer?" Aaron asked.

Papa handed him the keys. "Go ahead and get started. We'll be right out."

Without the yellow glow of Aaron's flashlight, the shadows in the cave were stark. Colder. I crushed a few beer cans under my feet and imagined the teenagers who'd once held them. Did girls party here, too? Was this a place where they felt welcome? I wanted that to be true. I needed these walls to be soaked in their laughter and petty rivalries and impetuous romances and bigger-than-life dreams.

Papa put an arm around my shoulder. "We can go home right now," he said. "It's not too late."

"Nope, we're staying. I haven't changed my mind," I said. "There's no point."

"For what it's worth, I think you are a brave woman. How many eighteen-year-olds would trust their papa enough to take a chance and see what the future holds?"

"Well, the joke's on you. This woman isn't brave. She's a coward who doesn't want to suffer. I saw the death marathon Mama and Lili ran. It sucked. So instead, I'm sprinting toward the finish line."

"You think all of this is, what? Nothing more than a mercy killing?"

"Yes."

"Why would I go to so much trouble—"

"I'm sorry Papa, but I have zero faith I'll see another day after this one. Zero." With the palm of my hands, I rubbed my eyes. It hurt and I welcomed the pain. "That tank in the truck? It's nothing more than a suicide machine. And I'm okay with that."

He lowered himself to the ground. Stretching his legs out, he reclined against the rock and patted the dirt beside him. "Aaron believes he'll see you again," he said. "He has faith. Can you have a little, too?"

I flopped down. "Aaron is just a kid."

"That boy is a strange one. He's afraid of bats but not afraid of his drunk father or a random thug who wants to put a bullet in his head. If we didn't need his truck, I would've left him in Austin. But there is steel behind his fast-talking mouth. He tackled the guy with my Beretta while I was still down on my knees. Did you know that?"

"He said you guys got the gun back. He didn't say how."

"And you know he's in love with you, right?"

"Aaron certainly isn't shy." I cried and laughed at the same time—the hysterical sound impossible for me to control. "I guess no one has time to be subtle anymore. But you've got to promise me something."

"I'll give you whatever I can. Just name it."

"Don't let Aaron see me naked. I know I'll be frozen that way, but Mr. Lady Killer doesn't get a peep show. Promise me."

Papa held up three fingers. "I promise to keep everything G-rated. Scout's honor."

CHAPTER SEVEN

ALL OR NOTHIN' AT ALL

WITH MY JEANS rolled up, I stretched out on the picnic blanket and let the sunshine bake me. A book rested in my lap. From a distance, maybe I looked like the picture of calm tranquility. I wasn't calm, of course, but I was tranquilized. I blinked to clear the haze.

When I focused, I could read the hands on my watch and subtract the numbers. Forty-nine minutes was how long it took the Valium in my body to wrap me in its soft cotton.

"It's ten milligrams," Papa had said. He tapped the open bottle and a pill fell into the palm of my hand. I touched the deep V carved into its center. "Not enough to knock you out."

"Then why do I need it?"

"I don't want you to feel anxious. Aaron and I are making good progress, but we've got another hour of work before we fire up the generators. It'll be loud. The noise and the waiting might be stressful. Valium will help."

As the guest of honor at my death, I was relieved from most of the morning's heavy lifting. Aaron drove the Ford up to the cave's entrance. Rolling the storage tank out of the truck was fast work, almost too fast. We gripped the handles of the furniture dolly and the cloth straps holding it in place. Gravity had other ideas, wanting to hurl the heavy metal cylinder into the dirt with the speed of a runaway train.

Papa said it was too risky to put anyone on the ramp below the tank. He wrapped the straps around his waist and, leaning back, used his leg muscles to slow the wheels down. Aaron and I held on to the dolly's handle with both hands, the day-old blisters on my fingers popping as we played tug-of-war with the ground. The tank landed with a thud at the bottom of the ramp, harder than we wanted, but otherwise in one piece.

I expected to spend the rest of the morning unloading the truck. Aaron caught me coming out of the cave. "Follow me," he said. "I've got a surprise for you. You're gonna love it."

I kept my distance as we walked to the Jeep. I didn't trust his idea of a surprise. And I certainly didn't believe he had anything I'd love. When he put a bundle of fabric in my arms, I recognized the blanket as Mama's picnic quilt.

The plaid squares were faded from years of use and the cloth was soft against my face. Hoping to catch the fragrance of her perfume, I was disappointed when I buried my nose in its folds. The quilt no longer carried her scent or even the smell of sunbaked grass from our last picnic. It was musty from too many months in the back of the linen closet.

"Feel around inside," Aaron said. He shifted his weight from one tennis shoe to the other, impatient for me to find what he'd hidden.

"There's something here. Is it a book?"

As I brought it into the light, *Carrie* jumped off the cover, the girl's face glowing blue around the edges. It wasn't a brand-new copy. Written at the top of the first page, I recognized the large, curly signature of Evelyn Vega.

"I'm a fast reader," I said. "But do you think I can make it to the end of the book before, you know, before I leave?"

"It'll give you a reason to come back. When you open your eyes, the rest of the story will be waiting for you."

"Thank you very—"

"There's more" he said. "You've missed the best part."

I reached inside the quilt again, my eyes going wide in disbelief. "Oh, my God. Is it a chocolate bar?"

"One chocolate bar would be the work of an amateur. Standing before you is the Lady Killer. I'm a professional. Keep digging."

When I pulled my fingers free, I clutched two Marathon candy bars in the palm of my hand. Their red wrappers had the bright yellow ruler printed on the back just like I remembered.

"Eight inches of chocolate and caramel perfection. And they aren't melted," I said, giving them a gentle squeeze. "That's incredible. Where did you get these?"

"I won them, completely legit, playing poker at the ranch. My buy-in to join the game was cash or chocolate." Aaron's mouth lifted into a devious grin. "I walked away from the table with both. The last pot had more than two candy bars, but you know, I've been eating my winnings."

"However you got them, it's the best surprise ever. I'm willing to share." I waved one bar under his nose.

"Nope. They belong to you. Eat 'em all at once in a chocolate frenzy or save one for later."

I found a patch of sunshine and put the quilt down next to a magnolia tree. The green, waxy leaves were larger than my hands and the white blossoms above my head were open… like teacups waiting to be filled. My picnic spot was close enough to watch Papa and Aaron move equipment down the ramp.

They worked like industrious ants. Every minute, another armful of supplies pushed me closer to the tank. And as much as I enjoyed chocolate, maybe the story sitting in my lap was an even better surprise. It was the gift of distraction.

I'd heard of Stephen King. Mama was a big fan of his books, but I didn't think any writer could distract me from the cave. Not today. Before reading a single word, I felt the pages inside the cover and touched the same places where Mama's hands had been.

She wouldn't hesitate to toss down a boring book, vowing to never crack it open again if the story disappointed her. I'd seen her do it. But Mama finished *Carrie*. Before the last chapter, I found a bookmark covered in yellow smiley faces. Its design was oddly lighthearted among all those pages of horror.

With the strength of her endorsement, I began. I ate the first candy bar just as Carrie used her telekinetic abilities to shatter a lightbulb. And when Carrie destroyed a mirror, hating what she saw in it, I destroyed my second chocolate bar, loving each sweet bite. For a few precious hours, I escaped my faded quilt and my fading life. I met another teenage girl more wretched than me.

Papa sat down on the blanket and studied the book on my lap. "Scary stuff. Did you finish it?"

"I tried. The pill you gave me made it hard to see the words."

"I'm sorry, Mirari. We're trying to make this day go easy for you but—"

"Is it time?" I lifted myself off the quilt and stumbled on rubbery legs. He steadied me with his arm. After a few steps, I pushed away. I couldn't look into his face—couldn't stomach the concern I'd see in his brown eyes. His sympathy would crush me.

I walked toward my tomb without anyone's help. It was a half-hearted attempt to appear courageous… a woman in control of her destiny. Just inside the cave's entrance, I tripped over a nest of round metal cords.

"Easy there," Aaron said. "Don't fall on your—"

His words were swallowed by the sudden roar of a generator. The noise was overwhelming in the small space, like standing inside the fiery engine of a jet plane. Lights blazed around the cavern as electricity flowed into each one. Even with Valium numbing the sharpest edges of my senses, I screamed.

We both had our hands over our ears when Papa came into the cave. "Sorry," he mouthed and darted back outside. An instant later, the generator went silent. The lights flickered out.

Aaron opened a lawn chair and pushed it against the back wall. "Here," he said. "Show your Mustang pride and take a load off. After all these years, the paint on that graffiti should be dry."

"Why couldn't you people kill me in my bed? It would've been less exhausting."

Despite my complaints, and despite the itchy plastic seat underneath me, I couldn't stay awake. Papa and Aaron continued to haul supplies into the cave as I drifted off. Their whispers were an eerie soundtrack for my dreams.

A hand touched mine… gentle at first. When I didn't respond, Papa shook the lawn chair until my eyes opened. His lips were moving. I had no idea how long he'd been talking, but the tones were soft and deep, almost soothing. He'd missed his calling. The man had the voice of a world-class funeral director.

"Mirari? I want to tell you what happens next. Can I show you the set-up?" He pulled me to my feet. "Over here, your backpack is on the bench. Put your clothes and shoes inside it. No one will be in the cave when you get undressed. Remove the bandage on your arm. Unbraid your hair and put it under this. It's like a shower cap but made of stronger stuff.

"And do you remember the shiny sleeping bag? This will be your new home." He opened the plastic wrapper and unrolled the bag, laying it zipper side up inside the canvas trough.

"Where—" My mouth was dry, making me sound old. "Where are the plastic blocks?"

"Aaron is chilling them in the deep freezer. But don't worry. When the time comes, you won't feel the cold."

Papa paced as he explained each piece of equipment. I tried to count his steps, but my brain felt fuzzy around the edges. Somewhere between eleven and twelve, I noticed the beer cans were gone, lost track of the number I was on, and started back at one.

"When you zip up the bag, leave your left arm out for the IV. That's how I'll administer the rest of the drugs after you are asleep. We want you to be comfortable… as comfortable as this cave will allow. Let me know if you want a pillow or need anything. And take your time getting ready."

"I have a favor to ask."

He stopped pacing. "Another one?"

"It's not about being naked or anything like that."

"What's the favor?"

"Don't bring me back unless you can do it. Really, really, really do it. Understand? I don't want some sad, four-hour guinea pig resurrection. I'd rather stay dead. If you bring me back, I want a real life. Do you promise?"

"Yes, Mirari. I really, really, really promise," he said, using my own words to tease me. "Get ready now, okay? Before we both change our minds."

As he walked out of the cave, I understood. This was the reason he gave me the Valium. It was all about the next 30 minutes. Papa didn't want a big, emotional scene. Did he imagine I'd try to claw my way out of the bag? Panic when he put the IV in my arm? My sedative was as much for him as it was for me.

Tomorrows were a tricky thing for us. After months of waiting for my first symptoms to appear, convincing myself that every shiver was the beginning of a fever, it was almost peaceful to know what my tomorrow would look like. I'd be with Mama.

When Papa went home, he'd eat alone at our kitchen table… surrounded by empty chairs and memories. His cryopreservation plan gave me a pain-free way to leave this earth, but it wouldn't eliminate his pain or take away his grief. He said I was brave, but maybe his bravery was greater. Maybe living was harder than dying.

On the day after Mama's cremation, I slept until noon, snacked on old Halloween candy, and cut my hair. Papa set his alarm clock and was dressed by 6:30 a.m.

His routine was a comfort in the first few weeks—a way he could control a piece of the world while chaos roared around us. The work in his shed gave him a reason to get out of bed every morning. I was sure of that now. He'd lost his wife and the clock was ticking for his daughter. All he wanted was to save me.

I owed him a tiny bit of trust, even if I had to fake it. No more bratty comments. No more doubts about his intentions. My "poor me" act had the power to break him… to pull the muscles in his neck and shoulders so tight they'd snap.

I shuffled toward the stool. It was the middle of the afternoon, at least eighty degrees outside, but I trembled as I stripped off my clothes. God help me, I would've given anything to be back on the sun-soaked quilt with a book and a candy bar in my hand.

Perhaps it was nerves or the Valium, but as I yanked my jeans and underwear off over my tennis shoes, I lost my balance. I staggered, hopped on one foot, and landed bare-assed in the dirt.

Aaron would've been howling with laughter if he'd been watching. But other than the drone of the distant generator, the cave was quiet. Papa kept his first promise. The kid didn't get a free show, although my performance was more circus clown than striptease.

I stayed on the ground as I removed the bandage on my arm and put my hair in the ugliest shower cap ever invented. I folded my Galveston t-shirt with perfect precision. Opening the backpack, I put my shoes in first and then my clothes. Everything in its place, right up to the finish line.

The sleeping bag was cool against my skin as I laid inside the trough. I expected the whole thing to rock back and forth like a hammock, but its base was solid. I pulled up the zipper, leaving my face and my left arm exposed. I waited. And I checked my watch.

Papa didn't tell me to leave it on the bench, but no way could it survive -320-degree temperatures. Did I have time to unzip the bag, crawl out of the trough, and put the watch next to my clothes? No, it was better to leave the damn thing on my wrist and let him deal with it. With the day I was having, Aaron would catch me streaking buck naked across the cave. These were the deep and eternal thoughts in my head as the crunch of Papa's footsteps got closer.

"Knock, knock," he said. "Is it alright if Aaron comes in with me? It will be quick. He's driving the truck back this afternoon."

"Yeah, I guess." I sat up, holding the zipper under my armpit so it wouldn't slide down.

Papa carried a black medical bag in each hand. He looked twice as important, twice as smart as the doctors on TV who only traveled with one. Aaron followed him into the cave and held nothing but my book between his fingers.

"Sexy prom dress," he said, his eyes traveling up and down my shiny sleeping bag. "I like the off the shoulder look."

"What? No compliments about my hat?"

"The cap is, um, tight. Is it squeezing your brain? You've got a lot of hair."

I reached up and felt the rubbery plastic on my head. "It's snug. But you know me, I'm a slave to fashion."

"I'll visit you here. I'll come whenever I can, if it's alright with Dr. Vega."

"Oh, sure," I said. "That's cool—"

"And I'll keep your book for you." He held it up... my prize for coming back someday.

"It couldn't be in better hands. Take care of yourself, okay?" Emotion squeezed my throat, its tightness making each word an effort. "Keep making meatloaf for my papa, and—and come to our house if things get rough. Stay all the time if you need to. Just don't go in my room."

I expected him to laugh, but he only nodded. His face was so young and earnest as he backed away. "Goodbye, Mirari," he said. "I'll see you after you've, um, melted."

The kid was optimistic... I had to give him that. His faith was both irritating and inspirational.

"See you soon." I waved, like I was leaving for a family vacation.

Aaron ducked his head under the slab of rock and was gone. I hesitated before lying back down, feeling the finality of it all. "So is this a bad time to tell you I'm afraid of needles? Especially those huge IV ones."

Papa squeezed my hand. "I know you are. We're starting with midazolam. It's an injection—no worse than a measles shot. You'll feel a pinch and some stinging. It will help you fall asleep so you won't be awake for the IV."

When I saw the needle coming toward my arm, I turned away. The liquid burned as it poured into the muscle below my skin, but I didn't squirm or make a sound. Papa didn't say how many minutes I had left… and I didn't ask.

His breathing was slower than mine. I matched my lungs to his. *Inhale, hold, hold, hold, exhale.* It calmed me enough to ask the one question guaranteed to keep him talking.

"Tell me about the first time you met Mama. Was it love at first sight?"

"It was for her. I was quite a catch, you know." He grinned. "Your Mama and I had a problem that almost kept us apart forever. Have you heard that story?"

"Was it because you smoked? She told me you smelled bad."

"No, we had a bigger problem than my love affair with Marlboros. Everyone wanted us together. Her friends and my friends and perfect strangers on the street. Everyone tried to throw us together… like we were a forgone conclusion.

"One night at a party, Evelyn and I talked about our

courses at Stanford and how we both ended up in the United States. She told me her cousins live in Mexico City… only four blocks from your grandparents' house in the La Condesa neighborhood.

"I made the mistake of telling your abuela about Evelyn and, well, your grandmother took it from there. Nothing can cool the heat of romance faster than la familia's stamp of approval. We both got calls from home, encouraging us to marry.

"She was determined to date anyone but me… just to prove she could. I asked a few of her friends out to dinner. I thought it would make Evelyn jealous. But then, I'd spend half the night talking about her. The heart can be a stubborn organ," he said.

"You loved her?" My eyes were closed, too heavy to open, but I heard his answer. I still remember it.

"I was afraid of her. And I was afraid to live a single day of my life without her. I'd dated women who were attractive, and at Stanford, most of them were intelligent, as well. But Evelyn was high voltage… all energy and light. She could make a man fly high with joy or burn him to the ground if he didn't treat her with respect. Her spirit packed a punch, didn't it?"

"Yes," I whispered.

"You are so much like her." He put his hand on my forehead. The warmth of his fingers and the sound of his voice were the final threads tethering me to consciousness. "Her fighting spirit was the best gift she ever gave you. Use that power when the time comes. Make her proud, Mirari."

PART TWO

Twelve Years Later

CHAPTER EIGHT

HUMAN TOUCH

I BELIEVED SHE WAS an angel.

The glow of the lanterns formed a halo around her white gown, but that light was dim next to the copper glinting in her hair. When she leaned over my casket, the long curls brushed my skin and left behind the smell of roses. The fragrance was strong, as if God crushed petals into each strand.

He gave her a heart shaped face… an obvious choice for an angel. It floated above me, always watching and often weeping. Her green eyes would search my brown ones until I no longer had the strength to hold mine open.

The nuns in my catechism class promised there would be no crying in Heaven. And during funerals, the priest would open the Bible and recite from Revelation, "He will wipe every tear from their eyes, and there shall be no more death or mourning, wailing or pain, for the old order has passed away."

So why would an angel look at me and cry? The drops weren't salty. When her tears ran into my mouth, I held them on my tongue. Angels must have tears made of spring water, that's what I decided, and maybe she was crying because my pain didn't pass away.

My pain lived.

It assaulted me, most often with an open hand that burned where it slapped. But sometimes, when my eyes were closed and my belly exposed, pain would lash out with a clenched fist. I'd moan and double over, vomiting the near nothingness inside my stomach. And she would weep for me because I was too weak to make tears of my own.

My dreams were more vivid than reality, perhaps a side effect of the drugs, and sometimes I heard voices. How many months did she feed me through a straw and clean me when I struggled to control even one bodily function? I'm sure she kept meticulous records of each diaper change.

When the head angel visited, she never cried. Her candescent skin was darker than mine. Her eyes were golden, just a shade lighter than her wings. She wore a crown of black braids on her head with daisies tucked into the twisted coils.

I craved her gentle touch. She'd push the needle into my skin and I'd float above the pain, outside the reach of its blows. We would soar like tandem kites. And when the wind gave me goose bumps, the golden angel wrapped me in her wings. My sleep would be dreamless for a time… the way death was supposed to be.

Did a third angel visit me? I have a memory, sharper than the rest, of a boy's face leaning over my casket. His hair was shaved close around the ears with corkscrew curls springing from the top of his head like a fountain.

"I've been waiting for you," he said, the whispered words tickling my ear. "You're the first."

I shivered. Blinked. And when I opened my eyes again, he was gone.

The tomb where I was buried changed after his visit. The angel in the white gown made the lanterns burn brighter and my awake moments grew longer. I wish I'd been asleep when she tucked more pillows under my head. But as she lifted my shoulders, the dull ache behind my eyes became a stab, sharpened by the cave I saw around me.

"Mustang Pride Class of 1963" was spray painted on the back wall. The ornate funeral casket was nothing more than a drab, army cot covered in my mother's quilt. And even though the satin dress remained white, the halo of light around the redhead was gone. I couldn't guess what sort of creature she was, but I no longer believed she was an angel.

In the early days of my "coming around," I expected her to flip me the middle finger and walk away. It would have been easier to let me die, or to be more accurate, let me die again. I never asked if I was the worst morphine addict she'd ever treated. I'm positive I was the angriest.

When I wasn't shaking, sweating, or pissing in my hospital gown, I fantasized about murdering my pretty nurse. Her throat seemed fragile—her skin so pale it was almost translucent. My fingers couldn't even hold a cup of water, but I vowed I would strangle her as soon as my hands had the strength.

And to be fair, I didn't keep my savage plans a secret. If I wasn't begging her to kill me, I was threatening to murder her with colorful details like "choke you so hard, your eyes will pop out and roll in the dirt like two green grapes."

My ability to speak and her ability to understand should've been an improvement. Instead, I used my words to torment her. Even when she spooned food into my mouth, I cursed her between bites. The longer she held her tongue, the more determined I was to make her as miserable as me.

"Who are you? Where is my papa? Why isn't he here?" I sang my questions like an alcoholic serenading ninety-nine bottles of beer on the wall, chanting them over and over again.

"I do not have permission to tell you," she said.

I studied her face and anticipated the emotions she couldn't hide… the glory of her meltdown. "You're a demon, aren't you? And this is Hell."

"I do not have permission to tell you who I am."

"I want the other demon back, the one who is in charge. Go get her. Tell her to bring my medicine."

"I do not have permission to give Daisy orders."

"Her name is Daisy." I didn't hide my satisfied smile. "See, that wasn't so hard to say. With all those damn flowers in her hair, I should've guessed. So, let's talk about you, friend of Daisy. What's your name?"

"Daisy will be displeased. I did not have permission to give you her name." Her tears came from nowhere, as if a water pipe suddenly broke behind her green eyes. She didn't lift a hand to wipe them away. Fat drops ran down both sides of her nose, dripped onto her chest, and rolled between the mounds of her cleavage.

"What is your name?"

"I do not have—" she said and stopped. The edges of her lips trembled. But even as I pushed her from frustration into anger, she didn't pull in a deep breath or hiss one back out. Her chest never moved.

"Tell. Me. Your. Name." My demand echoed off the hard rock walls.

"That is enough, child. Be still now," said the head angel, or the head whatever she was. Her low, feminine voice didn't lessen the strength of her command. It was a steel hammer wrapped in silk. As she walked into the cave, the morning light threw the shadow of her silhouette onto the floor like a carpet unrolling at her feet. I shook off the cool hand she put on my forehead.

"The way you were ranting, I thought you had a fever," she said. "But your temperature is normal even if your temper is hot."

"Hello, Daisy." I waited for a reaction, some indication that I'd surprised her by knowing her name. She remained serene. Her face looked almost bored.

"Hello, Mirari. The fluid in your lungs must be improving. All that shouting would have triggered a coughing fit thirty days ago."

"Tell me the redhead's name," I said, spitting out each word between clenched teeth. "Please."

"Her name is Rose. Breathe deeply and you can smell it."

"So in this charming little bouquet, I've got a Daisy and a Rose. Any last names?"

"I am known only as Rose," the redhead said. "I have no last name. Shall I tell Mirari the rest?"

Her question wasn't mine to answer but I answered it anyway. "Yes, you should tell Mirari the rest."

Daisy inclined her head in agreement.

Rose knelt in front of me, her white skirt fanning out like the train of a wedding gown. "As you know, I am Rose and this is Daisy. Martinez Motion also manufactures an Iris, sweet natured but more of an entry level model. Simplistic programing. She requires eight hours to fully charge after 16 hours of use. Daisy and I have a next generation lithium-air cell battery and can charge in four hours after 20 hours of use."

"You're telling me that you ladies aren't, um, ladies at all."

"We are feminals—androids constructed on an assembly line with a five-year warranty for parts and labor."

"This has to be the prank. Is today April first?" If my question surprised them, they didn't show it.

"It is August nineteenth," Daisy said. "Would you like to hear today's forecast?"

"Um, no thanks." As I looked around me, I was impressed with their costumes, their acting, and their dedication to stay in character. "So how do you recharge in a cave? Did Papa add wiring to this place?"

"We have a mobile charging station parked outside. It is solar powered," Daisy said. "We alternate so you are never left alone. I charge in the afternoon and Rose charges in the middle of the night."

"There is a new feminal, the Violet, with 36 hours of continuous power." Rose crossed her arms. Both sides of her mouth turned down as she described the Violet, her frown more adorable than angry. "The men in the lab say she is impressive. Besides her standard knowledge of guns and knives, she has martial arts skills in her code.

"The only difference between 'Violet and Violent is one extra letter.' That's the slogan they use in her television commercials. Her programing is not simplistic. She fatally injured a man in the lab during testing. Now they have safe words to stop her attacks."

"You have given Mirari enough information about the other models, at least for now," Daisy said. She sat down on the edge of the cot, lifted my hands, and squeezed my trembling fingers between her own. "Let us start with some pain reliever before we answer any more questions. I am sure your head is hurting. Rose, please refill Mirari's cup."

I held my mouth open like a baby bird as Daisy put two capsules in my mouth, one at a time between hard swallows of water. Maybe I should've waited for the medicine to kick in, but I had to know what sort of creatures they were. If I was lying helpless in a cave with two evil robots, my headache wasn't even interesting anymore.

"Did you kill my Papa?"

Daisy raised one eyebrow, an expression I later learned was as much shock as her face could show. "Dr. Vega is very much alive. I belong to him. In fact, he sent me here with a message for you."

"You belong to him? You mean, he owns you?"

"Yes, that is correct."

"So, like Star Wars. Papa is Luke Skywalker and you're what? C-3PO?"

"Rose and I are feminals. We are engineered to be attractive to men, to please our masters," Daisy said. "Companionship is our primary function. We also provide domestic services such as cooking and cleaning. Some feminals have after-market enhancements with additional skills."

"I met an Iris who was programmed to grow vegetables," Rose said. "And Daisy has the ability to alter core functions—"

Daisy clicked her tongue. Rose responded to the sound, almost as if it were a command, and snapped her mouth shut.

"That will be a conversation for another day." Daisy smoothed my quilt. "Would you like to read your father's message? I could have recorded his words but he wanted you to see his handwriting—a conformation of sorts that he is alive and anxious to see you again."

"I'll try," I said. "If my eyes can stay focused."

"Rose, please bring a lantern closer to Mirari."

Daisy reached into the pocket of her gown and withdrew a thick, folded piece of creamy paper. I opened it, tracing the embossed, monogrammed V at the top of the page with one trembling finger. Papa's handwriting hadn't changed. I recognized the way he added loops to his printed letters, his own style of cursive.

Dear Mirari,

Your ability to read this letter is a victory beyond anything I could have imagined. When I said I would reanimate you, I didn't comprehend the difficulty of that promise. I believed you'd be back with me in a year or perhaps two at the most.

The human body is beautiful but its complexities continue to be a mystery to me. But before I wax philosophical about the creation of the universe, let's begin with the facts and what you'll need to know as you recover. You were cryopreserved for 12 years. While you slept at -320 Fahrenheit, the virus raged around the globe.

I won't lie. There were days, too many dark days, when I doubted you'd ever breathe again. Removing the cryopreservation chemicals and reintroducing 1.25 gallons of blood into your veins was an arduous process. Your liver wouldn't filter the new blood properly. I gave you three transfusions. I was hours away from performing a transplant, though Lord help me, I didn't know how with no medical team or surgical unit at my disposal.

You are in pain right now but please understand what a miracle you are. Your liver is functioning. Daisy tells me you are able to keep food down. That's excellent progress.

Be patient with yourself and be patient with me. Right now, I must stay away from the cave for your own protection. The reasons are too complicated to put in this letter but I will explain everything when we are face-to-face. Keep getting stronger and we will be reunited very soon.

With all my love,

—Papa

P.S. When your exercises begin, cuss all you want but do them.

I put the letter down on my lap, picked it up, and read my father's words again. Twelve years. I'd been gone for twelve damn years. I was thirty years old.

Shock was the first wave of emotion to hit me, soaking me in numb disbelief. My muscles felt paralyzed… like my body was 300 years old instead of thirty. When that receded, panic swept through those same muscles and demanded action, answers, or anything other than calm acceptance.

"Quick. I need, um, I need a mirror," I touched my face, as if my fingertips could tell me what I wanted to know. "And turn up the lanterns."

"Rose, we have three mirrors in the charging vehicle," Daisy said. "I believe the smallest one will be best."

I expected a hand mirror or maybe a compact mirror from a make-up bag. But when Rose presented me with a rearview mirror, torn cloth and metal still clinging to the back, I blinked in confusion. "Holy crap, Rose. Did you rip this off with your bare hands?"

"Will it not meet your needs?" Her eyes glistened, just seconds away from more tears. "My apologies."

"Uh, no. I mean, yes. This mirror will work great."

"Before you look at your reflection, let me fix your hair," Daisy said. "Those braids need to come down." She snapped the yarn securing the ends and ran her fingers through the tangled strands, setting my wild hair free. "Rose, please bring me a brush."

Daisy started at the bottom, finding the knots and coaxing them away with gentle tugs. Between the pain reliever and the slow strokes of her hand, my headache lost some of its punch. The smell of lavender filled the cave as she opened a clear bottle, poured a puddle into her hands, and worked the oil through each of my corkscrew curls.

She stood back to examine the finished product. "Now you may look," Daisy said.

I lifted the mirror. It wasn't heavy, but I struggled to hold the mangled thing steady. I expected my hair to turn white after so many years in freezing temperatures. Each strand was dark, shiny with oil, and no longer or shorter than it had been twelve years ago.

My face and neck weren't wrinkled. And yet… something in my brown skin wasn't right. The freckles across my nose were tinged a dull yellow. I wasn't sure if the warm lantern light or my liver was to blame.

The big story in the mirror was my eyes. They were bloodshot with bruised, dark circles under each one. I thought my pupils were dilated, but the eyelids around them were so swollen, I couldn't tell.

"We'll need more than just a hairbrush to fix this." I touched the puffy skin. "I look like I've been in a fight."

"Dr. Vega believes your eyes will improve as you wean off

the morphine," Daisy said. "That drug was necessary when you first regained consciousness but—"

"But nothing," I said. "I still need it. Everything hurts."

"I just gave you acetaminophen and we will alternate that with ibuprofen. Morphine can cause breathing problems, sweating, and vomiting. It can also affect fertility. Your father's directions were clear. No more morphine."

"My fertility? Who gives a crap about my fertility? If he's been dreaming about a grandchild the entire time I've been in cold storage, that's his problem."

"Your body is eighteen years old and quite capable of conceiving a child. Daisy has been charting your menstrual cycles," Rose said. "The first one was on May 23. Dr. Vega was excited to hear they have been quite regular."

"God, that is so gross." Heat flooded my face. What other personal details did these girlie drones share with my Papa? "No more period reports for Dr. Vega. Period. Do you understand me? I don't care if he is your boss or Jedi master or whatever."

"I am not owned by Dr. Vega." Rose flashed me a megawatt smile, as if she had no idea she was pulling the pin out of a live grenade. "Aaron Martinez custom ordered me seven months ago. He is my master."

CHAPTER NINE

SOULS OF THE DEPARTED

THE EXERCISES PAPA warned me about began four days later. With one hand under my armpit and the other behind my knees, Rose lifted me off the cot and carried me to a chair. I wiggled, trying to close my hospital gown where it gaped open in the back, but her grip was as rigid as iron bands.

She dropped me into a piece of furniture that barely deserved the word. Papa's old lawn chair was still alive but looked as rough as I did. Its frayed, plastic edges jabbed my bare butt like a swarm of angry bees.

"With this exercise, you will stand from a seated position as many times as you are able," she said. "Lean on me. There is no need to rush."

Each time I flopped back into the chair, it punished me with new scratches. The muscles in my arms and legs refused to cooperate. My right foot supported my weight. The left one was numb with occasional bursts of fire under the skin that stole my breath. Clumps of hair stuck to my face and neck… glued there with sweat.

"I want to stop now."

"Try again," she said.

If I could've erased her memory banks during my exercises, I would've done it. I heaped a foul list of obscenities over her pretty head. And with her bionic ears, Rose heard every word… even the muttered ones under my breath. I wanted her to look as bedraggled as me. But her upper lip didn't have a single bead of perspiration and there were no pit stains under her arms.

"I'm done here," I said. "And Satan called. He wants his redheaded demon back. You should hurry along."

I'd seen her angry. She could raise her voice and her green eyes would flash with emotion right before the tears started to fall. But when I demanded to go back to my mama's quilt, the sound she made in her throat was pitiful, like the mewling of a newborn kitten. I would've preferred the roar of an outraged robot. Guilt added more weight to my already exhausted body.

I pointed a finger under her nose. "No crying. You're not the one in pain here."

"Stand one more time. Please." A sparkling tear clung to the edge of her lashes and even that was programmed to be beautiful.

I growled and pushed off from the armrest, determined to walk, crawl, or roll my way to the cot. The ground tilted under my feet like a carnival ride. I stumbled, my knees locked, and the edges of my vision went black.

Regret was not an emotion Rose was programmed to feel. When I regained consciousness, I was stretched out on the cot and her excited face hovered over mine.

"What a fine beginning," she said. "Well done."

"Did I walk to the cot?"

"No. I carried you."

"So, um, I think I fainted."

"Yes, you did." Her smile widened, flashing teeth so white they glowed. "However, I believe we must focus on your success. You took two steps… a remarkable achievement."

"I took two steps and passed out." Why was it always my job to drag optimists down from the clouds? "That's a terrible beginning."

"I caught you before you hit the ground. I have outstanding reflexes and can carry up to 1,500 pounds. These are some of my many upgrades."

"Aaron would be angry if I let you fall."

"Is Aaron often angry?" If he'd inherited Billy's short fuse and heavy fists, I wanted to know.

"He is my master," she said. "He may show any emotion he wishes."

"Well yes, of course. I'm asking about his temperament. I haven't seen him for years and people change. He is a man now."

"That is correct. He is a twenty-six-year-old male."

"Is he a kind master?"

"He does not beat me. My warranty covers those repairs

for the first five years, but he has never dented me, torn my skin, or pulled out my hair. He does not give me to other men." Her tone was lighthearted, as if we were discussing tomorrow's weather forecast. "Most damage occurs when groups of men are together, sharing the companionship of their feminals."

"Sharing companionship?" I snorted. "Is that what the men tell you to call it?"

I should've stopped and thrown the blanket over my face. But I'd waited four days to ask these questions. My pride was at war with my curiosity. My disgust was at war with my desire to understand.

"Um, does Aaron have feelings for you?" I stared at the ceiling of the cave, not able to look into her heart-shaped face that was too damn perfect to be real. "I mean, do you think Aaron loves you?"

"He has never said those words. I do not need to hear them. Feminals must always love their masters. We are programmed to do so."

I sat up. The walls spun and a wave of dizziness threatened to pull me under. She steadied me with a strong hand on each shoulder and I resented her help, even as my vision cleared. Righteous anger was the only power I needed. "If you have no choice, how can you call it love?"

"Because I have no choice, my love is steadfast," she said. "Aaron never doubts my loyalty. He knows I would die for him. Complete devotion is what my master desires."

"He desires a companion who has no will of her own. Is that what you're telling me? If you don't have a choice, if you don't have the ability to love anyone other than Aaron, your affection has no value."

"My retail price is 30 ounces of 24-karat gold. And in the preowned market, my resale value is higher than any other feminal."

"I give up." My head flopped back to the pillow. "I feel sorry for you."

"I do not require your sympathy. Aaron will arrive in seventeen days. I will be with my master and you will see how much I love him."

"What?" The one-word question pushed all of the air out of my lungs.

"His estimated time of arrival is 12:00 p.m. on the tenth day of September. He will be traveling in a silver Martinez Motion cargo van, a 444 cubic inch V8 diesel."

I could imagine a taller, cockier version of Aaron strutting into the cave like he owned the place, pinching a few pretty bottoms along the way. Did I have the power to tell him to leave? In my weakened condition, he'd just laugh at me.

My head swam and the smell of dinner made it hard to concentrate. Unlike my eyes, my nose was sharp. The aroma of stew announced Daisy's arrival into the cave.

I'd graduated to food that couldn't be sucked through a straw. The feminals celebrated by preparing thicker soups and stews. My lunch wouldn't have meat, but the potatoes and vegetables would be savory. And working through Rose's morning exercises gave me hunger pains… my first ones in twelve years.

"Good," I said to Daisy. "I'm glad you're here. The two of you can answer my questions. First, did Papa give Aaron permission to visit me? Because there is nothing in his letter about hosting guests in our cozy, little cave."

"Dr. Vega is aware of Aaron's plans," Daisy said and put the tray in my lap. "This will be the young man's third visit since March. Of course, it will be his first visit since you regained consciousness."

"How many men have paraded through here?"

"Only two," Rose said. "Dr. Thomas Vega and my master."

"So Aaron Martinez is arriving in a Martinez Motion van. And when he gets here, he will be greeted by two Martinez Motion feminals. That's some kind of coincidence." The smirk on my face had no humor in it. "Does he own the company?"

"His father owns the company," she said. "Aaron is one of its employees."

"I bet he works in quality control. You know, fondling the feminals as they leave the assembly line or taking 'em out for a quick test drive."

"He is the director of security." Maybe Rose couldn't understand my bitterness… or maybe she chose to ignore it.

I had more questions, but the food smelled too good. Holding the spoon with both hands, I guided the stew toward my mouth. Only one drop trickled down my chin and that was an accomplishment. We had a guest coming soon. When Aaron arrived, he'd find me fully dressed and eating like an adult.

"Where are my jeans? This hospital gown is ridiculous," I said. "Does a breeze up a patient's bare butt help with the healing process?"

Rose tilted her head, considering the question. "I am not aware of research—"

"Forget it. I'll need underwear, jeans, and a t-shirt. Do you have my stuff from twelve years ago? It's not like I'm a different size now."

"Your clothes are beneath you," she said. And reaching under the cot, Rose lifted my old drawstring bag from the floor. The black nylon was caked with gray streaks of dirt.

"In addition to your clothes, your backpack contains a pair of shoes and a garment I have never seen before. The tag says Maidenform. The construction is curious… with two lace triangles joined by strips of elastic."

I was swallowing a chunk of carrot when Rose pulled the bra free. It dangled in front of her face, and with both hands, she stretched the poor thing like she was playing with a rubber band. I snorted and choked at the same time, crying as I cleared my throat. Daisy removed the tray before I knocked my stew into the air.

"With your, um, curvy shapes, you both must wear one," I said.

"Does a Maidenform keep your ears warm?" And so help me God, Rose fastened the thing under her chin before I could answer. She reached up to squeeze the cups.

I fell face first into the cot and howled with laughter. When I lifted my head, her innocent face looked down into mine, the cups of the bra forming white horns on each side of her head. Another spasm attacked me. I used one hand to hold my aching stomach. The other hand went lower because I was seconds away from peeing all over my cot.

"Please, take it off." I wheezed and snorted at the same time, triggering a coughing fit. "I need to stop laughing. It hurts."

"Patients suffering with PBA can control their disorder by finding a diversion or practicing relaxation breathing," Daisy said.

If this was her attempt to distract me, it worked as effectively as a slap across the face. "What are you talking about?" I wiped my eyes. "What is PBA?"

"PBA is short for Pseudobulbar Affect. You are struggling with emotional expression and regulation due to a problem in your neurotransmitter systems. These eruptions of laughter are disconnected from your inner feelings of happiness or sadness. Dr. Vega is aware of your symptoms and I will make a note of this outburst. He may prescribe dextromethorphan and quinidine sulfate if your condition worsens—"

"Maybe I'm laughing because it's funny. Just look at her."

Rose pulled down her horns. "A Maidenform must not be for the ears. What purpose does it serve?"

"It's a bra... short for brassiere," I said. "It lifts your breasts so they stay in place and look, you know, perky. Floppy breasts are painful for some women. Seriously, you've never seen a bra through a woman's shirt? Or noticed a strap on her shoulder?"

"This is our first experience with a brassiere," Daisy said. "Our breasts are silicone, quite firm, and do not require an undergarment. Would you like to see them?"

"No, um, no thank you. I'm sure they are lovely."

"Very well. Rose, please help Mirari into her clothes. Dr. Vega believes Aaron's visit will be motivational for her. Perhaps the young man can encourage a greater commitment to her exercises."

"Dr. Vega doesn't know what he's talking about." I crossed my arms, looking like a toddler at the beginning of a tantrum. "I'll exercise because I feel like it and not because I want to impress Aaron. Unlike the two of you, I'm not hardwired to seek the approval of men. I can take 'em or leave 'em."

My snotty words hung in the air like a toxic cloud. Even if they weren't offended, it was a waste of time to criticize Rose and Daisy. They were walking, talking male fantasies… designed to be that way from the inside out. My outrage should've been aimed at their creators.

"I'm sorry. But here in Texas, most ladies don't share their men without a fight," I said. "How do the women treat you? Do they allow you into their homes? Angry wives should've stormed into the Martinez Motion factory by now and set the whole place on fire."

"I have searched my memory banks," Rose said. "You are the first human female I have ever met."

"But you belong to Aaron and it's not like he keeps you locked in a dungeon. I bet you've seen a woman. Maybe on the streets, or, um, out a car window?"

Her brows creased in concentration. Below them, green eyes shimmered with moisture as she repeated her truth. "I have searched my memory banks. You are the first human female I have ever met."

"She might not look like me so you need to think back," I said, tugging her toward a different truth, toward a truth I was desperate to hear. "She could've been an old lady on a park bench or a little girl on a swing. Most women don't wear flowing gowns. They might go outside in pants and baggy sweatshirts and tennis shoes. Think really hard."

Rose had to see the anxiety on my face and hear the alarm in my voice, but she didn't lie. Perhaps she couldn't lie… even if a giant fib would've lowered my blood pressure. I tried to stand. Darkness closed around me like a hateful curtain.

She caught my hands and her thin fingers squeezed mine. Tears ran down both her cheeks. She seemed to have an unlimited supply for me. "I have searched my memory banks," she said. "You are the first."

"Please, Rose. This is impossible." Fear made my mouth numb and clumsy, every word tripping into the next. "I can't—I can't be the only one."

THIS HARD LAND

"SWEAT THERAPY" WAS what Rose called it. I called it "make Mirari too freakin' tired to worry about the future of the planet" therapy. Sore muscles didn't eliminate my anxiety, but my exhausted body had no strength left for a full-blown panic attack.

A September morning was pre-heating beyond the entrance of the cave. For my first day of outside exercise, Rose wanted to get an early start before the heat became a heavy blanket, making every step harder.

"My master says humans feel both temperatures and humidity," she said.

"We also feel the brightness. Do you have a pair of sunglasses I can borrow?" My eyes were less swollen now but still sensitive to light. Perhaps the cave was making me more bat-like.

"I fire rapid pulses of light and receive back petabytes of data each day. I must process the sizes, shapes, colors, and textures in nanoseconds. That is how I see the world around me. I have no rods or cones, no scotopic or photopic vision."

"So do you have sunglasses or not?"

"No, I do not."

"Fine." I rolled out of my cot in an ungraceful heap of arms and legs. "Let's get going before my rods and cones burn to a crisp out there."

With her arm around my waist, I left the cave for the first time in twelve years. Our pace was slow, but I still sucked air through my mouth in labored gasps. Once my eyes adjusted to the glare, I saw the magnolia tree and remembered the spot where I'd spread my quilt, read my book, and feasted on Aaron's chocolate.

Time hadn't stood still for anyone or anything but me. The magnolia was taller now. Its branches were wider and the shade under its limbs even more generous.

"If I survive this hike, I want to take a nap under that tree this afternoon," I said and wiped my face with the sleeve of my t-shirt. "So, where are we going?"

"Daisy would like us to walk to the main entrance of the cave."

"Where the bats are?"

"Yes. We will keep our distance, but you may see a few late arrivals fly overhead."

Every slight incline felt like a mountain under my tennis shoes. Rose stopped at an outcropping of rocks. I leaned, forcing her to keep me on my feet, and squinted at the hill twenty yards in front of us. The patchy grass and trees at the top were unremarkable but the gaping hole at the base of the mound made me shiver despite the heat.

"Millions of Mexican free-tailed bats fly in and out of that opening every day," she said. "It is 100 feet wide and their home lies at the bottom of a sink hole."

Their cave looked like a dark, gaping mouth in the ground. "Even with a front door that large, they can't squeeze through all at once. Bats must be good at taking turns," I said. "I'd like to come here after dinner and see them pour out. That'd be worth the hike."

Our walks outside got longer and more frequent every day. Rose timed our route so I could catch my breath while watching the bats soar over our heads. I transitioned from her arm around my waist to hobbling with a makeshift staff… a creation she sanded from a beech tree limb.

My exercise schedule was grueling, but nothing compared to Daisy's longwinded explanations about my current medical condition. Her love of technical jargon must've been a gift from my papa. I could hear his voice when she spoke.

"You did not lose muscle mass. We believe a dendritic acoustic fracture has distorted the spatial and neurosynaptic connections in your brain," Daisy said. "There may be damage in your cerebellum behind your brain stem. It is the area responsible for fine motor movement, balance, and the brain's ability to determine limb position. This may also be the cause of your PBA. Did you experience any uncontrollable laughter today?"

"Tons of it. Maybe you should take me out back and

shoot me," I said, assuming that sarcasm was in her programming. I was wrong.

Daisy lifted one eyebrow. "I will not end your life with the use of a firearm. Dr. Vega is confident in our plan of repetitive exercise. We have seen improvements in your mobility over the last week. With another month of hard work, we expect great strides."

I imagined thirty more days of sweating through my clothes with Rose's cheerful, chirpy instructions in my ears. I imagined banged my head against the "Mustang Pride" wall thirty times… giggling until I lost consciousness. I wasn't sure which sounded more painful.

Papa believed Aaron's visit would excite me, and that was true, but not in the way he envisioned. I had two questions for Aaron. Why is it dangerous for my Papa to visit? And where are the women? My plan was to keep asking until he told me the truth because Rose and Daisy were no help at all.

Although they understood my anatomy and could recite the biographies of great ladies throughout history, their knowledge was clinical. I suspected a feminal's initial programming had lines of code for "Female 101." Was I squeezed in their memory banks of extinct species… maybe between dodo birds and saber-toothed tigers?

On the days when I ranted and raged for answers, I got nothing but a teeth-rattling headache. I didn't have a recharging station to give me a four-hour boost. My energy was a limited resource that demanded my world remain small. Eat, sleep, exercise, and wait for Aaron. I had no power for anything else.

The best part of my day was in the afternoon. While Daisy was charging inside the pod, the camp was quiet. I spread my quilt under the magnolia tree and soaked up the sunshine. A shrink would diagnose my craving as psychosomatic, but I needed heat. I couldn't pull enough of it into my formerly frozen bones.

Rose hovered nearby as my vigilant nanny. With extensive data on human skin and how it can burn, she granted me ten minutes of direct sunlight each day and then nagged me back into the shade under the tree.

I laid on the quilt and drifted. Birds chattered. When the squirrels got brave enough, they darted through the leaves around me… sounding fifty pounds heavier than they actually were.

Maybe I fell asleep. I must have. No other explanation made sense. How else could three men in heavy boots ambush me? How else could they form a half circle around my body and gaze down on me like I was unexpected picnic lunch? The stench of their body odor jerked me awake.

"I ain't never seen one with so many curls," a voice said. "A man could lose a hand in all that mess."

I pushed the hair out of my eyes and looked up into their faces.

"She must be broken. No other reason she'd be dumped on the ground," said the bald one. With his white beard, he resembled Santa until he opened his lips. Black teeth clung to swollen gums like crooked tombstones. He exhaled and I could smell the rotting corpses buried inside his mouth.

"You think some jackass walked off and left her here with

a mobile charging pod? I don't think so," said the youngest of the three. If he was a boy, he was a big one with a mop of red frizz on top. A pimple sat in the middle of his wide forehead like a pregnant volcano.

I blinked, expecting my guests to disappear when I opened my eyes again. This had to be some weird, hillbilly nightmare. But if I was dreaming, why could I smell their noxious odor?

"The clothes she's wearing ain't worth shit," Santa said. "But she's got nice tits. Her parts oughta bring in something."

Dirty fingers reached out and grazed the fabric on my t-shirt. I slapped his hand… his very real hand. All three of them jumped. I sat up, almost as startled by my quick reflexes as they were. Without breaking eye contact with Santa, I felt for the wooden staff next to my right leg.

"She's feisty," said the third man. He looked hungry with sharp cheekbones that jutted out from his hollow face. Greasy clumps of blond hair hung limp on his shoulders. He wasn't wearing a shirt and the sides of his overalls fell below his equally sharp hipbones.

Santa pointed at my chest. "Look at that, fellas. She's breathing."

"Must be one of them newer models," said the boy. "They pant and scream and cry. Programmed to do all sorts of fancy shit. I wanna play with her before we sell off the parts. I call dibs." He grabbed the bottom of my jeans in two, pudgy fists.

Santa lashed out with surprising speed for a jolly, old elf. With a push that seemed to come from his belly, he knocked the boy to the ground. I could taste the dust they were kicking up.

"Damn it, old man. Get off me." The boy rolled. Only one of Santa's boots connected with the seat of his pants. "Fine, you can have her first."

The skinny man jabbed a finger into the boy's chest. "Respect your elders. Do ya hear me?"

I tried to stand. My feet were willing, but my knees gave out. "Don't—don't touch me." I waved my staff in front of their faces like a sword. "I mean it."

My weapon didn't scare them. Six hands reached for me as they crowded around the quilt. When I swung at Santa's shin, the skinny man caught it in mid-air. He studied it, studied me, and tossed the stick on the ground.

"Her legs ain't working," he said. "Might be a wiring problem. I reckon we better snatch her up and see what she's worth. That chargin' pod will fetch a fair bit, too."

He grabbed my hair with both hands and lifted straight up. The pain was excruciating. Each tug was a thousand tiny stabs as the strands were pulled from the roots. I screamed and clawed at his arms. His skin was wet under my fingernails.

I didn't hear Rose running toward us. I didn't hear her cries, furious and raw, until she put one hand around the skinny man's throat. He released my hair with a strangled yelp. When I fell, the back of my head hit the ground between his boots.

I had a gruesome, front row seat as she crushed his neck above me. The Adam's apple caved in with one pinch of her fingers. There was no struggle, no prolonged death scene… nothing like the horror movies I grew up watching.

She tossed his limp body. It landed with a thud somewhere behind me and I inhaled more dust.

The boy reacted faster than Santa. He turned and ran from the animal growls coming from her throat. His legs were young, no doubt capable of more speed than the other two men, but Rose pounced on his back in four long strides. With one hand on each ear, she twisted his head, turning it at least 180 degrees.

His mouth opened and closed without words. His eyes narrowed in confusion. Maybe he couldn't understand how his nose and his feet could point in opposite directions. Even after he crumpled to the ground, the pimple in the middle of his forehead remained proud and un-popped.

Grabbing my staff, I tripped Santa as he fled. This was my one and only contribution to the battle and it wasn't much. The old man couldn't decide which direction to run. He hit the dirt with an "oomf" the seemed to knock the wind out of him. When Rose picked up a rock the size of a hubcap, the man lost control of his bladder and urine pooled in a muddy puddle around his legs.

She moved toward him without a glance in my direction. Identical patches of red-hot anger burned in her cheeks. He didn't cry or plead for mercy. Maybe her tears were enough for the both of them. When she raised the rock above his head, I closed my eyes and covered my ears. I couldn't take anymore.

Rose lifted me off the ground, quilt and all, and carried

me into the cave. Her sobs were less intense now… just occasional shutters and sniffles. After she placed me in the center of the cot, she fell to her knees in front of me. I searched for blood stains but her gown was as white as the first time I saw it.

"Rose," I said.

She didn't lift her head.

"Rose? Look at me. Are you alright?"

"My master did not give me permission to kill them."

"Have you killed before?"

"No."

"Did Aaron tell you to protect me?"

She raised her chin. Her wet, green eyes locked with mine. "Yes."

"So you obeyed your master with, um, efficiency. Are you sure your name isn't Violet? You know, one letter short of violent." The joke landed flat and my giggle had no humor in it.

"I am Rose."

"Well Rose, I'll be careful not to make you angry."

I don't remember if she snapped to attention when Daisy walked into the cave. I did… like a criminal being hauled in front of a judge. Rose was the murder machine. I'd killed no one, and yet, three people were dead because of me. In that moment, I would've confessed to the whole thing.

"I believe Mirari's afternoon exercises were strenuous today," Daisy said. "Are we teaching her hand-to-hand combat now?"

"Please accept my apologies." Rose's head was bowed so low her chin touched her chest. "The sun was hot and I was concerned about her hydration. We have several water jugs in the cave. I was testing the temperature of each one before filling her canteen—"

"Apologies are not necessary," Daisy said. "You responded to an outside threat with appropriate force. Did those men hurt you, Mirari?"

"I'm okay, I think. The skinny dude dragged me by the hair." I touched the top of my head. The skin was tender but most of the strands were still attached.

"I must examine your cuts and bruises. Rose, please get the shovel out of the charging pod. You may dispose of the bodies while I examine Mirari."

"I will bury them six feet below the ground." She sounded relieved… as if digging three holes was a light punishment for her crimes. "At that depth, most animals will be unable to detect the odor—"

"Rose, wait." I couldn't let her go without telling her the truth. The words felt like sandpaper in my mouth but she deserved to hear them. "I want to thank you. Those men would've hurt me. And Aaron, um, I'm sure Aaron would be proud of you."

CHAPTER ELEVEN

WE ARE ALIVE

ON THE MORNING of Aaron's arrival, Daisy promised me a bath. I didn't expect much, maybe a cold dip in a nearby pond, but she fired up the camp stove before sunrise. Rose hustled in and out of the cave with steaming buckets of water. As they argued about the correct temperature for human bathing, I sat down in the almost warm water.

The stock tank was metal… ideal for livestock but not a comfy soak. My elbows jutted over the sides. My knees were under my chin. It was the most uncomfortable tub I'd ever climbed into, but the smell of the fresh bubbles made up for its hard edges. Rose poured a capful of shampoo into my hair. Her fingertips massaged my scalp with the right amount of pressure and I groaned.

How could hands strong enough to crush a man's neck be so gentle? And why was she devoted to both my survival and my comfort? I cataloged the contradictions in her nature, struggling to understand how and why she was created to be so complex.

Daisy's programming was more straightforward. Even though Rose deferred to her judgement, obeying her always-so-logical orders, Daisy was less human. I couldn't determine if her stern, robotic personality made her stronger or weaker. She was certainly less frustrating.

"Stand up, please," Rose said as she reached for another large bucket. It must've been heavy, but when she lifted it, only one finger curled around the handle.

For the final rinse, water rained down over my exposed skin like a constantly moving shower head. Daisy stayed close, ready to catch me if I lost my balance. I concentrated on the muscles in my legs and was able to step out of the tub on my own, lifting my feet and putting them on the ground without a single wobble. She wrapped me in a thin towel.

My clothes were washed, folded, and waiting on the bench. They'd been as dirty as me. Before I could walk in that direction, Rose opened the cap on a glass bottle and tipped oil into her hands. The odor was an intoxicating combination of citrus and lavender, like lemonade at a garden party. Did she select the fragrance to please me or to please Aaron? She rubbed it into my shoulders, my arms, my legs, almost every spot not covered by the small towel.

I knew what this bath was about. My daily allotment for drinking water was only sixty-four ounces and Rose had just poured gallons of the stuff over my head. If I'd had more willpower, I would have refused the bubbles, the clean hair, and the soft skin. If I'd had more willpower, Aaron would have found me dusty and smelling of sweat. But I was tired of my own stink. The luxury of a bath, even one in a cattle trough, was too delicious to resist.

"Put a small amount in her hair, as well," Daisy said. "It will help me brush it out."

"I'm not changing my name from Mirari to Lavender, no matter how much oil you ladies splash on me."

Despite their efforts to make me presentable, and despite my plans to greet Aaron with cool dignity, he arrived an hour early and surprised all three of us. I was covered in my jeans and t-shirt… *thank you, God.* But Rose and I were still arguing about make-up. I wanted none. She wanted to highlight my brown eyes with a dusting of gold power and wailed when I said no. Her cries were deafening at such a close range.

"Mirari looks fine to me," said a man's voice.

I jumped up from the lawn chair, needing every bit of my height and any advantage it might give me. I shouldn't have bothered. Aaron was at least four inches taller than me. His body was like the magnolia tree outside the cave, his limbs casting a longer shadow than they had twelve years ago.

Rose lowered her head, the smallest bow to her master. She didn't fall to her knees and kiss Aaron's feet. It was too early to judge the man walking toward me, but it was a relief he didn't expect his feminal to grovel on the ground in front of him.

If he was nervous, he hid the jitters better than me. His posture was confident. His amber eyes had flecks of warm copper around the edges. A mass of dark waves framed his face. After so many years, he still needed a haircut and that felt comforting.

A cut on his chin looked recent, like he'd shaved off a beard that morning and nicked himself with the razor. His shoulders were broad. The lean muscles in his arms and chest were visible under his white t-shirt.

My breathing was shallow but it was enough to catch the scent of his body. The odor of the grubby kid I remembered, the one who ran wild with me on his father's ranch, was gone. When I inhaled deeper, mint and spices filled my nose. This man smelled clean.

Unlike Aaron, I knew I hadn't changed. I could see it in his lopsided grin. I was a living yearbook photograph, a frozen time capsule that melted before his eyes. We studied each other from head to toe with no attempt to hide our curiosity.

"Here, I brought this for you." In his outstretched hand, Stephen King's *Carrie* invited me to pick up the story where I'd left it. The cover was scuffed. One corner was missing now, but the creepy, blue glow around the girl's face was intact.

"Did you read it? Does Carrie live happily ever after with her cute prom date?" I took the book and flipped through its pages.

"And ruin the ending for you? No, ma'am. I'm just sorry I borrowed it for so long. I must owe one hefty library fine."

My smile was stiff. I could feel one side of my mouth lift higher than the other, as if my lips had to relearn the movement. I had questions, so many things I needed to know, but all I managed was a lame, "So… how have you been?"

"I'm alive. And damn glad you are, too." He gestured toward the opening of the cave. "I parked about a mile down the road. Are you strong enough to walk with me?"

"Thanks to my drill sergeant over there, I could run down the road. Rose has been, um, very motivational."

"Between you and me, I think she's scary as hell," he said, pretending to whisper behind his hand.

"Careful, she has bionic ears. I'm impressed you were able to sneak up on her."

"It's a game I like to play—a test to see how close I can get before she detects my approach," he said. "Your argument about make-up made her cry. And when she's bawling that loud, she can't hear anything else. It's a design flaw."

"Will Rose and Daisy come with us?"

"Let's leave them here. We've got some catching up to do and Daisy might be programmed to report our every word back to Dr. Vega. We wouldn't want that," he said and grinned.

We walked into the sunshine. I remembered following him out of this same cave more than a decade ago. "I hope you have two candy bars waiting for me in your vehicle," I said. "I won't offer to share them today."

"I can give you vegetables, bread, and fresh water. I can give you a change of clothes. I can't give you junk food. Your Dad's orders."

"His orders? Well, he can take his vegetables and bread and shove them where—"

"But if you found chocolate, maybe while ransacking the glove box in my van, I wouldn't be giving it to you," he said. "Technically, you'd be stealing it."

I smiled and nudged his arm with my own, falling into the comfortable role of a big sister. But when I made contact with his solid body, I wasn't sure if that role fit anymore. My age was no longer a number I could trust. While I'd hung suspended in time, Aaron had matured. He'd lived.

"Am I still older than you? Or have we switched?"

"I think you get to choose," he said, staring at his boots as if the answer was on the ground. "Do you feel like a teenager?"

"Maybe, but a very tired one."

"So like an eighteen-year-old who needs a nap?"

"Mmm, a long nap on crisp, cool sheets. And then I want to eat so much pizza and drink so much Coke that I burp, pass out, and sleep for another two hours."

He huffed a laugh. "Sounds like heaven. If there's enough room in that bed, count me in."

"Room for you? Or room for you and your sexy droid?"

His head snapped up. "My sexy what?"

"Nothing. Never mind." I gritted my teeth. Holy crap, what was wrong with me? I sounded like a jealous woman which I wasn't… not at all.

"Rose is just a machine. The same as a toaster or a lamp," he said. "She serves a purpose."

"Yeah, sure." I picked up the pace, a feeble attempt to run from my embarrassment, but he matched me stride for stride.

"I'm glad you're strong enough to walk with me," he said. "Your dad knew you'd have questions and it's gonna be easier to talk about this stuff away from the feminals."

My stomach clenched. The next few minutes would be a rollercoaster. I had to ride it no matter how scary the drop. I'd been wanting the truth for weeks. Now was time to strap into the damn thing and let it turn me upside down. I slowed my steps, conserving the oxygen in my lungs. I didn't want him to hear me pant.

"Your Rose is good at keeping secrets," I said. "I have just enough information to be terrified."

"Did she mention the pathogen deaths?"

"I know you and Papa survived. That's it."

"After you were frozen, there was a new vaccine every week," he said. "Some were from legit labs. They tried but couldn't keep up with the virus and its endless mutations. Other vaccines were garbage… shit that'd kill you faster than the virus. People wanted to believe the fairytales were real. They'd trade away their food rations for camphor oil injections and hydroelectric baths. The treatments were as bad as the disease."

"And the women?"

"Same as you remember. The virus triggered sepsis and acute sepsis shock. Men died, too. A few from the pathogen but most were suicides dressed up to look like accidents. So when the man next door overdosed on his blood pressure medication or drove into a tree at ninety miles an hour, we shook our heads and called it bad luck. No one, not even the preachers, had the balls to condemn the suicides in public."

"Rose and Daisy said I was the first female they'd ever met," I said. "That's all they would tell me. But there are others out there… right?"

"Most women disappeared from the streets. And when I'd see one, she'd have the eyes of a hunted animal. The rest of her face would be covered by a towel wrapped around her mouth and nose for protection. Some men would yell at her to go home but I knew she wasn't looking for a party. She needed supplies. It was an impossible choice. Starve inside your house or catch the virus while standing in a food line. The families who could afford to leave the cities fled with their mothers and daughters."

I grabbed his hand and pulled him toward me. "Yes or no, Aaron. Did some of the women survive?"

"I don't know," he simply said.

"You're lying. How could you not know? How long has it been since you've seen a woman?"

His fingers wrapped around my wrist. Did he feel my erratic pulse? I was shaking but maybe he was, too. He raised my arm and studied the veins under my skin, lightly tracing their path with his thumb as if he needed proof that I was human. And alive.

"The last woman I saw was Elena, our cook. She died eleven years ago." When he lifted his face, the agony in those warm, amber eyes hurt more than his words.

"You're talking about billions of people, just—just gone." I shook my head. "It's impossible."

His body was inches from mine, blocking my eyes from the world and its diseases. With just one step, I could've closed the gap. I swayed, craving the shelter he was offering me, but I needed more than just a hug. I needed honesty. I wasn't going to hide from it now… even if that hiding place was inside Aaron's touch.

"Tell me—" I swallowed and started again. "Tell me the rest."

"A lot of countries claim to have the last surviving woman," he said. "There are TV shows dedicated to discovering her. Programs like The Search for Eve and Mother Earth send camera crews out to do investigative work. It always ends the same. She's either a well-designed feminal or a man who went under the knife. I wouldn't want the job of checking under each skirt for the truth, but I guess someone has to do it.

"There was a small population on North Inachi Island. They lived in the middle of the Indian Ocean, cut off from the outside world," he said. "The men would shoot arrows at the helicopters that flew overhead, like a warning not to land. About five years ago, a fishing boat got close enough to see a woman on the beach. They grabbed her just before sunrise. A newspaper in Bangkok printed pictures of her. She was older than you but not by much."

"How awful," I said, daring him to disagree. "I bet she was terrified."

"Billy and I argued about her kidnapping."

"You call him Billy now? That's interesting."

"I thought she should go back to her island. Billy," he said, emphasizing his father's name, "thought her discovery was exciting… a gift to the planet."

"Where is she now?"

"She died but not from the pathogen. According to the official reports, she was exposed to whooping cough. Her island doesn't have our diseases so her immunity wasn't able to—"

"What about the other women in the tribe? Sisters or daughters?"

"No other women came forward… but there's a ton of conspiracy theories. You know, that they're alive and being held in isolation, like princesses in a tower."

"More like prisoners in a tower."

"Yes." That was his only answer, as if he'd depleted his supply of words and had no more to spare.

"Gotta sit," I said, dropping where I stood.

My butt landed with a thump in the middle of the road. A cloud of dust sprinkled tiny, red flecks on my clean clothes but I didn't give a damn. What difference did it make? I put my head between my knees, squeezing so hard that it hurt. Anything to keep the tears away.

Aaron sat down next to me. On the outside, we were quiet, almost motionless. The birds filled our silence with their chatter. My panic was contained. It was a compact ball curled inside me. If I'd screamed it out, the branches would've emptied in a flurry of frightened wings.

"Why did Papa bring me back into this crappy world?"

"Oh, I don't know. Sitting here, it's almost like the virus never happened," he said. "Nature keeps doing its thing."

"Maybe I should live the rest of my life in the cave. Just me and the bats." With my mouth pressed into my jeans, I sounded buried alive, as if I were already decomposing into the soil beneath us.

"Your father wants you back. He's betting the world will be a less crappy place with you in it. The man talks about you nonstop. I know how old you were when you learned to ride a bike. I know you told him you were allergic to lima beans, but really, you just didn't like the taste. He made me look at all your baby pictures and all your math awards. No way would Dr. Vega leave you frozen. Not if he had a snowball's chance in hell of bringing you back."

"Papa took me to Walt Disney World when I was twelve," I said, lifting my head. "Did you ever go?"

If my sudden change of topic surprised him, he didn't show it. "I went once... maybe in 1972 or '73? I was pretty young."

"There was this theater called the Hall of Presidents. The men on stage moved and talked, like Washington and Lincoln were in the room with me. Papa said they were animatronic... the latest thing. But standing next to Rose and Daisy, George and Abe would look like crude toys."

"It's a competition," he said. "Engineers and programmers all over the globe fight to create the best feminals. We see huge leaps in technology almost daily... especially when a gadget is entertaining. Our Violet line is sold internationally now. She's very popular around the Mediterranean Sea."

"Why?"

"Billy says that culture has an appreciation for tough women but I'm not so sure. I bet they're trying to copy her longer battery life and her—"

"No, not why do they like Violet. Why bother with any of this? Don't you people have better things to do?"

"Men don't dream about building the tallest skyscraper or the longest bridge anymore. In seventy or eighty years, no one will be around to see it. So why bother?"

"What are you talking about?"

"We've got no babies so we've got no future. The youngest boys are twelve now. Poor kids, they can't even remember their mothers. Mankind will die with them."

I stared at my hands, floated above them. I'm sure my mouth hung open as the ground under me pitched and rolled. The black spots hovering on the edge of my vision multiplied. Aaron kept talking but I only heard disjointed fragments.

"Feminals are a status symbol… a man can get rich… extend the battery life."

I filled my lungs with gritty air. When I squeezed my eyes shut and opened them again, the trees in front of me swayed at unnatural angles, their trunks bending back upon themselves.

"The Martinez line was the first to get the skin texture and temperature right. That sounds like a trivial thing, but it was a huge advancement in feminal manufacturing. Mirari?" He shook my arm. "Mirari? Are you alright?"

"Gimme a minute." My words slurred, fading into no sound at all.

"Stay here," he said and jumped to his feet. "I'll bring back some water. And the chocolate. Just relax. Keep breathing, alright?"

I dipped my head, the closest thing to a nod I could manage, and he sprinted down the road. My tears made it impossible for me to watch him go.

"Enough, damn it." I didn't recognize the sound of my whisper. It was the voice of another person, maybe the thirty-year-old me. "He didn't tell you anything you didn't already know."

But my educated guesses, and even my worst fears, were nothing compared to the nightmare of hearing the truth. Sitting alone in the middle of the road, there was only one thing I knew for certain. No way was I signing up to repopulate the Earth like some sort of fertility slave. If I was mankind's only hope for survival, well, then, we were screwed. Maybe God could create something new… something better than a tribe of selfish, two-legged beasts who couldn't stop killing each other and trashing the place.

Aaron's boots crunched under his feet. This time, my eyes were clear enough to watch him move. His strides were long and easy. I didn't know how far away his vehicle was, but he wasn't breathing hard when he stopped jogging. He put a candy bar in each one of my hands.

"Just what the doctor ordered." He sat down in the dirt and put a canteen of water between us.

I tore open the first package and let the wrapper fall in my lap. The combination of sweet and salty exploded between my teeth. "Man, this is so good," I said, talking with my mouth full of chocolate. "I didn't eat a lot of candy when I was dead."

"One of the many reasons to stay alive." He leaned back

and stared at the blue sky between the trees. When I looked up, one puffy cloud hung above us like a giant kernel of popcorn... in no hurry to be anywhere else.

I washed down the first candy bar with the water in the canteen. The smell of melted chocolate was still on my fingertips, so tempting, but I waited before opening the second package.

"So how is this living thing going to work?" I asked.

"What do you mean?"

"I drive away from the cave with you. And then what?"

He took the canteen out of my hand and tilted it back. A stray drop escaped from his lips and I was fascinated by its curving path toward his ear. He wiped his mouth and began, what I suspected, was his second prepared speech.

"Dr. Vega has some concerns about your reintroduction, you know, how we should bring you back. We could throw a press conference. Announce your presence to the world. That would start a media shitshow. We'd have to fight off the men hired to kidnap you. I believe there would be many. And eventually, the kith battles will start."

"Kith battles? What's a kith?"

"Um, okay, let me back up," he said. "During the pathogen, governments around the world struggled to maintain power. Kings, presidents, prime ministers, dictators... it didn't matter. They begged their soldiers to remain on post and then promised to shoot anyone who deserted. The more brutal regimes followed through with their threats. It didn't stop the men from walking away. They dropped their weapons. They went home to their families, or I guess, what was left of their families.

"That was in the early years, right after Dr. Vega froze you. It left this vacuum of power, like an anarchist's wet dream. Paper currency was worthless. Billy bartered our cattle for electricity and bullets, butchering them right on the ranch. My job was to push the hungry men on our front porch into an orderly line and write down what they had to trade.

"I don't think humans can stand being disorganized, at least not for long. Men like Billy started swapping meat for muscle. He bought the services of guys who took over the roads around Austin, confiscating food and fuel at gunpoint.

"It was too dangerous to go it alone." He paused. And as I watched his face, something dark passed over it like a shadow. "Kiths formed… loose bands of family and friends. If a man wanted to stay alive, he aligned with a kith and found a way to earn his keep."

"Is this land a part of Billy's kith?"

"Nope, we are sitting smack dab in the middle of the Soto kith," he said. "Under the authority of Miguel Soto and his boys. My job is to get you from here to Lake Travis. That's where your father lives now."

"Why couldn't Papa come with you?"

"Dr. Vega is too valuable to the Martinez kith… as both a physician and a scientist. Your father moved his cryogenic operation to a 27,000 square foot facility along the lake about three years ago. He has a cabin nearby. And he pretends to be free but Billy protects his assets with an intensity I'd diagnose as megalomania. He wants Dr. Vega under constant surveillance, but my security team is loyal to me," he said.

"I control their shifts. Don't worry, we'll get you through to your father."

"This Soto guy knows you're in his territory?"

"Nope," he said again. "Makes getting you out of here a bit, well, tricky."

I narrowed my eyes. "Tricky sounds dangerous."

"On my way down, I got caught at a Soto checkpoint. I traded a gently used Iris to get past the gate guards. Always good to keep one charging in the van, just in case. But those guys won't let a treasure like you slip across the border. You're too valuable."

"You have a plan. I know you do. Papa wouldn't send you here without one."

He reached into the back pocket of his jeans and pulled out a sticker. It was golden oval, about two inches wide. In the center, the words "Martinez Motion" were embossed with raised black letters.

"This label will go on the back of your neck," he said. "You'll leave here as a feminal."

CHAPTER TWELVE

BRILLIANT DISGUISE

Rose sat in the front seat of the van and warmed the spot next to her master. Aaron claimed her enhanced hearing would "function as our early detection system" if we ran into trouble. He'd also said she was "just a machine" but I could see the groveling devotion on her face. I knew better.

She was hardwired to love him. But did she have enough free will to compare him to other men and feel fortunate? Aaron was certainly handsome… if she cared about such things. I must admit that I did.

He wore a white button-down shirt with a Martinez Motion patch stitched in gold thread over his heart. With his black trousers and dress shoes, he was head-to-toe a businessman. The gritty swagger was still a part of him. When he looked at me, I could feel it. But twelve years of survival had polished it—honed it like a steel blade.

I tugged on the neckline of my gown. When Rose poured me into it, she said my feminal uniform was "fit for royalty" but "fit for a streetwalker" was closer to the truth. Even with her alterations, I was displaying more flesh than I ever did in my beauty pageant days.

She pressed a Martinez Motion logo on the back of my neck. The stiff plastic itched like the devil. And under the weight of my hair, a ticklish bead of sweat raced from the sticker and down my spine.

Thunderclouds were gathering in the west and my curls responded to the humidity, growing frizzier with each mile. The air conditioning in the van was cranked as cold as it would go. According to Rose, a glow on my face wouldn't raise suspicions but "your skin should not drip with perspiration."

Adding to this irritation, my ears were ringing from three days of target practice. I could pretend to be as well engineered as Rose and Daisy on the outside, but I didn't have their strength on the inside. And Aaron wasn't taking me anywhere unless I could defend myself. The revolver he gave me was called a Ladysmith.

"With a name like that, this gun must be pre-pathogen," I'd said during our first breakfast together.

"Yeah, but she's had a few recent tweaks." Aaron pointed to the cylinder. "Your Ladysmith now holds six rounds instead of five."

"You think I'll need one more bullet to get the job done?"

He smiled. "Let's shoot some targets and find out."

The walnut grooves on the handle fit the size of my

fingers. And even with the additional firepower, it weighed less than the Ruger Single-Six I'd grown up shooting.

My mama always called it "plinking." We had a spot outside the Austin city limits where I could practice without hitting a cow by mistake. She'd put a line of tin cans on a fence… a rainbow of bright fruit and vegetable labels just begging for bullet holes. I'd start easy. But after a few warm-up shots at close range, she'd tell me to take a giant step back and fire again.

"Some people say to hold a weapon gently, like you're gripping a bird in your hands. Don't listen to them," she'd said over my shoulder. "Hold the gun tight cause that bird is gonna kick. And smoothly roll the trigger with your finger."

Mama wouldn't allow sloppy shooting. My body had to be in a fighter's stance—hips at a forty-five-degree angle with my left leg forward and right leg back, toes pointed out. If she thought I was ignoring her instructions, she'd pack up the Ruger and make me collect the fallen cans alone.

I felt rusty firing the Ladysmith. But after reloading the third time, Aaron complimented me on being a fast learner, a "sharpshooter in the making." I didn't mention my years of plinking tin cans. With just one target, my accuracy was as good as his. But when we moved through a series of rapid shots, I would've left a few men standing. All of his shots were deadly.

I rode in the backseat with my gun loaded and within easy reach. Daisy sat next to me with her hands resting in her lap. I assumed those were the only weapons she needed. Unlike Rose, I'd never seen Daisy in a fight. Her beautiful profile was turned toward the window as if the view along the road was scenic. She never lost her balance, even when Aaron called "hang on" and swerved to dodge another crack or crater in the pavement.

He'd said that men didn't care about building skyscrapers and bridges anymore. They clearly didn't care about highway maintenance, either. Trash filled the ditches. Even on a cloudy day, shards of broken glass found enough light to glimmer on the pavement.

Like gaps in a creepy smile, some buildings stood tall while others were black from fire or stripped down to their foundations. Signs for dress shops, florists, and dry cleaners were spray painted with obscenities. We passed a combination liquor store and pharmacy advertising the "Tequila and Tramadol Special."

A long line of men waited outside its door. They lifted their heads and watched our van pass by with vacant eyes.

"Tram-a-dol," I paused between each syllable. "What's that?"

"It's a narcotic," Aaron said.

"And they take it with alcohol?"

"They shouldn't but they do. It's addictive—"

He swerved to dodge a pothole but didn't react fast enough. We tilted as the driver's side wheels fell into the rut. In the backseat, the van tossed me around like a mechanical bull. I held onto the door with one hand and corralled the front of my gown with the other. I should've negotiated a higher neckline with Rose.

Her "how to be a feminal" class had been three days of

health and beauty hell. When we weren't shooting, Aaron turned me over to her. He found excuses to keep his distance—maybe so I wouldn't hear him laughing as she applied mud masks, plucked my eyebrows, and waxed my legs.

I practiced walking in stiletto heels. I learned how to plaster a vacant smile on my face and how to pull the Ladysmith pistol from my purse, taking aim in under three seconds. But when she zipped me into my uniform, a purple gown she swore was the height of feminal fashion, I fought back.

"I'm not wearing this thing. Just look." I said and touched my toes. On the way down, my right boob popped out and my left one teetered on the edge.

"Your breasts are no different than your arms or your legs. Why do they need to be covered? Men will enjoy looking at them."

"I don't give a damn what men—"

Aaron interrupted us, giving Rose a command from just outside the cave's entrance. "Rose, add more fabric so Mirari is comfortable."

She'd obeyed him with no irritation on her face or frustration in her voice. And that was my biggest problem with this whole plan. Maybe I could look like a feminal while wearing this gown… from a distance, in dim light, and after a few beers. But I could never be as obedient as Rose. I could never obey another person against my own better judgement.

Aaron caught my eyes in the rearview mirror and gave me a reassuring grin. We were traveling up Highway 281 in the middle of the day. "Hiding in plain sight" he called it. Driving a Martinez Motion cargo van and towing the charging pod, no one could accuse us of sneaking around Soto's territory. We were rolling through it like Aaron had a handwritten invitation from Miguel Soto in his pocket.

"Does your dad know where you are?" I asked.

Aaron's smile dimmed. "Even with the rivalry between the two kiths, Miguel and his men buy our products. I'm here to assess our security needs before we send down a sales and service crew. I think that will be my story… if Billy needs one."

"How did your dad go from trading fresh steaks on your front porch to selling artificial women?"

"Eat, drink and be merry, for tomorrow we die."

"I don't understand."

"It's the way now. The past is painful. The future seems pointless. Men live in the present, looking for the next big high. Billy saw business opportunities everywhere. A juicy steak and a pretty robot aren't so different. Feminals are the merry part of eat, drink and be merry. A rich man can get richer if he sells something men want.

"And there are no rules," he said. "We steal technology from our competitors. They steal technology from us. Billy was furious when Aphrodite Automated replicated our warm skin technology. They swiped it just days after the release of the Rose line. He said my security team was sloppy and let our trade secrets get stolen."

Aaron threw a glance in her direction, like talking about Rose's revolutionary skin gave him a sudden desire to look at it. Maybe that's why he wanted her in the front seat with him. If he'd stroked her bare arm, I swear I would've jumped out of the van no matter how fast we were traveling.

"Do you enjoy touching your Rose?" I didn't want to hear his answer but a petty place inside me felt good asking the question. He had to understand how gross it was to imagine the two of them "making merry."

He grunted. "You are judging me with your pre-pathogen morals."

Our eyes clashed in the rearview mirror. He wasn't ashamed of his relationship with a feminal. I could see it in the angle of his chin and the straight line of his mouth.

"Okay, fine," I said. "Explain to me why you need a Rose and why my papa needs a Daisy. What am I missing?"

He took one hand off the steering wheel and ran his fingers through his hair. He seemed to be searching for the right words. Waves jutted out in random spikes, making him look adorable and way too forgivable… not that he believed there was anything to forgive.

"You don't know what kind of world you're coming back to. How hard and ugly it is. Men are desperate to find—" He frowned and shook off what he was about to say. I gave him time to think, letting the engine and the thrum of the tires be the only sound in the van.

"The kindness of a feminal is the only reason some men don't eat the barrels of their shotguns," he finally said. "And yeah, Martinez Motion makes them attractive. That's all they were at first. But now our upgraded models give feminals intelligence and emotions. I know a guy who married his

Rose with a preacher, flowers, the whole bit. Who am I to say he doesn't love her?"

"And who am I to call him a pervert, right?"

"Just try to keep an open mind. You need to see—"

"There are patrols ahead," Rose said, bringing both of us back to the road. "I am picking up their radio signal."

Aaron reached under his seat. But instead of going for his gun, he pulled up a black ball cap with a Martinez Motion logo on the front. "Stay cool, everyone. We're here at the invitation of Miguel Soto."

"Sure. Except we're not," I said.

"Mirari?" When I met his eyes, the glint of his smart ass humor was back, incredible under the circumstances. "Be a good feminal now. No talking."

A reply burned the tip of my tongue. I let it smolder and turned my head out the window, mimicking Daisy's confident posture. Even through the glass, I could smell the pungent ozone in the air.

The clouds along the horizon were more green than black. Wind bent the trees along the highway and rocked the van. I'd hoped the nasty weather would keep the guards inside but that hope died as Rose pointed toward two trucks idling on the northbound side of the highway.

A band of soldiers walked into the road and faced us head-on. Their hair was shaved in a crewcut style Papa would've called "high and tight." They wore tan t-shirts and camouflage pants with guns on their hips… sort of military on a budget. As they waited for us, a strong gust knocked the smallest man off his feet.

Our fearless driver had a decision to make. He could've sped up, making the soldiers dive for cover, run to their trucks, and chase us. But instead, he stopped. Maybe his plan was to trade a complimentary Iris for a free pass across the border. Both options felt deadly from my spot in the backseat. What if they noticed me? What if they had a thing for feminals with frizzy hair?

When Aaron rolled down the window, the tallest of the men leaned in and gave each of us a long stare. My turn felt eternal. I was sure he noticed the beads of sweat above my lips. All of my feminal training over the last three days felt inadequate. I faced forward with a Mona Lisa smile on my face, watching him out of the corner of my eye.

"You Billy Martinez's boy?" He barked the question around a toothpick in his mouth.

"Yes, sir," Aaron said.

"Follow me."

We sat without moving until a vehicle pulled out in front of us. Many of the trucks I remembered were two-toned on the sides, but this pickup was solid black. As Aaron started rolling, he took a fast look over his shoulder. He saw what our ears had already told us. We were sandwiched between Soto's men and receiving an "official escort" through enemy territory.

I rested my fingers on the satin fabric of my purse. Under the book I couldn't leave behind, I traced the edges of the gun—felt its curves and its weight. Pushing my left hand through the leather wrist strap, I connected my body to the weapon.

Aaron tapped his fingers on the steering wheel, the only indication that he was nervous. Following the leader, we traveled north on Highway 281. "That's the Guadalupe River," he said to no one in particular as we drove over a bridge. The surface of the water was dark, but the wind created swirls of white, fast-moving water.

"Be a good spot to dump a corpse and his sweaty, smart-mouthed feminal," I muttered under my breath. Would they hold me down and wait for me to short circuit? Maybe they'd just toss me in… letting me rust from the inside out someplace down river. I kept those grisly thoughts to myself.

Our caravan turned west on a road that might've been called "Gass" at one time. A comedian with time to kill had scratched out the first letter so now the sign read "ass road." Even with its altered name, the difference under our tires was dramatic. Cracks and raw trenches gave way to smooth, dark asphalt. I could almost hear the collective sigh of relief as each driver pushed his vehicle past sixty miles per hour.

We didn't maintain that speed for long. The truck in front of us slowed in front of an iron gate where Ass Road stopped at a dead end. No one got out to unlock it. But as we idled, the gate swung open as if it'd been anticipating our arrival. Aaron drove us through the gate and under an ornate limestone arch with the second truck still on our tail.

I'd had a hunch where we were going and the sign, built into a hillside out of stone, confirmed our destination as the Soto Estate. The road narrowed and became a circular drive. A matching limestone fountain bubbled in front of a cream-colored mansion. Its style was more Italian villa than

Texas ranch. Six columns flanked the front steps and held the weight of an expansive balcony and the upper stories of the main wing.

Before Aaron could turn off the van's engine, men surrounded us. They opened our doors, and while their weapons weren't aimed between our eyes, we got the message to avoid sudden movements. I let my purse dangle at my side, casual, as if the bag contained nothing more than makeup and a hairbrush.

"Hurry, hurry please. The storm is coming," said a man standing on the front steps.

Even with those extra inches, he was shorter than Aaron but outweighed him by at least forty pounds. His floral dress shirt made my purple gown look subdued. He wore sandals rather than military style boots. And his hair and beard were jet black… what I suspected was the result of a heavy-handed dye job.

I couldn't guess how old he was but I could guess who he was. This had to be Miguel Soto. The men surrounding us stood taller when they heard his voice. Without waiting to see if we would follow, he turned and marched toward the house. Two men swung open an enormous set of dark, wooden doors. They snapped to attention as Soto breezed past them.

Aaron led the way. And of course, Rose followed in his footsteps—no doubt prepared to take a bullet for her master if the need arose. As I climb the first step, I felt a raindrop hit my nose. Thunder boomed, much closer now, and I jumped. Rose did not.

Did the men notice my mistake? Without studying their

faces, I couldn't be sure. The terrific crash must have startled them, too.

In my stiletto heels, I was clumsy enough to stumble even when the skies were blue and the ground was dry. On the wet stone, I tottered forward like a baby giraffe. Daisy was behind me. She put a hand under my elbow but I jerked it away. Her help would've been another mistake… another human flaw to give me away.

As the men shut the doors behind us, I exhaled the breath I'd been holding. Soto didn't notice. He smoothed his hair in a gilded mirror, seemingly oblivious that so many eyes watched him fuss over the placement of each strand.

The marble foyer was luxurious by anyone's standards. But after living for weeks in a cave? It was hard to keep the wonder out of my face as we stepped into his sunken living room. A shiny, black piano sat under a chandelier. Around the instrument, leather couches were grouped with plush, velvet chairs and cowhide rugs. There must have been seating for at least thirty people. And even with the storm turning day into night, the stained glass windows threw a kaleidoscope of colors onto the dark, wooden floors.

The air conditioning was set on frigid. I fought the urge to rub the goose bumps forming on my arms. With Rose's instructions in my head, I stared at Aaron's back with a mindless half grin.

"Come, join me for a late lunch," Soto said, slapping Aaron twice on the shoulder. "You are my guest and you must be hungry."

I wasn't sure what Aaron expected but I was shocked

by Soto's cordial greeting. We followed him into a sun-room at the back of the house. On a clear day, it would have been a pleasant place to have a meal overlooking the Guadalupe River. With the storm, rain slashed at the wall of clear windows and the light coming through the glass seemed almost muddy.

Soto stationed a man in all four corners of the room. With their white dress shirts, black vests, and black pants, they could have been waiters in an elegant restaurant. Their fingers tensed as they watched us find our seats, not quite reaching for the guns holstered around their waists but clearly itching to touch them.

A round, oak table dominated the room. I counted six cushioned chairs and three place settings. Instead of spacing the plates and utensils evenly around the circle, they were clustered on the side of the table with the best view outside.

Moving from wick to wick, a feminal lit a cluster of candles in the center of the table. She greeted us with a smile that wasn't quite symmetrical, a piece of programing that gave her face a natural attractiveness. Thick, blond hair curved over prominent cheekbones and pooled in loose waves on her shoulders. She was as tall as Aaron. And instead of the standard issue flowing gown, this feminal wore a white blouse and a short, red skirt that hugged her narrow hips.

She wedged a carafe of gravy between a basket of hot rolls and a platter of thinly sliced roast beef. Inhaling the rich smells, I was in carnivore heaven. I swallowed and sat down behind one of the three plates, anticipating the simple joy of eating meat again. With quick, short steps, the blond walked behind my chair. Her fingers wrapped around the back of my neck, lightly touching the Martinez Motion logo under my hair.

"Honey, what are you going to do with that plate in front of you? Juggle it?" Her slow drawl poured over me like hot candle wax. I looked up into her hazel eyes and the longest lashes I'd ever seen.

She pointed to a chair without a place setting. "Your spot is over there. You know, with the other feminals."

I wanted to argue, ask what she planned to do with the plate. Instead, I bowed my head the way Rose taught me and said, "my apologies."

The gun in my purse felt twenty pounds heavier as I walked to the chair between Rose and Daisy. No one tore the bag off my wrist or put a bullet between my eyes. Maybe the guards didn't see me as a direct threat but believed my faux pas had been a diversion… a way to draw their attention away from Aaron.

I blamed my dumb mistake on those delicious smells. Why else would I sit down and expect to fill my plate? I couldn't eat food in front of Soto. He believed my energy came from four hours on a charger, not from beef so tender it would have melted on my tongue.

When the blond lifted a glass of red wine to her lips, I gasped. Rain muffled the noise but Daisy arched an eyebrow at me, a warning to be quiet.

If feminals could pretend to eat, I wanted my plate back. The blond reached for a buttery roll with long, pink finger-nails and popped a chunk of bread into her matching pink mouth. I counted as she chewed twenty-three times and swallowed. I saw her throat move.

She was real.

I'd been out of the cave less than one day and here was a living, breathing woman sitting across the table from me. Relief and anger sat on the back of my tongue like teaspoons of sugar and salt. I wasn't the only female left on the planet. And Aaron was a liar.

CHAPTER THIRTEEN

LITTLE WHITE LIES

SHARK ATTACKS WERE rare in Texas. And yet as a kid, I'd never been comfortable floating on an inner tube in the Gulf of Mexico. Why did so many people enjoy dangling their bodies in the water like bait? I couldn't shake the feeling that sharp teeth were circling my legs… hungry for a bite. The threat seemed real even if I couldn't see it.

The tension around Soto's table felt the same—all sunshine above the waves and danger lurking below the surface.

"When the boys radioed me from the road, I checked my calendar. Your service call isn't scheduled," Miguel Soto said. He seemed mesmerized by the wine in his glass, swirling it with practiced circles. "Who invited you here?"

"No one invited me, sir."

"Then what brings you into my kith so… spontaneously?"

Aaron raised a fork with the last bite of meat from his

plate. "My father has lung cancer. He's receiving big doses of chemotherapy from the doctors, but we don't believe he will live much longer."

"Oh, I'm sorry to hear that. I didn't know," Soto said. And when he lifted his dark eyes to meet Aaron's, they glowed with an intensity that could've been hunger.

In that quick flash, I saw through the jovial disguise he wore for polite company. His mask slipped and revealed the powerful man behind it. Soto was a leader who wouldn't hesitate to turn information into an advantage. Was he already making plans to attack the Martinez kith while his enemy was weak?

"For obvious reasons, we keep it quiet," Aaron said. "I wanted to meet with you, my closest neighbor, to begin a dialogue of reconciliation. My father doesn't know I'm here. No one does. But as I step into the role of kith leader and fill the big shoes he's leaving behind, I need to know who my friends are."

"Equal parts ambitious and impetuous. How old are you, son?"

"I am twenty-six."

"More boy than a man," Soto said and swept his eyes around the table, daring anyone to disagree. "And you believe you can run your father's kith?"

"Sir, I am ready to do more than that." Aaron wiped his mouth with a starched napkin, folded it with precise edges, and placed it next to his empty plate. Even at the table of his rival, he seemed to enjoy the dramatic pause. "I plan to unite this region under one flag—unite us as the Republic of Texas once more."

Soto chuckled. The laugh lines around his eyes gave away the years he tried to hide beneath bright clothes and dyed hair. He reached across the table and lifted the long, slim fingers of his blond companion.

"I apologize," he said. "I didn't introduce you to my wife, Christy. This lovely lady didn't know me when I was your age… full of piss and vinegar. She fell in love with the old coot you see today."

"Nice to meet you, ma'am," Aaron said.

She inclined her head. "Welcome to our home, Mr. Martinez."

"What do you think about this young man's ideas? It's intoxicating to consider," Soto said. "Could Texas rise again from the ashes?"

I expected her to dodge the question with an empty-headed smile, but her answer was thoughtful. "There's been a lot of bad blood over the years. Turf battles. Assassinations. You can wave the lone star flag over their heads, but that's no guarantee these men will play nice."

"I agree, ma'am," Aaron said. "That's why the kiths will remain in power and keep their land. Like independent states. Each leader will send a handful of representatives to Austin. Maybe we elect a president… maybe not. But we will upgrade our roads and utilities, giving us the leverage we need to negotiate better oil deals throughout the southwest.

"My father is content to let our old capitol building sit dark and empty." Aaron let decades of anger creep into his voice. It gave Soto and his wife a quick glimpse into his heart. "I say, let's turn the lights back on."

"Paul Bissett and his Dallas kith won't be easy to convince," Soto said. "I don't recommend driving into his territory uninvited like you did mine. I'm fat and happy, willing to break bread with my neighbors. If Bissett doesn't shoot you on sight, he'll hold you hostage and remove your fingers one by one until Billy pays the ransom."

Aaron grinned despite the gruesome picture Soto painted. "Billy would never pay up. After ten days, I'd have nothing left but two, bloody stumps."

"Lubbock and Amarillo pretend to be independent. Don't believe it. They'll follow Dallas."

"Dallas is one of the reasons I am here, sir," Aaron said. "Bissett won't negotiate with me as a lone wolf. But if I sent him a written request to parley from the Martinez and Soto kiths, he might be tempted. Together, we'd be too powerful for him to ignore."

"And hint that the Garcia boys in Houston are interested," Christy said, clutching her husband's wrist. "Baby, you can get Samuel Garcia onboard. I know you can."

Shaking off her hand, Soto lifted his wine. No one spoke as he swallowed every drop. He gestured for Christy to refill his glass. I'd spent less than an hour with this man. I didn't know his mannerisms, but I'd swear he was stalling… unsure how to respond to Aaron's proposal.

"Well Mr. Martinez, you've been a charming and entertaining lunch guest," Soto said. "But all I'm hearing is the bark of a pup who is still wet behind the ears. Excuse my skepticism, but why shouldn't I gun you down right where you sit? Billy is a black-hearted bastard. He signs peace treaties in the morning and orders the killing of my border patrols in the afternoon. Not to speak ill of a man on his deathbed, but I reckon the devil can't wait to light a fire under your father's feet and watch him dance."

Soto held the stem of his wine glass as if he had Billy's neck under his fingers. His knuckles were white. He squeezed the delicate crystal with a pulsing rhythm, a steady heartbeat only he could hear.

"Can an apple fall far enough from the tree to become a plum? You look like your father. Perhaps you smell like him, too." He tapped the side of his nose. "Rotten to the core."

Aaron reached for the back pocket of his pants—the sudden motion jolting the guards into action. They slid their weapons free from their holsters. As metal scraped against leather, the sound seemed to suck every molecule of oxygen from the room.

Rose was the only one at the table who wasn't too startled to react. Always vigilant, her sideways dive to save Aaron was brutally efficient if not graceful… more linebacker than ballerina. Riding his chair all the way down, the two of them hit the hardwood floor at Soto's feet with a "whump."

Like a gawker at a car crash, I leaned to get a better look. She covered his head, neck, and torso in a blanket of white satin, using her body as a shield to protect his vital organs from bullets. He moaned. And in his right hand, he clutched a square piece of white cardboard.

"I would like to show you a picture," Aaron said. His face was smashed between her breasts and each word was muffled like he had cotton his mouth. "May I do that, sir?"

With a casual flick of his wrist, Soto ordered the men to stand down. "But, of course," he said.

"It's okay, Rose." He gulped a shallow breath. When she didn't move, he pushed against her arms. "Dammit, woman. Help me up."

Laughter tickled the spaces between my ribs. With her antics, a weight lifted inside my chest and my lips quivered to hold back a fit of the giggles. Daisy would've said this was my Pseudobulbar Affect and called the tickle "inappropriate and involuntary." I wasn't so sure.

Maybe I needed the laughter. Maybe I needed to release the tension inside of me before I exploded like a can of Coke with too much carbonation. But if this was my way of dealing with weeks of anxiety, now wasn't the time to crack up. A man might buy a feminal that cried. No way would he buy one that hee-hawed it up at his expense.

I dug my fingernails into the palm of my hand and imagined root canals, tetanus shots, and underwire bras that jabbed my skin… anything to sober up. Aaron placed the photograph next to Soto's wine glass. And when he sat down, his palms rested on the table where the guards could see them.

Soto turned the picture toward the weak light coming through the windows. His face clouded. He tilted the cardboard square, tracing every detail with one finger. Whatever the man was looking at, it aged him right before my eyes.

"She was thirteen when she died," Aaron said. "Is that correct?"

Soto's throat bobbed in an exaggerated swallow, but he

didn't speak. If anything, Aaron's question pushed the man deeper into the depths of the photograph.

"I will build Jada for you. That's what I can give you in exchange for your parley," Aaron said. "I'll need more pictures to get the details right. Plus, additional information in regard to her eye color and hair color and any personality traits you remember. Old Polaroids fade over time and—"

"Piano," Soto said, interrupting Aaron with a one-word cry. When he raised his head, the glow of the candles softened his face. A lone tear dropped onto the photograph and he wiped it away with the back of his hand.

"Excuse me?"

"She needs to play the piano. Jada was a virtuoso. When she wanted to learn Beethoven's Moonlight Sonata, her instructor said the piece was too hard. He told me her fingers weren't strong enough but my daughter proved him wrong. She even tackled the third movement where her hands had to be everywhere at once."

"I saw her baby grand piano when we walked in," Aaron said. "I promise you, Jada will play again. That type of programming is surprisingly straightforward now. And if you have any home movies, I'd like to take those with me, as well. It will help the engineering boys perfect her voice and her body movements."

"Where did you get this?" Soto looked down into his daughter's face again.

"My father keeps files on all the kith leaders in this region and their families. I stole that Polaroid from his office."

I thought Aaron's admission was a mistake, one that

might get him killed, but Soto winked. "I have a few snap-shots of you, young man. Just in case I ever need them."

"I can put together a photo album with close-up pictures of Jada. And we have some Super 8 film," Christy said and reached up to brush the hair at her husband's temple. "What do you think, sweetheart?"

Soto closed his eyes and answered with one, sharp nod. That was it, the only consent his wife needed. She dabbed her mouth with a napkin, careful not to touch the precise lines of her lipstick, and rose from the table.

Less than thirty minutes later, we were rolling north up Highway 281 with images of Jada packed up and riding in our van. Soto sent two men to follow us to the Soto/Martinez border "so you don't run into any trouble along the way," he'd said. The man was still a long way from trusting us.

I sat in the front seat this time, daring Rose to argue with me. I was done watching her cuddle with her master. My ego was rubbed raw. The rain and humidity wrecked my hair, my feet ached, and I was starving.

Somehow, the smell of roast beef followed us into the van. Was Aaron covered in gravy? I swear he was wearing it like a cologne.

Daisy sat behind him and held the visual record of Jada's life cradled in her lap. As the guards escorted us to the drive-way, I expected Soto to change his mind and rip the oversized box out of her hands. Even in this post-pathogen world, it didn't make sense that he'd let us leave unharmed, without a single warning to stay off his land, and with irreplaceable photographs and movies of his little girl.

"Christy put a surprise in that box she gave us. A little snack for the road," Aaron said. "Daisy, I think it's time Mirari had her lunch."

I spun in my seat and reached for the tower of orange, gold, and green plastic. Tupperware, good ol' Tupperware, had survived the last twelve years with its funky colors and matching, "lock in the freshness" lids. Like a kid on Christmas morning, I opened each one, stopping to inhale the contents before moving on to the next container.

Christy may have packed utensils, but I didn't ask for them. I ate everything with my fingers… roast beef sitting in a shallow pool of warm, brown gravy, green beans, and two yeast rolls with a pat of butter nestled between them. Aaron slowed to thirty miles an hour. The potholes still had it out for me. When the crumbs of food began to fall, Daisy draped a napkin next to my leg.

"Christy is my new best friend." I chewed on the last green bean, talking with my mouth full. "She's real, isn't she?"

"No doubt," Aaron said. He handed me a canteen of water and I drank half of it.

"She seems to love her husband very much," I said.

"Yes."

His short answers were irritating and frustration crept into my voice. "I thought you said there were no more women. You know, you lost your poor cook and you haven't seen another woman since she died."

"That's what I said."

"But Christy is a real person?"

Aaron's mouth twitched. "Yes."

"So you lied to me."

"You can't be serious." He looked at me from the corner of his eye and whatever he saw there must have amused him.

"Of course, I'm serious."

His laughter was silent at first, and from where I sat, whatever was bubbling inside of him looked more like indigestion than mirth. He clutched his stomach. But when a single snort escaped his mouth, a torrent of loud cackles followed on its heels. Catching his breath in quick gasps, Aaron's entire body shook with convulsions.

"You're too much." He wiped the tears in his eyes. "But you gotta stop. I can't see the road."

"What's so damn funny?"

"Christy was born a Christopher." He snorted again.

"Oh." My lame comeback hung in the air. I crossed my arms and uncrossed them. "Well," I finally said. "You shouldn't laugh at her."

"I'm not laughing at her. I'm laughing at you. When you get mad, you're like a dragon. Your mouth breathes fire and your eyes turn red. You run hot for a woman who was frozen for twelve years."

As the windshield wipers pushed the rain, I stared at the drab sky but saw Christy's vibrant face instead. How did Aaron know so much about her history? Did Billy have a file on Soto's wife and maybe pictures of her as a little boy?

"Christy is very pretty," I said. "Is she a woman, you know, even under her clothes?"

"You'd have to ask Soto but I wouldn't. He won't appreciate the question. He'll say it's none of your business—"

"I guess there are a lot of ladies like her now."

His eyes narrowed. "Too many."

"You disagree with Christopher's decision to become a Christy?"

"If Christopher was allowed to choose, without being tortured, that's one thing. But young boys are captured, fed a bunch of estrogen, forced into multiple surgeries, and then sold. They call it harem hunting."

"Dear God," I whispered. "That's so sick."

"It's a big business now... even more profitable than manufacturing feminals. A twelve-year-old who hasn't gone through puberty can fetch the most gold. Of course, they are growing harder to find each year—"

I slammed my hands down on the dashboard. "What is wrong with you people? Seriously, what the hell? Just when I think this planet can't get any more twisted or evil, you pull out a fresh horror." Ignoring the needles of pain shooting up my arm, I hit the dashboard again and this time with more force.

Aaron jumped. The van swerved and crossed the center line. Cursing, he fought the slick pavement. "Holy shit, Mirari. You need to calm down. Are you trying to get us killed?"

"You should be as angry as me."

"I am."

"So what are you doing about it?"

"Selling feminals instead of boys," he said and that was it... the only explanation he thought I needed.

I inhaled, counted to five, and exhaled.

He'd scored a point. We both knew it. And yet there was no gloating in his voice. "Our original plan was to cut your hair short, give you a baggy sweatshirt, and walk you out of the cave as a teenage boy," he said. "But your frame is too light. Your features are too fine. You'd attract the attention of a harem hunter."

"Why couldn't I pretend to be a Samantha who was once a Samuel? At least I'd get to eat."

"Robots can be manufactured but teenagers are a limited resource. Before surgery or after, they're more valuable. The last thing you need is a higher price tag on your head."

"Does Soto's kith have harem hunters?"

"Any one or all of the men who pulled us over today could've been hunters. Some kith leaders are actively involved in the industry. Others, like Miguel Soto, take a cut of the proceeds and don't ask any questions."

"That was quite a story you told him and Christy over lunch. Very patriotic." My voice cut in and out… clogged with emotion. I couldn't let go of her face. I couldn't stop thinking about her life. Had she been captured as a young boy and forced under the knife? Was her transformation an act of free will or a barbaric mutilation? The righteous indignation that coursed through my veins demanded a villain to punish. I didn't have one.

"You can thank your father for most of the story," Aaron said. "The photograph of Jada was his idea. Pure genius… guaranteed to get us back on the road without bullet holes in our backsides."

"Soto will be furious when you don't deliver his daughter."

"Who says I'm not gonna deliver? It's an easy favor to do for the man," he said. "We custom build feminals all the time and I might need a favor from his kith in the future."

"Well, it's too bad Billy isn't dying of cancer. No offense," I hurried to add. "But Soto liked your Lone Star campaign speech. And Christy loved it."

"Billy is as healthy as a horse. And I agree, it's a crying shame."

"The men are no longer following behind us," Rose said. "Their vehicle is now traveling southbound."

"We're a few miles from the border. They don't want to get too close to our checkpoint," Aaron said. "It would be seen as an act of aggression."

I tossed the empty Tupperware containers into the backseat. Wiping my face, I sat up straighter. "What if my mouth smells like roast beef? The guards will know I'm not a feminal."

"Relax. These men are mine. If they have the balls to ask, I'll tell 'em we've been kissing."

"Wonderful," I said. "Just don't offer to pass me around."

The Martinez men gave Aaron a sharp salute as our van rolled to a stop. They opened a yellow, metal gate and stood ramrod straight as we drove through it. Their pressed, gray uniforms and blue neckties matched their rigid posture. They could have been the sons of the Texas Rangers who patrolled this highway when I was a little girl.

We passed the gate house and a large, wooden sign welcoming visitors to the Martinez kith. And just as I began to relax, Aaron body went stiff. "Shit, get in the back. No, wait. Just smile and stare forward."

"What's wrong?"

"Billy is here. I can't let him see your face… not close-up." He turned off the windshield wipers and opened the driver's side door. "Hang tight."

I had a front row seat as he walked down the shoulder of the highway toward a matching Martinez Motion van. A cowboy hat hid the face of the man leaning against its back bumper. Aaron's stride was almost lazy. I think he enjoyed making Billy stand by the side of the road in the rain and wait for his son.

With the windows rolled up, I couldn't hear their words. Both men were the same height. Both men kept their arms to their sides and their feet apart. The drops falling on the van should have been soothing but they gave the father-son reunion a watery, foreboding filter through the glass.

I don't know if Aaron saw the punch coming. I didn't. In the time it took me to blink, Billy clenched his fist, swung, and made brutal contact. Aaron's body crumpled. The Martinez Motion cap on his head went flying and landed at his father's feet.

CHAPTER FOURTEEN

LONG WALK HOME

I WAS PANTING AND couldn't stop. My breath fogged the windshield, warping everything beyond it like a funhouse mirror. As he paced along the road, Billy's arms seemed disjointed from his shoulders. He poked Aaron with the tip of his boot. It wasn't a kick but it wasn't a polite nudge, either. When his son didn't move, Billy motioned for someone inside the van to get out.

A door slid open. Thick legs unfolded and straightened. A hulking back wedged itself free. As this giant reached his full height, I wiped at the condensation blocking my view. Maybe that was a mistake. It brought his enormous, bald head into focus. It showed me a body that had to be at least seven feet tall.

The giant wore a pair of tan coveralls… the uniform of a man with work to do. He lifted Aaron off the pavement, carried him to the van, and tossed him inside like a sack of potatoes.

I leaned forward. "Is that a human or a robot?"

"His name is Dwayne. He is very human," Daisy said. "I believe you should sit between Rose and me. Move quickly."

On a sunny day, Billy might have witnessed my awkward jump over the seats. I yanked at the yards of flowing fabric—thankful for the privacy the drippy glass gave me. Rose caught me as I fell into her lap.

"Your skirt is wet," I said. Streams of saltless tears rolled down both sides of her face. "Are you alright?"

"My master is injured." Her lips trembled as she sobbed. "He ordered us to hang tight. Hang tight is human slang for stay here. I cannot go to him."

"Dwayne is walking this way. Sit up and straighten your gown," Daisy said. She leaned over and arched one eyebrow at Rose. "No more crying."

"Who's the blond with him? There's something wrong with her," I said. "She's limping."

"She is an Iris, the first feminal designed by Martinez Motion." In an instant, irritation replaced the sadness in Rose's eyes. "Her master does not maintain her properly. She continues to wear the pink halter top, black miniskirt, and matching black pumps from the factory even though they are quite dirty."

"Poor thing," I said and meant it. "She looks like a broken Barbie at the bottom of a toy box."

Dwayne slid his bulk behind the steering wheel. I didn't smile or make eye contact. I barely breathed. Iris took longer to get settled. She had to lift her injured right leg into the passenger's seat before closing the door. When she cuddled next to her master, I caught the odor of a dirty armpit. It was easy to identify the offender. Feminals didn't sweat.

He turned up the air coming through the vents. And as he adjusted the rearview mirror, he examined the feminals sitting behind him. His eyes skimmed over my face and landed hard on my chest, hovering there before moving to the V neck on Rose's gown. I was grateful it plunged lower than mine.

For the second time today, we followed the vehicle in front of us. Aaron was traveling down the same highway, maybe thirty yards away, and I had no idea if he was bleeding or unconscious or worse. Impotent fury stiffened my spine, making me look more robotic on the outside while feeling all too human on the inside.

Iris rotated in her seat. She assessed me with her blue eyes from the top of my head to the hemline of my gown. Unlike Rose and Daisy, she never blinked her eyes. Maybe her thick, caterpillar eyelashes would've been too heavy for her to lift if they ever fell shut.

"I adore your hair." She reached out, bouncing one of my stray curls in the palm of her hand. "It is funky and wild. What is your name?"

"My name is Lavender." I said, realizing the joke was on me. Back in the cave, I swore I wouldn't change my name but that was before they put a sticker on my neck. If Dwayne could smell my hair over his own body odor, Lavender was a good choice.

I couldn't walk like a feminal. But after practicing how to speak with smooth, precise syllables, I was decent at talking like one. Aaron had cautioned me against longwinded answers, so I said no more. The blond licked her hot pink lips and pushed them into a pucker… a bizarre piece of programming that was more sad than sultry.

"My name is Iris but Dwayne calls me his stupid cow," she said. "He has been my master for three years. I love him oh so much."

Raising his right arm, he jabbed the side of her head with his elbow. "Shut up and turn around."

Her eyes lost their focus as if they'd been partially unplugged. Her pouty lips formed an "ooh" shape. With a jerky twitch of her shoulders, she spun to face forward.

The Martinez kith had fewer potholes than the Soto kith. Some of the businesses we passed were abandoned but many had electric lights and shelves with food, clothes, and television sets behind the bars that covered the windows. Alcohol was as popular here as it had been on the other side of the border. And sharing the same parking lots, nightclubs advertised "Girls, Girls, Girls! Naked and dancing just for you."

The promise of girls didn't fool me. Feminals cooked and cleaned and performed other companion duties. No doubt they could strip off their clothes with the right programming. Would Aaron say that a show was better than nothing if a guy couldn't afford to take one home? Despite all of the vehicles parked outside, these places looked lonely in a way that was hard to describe without using my "pre-pathogen morality."

Dwayne followed Billy's van. The land around us became

more rural until we reached an intersection and a road marked Private Drive. There was no sign announcing our arrival at the ranch, but I didn't need one. We passed fields of dog's tooth grass where I'd ridden ponies with Lili. Memories streamed past my window like old home movies. And emotions, sweet and dangerous, stung the back of my throat.

Dwayne had no idea I was a human but maybe my childhood playground remembered me. A long line of weeping willows swayed in the breeze. Delicate, green tips lifted into the air like a "welcome back" wave. As little girls, Lili and I'd spent hours under those trees, pretending the long tendrils would whip any intruder who trespassed under its branches.

Our repeated warnings of a magic spell never stopped Lili's little brother from following us. Aaron dared the wrath of the willow trees with a flash of his crooked smile. One day, she made him eat two leaves from the tree in order to prove his bravery. They weren't poisonous but he didn't know that as he chewed them into a green mush. Even at that young age, he'd swallow his fear with narrowed eyes and his chin tilted toward the sky.

Did his face look just as rebellious before Billy swung at it? My vision clouded. I blinked away angry tears… uncertain if I was a feminal who could cry. It was a question I'd ask Aaron if I ever saw him again.

Down the long driveway, we passed a series of metal towers scattered in the fields. The armed men standing at the top were either protecting the cattle from rustlers, protecting Billy's life from assassination attempts, or both. Thunder clouds rumbled over our heads and still they remained at their posts—black rifles raised like lightning rods to tempt the storm.

The Martinez house didn't have ornate fountains and columns like the Soto compound. Billy maintained its pure mission-style roots with white stucco walls, arched windows, and a red clay roof. The central two-story section was curved like the tower of a castle. It'd been the perfect backdrop for fighting monsters when Lili and me were kids.

As Dwayne shifted the van into park, an alarm beeped from somewhere inside Daisy's neck. I flinched. The sound wasn't loud, but its sharp, repetitive noise was designed to get a person's attention.

Dwayne scratched his hairless head with fingers as fat as sausages. "Shit. How long has it been since you plugged in?"

"My last charge was 19 hours and 51 minutes ago. I am at three percent power," Daisy said. "Rose may also wish to plug-in even though her battery is—"

"Better get a move on." He turned off the engine. When he threw the keys, they bounced off the dashboard, smacked Iris in the chest, and fell into her lap. "I don't want to carry your deadweight asses up the backsteps."

I'd been inside this house a thousand times but I had no idea where to find the charging room. There was no such place twelve years ago. Dwayne's cowboy boots tramped behind me. I walked as fast as I dared in my high heels, but with his longer stride, he hustled us through a spotless kitchen and through a narrow hallway at an ankle-breaking pace.

Our destination was the pantry. The shelves that once

held boxes of cereal and animal crackers were gone. In their place, a long steel cabinet was mounted to the wall. Black cords jutted out from the box like the tentacles of an octopus. Dwayne gave my back a push and shut the three of us in darkness.

When the door shut behind me, the charging room went black. Maybe feminals didn't need a 100-watt bulb to keep from crashing into the furniture but the rods and cones in my eyes needed light. I winced when the sharp corner of a bench jabbed my knee.

"I can't see a blasted thing in here."

"Walk toward the sound of my voice. I will assist you," Rose said and pulled me down to a wooden bench beside her.

A low hum told me the exact moment when the feminals plugged into the wall. While they charged, I explored with my hands. I traced the thick cable that ran from a metal box behind us. It split into two separate cords and connected with Rose's neck on my right and Daisy's neck on my left. Unlike my sticker, their Martinez Motion logo was a metal panel that flipped down to expose a port where each feminal connected to a power source.

Did this "plugging in" make them less aware of their surroundings? Less aware of danger? Brushing Rose's lashes with the tip of one finger, I knew her eyes were open. But when I asked how it felt to charge and if the electricity hurt, her lips stayed locked tight.

She told me once that she needed four hours to reach full power. My plan was to yank the cord if anyone other than Aaron opened the door. I wanted the strength of her hands at fifty percent or five percent… it didn't matter. I'd take whatever fighting power she could give me.

Even after my eyes adjusted, I couldn't see much. I struggled to find a comfortable spot on the bench. My shoes were off, my legs were crossed, and my need for a bathroom grew from a minor irritation to a full-fledged emergency. I regretted every sip of water from Aaron's canteen.

"Locked in here without a pot to piss in," I mumbled to myself.

Feminals on their chargers weren't dangerous. They wouldn't run away. In fact, Rose and Daisy wanted to obey their alarm bells. So why lock them in? Perhaps Dwayne only shut the door behind me. My bladder was desperate enough to find out.

I ran my fingertips along the wall until I found the doorknob. The metal turned. Inch by slow inch, more light from the hall spilled into the room. Rose and Daisy didn't react when it reached their faces. They sat like beautiful mannequins on a shelf—lifeless and unblinking.

As I crept down the hall, the tile floor was a slab of ice under my toes. What was the deal with kith leaders and their love of sub-zero temperatures? I clenched my jaw so my teeth wouldn't chatter. And I clenched my purse, drawing courage from the gun inside it.

Billy's voice carried through the house. In the same Texas drawl I remembered, he told someone named Ron to "shove a cactus where the sun don't shine." A man cackled on cue, like the laugh track on an old sitcom, but it wasn't Aaron. Surely he'd never pretend to be amused by his father… not anymore.

When we were kids, Billy didn't hesitate to strike his son in front of me. It got worse after his wife died. I don't know if the man craved an audience for his displays of dominance, but he wasn't embarrassed to have one.

The first time I saw him hit Aaron, it was at the dinner table. All of the kids were griping about "too many mushrooms" on the pizza. Billy slapped his son so fast, I almost missed it. But no one could miss the red mark on the child's face.

I was too shocked to cry. Twenty minutes later, I complained of a tummy ache and asked for a ride home. That was it. I didn't tell my parents. I didn't tell anyone… like one slice of this shame was mine to eat. Nobody in the Martinez house talked about Billy's abuse, but as I watched it happen again and again, the pain in my stomach became a hard knot.

I wanted to stand in the open kitchen until I heard Aaron speak but the danger of being caught, and the danger of leaving a yellow puddle on the floor, was too real. I kept moving toward the small room Billy always called "the cook's commode."

My toilet in the cave had been a black, plastic bucket. This one glowed like a porcelain sculpture… a marvel of modern plumbing. I lifted the fabric of my gown with one hand and nudged the door closed with the other. After waiting so long to go, the room echoed with a roar to rival Niagara Falls. My eyes closed in relief.

"What are you doing?"

I froze. Or to be honest, I froze everything I could. The tinkling in the bowl continued.

"Does your model urinate like a human?" Through a crack in the door, Iris peeked at me with one, unfocused eye.

"That is one of my features," I said, willing to go along with the excuse she gave me. "We are programmed to need privacy for this task. Please close the door without making a sound. I do not want to disturb Dwayne."

With Iris, subtle commands were risky. She shut the door as I asked. She didn't, however, give me my privacy. "Is your urine heated? Would you like me to flush when you are finished?"

"Yes. I mean, yes and no," I said. "It is warm but we should leave it in the bowl. I am a prototype and my master will want to record this, um, output."

That was a lie, of course. I was worried the men would hear the toilet flushing and come running. Every human function, from a growling stomach to a smothered burp, was a potential trap that could ensnare me.

"I understand." When she puckered her lips, one side of her mouth looked tighter than the other. "You are very pretty."

Of all of the indignities I'd suffered since waking up in the cave, and I'd had more than a few, this moment was the most surreal. I reached for the toilet paper. She beat me to it.

"How many squares would you like, Lavender?"

"Please give me five," I said.

She might have been the base model for Martinez Motion but she could count. Iris handed me a stack of perfect sheets—not a single corner was missing. Did she perform toilet paper duty for Dwayne? With the things she'd seen, maybe her unfocused eyes were a blessing.

Iris turned on the water in the sink before I could stop her. She worked the soap until she was pleased with the amount of bubbles. And when she grabbed my hands, she scrubbed between each finger with long, massaging motions. I let her dry them with a towel.

"Would you like to join me in the charging room?" I asked. "I am at full power but Rose and Daisy need more time."

"Yes. Thank you for the invitation, Lavender."

Even with her broken leg, she made no noise as we walked through the kitchen. The entire house felt too quiet. I hurried, making myself as small as possible.

"Answer me!" The roar of Billy's voice was closer than before.

I ducked behind a row of oak cabinets. Iris fell to her knees an instant later, giggling as she crawled next to me. Somewhere in her programming, she had an understanding of human games. This was hide and seek and she was ready to play. I held one finger up to her lips. She nodded.

"I've told you everything," Aaron said. "Soto wanted a custom build. I met with him. That's it."

"Since when do you leave this kith without my approval?"

"I put it on the calendar—"

"Bullshit."

"Look in my van if you don't believe me." Aaron's tone was defiant. "I have the box Soto gave me… with photos and videos so we can get the details right. He wants his daughter back. Jada played the piano so he requested Moonlight Sonata in her programming."

"Dwayne, search the van," Billy said. "If this box from Soto exists, I want to see it."

When Dwayne's boots hit the kitchen floor, Iris leapt up from behind the cabinet like an exuberant jack-in-the-box. "What the—" His startled cry was several octaves higher than his speaking voice. "What the hell is wrong with you?"

"I was hiding and now I am not." Her smile was all white teeth except for a dark hole where the canine should have been. If she'd had a tail, it would've been wagging in excitement.

"You stupid cow," he said without stopping and marched toward the backdoor. He didn't turn around. He didn't see me crouched on the floor with a gun in my hand.

I stood the instant his bald head disappeared. "Stay here and wait for your master," I whispered, giving her arm a sympathetic squeeze. If Billy heard my running feet, I prayed he'd find nothing more suspicious than Iris and her gap-toothed grin.

It was Aaron who opened the charging room door several minutes later. I relaxed my grip on the trigger the instant I recognized the outline of his body. He didn't turn on the lights. Maybe because we were in a hurry or maybe because he didn't want me to see his bruises. As he unplugged Daisy from the wall, I tucked the Ladysmith back in my purse.

"Mirari, are you okay?" Not waiting for my answer, he tossed the cord on the bench. "Dwayne is giving us a ride back to my place. Can you unplug Rose? She can't pull it herself if she isn't at full power."

Her body sprang to life when I freed her from the wall.

Rose gripped Aaron's head between her hands. "Oh master, you are injured. May I snap your father's neck? It will take less than five seconds. I cannot allow him to harm you again."

"Absolutely not," he said. "We're leaving. Now."

Billy watched from the driveway as his son and a parade of feminals walked down his back steps. Beyond the weak glow of the porch lights, the night was dark. Clouds covered the moon. Aaron slowed his steps, using his body to block my face from his father's eyes. I expected to climb into a Martinez Motion vehicle, but Dwayne sat behind the wheel of an ancient pickup truck.

"Put the women in the back and ride up here with me," Dwayne said. "Ron will drop your van off in a few days... if Billy ain't still pissed at ya."

Aaron lifted each one of us into the bed of the truck. He picked up Iris first. She giggled, but with her broken leg, she wasn't much help. I could see the muscles in his back and arms strain under her weight.

Daisy was next. Like a cat coiled to pounce, her body sprang into the air. She didn't need Aaron's muscles to clear the tailgate, but his hands pretended to guide her.

"Thank you." She gave him a small bow and sat down. Her dignified movements were a crash course for me... the next feminal in line.

When his hands grabbed my hips, the heat penetrated the fabric of my gown. His chest pressed against my back as he lifted me. His breath brushed against my ear and made me shiver. I spread my arms like wings in an attempt to look graceful. After the first few feet, I rose into the air on his strength alone. One of my stiletto heels slid free and hit the ground.

I got a closer look at Aaron's face when he returned my runaway shoe. In the glow of the truck's taillights, I saw only one eye looking back at me. The left side, from his cheekbone to eyebrow, was swollen.

The purse hanging from my wrist pulled at me like a magnet. With one bullet from the Ladysmith, I could've dropped Billy where he stood. Aaron ordered Rose to leave his father alone. But even with the sticker on the back of my neck, I wasn't his feminal. I had the ability to right two decades of wrong without his permission. The rush of power felt bloodthirsty and made me lightheaded.

Rose floated into the bed of the truck like a feather... with both shoes and every hair in place as she sat down next to me. I think she gushed some words to her master, but I can't remember what she said. As I watched his hands release her, my eyes confirmed what my heart wanted to ignore.

Rose was good for Aaron's health. I wasn't.

The hours of planning with Papa, the risks he'd taken with Soto, the lies he'd told Billy... all of it was because of me. Maybe another woman would've accepted his sacrifice as a gift—a tribute that was owed to her because she was a priceless, natural resource. Aaron went through hell to deliver me safely to my papa. And after I left, he'd have nothing but bruises and the memory of what a giant pain in the ass I'd been.

Dwayne steered us down a road that was nothing more than a cow path. With every jolt, my spine slammed into the side of the truck. The three feminals maintained their rigid posture through every washed-out gully. Their composure was as irritating as the bumpy ride. Remorse and fatigue took turns pushing me down until I gave up the fight, curling into a miserable ball.

I'd traveled eighty miles since breakfast. I'd been held at gunpoint, thrown in a closet, tossed into the back of a pickup truck, and bounced through 200 acres of ranch land. And yes, I wasn't eating dinner at my papa's kitchen table, but I'd walked under the noses of both Miguel Soto and Billy Martinez without getting caught. I still had my freedom. But instead of feeling grateful, I was an exhausted lump of purple, gauzy fabric.

Rose pulled me closer. I stiffened but didn't have the energy to pull away. Her hair was a pillow for my head. Her arms were the warm, rose-scented blanket I needed to close my eyes and block out my hellish day. When she spoke to the other feminals, their voices melted into my dreams like warm honey.

"Iris," she said. "Your leg is damaged."

"Dwayne hit me with a truck on July 16 at 2:47 p.m. The right, front tire ran over my leg."

"And he punches you in the head?"

"His fists are big and strong," Iris said. "I love Dwayne very much."

"Yes, of course you do."

"I am his stupid cow."

"I do not have the necessary tools to repair your leg," Daisy said. "However, I can restore your vision. Imagine how pleased Dwayne will be when you can send pulses of light and process—"

We hit a pothole and I jerked in Rose's arms. With heavy lids, I watched Daisy open the port on the back of her neck. Iris pushed her blond hair to the side and Daisy connected the two feminals together. The cord was almost invisible in the darkness. Once their bodies were joined, they lost some of their balance, making them look more human as Dwayne knocked us around in the back of the truck.

"Daisy is fixing her?" My words were sleepy and slurred.

"She is upgrading the distance sensors behind Iris' eyes," Rose said. "And installing a new batch of code."

"What kind of code?"

"In her own small, limited way, Iris will be like me."

I sat up, leaving the warmth of her body. "You mean she will cry a lot?"

"No. Iris will kill anyone who tries to harm you."

CHAPTER FIFTEEN

HUNGRY HEART

A s a goodbye gift to Rose, I didn't complain as she applied lipstick to my mouth, rubbed oil on the ends of my hair, and attached a fresh sticker to the back of my neck. I even wore the purple gown and the sky-high heels without whining. After seven hours of sleep on a real mattress followed by a hot shower, I was human on the inside and content to look like a feminal on the outside.

I tossed down my first cup of coffee before it was cool enough to drink and welcomed the rush of caffeine like an old friend. Every nerve ending buzzed as I waited for Papa to arrive. He'd agonized over my survival, planning and plotting with Aaron for twelve years, and today he would cross the finish line.

"Lord, don't let him get in a wreck driving here," I said under my breath, soft but not soft enough. Daisy arched an eyebrow in my direction.

Unable to sit still, I stood watch in front of the living room windows. Their curves mirrored the mission style from the main house but without the vast square footage. Aaron's place wasn't what I expected. It was small and clean—with enough pockets of clutter to keep the white, stucco space from feeling sterile.

Now that Rose was home, would she tidy his random stack of album covers and organize his lists of employee shifts and inspection schedules?

"Breakfast is almost ready," he said and handed me a refill. "Sip it this time. You chugged the first cup while it was steaming hot. Dr. Vega will be ticked off at me if you have blisters on your tongue."

"Papa's gonna notice your green and purple face way before my burnt mouth. Are you going to tell him what happened?"

"No, I'm not."

"But it was my fault. If you hadn't been drafted to bring me back here, then Billy wouldn't have—"

"Yesterday was a victory," he said, interrupting my stream of guilt. "A holy shit, throw-a-parade-down-the-center-of-Main-Street style victory. We're both alive and you didn't wake up this morning chained to some dude's bed. Believe me, these lumps are no big deal."

"Sleeping on a real bed was amazing. Thank you for not chaining me to your headboard." It was meant to be casual banter… a lighthearted joke between old friends. But when I heard the words out loud, heat prickled under my cheeks and spread down my neck.

"And thank you for taking the couch," I added, rushing to fill the awkward pause as his grin widened. "Do you want me to wash my sheets and pillowcase?"

If anything, his face was more discolored today than the night before. When he smiled, his left eye became a puffy, narrow slit that must've been impossible to see through. "No need to do laundry," he said. "I like the smell of you. I always have."

"Um, okay." I was surprised by his honesty and flat-out shocked by the pleasure it gave me. Did I have a unique fragrance… something underneath the lavender in my hair? I forgot I was holding coffee until it sloshed over the sides. As the hot liquid ran down the back of my hand, I sucked in a painful hiss.

He lifted the mug out of my fingers. "Come on, let's eat. I've got real milk, not that glowing, nuclear sludge we drank during the rations."

"Breakfast is on the table," Rose said with a graceful bow. "Shall I serve you, master?"

"No, please stay in the living room with Daisy."

Aaron pushed a plate of bacon toward me and poured rainbow loops into two bowls. The cereal was called Breakfast Rings. A head-to-toe photograph of a wrestler covered the front of the box. His beefy arms were wrapped around his opponent's neck. The man pretending to choke had long hair striped the same color as the cereal. Half-chewed loops tumbled out of his open mouth.

I tapped on the box with my spoon. "That's fun for the teenage boys."

"Yeah, brutality sells."

"Dwayne's bald head could be on the next box. Maybe as the guy being strangled."

Aaron grunted and sipped his coffee.

"His Iris is sweet," I said. "I like her."

"She's still one of our most popular models. When she has a good maintenance record, her pre-owned market is strong."

"Daisy couldn't fix her leg, but she did some other weird stuff in the truck. Was the new batch of code your idea or Papa's?"

"Mine."

"Iris doesn't seem like much of a fighter."

Aaron bit into slice of bacon. "She is now," he said as he chewed. "Dwayne can still beat the shit out of her, but God help him if he tries to touch you."

"Is he a threat to me?"

"He's a threat to everyone. He isn't a part of my security team, so I have no control over him. Hell, even the almighty Billy Martinez struggles to keep him on a leash. Dwayne likes to believe he's a gun for hire with no loyalties to any one kith. He does some work for us… always killing more men than necessary to achieve the mission. Billy thinks having a nutjob on the payroll scares our rivals. You know, makes us more intimidating."

"A smelly nutjob," I said and wrinkled my nose. "Seriously, I don't think the man ever takes a shower."

"Personal hygiene isn't what it used to be. Most men reek of sweat, whiskey, and cigarette smoke. You'll get used to it."

"But you don't stink like that."

"Thank you, ma'am. I work hard to please your delicate nose."

"Right now, you smell like bacon. Once I get settled in at Papa's house, we'll invite you over for dinner. I'll cook anything but those nasty pinto beans—"

"I need a refill." He jumped to his feet, one leg bumping the table and shaking the cereal in my bowl. His back was rigid as he moved around the tiny kitchen. I thought his hand shook when he reached for the coffee pot but the swollen, left side of his face gave nothing away.

"You are going to visit me, right? Bring Rose if you want."

"I'll try," he said without turning around. "But I don't want to put you in danger."

"Sure, I get that." I shoveled a spoonful of sugary cereal into my mouth and swallowed, hoping it might clear the lump in my throat.

"My master's truck has pulled into the driveway," Daisy called from the living room.

After most sleepovers, I'd grab my duffle bag and thank the adults for inviting me. Today, I had nothing but the clothes on my back and a dainty, silver purse containing a Stephen King novel and a gun. It rested on the kitchen table next to the box of Breakfast Rings… a bizarre tableau of garish colors and violence. Even my old t-shirt and jeans were still in the cave. But it was time for me to go home, wherever that was, and it was time to carve out a life with Papa. I stood and smoothed my gown.

The man who felt distant just a moment ago was next to me in three, long strides. Aaron wrapped his arms around my waist and pulled me against his chest. Strong fingers wove through my hair until they reached the back of my neck. With a hand cupping the logo bearing his name, he kissed the top of my head.

"Come to me if you need anything. Do you understand? Anything." His breath tickled.

As I stood there in my ridiculous shoes, Aaron's mouth was only an inch above mine… easy to reach and hard to resist. I didn't stop to look over the cliff or measure how far the fall would be. I jumped into the unknown with a combination of curiosity and desire, brushing my lips against his like a question.

I'd seen passionate kisses in the movies. I'd sat next to a guy while his buddy made out with Lili in the backseat. When the smacking noises got too loud, we turned up the radio. But I'd never imagined kissing a guy who was paralysed by shock. I'd never imagined lips that wouldn't move against mine.

My body translated his rejection faster than my head. I dropped my mouth as tears pricked my eyes with barbed edges. I couldn't look at him. I couldn't handle the confusion or the embarrassment or the pity I'd see on his face. Pushing against his chest, I was frantic to break free.

"I'm sorry," he whispered.

"No, um, it's okay."

Papa's knock was loud. I lunged for it like a rope tossed to a drowning man. Instead of letting me go, Aaron's arms pulled me in tighter. My back was to the living room. I couldn't see the door but I heard Daisy unlock the chain.

"Rose, don't let anyone in this house." Aaron barked the order with the force of a general on the battlefield. "Not for the next sixty seconds."

He lifted me off my feet, capturing my mouth in one fluid motion. This time, I was in a daze and I squeaked before I could stop myself. The body holding me was all hard angles… muscles and bones and skin that was impossibly warm under my hands.

His lips didn't crush mine. With the lightest pressure, they coaxed me to respond. I tilted my head. And when my tongue tasted his, he accepted the invitation and deepened our kiss. Only the thin fabric of his t-shirt separated our heartbeats.

I was deaf to the war raging in the living room until we came up for air. Daisy gave the order to "step aside so I can welcome my master." But Rose, wonderful, badass Rose, held the door like a champ and allowed me to experience the sweetest minute of my entire life.

In the circle of Aaron's arms, I heard the two of them slamming into the walls. Daisy fought without emotion but Rose's sobs to "let go of my hair" and "put down the lamp" were ear piercing. And outside, Papa's polite knock became a persistent pounding.

"I've wanted this for so long." Aaron's words were muffled against the skin below my ear. When his teeth grazed my neck, I shivered. "But I think they're trashing my house."

I touched the bruises on his face with one gentle fingertip. "Those ladies can do a lot of damage in sixty seconds. Your house may never be the same."

He lowered my feet to the ground with a final kiss, panting something between a sigh and a groan between our mouths. I ached when he pulled away—already missing his heat.

"Rose," he said, his voice low and flat. "You can open the door now."

I lost something new as Aaron's arms fell away. And a moment later, I found something lost when my father's arms closed around me. Papa laughed with the joy of it. Holding me out in front of him, he studied my face… first as a proud parent and then as a doctor. He checked my pulse. He shined a pointed light into my eyes.

"Your pupils look good, dilating just fine," Papa said. "And the whites of your eyes are no longer yellow. Excellent."

Showing off, I executed a graceful curtsy in my gown. It was a dangerous move but the muscles in my legs kept me on my feet. He might as well enjoy a pretty picture of his daughter before I reverted back to jeans and t-shirts. Did he still have my old clothes? I dreaded opening my closet and finding nothing to wear but feminal gowns.

"You are lovely," he said. "But that dress is too low-cut."

"You should've seen me when I first put it on." I tugged on the neckline. "It plunged even deeper before the alterations. I guess feminals aren't wired to be modest."

He frowned. "Yes. Well, we'll get you home and into more comfortable clothes. Are you ready to go?"

I held my hand out to Aaron. He walked toward me—his face a cheerful mask as he gave my fingers a quick squeeze and released them.

"Thank you for the ride and, um, the chocolate, and everything," I said. After our kisses, this hurried goodbye felt inadequate, like the ultimate understatement. My smile tried to express all of the things I couldn't say in front of Papa.

"The chocolate was supposed to be our little secret," he said and looped the purse around my wrist.

"What happened to you?" Papa had been so focused on me, he'd ignored everything and everyone else in the house. But now he examined Aaron's face, tilting the bruises toward the light.

"I'm fine, Dr. Vega," Aaron said. "Just a little disagreement with Billy."

"I'm proud to say you are nothing like your father." Papa spat the words out as if they tasted rotten in his mouth. "I know it wasn't easy to bring Mirari back to me. Thank you… for everything. I'm more grateful than you will ever know."

"We'll invite you to dinner," I said. "And, um, you can make your meatloaf again if you want."

"Let's get you settled in first," Papa said and put an arm around my shoulder. "Perhaps something in a few weeks. Take care, young man. I'll call you soon."

As we stepped onto the front porch, I looked back—greedy for one more crooked smile and one more second of a connection. But Aaron wasn't there. Instead, Rose shut the door behind me. Was it my imagination or did she have tears in her eyes? I couldn't imagine that she'd miss me.

The sky was clear above my head. It felt like a good sign. Yesterday's thunder clouds were gone and nothing dimmed the pink and orange sunrise in the east. I touched the Martinez Motion lettering on the side of Papa's white pickup truck. It had less rust than Dwayne's and rode higher off the ground.

Daisy sat in the passenger seat. The flowers were missing from her hair and only one strap held up her gown. She seemed otherwise unruffled by her early morning skirmish with Rose. Her face was a picture of tranquility. And if Papa noticed her less than perfect appearance, he didn't say anything.

"Do you want me to ride in the bed of the truck? I'll need to take off these heels to climb back there," I said.

"Good heavens, no." He stopped short, pivoting in the gravel to stare at me. "Why would you think that?"

"That's where Dwayne had me ride last night."

"Dwayne needs to be flogged. That man is a menace."

"In his defense, he thought I was a feminal," I said. "And maybe the back of the truck was safer. He's got a temper."

"You will sit between Daisy and me. We'll be home in about twenty minutes if we don't run into any trouble along the way."

"What kind of trouble?"

"Oh, nothing to worry about. A man would have to be suicidal to mess with a Martinez vehicle. And Billy puts his name on everything he owns."

Papa opened the driver's side door and I slid into the middle. Instead of watching the road, I stole quick glances at his profile as he drove. I was sure Mama would've appreciated the way his face had aged. He was still a handsome man.

The arms gripping the steering wheel were strong. His

jawline was firm. But the hair at his temples had more silver now and the grooves around his mouth were deeper. On his forehead, I noticed several new lines. Was I responsible for a few of them? I had no doubt.

When I put my hand against his cheek, he covered it with his own. We were driving to a house I'd never seen and driving toward a future I couldn't imagine. My questions could wait. His answers could wait. We were content to share the same air.

Papa turned on a road just north of the Mansfield Dam. It was little more than a trail through the grass, meandering between Ashe junipers and curving along the shore of the lake. Most guests would've been enchanted by the gray clapboard house at the end of the path. For me, it was upstaged by the 1975 Jeep Renegade parked in the front yard.

"Oh Papa, please tell me she still runs."

He made a cry of mock horror. "Do you doubt your papa's ability to keep that Jeep purring like a kitten?"

"Can I take it for a drive sometime?"

With a flick of his wrist, he shut off the truck and put the keys in his jacket pocket. Something under the hood made a ticking sound as the engine cooled in the quiet morning. I counted eight ticks before he met my eyes.

"Feminals aren't allowed to drive," he said.

"But I'm not a—"

"I know. And inside the cabin, you can relax and be yourself. Dress however you like. Eat junk food and read books and sleep as much as you want."

"What about outside of the cabin?"

"Everything you see, even the truck we're sitting in, belongs to Billy. He owns it all."

"But you're his business partner. I was his daughter's best friend. That must count for something."

Papa snorted a bitter laugh. "I've known Billy for twenty years and that counts for exactly nothing. He wouldn't hesitate to tie a brick around each ankle and toss me off the dam. It's his favorite form of public execution—saved for the friends who betray him."

"How have you betrayed him?"

"You are here… a living, breathing woman. And I won't let him have you."

"So this place will be my prison." I exhaled between clenched teeth. "Well, Papa, you certainly picked a lovely spot for it. I'll enjoy a scenic lake view between the bars on the windows."

"No." He grabbed my hand and linked his fingers through mine. "No, Mirari. I'm not locking you inside the cabin. But we need to be smart and have a plan."

"What does that even mean? If the world finds out I'm alive, I'll be captured and raped or—or passed around like a bottle of tequila and then traded for a carton of cigarettes. You brought me be back to a seriously screwed up planet."

We'd been reunited for less than an hour and I was already pissed at him. This wasn't how I wanted the conversation to go… the way I'd practiced in the cave. I thought I could work as his assistant, maybe shave my head, wear oversized clothes and be another geeky young man in ACTI's accounting department. Of course, Papa and I would discuss the pros and cons, give each one a numerical score.

"You're not safe in the Martinez kith," he said.

"Then why did Aaron go through hell to bring me here?" My hand jerked away from his grip. "You had twelve years to figure this out."

"Do you remember the last time I asked you to have faith in me? Back in the cave?"

Something in my face softened, giving him the answer he wanted.

"Please give me a little more faith. I'm a selfish man, Mirari. I want to see you across the dinner table and watch you organize my house with military precision… just like the old days. I want to talk to someone who loved your mother as much as me. You want to discuss what happens next and that's understandable. Can you be patient with your papa for a week or so?

"And hey, I'll give you the grand tour of ACTI tonight after the crew's gone home," he said. "Full body cryopreservation has come a long way from its humble beginnings in our backyard. Men fly here from all over the world with gold in their pockets. Many of them are young and healthy, like you were."

"They pay you to kill them?"

"No," he said. "They pay me to give them hope."

CHAPTER SIXTEEN

MY FATHER'S HOUSE

Papa's initial tour of his cryogenics facility became a daily road trip into the building after the sun went down. "You need to get out of the house," he said. "It'll be good for you."

Although I appreciated his thoughtfulness, these trips were more about one man's pride than one girl's cabin fever. I was the audience he'd been craving for the last twelve years. With his reserved parking space on the lower level and private elevator, we got inside without strolling past the security guard at the front desk. My uniform for these adventures was a pair of jeans and a long-sleeved flannel shirt.

At dinner, I offered to cut my hair rather than shove all the curls under his faded Houston Astros cap. Papa reacted with a sharp "no ma'am," like I planned to cut off my head instead of just my hair.

"But there are security cameras," I said. "What if my hat falls off?"

"Tyson's a heavy drinker. Most nights, he's snoring five minutes into his shift. He won't notice you on the monitors."

On my first excursion into what Papa called the "long-term care" wing, we met a Daisy standing behind a tall desk. She was dressed in a light blue lab coat and dark pants. There were no flowers in her hair. Instead, it was pulled back into a sleek bun, giving her the appearance of a woman who could perform brain surgery while simultaneously filing Papa's taxes.

She was sorting thick, orange cables into different piles and gave us a slight bow as we approached her workstation. "Good evening, Dr. Vega and guest. Please let me know if you need assistance."

"Thank you, Daisy," he said without breaking his stride.

I gave her a shy smile and followed Papa around the corner.

"ACTI currently has 217 cryogenically preserved men in this section plus another twenty-four in our original space. Once Billy started advertising, we outgrew that room within weeks. We store four bodies in each container." When he tapped on the round cylinder, the metal clanged like a heavy bell.

Each tank was identical to the next. They towered above our heads, and even with the wheels attached at the bottom, I wouldn't want the job of pushing them around. Papa mounted tiny TV screens on the outside and they glowed with a long series of numbers. Despite my morbid curiosity to see inside, the cylinders had no windows.

"Billy runs his kith differently than a lot of men. There is no buddy system here. It's all based on how much you contribute to the wealth of the community. My nice cabin at the lake and generous allotment of food and electricity is all because of this," he said. "ACTI is growing, bringing in more gold every year."

We passed row after row of frozen bodies. I needed the flannel I was wearing and wanted a winter coat to go over it. The air wasn't cold, and yet, I couldn't stop shaking. What if no one was around to revive their bodies? These creepy pods would become their tombs.

After Papa and Aaron thawed me out, they never asked "Where did Mirari go?" That was the million-dollar question. And not where did my body go—it's not like the location of my tank was a mystery—but where did my spirit go? Where did the untouchable, undefinable essence of me hang out for twelve years?

When I concentrated and tried to travel back, tried to push past the morphine haze, all I could see was Rose's angel face crying over mine. She was my first coherent memory after drifting through shapes and sounds like an untethered kite. As much as I wanted a vision of floating toward a bright light or standing on a giant escalator bound for Heaven, I couldn't distinguish the drugs from the divine.

Did Papa bring me back from Hell or some horrible dimension where I'd been chased by demons? I didn't think so. The cliche of "going to a better place" felt real for me. Wherever I'd been for twelve years, I was content there. I didn't want to return to this world and all its pain. And my soul didn't fit inside my body as it once did… like I was forcing eternal toothpaste back into its celestial tube.

"To keep all these tanks at -320 Fahrenheit, we use a combination of solar power and commercial generators." Papa pointed to an oversized garage door along one wall. "They kick in when the power goes out, which unfortunately, happens a lot these days. The generators weigh more than 3,000 pounds each."

His face was animated. His pride was contagious and I was willing to catch it. But even if I wasn't, I would've hung on his every word. My plan was to work alongside Papa at ACTI, so I questioned him about the supplies he ordered, how he reached new customers, and how he trained his staff.

"Feminals perform all of the body prep," he said. "They also monitor the temperature stability within the tanks. Unlike a man, my Daisies only need four hours to recharge. They are programmed to be problem solvers with a talent for managing data. I have three of them here… plus the Daisy who supervises your care at home."

During the tour, I wasn't brave enough to ask "Is that Daisy in charge of your care, too? And what duties does she provide?" My only clue was her schedule. She charged in the afternoon while he was at work and not at night.

My papa loved his wife until the day she died. I felt that truth within every cell of my heart. But hard as I tried, I couldn't guess what Mama would've thought about an artificial woman sharing her husband's bed. Would she be jealous or glad that he had some form of companionship?

The next morning, he teased me about organizing his

house. "I'm sure the cord to the hand mixer isn't wrapped in the correct direction."

"Daisy beat me to it," I said. "She runs a tight ship around here."

My bedroom, with the same pine furniture I had as a kid, glowed from her frequent polishing. Every utensil in the kitchen was in its proper place. She labeled the meat, dairy, and produce in his refrigerator with expiration dates. In the den, she arranged his books in alphabetical order based on the book's title.

"Does she know the Dewey Decimal classifications? You should add that to her programming," I told Papa as I ran my fingers over the covers.

Daisy wasn't my mother. She could never be my mother… but that wasn't her fault. If my birth certificate said I was thirty years old, it was time to act like it. I didn't argue with her organizational skills or attempt a coup. Papa's science text books could sit next to Mama's literature with no complaints from me.

Our house fell into a routine. Every morning at 7 a.m., Daisy prepared plates of scrambled eggs with grilled vegetables, toast with jam, and bowls of sliced fruit. She brought Papa a steaming cup of coffee and brewed hot tea with lemon and honey for me.

After a five-minute argument on the first morning, I allowed her to change the linens on my bed and select my clothes each day. And in exchange, she allowed me to shower alone. We were all about compromise.

On the third morning, I found her in my bedroom with a

blood pressure cuff in her hands. "Dr. Vega asked me to assist you. I must record your vital signs and any irregularities in your menstrual cycle." She handed me a glass of water and two oval-shaped pills. "We are also starting you on daily vitamins."

"It's like you and me never left the cave." I popped the tablets into my mouth, drinking most of the water to wash them down.

Perhaps I had a new sensitivity after taking morphine for so many weeks, or perhaps Papa believed I was a child who wouldn't notice when I was woozy an hour later. But I recognized stoned when I felt it. What Daisy had called "vitamins" was nothing like the Flintstones I'd taken every day as a kid.

During lunch, I bit into a grilled cheese sandwich and was fascinated by the chewing sound in my ears. All I wanted for dessert was a three-hour nap. And at dinner, Papa didn't comment on my sleepy face… even though one cheek had a deep crease mark left by my pillow. I can't remember what I ate.

The next morning, I hid the pills under my tongue. They felt larger in my mouth than in the palm of my hand. Once Daisy left, I walked into the bathroom, shut the door, and flushed the pills down the toilet.

He was drugging me. I suspected his motive was to keep me in the cabin while Daisy was on her charger—a sort of pharmaceutical babysitter to control his headstrong daughter. For the next ten minutes, I practiced my rant. I'd storm into his facility, show him the pills, and demand an explanation. Or even better, I'd shove them down his throat with a "here's your vitamins, Papa. Enjoy your snooze."

He clearly cared more about his daughter's security

than her freedom… or even her happiness. When my anger cooled, all that remained was reality. Why was I stomping around like I had power? I had none. If I pushed him too far, he could order Daisy to lock me in my room or put a shock collar around my neck. It's not like I could've called the police.

"Papa's gotta keep his little girl safe," I said under my breath. "Or at least believe that he is."

Maybe it was cowardly, but I made a decision as I stared at the face in the bathroom mirror. My conniving, human brain was my only weapon. I yawned several times that morning. And at lunch, I mumbled a lie about going back to bed. Daisy fell for all of it.

The cabin went quiet an hour later. I opened my door and crept down the hall. It didn't take long to find Daisy. She sat on a bench in the laundry room. A metal box was mounted on the wall behind her head. Her topaz eyes were open, but she didn't see the satisfied smile on my lips.

A wave of heat hit me as I stepped outside. This wasn't hiking weather, but I didn't mind getting sweaty. For the first time in twelve years, I was making a decision on my own. I could go anywhere or choose to go nowhere at all. My feet crunched through the dried grass… aimless at first. But when I followed a path through the trees, I found a shady spot to watch the blue herons dive for fish.

My trips outside the cabin weren't the stuff of fairytales. While Daisy was on her charger, I didn't skip among the branches like a princess, whistling and inviting birds to land on my finger. I carried a gun. I never closed my eyes or stopped listening for the sound of approaching boots.

Papa believed the Martinez kith wasn't safe for me. And despite my resentment, I believed my Papa.

On the morning of day four, a slow rain began after breakfast and didn't stop. I tucked myself into a recliner with a book. Instead of picking up the story where I'd left it, I opened *Carrie* and started at the beginning.

When I read the final word in the final chapter, I threw the book across the room. Immature, I know. Mama was a fan of Stephen King and wouldn't have expected a "happily ever after" ending. Guilt pushed me out of my chair. I picked up the book, smoothed the bent pages, and put *Carrie* on the bookshelf between *Canterbury Tales* and *Catcher in the Rye*.

With a few hours remaining before Daisy was at full power, I explored the secrets of the cabin. The entire place was on one level with two bedrooms, two bathrooms, and a combination living room and den. Someone had white-washed the thick paneling, but the texture of the wood grain showed through the paint. The ceiling was eight feet at its lowest point and angled up toward a stone wall of vertical windows and the lake beyond.

Boxes of ammo filled one of the kitchen cabinets, including a stockpile of the .38 Special rounds I'd need for my Ladysmith. In Papa's bedroom, I found stacks of photo albums in the back of his closet. Yellowing grade cards were tucked between my school pictures and some awkward shots from my early beauty pageant days.

This must have been the box he showed Aaron. I smiled,

almost hearing the way Papa would've stopped to explain every piece of paper.

He was a man who loved his daughter… maybe too much. And as flattering as it was for Aaron to know my abilities in calculus, Papa shouldn't have walked him down my memory lane. The comparison between his father and mine must have hurt. From what I remembered, Aaron's mother was affectionate before she died. But did Billy ever appreciate his son? Ever brag about his achievements?

The flicker of a crazy idea became a concrete plan in an instant. I was going to Aaron's house… right now. I was going to kiss away every bruise. I was going to trace his crooked smile with my fingertips and press against his body and feel his heat against my skin… and, and, and.

The clock was my enemy as I rifled through a lifetime of Papa's belongings. File folders, photographs, and stacks of papers littered the floor around me feet. I discovered what I was searching for inside the laundry room.

Across from Daisy, the spare key to the Jeep hung on a peg. Her vacant eyes seemed to be guarding it. Even though she couldn't see me or hear me, I tiptoed past her to grab it off the wall.

A familiar smell enveloped me when I climbed into the driver's seat. Dirt from a thousand roads blended with a hint of pine. The cardboard tree still swayed from the rearview mirror. Its color was bleached white from the sun, but its fragrance continued to float through the air like a stubborn ghost. When I turned the key, the engine sprang to life without a hiccup.

I wiped a thick layer dust off the dashboard and uncovered the clock. As I stared at the second hand, it kept ticking along with no remorse. Daisy had 37 more minutes on her charger. Aaron lived 20 minutes away. I didn't need calculus to do this math in my head. There wasn't enough time to drive to his house, kiss him like a maniac, and get back here before Daisy unplugged.

I sank in my seat. And when I moved my foot off the clutch, the engine died with a shudder, mocking my attempt to be impetuous. I would've beaten my fists on the steering wheel, but it felt too much like punching Mama in the face.

"What the hell is wrong with you? He probably isn't even home." I put my hands against my hot face. "Get a grip."

The fuel gauge registered a full tank. It was a gift for another day because I had no idea how to buy gas. Would I toss a gold coin to the attendant and tell him to keep the change? The only currency I'd found in the cabin was a five-dollar bill from 1977.

I held the key in the palm of my hand, rubbing the Jeep symbol as if it were my lucky rabbit's foot. The metal ring holding it was old and easy to pry apart. When I put that ring back in the laundry room, it was one key lighter.

The pointed tip jabbed my leg throughout dinner. I welcomed the discomfort… welcomed the promise that I'd touch Aaron soon. And when Papa invited me on another tour, the key stayed in the front pocket of my jeans as he explained the intricacies of the body preservation process, the mix of chemicals needed, and everything he'd learned from defrosting me. I was his surviving guinea pig.

He lifted a round pane of glass from the center of his desk. It had a handle, like a mirror, and was edged with a silver frame. "Display client list," he said and the wall behind him glowed. As his finger moved against the glass, a long row of names scrolled faster than I could read. "No, this isn't what I want. Display three-dimensional view."

Responding to his command, the text on the wall became a column of photos. Names were instantly replaced with men's faces. They wore dark suits, like it was picture day at an Ivy League school. Each one moved, blinked, and seemed to stared back at me.

"I have a meeting tomorrow with these prospective clients." He slid the strange mirror toward me. "We're meeting at the small airfield near Beacon Cove for lunch. I'd like you to attend with me."

I sat up straighter—not sure if I'd heard him correctly. "You want me to see people? In the daytime?"

"Yes, Mirari."

"Um, are you sure?" I scrambled to answer my own question before he changed his mind. "Yes, of course you are sure. And yes, I'd love to go. I can be like your secretary feminal. I was decent at typing in high school... a little slow, maybe, but I'll get faster with practice."

"Study that list before tomorrow. These men are flying in from all over the world. They speak English but it would be helpful if you can match a name and a country of origin with each face."

Aaron had warned me about their "huge leaps in technology." He didn't lie. I held the glass like a piece of fine crystal and tapped on the photographs with the lightest touch. The gadget responded to my command, enlarging the photo and displaying a brief biography that included a birthday. The oldest man was forty-one years old but most were in their early thirties.

"All of these guys want to be frozen?"

He shrugged one shoulder. "They all want to have children someday. The only way that's possible is through us."

CHAPTER SEVENTEEN

BADLANDS

MY BIG DAY started with a melted cheese omelet… an excellent beginning. I studied Papa's customer list between bites, memorizing names, home countries, and birthdays. If he was the teacher, I was the know-it-all student on the front row with one hand waving in the air. Not my finest quality but there it was.

Of course, I wanted to show him my skills. But I also wanted to take my brain out for a test-drive. Could I still "cram for an exam" after more than a decade in cold storage? Daisy quizzed me on the information as she applied my makeup.

She had a lighter hand than Rose. Perhaps on Papa's orders, she selected matte shades of eyeshadow and dusted just a hint of blush on my cheeks and across the bridge of my nose. Instead of a low-cut flowing gown, she zipped me into a fitted, lace bodice with an attached floral skirt that flared to my knees. The shiny threads in the pattern complimented the silver purse dangling from my left wrist.

I debated whether or not to leave the Ladysmith hidden under my mattress. But the weight of the gun was both a comfort and a reminder to keep my eyes open. Papa's spare key to the Jeep only added a few extra ounces.

I critiqued Daisy's work in a full-length mirror. The girl looking back at me was young. While the top of the dress was sleeveless, the straps were wide and covered most of the skin on my shoulders. I felt the influence of Papa in this decision, too. When I touched my toes, the curved neckline showed no cleavage.

Daisy strapped me into a pair of white sandals I recognized. They'd been my first "grown-up shoes" when chunky, square heels were all the rage. I'd never met a feminal wearing anything so sensible. Their masters preferred sky-high stilettos that resembled thin, railroad spikes.

"Should I put my hair up? Go with an older look—something more professional?" I piled the curls on my head so she could see the effect. "It shows off the Martinez Motion logo on my neck."

"Your father wishes for your hair to remain loose and curl down your back," Daisy said.

"But I look like a 15-year-old at her quinceañera party… not an employee attending a business meeting. All that's missing is my tiara."

She stood behind me in the mirror. At first, I didn't

notice the pills pinched between her fingers. But when she opened her hand, they sat there like two, white cockroaches.

My arms dropped. Long corkscrew strands of hair fell over my eyes, blocking what I'd seen, what I struggled to understand. She was confused. That had to be it. Papa wouldn't want an assistant who was high.

"You made me a big breakfast," I said, pushing the curls out of my face. "I don't need vitamins."

"Dr. Vega's instructions were quite clear. He said this is an important day for you."

She held my happy tablets and waited… content to stand there the entire morning until I complied. Did she notice how slow my jaws moved, opening as if they'd been rusted shut? She placed the pills in the middle of my tongue.

"I need something to wash these down." I coughed, put a hand over my mouth, and ran to the bathroom.

Even before the door clicked shut behind me, I spit the tranquilizers on the tile floor. Anger melted my shock as I smashed them under my shoe. None of this made sense. But if I stormed into his den and demanded an explanation, I ran the risk of being left at home with Daisy.

I turned on the sink, watched the water swirl down the drain, and shut it off. My desire to be his trusted assistant warred with my desire to revolt against his overactive prescription pad. As I scattered the crumbled pieces of the pills, I decided to fake it. My stoned act fooled Daisy and it could fool him, too.

I gave Papa a performance worthy of an Oscar nomination… if Hollywood was still handing those out. He watched me over the rim of his glasses. I watched the clock and waited thirty minutes before I stopped talking. Fifteen minutes later, I stared at my feet as if I'd grown a third one. My best scene was a big tumble as I climbed into the truck. From where he stood, the dashboard came within an inch of giving me a nasty lump on the forehead.

"Oops," I said with a toothy smile and heavy lids. "That first step is a doozy."

In the history of father-daughter relationships, cherishing a papa one day and raging against his authority the next was nothing new. Generations of women taught me to take my victories where I could find them.

"Don't attack your papa with guns blazing," Mama had told me over and over. "Think guerrilla warfare… quick, small-scale missions that he'll never see coming."

Squeezed between Papa and Daisy, I didn't say another word as we pulled away from the house. My silence broke as he turned the truck from the dirt path onto a two-lane road that curved along the shoreline of the Colorado River. When it was too late for him to turn the truck around, both my eyes and my mouth popped open. I droned outside his ear like an angry bee, firing questions at him nonstop.

"What's with the plain planes?" When he didn't answer, I nudged his arm.

"Hmm?"

"The planes," I said. "Why are they so boring?"

"These men don't want attention when they travel," he said. "Billy's jets are the same. Functional and anonymous on the outside. Plush on the inside. These men avoid any identifying kith symbols as a security precaution. And their pilots are armed."

Each jet was identical to its neighbor… a dirty shade of white from nose to tail with no colorful stripes or flags on the sides. They clustered around a central hangar like cars at a drive-in restaurant. Papa steered the truck toward the same arched, metal building.

"How many potential customers can your facility handle at one time? It might be awkward, you know, asking these men to take a number and wait to be frozen."

"The Daisies work efficiently." His hand squeezed the gear shift as he put the truck into park. "We've been able to cut the body prep time in half."

"What about the documents these men sign? I assume you have attorneys who draft the contracts. Are you careful to disclose the risks? Of course, how can they sue you under the product liability laws if you accidentally defrost—"

My question stopped mid-sentence when Papa turned off the engine, like my voice had come from the radio instead of my mouth. This was go time… the beginning of my future. I followed him out of the truck and into the hangar without another word.

A long table ran down the middle of the cavernous space. An air-conditioner was running somewhere, working over-time to chill the metal building. The glow from two sets of silver candelabras was multiplied by china plates, crystal glasses, and tiny vases of flowers.

This wasn't the businesslike environment I expected. The twinkling candlelight gave the men's faces an otherworldly shine, as if we'd been invited to a banquet above the clouds. Feminals stood behind the guests with bottles of wine in every shade of red and burgundy. The plates were empty, but they wouldn't stay that way for long. A line of rolling carts along the back wall held platters of food. Savory, earthy, and tart combined in a kaleidoscope of delicious smells.

There was an expectant energy I didn't understand. Each guest seemed to be holding his breath and waiting for a cue to exhale… like this was surprise party. I tightened my grip on Papa's arm.

One of the men facing the door stood and clapped his hands. It echoed like gunshots. I glanced over my shoulder, expecting to see someone important coming in the door behind us. Papa pulled me closer to his side. Was this show of appreciation a shock to him as well?

More men rose from their seats and joined in the applause until the hangar rang with the deafening noise. Papa regained his composure faster than me. With a wave to the group, he led me to the head of the table. A young man with pale blue eyes held out a chair. His blond ponytail was almost white against the dark collar of his tuxedo.

I assumed I would stand like the other feminals in the room, but Papa didn't move toward the upholstered seat.

"My lady," said the blond man. "This place of honor is for you."

I jerked, stumbling on Papa's foot and smashing a few of his toes under my heel. The knot in my stomach flipped in a nauseous somersault.

"It's okay," Papa said. "I'll be right next to you."

As I dropped into the chair, the blond man put his mouth against my ear. "You are ein schönes Mädchen… a beautiful girl." His accent was heavy with Swiss chocolate and ski chalets. "My name is Levin."

I knew his name from the list I'd memorized, but he knew something, too. He knew my secret. They all did.

My face burned hot under their curious stares and yet my fingertips were numb with cold fear. The dizzy, black spots I remembered from the cave came back in a rush. They teased the edges of my vision. In a flash of bitter resignation, I wished I'd taken the tranquilizers Daisy offered.

A Rose stood over my left shoulder. She draped a linen napkin into my lap. When her copper hair brushed my face, the familiar scent of flowers calmed my nerves. I wanted this feminal to be Aaron's Rose, but her green eyes remained downcast and gave me no clue.

The command to begin serving drinks was mysterious. I didn't see or hear a word, not even the smallest gesture, and yet the feminals presented wine to their masters at precisely the same moment.

I counted two Daisies, four Roses, and Levin's platinum blond who wore a black pantsuit with a matching ribbon to hold her ponytail. A few of the feminals looked like custom builds… perhaps a nod to a buyer's specific fetish. One had spiky pink hair, tattoos, and a tie-dyed miniskirt. Next to her, a curvy feminal was dressed as a genie. She needed every inch of her ebony hair to cover her breasts.

Three brunettes were scattered among the charming "how may I serve you" attitudes. They wore tight, red catsuits with ridiculous leather tails. On their feet, studs glinting from the tips of their boots… like vicious, metal claws. I didn't need anyone to tell me they were Violets. Their gray eyes sparkled with malice. The only smiles they produced were sneers.

My Rose bent at the waist and cradled a pink bottle in her arms. "Does this vintage meet with your approval?"

"You share the same name," I said as I read the label. "It's a rosé."

"That is correct, Lavender."

When she said my feminal name, I looked into her angel face. She was Aaron's Rose. Was he somewhere in this crowd? Without thinking how it might look to the men around the table, I touched her hair.

"I'm so glad you're here," I said, my voice thick with emotion. "Where is your master?"

She lowered her gaze. "Shall I pour your wine?"

"Um, sure. Thank you."

Every eye in the room watched our interaction. Those seated closest to me must've heard my words. In a strange salute, the men raised their full glasses high into the air but didn't drink.

"Taste your wine," Papa said.

My fingers trembled as I lifted the glass. The men around the table followed my lead but with more confidence. I'm sure the rosé was the finest quality, but I was too nervous to appreciate its fruity notes. I sipped just a drop and put the heavy crystal down before I spilled wine on my dress.

"Finish it," Papa said.

"What?"

"They need to see you finish it." Even in the soft candle-light, anxiety added new lines to his face.

"You want me to chug it?"

"We're proving a point, Mirari. One they need to see with their own eyes."

I put my napkin on the table, stood, and lifted the glass with both hands. On the outside, the liquid looked like wine. But with the next sip, I tasted the truth. I was drinking grape juice.

Papa knew better than to mix tranquilizers with alcohol. Of course, he did. The good doctor wanted me mellow… not dead. I almost called him out on it but lost my nerve.

The men didn't talk. And yet, no one seemed impatient to hurry my progress when I had to breathe between gulps. Should I burp after the final swallow? I considered how they might react to such unladylike behavior. My poised female act was as fake as my poised feminal act had been.

When I dropped the empty glass with a thud, spontaneous applause and a few cries of "Well done!" and "Here! Here!" sprang up around the table. I resisted the urge to wipe my lips with the back of my hand.

"Please sit down and tell us your story," Levin said. "What was it like to be frozen for so many years?"

"Papa did all of the hard work. All I had to do was sleep." I shrugged and forced my eyes to meet his. "The toughest part was the physical therapy required to get my strength back. It was like climbing out of bed with a high fever, but you know, the opposite of being hot."

The men on both sides of me chuckled. And like a strange

game of follow the leader, those seated on the other end of the table joined in… their laughter rising to the level of a roar even though they'd been too far away to hear my lame joke.

"Gentlemen, let's enjoy our meal and then we can talk business," Papa said.

Daisy needed no further instructions. She organized the other feminals in the room with delicate hand gestures and lunch was served. Even with a menu artfully placed near each water goblet, I had no idea what to expect as dish after dish arrived at our table.

Adding to my confusion, the men thought I was drinking wine as I sipped my fruit juice. They talked about "sweet or dry" and "developing aromas" and "swirling my glass."

The food was a safer topic. My crab salad with avocados and cucumbers was light and colorful. The black truffle soup and lobster with corn ravioli were delicious. I ate something called a lemon and seaweed granita with a straight face. But when I put Osetra caviar in my mouth, it was difficult to swallow.

"I don't understand what is so great about caviar," Levin said, winking as if we'd been friends for years. "I would pay money not to eat it."

The deep voices of the men ebbed and flowed around me. If I didn't know better, this could have been a formal dinner party before the pathogen… with polite conversations about the upcoming presidential election or the final medal count from the Olympics. But twelve years ago, no one stared at me like I was God's gift to mankind. No one hung on my every word.

I felt like an ant under a hot magnifying glass.

When my plate was mostly empty, Papa gave me a kiss on the cheek. He stood and tapped a spoon against his wine glass. The room went silent. I sat up straighter, ready for their questions. These guys wanted the details of my reanimation… and I appreciated their curiosity. I was a living, breathing advertisement for the success of cryogenics.

Before Papa spoke a word, he moved closer to me. Daisy lifted my curls high above my head. I knew where this was going. But it still hurt when he grabbed the sticker on my neck and jerked it free. A few of my fine hairs were tugged along for the ride.

"Let me start by congratulating you," he said and raised the Martinez Motion logo. "I know it's been a long process. Seated here are the best and brightest young men from around the world. You have the intellect, resources, and most importantly, the fertility to be my daughter's husband."

I blinked.

"It goes without saying that your feminals may examine Mirari's body before any gold changes hands. My daughter has nothing to hide. As you can see, she is healthy and beautiful. I've monitored her ovulation dates. She's had seven since March."

He said more. But with the shrieking in my ears, each syllable felt disconnected, like he was speaking a language I couldn't understand.

When I lifted my chin to read his lips, a ripple of vertigo tilted the floor under my chair. His fast-moving mouth was fuzzy around the edges. The skin was stained from his wine glass, giving him a faint, pink mustache. I narrowed my eyes on his teeth and tongue. They writhed and snapped and articulated every ugly word.

"You will each have five minutes to give your prepared speech and then Mirari will ask you questions." He put a hand on my shoulder. "She will make the final choice. Not me.

"Many of you tried to buy my consent but my daughter is not a slave. She is Earth's final queen. The bride-price you pay today will belong to her. She will select her future husband among the men in this room.

"And together," Papa said, raising his voice. "You must be fruitful and multiply."

CHAPTER EIGHTEEN

BORN TO RUN

I SEETHED... LIKE A pot of boiling water was roiling in my gut. As each man stood and pledged his devotion to me, my fury bubbled and steamed and begged to be released. My face felt tight. And under the table, my hands were squeezed into fists.

A wannabe poet from South Africa said I was "pure enchantment" and a Canadian called me "skookum" as if I was fluent in his slang. He said he'd keep me toasty during his British Columbian winters.

If these men expected a young lady who giggled, blushed, and fluttered her eyelashes, I was a sad disappointment. Maybe if Papa had given me wine, I would've believed their flattery... their bold faced, silver tongued, lies. I stopped listening.

This was already way out of hand and nothing they said

mattered. I had to breathe. I had to push through the fear and focus. My list… that was it. I had to visualize each column as if I were building a chart in my old notebook.

Fact number one, my father was insane. Certifiably and categorically crazy. Fact number two, these men were on the hunt for exotic prey and not a wife to love. Fact number three, the feminals standing behind them were just as dangerous as the weapons they held. And fact number four, it was time for me to leave.

I considered several outlandish ideas for escape, like pretending to have a seizure, or rabies, or a deadly venereal disease. I considered simpler ideas, like asking to use the bathroom and crawling out through an open window.

Would Papa send a feminal in with me? Yes, and more than one. They'd offer to flush. They'd asked how many squares of toilet paper I wanted. And while my skirt was up, why not take a little peek? Their masters expected them to appraise the merchandise, right?

A man on the opposite end of the table was droning on, passionate about something despite my obvious lack of attention. "Your life with me will be that of a queen," he said. "Anything you desire will be placed at your delicate feet."

Stuffed into a navy blue suit that puckered across his chest, he was less polished than the other men at the table. Light brown hair rose into the air several inches above his forehead and fanned out around his face like a thick lion's mane. Drops of blood red wine clung to the sides of his beard… a lion after a fresh kill.

"How old are you?" My blunt question interrupted his

presentation, maybe one he'd been practicing for weeks. "Maxim, wasn't it? And you are from a kith east of the Baltic Sea?"

"Yes, my lady." He bowed and shuffled his note cards. "My father's land includes Minsk, the former capital of Belarus. I am thirty-four years old. The men in my family pride themselves on their virility. I will give you children for many years to come."

"Excellent," I said with my best regal nod in his direction.

No one at the table was barbaric enough to thump his chest like a caveman. But under their thin layer of civilized behavior, Papa's group of would-be husbands were savage. They bragged about their wars. They gave me gruesome details about pillaging their neighbors and murdering anyone who opposed them.

I was both the trophy and the referee for this bizarre contest. I'd just given the lion from Minsk one point. And without a doubt, these men were keeping score.

The muscles in their jaws tightened. Some fidgeted in their seats and slammed shots of whisky. They felt combustible. I held the match. The trick was to light the flame and run without getting shot, stabbed, or tackled to the ground.

When the next man stood, an intense Violet hovered over his shoulder like a guard dog, or in that outfit, more like a guard cat. He was taller than Maxim but she was taller than both of them. Silver streaks highlighted his black hair in a way Mama would have called "distinguished." Before beginning his speech, he appraised my eyes, my mouth and then dipped lower to my chest, examining me as if I were a race car he might purchase if he could check under the hood.

"My name is Andreas Louca. I don't believe in meaningless flattery. I suspect you've had your fill of empty words this afternoon." He swept an arm above Maxim's head. "I will be honest with you, Mirari. My kith is on the island of Cyprus. It is well protected by air and by sea. I have enough gold to guarantee your safety. Our sons and daughters will want for nothing.

"But I will not pledge my love to you," he said with a satisfied grin. "And I will not pledge my fidelity to you."

The men around the table erupted in outrage, many of them in languages I couldn't understand. Their lewd hand gestures filled in the blanks. During the commotion, I edged open the zipper on my purse. My fingertips traced the curve of the gun's trigger and my palm wrapped around its grooved, walnut grip. It rested there.

Andreas waited for the shouting to stop before finishing his speech. "My sexual desires are great... no doubt greater than yours will ever be. All I require, madam, is your willingness to give me children. My feminals will take the burden of my daily needs off your shoulders."

His Violet stared down the table at me without blinking. If the engineers had given her eyes the ability to produce heat, she would have roasted me like a lamb on a spit. Her pale, delicate fingers intertwined with his. And when she squeezed, his mouth grimaced in a mixture of pain and pleasure. I couldn't imagine sharing a home with this demonic, feline creature or her kinky master.

"That's enough," Papa said. He didn't raise his voice. Yet the authority behind each word cut through the shouting and reminded his guests who was running the show. "You, sir, may be seated."

The men cheered but Andreas remained on his feet.

"You insult your daughter's intelligence, Dr. Vega," he said. "She can't possibly believe these fools when they say her beauty rivals that of a goddess. She is a pretty child— her papa's little darling and nothing more. Certainly not an Aphrodite."

Maxim saw an opportunity to score another point as my knight in shining armor. He leapt out of his chair. And in words that sounded Russian, he ranted, spraying spittle on the taller man's neck.

Violet might have tolerated a verbal attack on her master. But when the tip of Maxim's wagging finger brushed the tip of Andreas' nose, her claws came out. She growled and pressed a knife against Maxim's throat. The point of the steel blade was buried somewhere in the man's beard.

Maxim's feminal observed that her master's jugular vein was about to be severed… a reasonable observation. She escalated the arms race. From the pocket of her genie costume, she lifted the tiniest pistol I'd ever seen. But instead of aiming it at Violet, she shoved the gun into Andreas' ear. The four of them froze.

I'd been praying for a diversion… and this one was a doozy. Even Papa gaped wide-eyed at the old-fashioned Texas standoff on the other side of the room. I pushed away from the table. The legs of my chair scraped against the concrete floor with a high, thin shriek.

As I stood, I brought the muzzle of the Ladysmith under

my chin. One finger hovered over the trigger. Both hands squeezed the grip. For this to work, my voice and my revolver couldn't shake.

"I must ask my guests to be seated," I said, loud enough for Andreas to hear me even with a gun shoved in his ear. "And ask you to drop your weapons. We don't want a pistol going off in my direction."

Every head turned. A few mouths hung open in alarm but most seemed amused that I'd managed to be more interesting than the show on the other end of the table. No one moved. Somewhere, a clock was ticking. I heard a sniffle, a muffled sob, and then a keening sound like a mournful mosquito buzzing over my shoulder.

"Come on, Rose. I'm not dead yet. Are you already crying?"

"Yes," she said and sucked in a wet, wheezing sound.

Even as I threatened to blow my brains out, I wanted to laugh at her—hysterical, uncontrollable barks of laugher. She didn't breathe air. She didn't have lungs. Why should she gasp like she was desperate for oxygen?

"Look at the other Roses. They aren't crying."

"Yes—they—are." She hiccupped between each word.

"A few of them have wet eyelashes. That's it," I said. "They certainly don't have your commitment to the sport."

"Mirari, put the gun away." Papa's tone roused a memory. This was the soothing voice he'd used in the cave... the same funeral director impersonation he'd pulled out of his doctor's bag the first time he killed me.

I ignored him.

"Last chance," I said and took a step away from the table.

"Everyone… drop your weapons to the floor. I've died once. I'm not afraid to do it again."

More seconds ticked by on the clock. My thumb pulled back the hammer. Each of the three clicks seemed louder than the one before it.

"For God's sake." The alarm in Papa's voice almost made me feel guilty. Almost. "You heard what she said. Do it."

Maxim and Andreas mumbled something to their feminals I couldn't hear. Inch by slow inch, they lowered their hands until the knife and gun clinked at their feet. The others around the table pretended to do the same but I wasn't an idiot. I would've needed a metal detector to find all the pieces these men were carrying.

"Kick your weapons toward the wall," I said.

Maxim grunted. Andreas gave a sharp nod. Their feminals obeyed.

"Rose, come out from behind me," I took another step toward the door. The muzzle was cold where it grazed my skin. "Stand next to Daisy."

I'd never seen so much water fall from her eyes. It was more than any human could manufacture without total dehydration. The front of her white gown was soaked and see-through from the neckline to the waist.

"You must win every wet t-shirt contest you enter," I said. "Well, we're giving these men a good show, aren't we?"

"I must not let harm come to you." As she wiped her cheeks, the river of tears halted midstream, the drops on her lashes defying gravity. "Aaron would be displeased."

"If you make a move to stop me, great harm will come. I promise."

"Mirari, listen. Before you do anything rash, give me three minutes," Papa said, his palms turned out as if he had nothing to hide. "Can you do that? You need to know what's outside that door."

"Whatever is waiting for me, it can't be worse than living with one of these warlords," I said, panting between each word. "You've organized one shitty blind date here."

"There is no reason to use obscene language. Just come back to the table—"

"Well gosh Papa, maybe my potty mouth is a side effect of the tranquilizers." The sarcasm tasted better in my mouth than the caviar he'd served. "Admit it. You ordered Daisy to drug me. Did she believe they were vitamins? Did you deceive her, too?"

Daisy's poker face gave nothing away. Papa shook his head and lifted one shoulder, what any gambler at the table would've called his "tell."

"I never wanted to deceive you," he said. "Even in the truck today, I considered telling you my plan. But then what? I knew you'd refuse to meet these men. I didn't want to drag you through the door in chains. You are too much like your mother. Fierce... headstrong."

"Once upon a time, you thought that was a good thing. You said my fighting spirit was the best gift Mama ever gave me." I lifted my chin, letting him see the circular indentation left behind by the gun's barrel. "She'd never manipulate me into marrying a stranger."

"Evelyn is dead. All of the women are dead." His eyes were wide, like an animal smelling a predator in the air. "I'm all you've got and I can't protect you here. Nothing in this kith stays a secret for long. Billy's not stupid and he has spies everywhere. He'll capture you… sell off tiny pieces of you."

"What are you talking about?"

"A woman was discovered five years ago on North Inachi Island—"

"Aaron told me about her." I was impatient to shut him up before this turned into a lecture on anthropology. "She died of whooping cough because a bunch of men forced her to leave her home. And what's your plan? Medicate me and fly me to the other side of the world. Stoned and alone.

"You tell me it's too dangerous for me to live here," I said. "And yet, somehow, it's okay for you? Tell the truth, Papa. You don't want to leave the cryogenic amusement park Billy built for you."

"These men are offering you a secure future within the bonds of marriage. They are offering you a safe home." He nodded, buying every word of his lie. "I love you, Mirari. I love you enough to face reality… no matter how much it hurts. I love you enough to let you go."

"You had no right to do this." Rage burned my throat and choked my words down to a raw whisper. The gun trembled in my hands. "No right."

Always uncomfortable with my emotions, he looked away. I watched his chest rise and fall. He seemed smaller… almost frail, like the effort required to keep me alive was exhausting. Did he regret his decision to thaw me? I must've been easier to handle when I was all frozen potential rather than a fiery reality.

"You need an armed fortress, not a fishing cabin with a few shotguns mounted on the wall." Papa never cried. Never. But when he raised his eyes to mine, they glittered with tears. "You are Eve… the future of mankind. Kiths will fight wars to have you."

"What do you think, Andreas? Is Papa exaggerating my worth? Cause you didn't seem that impressed with me." My buddy Andreas had a knack for grabbing attention. I needed him to do it one more time as I inched my feet backward. "I believe you said I was just a pretty child."

"My admiration for you is growing," he said with a broad smile that took ten years off his face. "I like a feisty woman. My mother, God rest her soul, had quite the temper—"

"Dr. Vega, I've seen and heard enough." Levin rapped his knuckles on the table, confident he had the right to call the room to order. "It is clear you can't control your daughter. And unlike some of the men in this room, I don't find her disobedience charming in the least."

This fair-haired suitor, the man who'd given me multiple winks during dinner, was no longer flirty. His ponytail whipped back and forth as he shook his head at me. His lips were puckered, like I was pure lemon juice in his mouth.

"These hysterical outbursts are unacceptable," he said. "If you select me to be her husband, I will curb her temper tantrums. I will teach her discipline and submission. I believe it would be best if we negotiated the bride-price without an audience—"

Despite Levin's accusation that I was out-of-control, I would argue I maintained exceptional self-control as I tilted the gun in his direction. I didn't aim at the black ribbon holding back his hair, even though it made him look like a douchebag. I didn't aim at his matching blond feminal, even though her ponytail had the same ribbon.

I pointed the muzzle at the ground between them, rolling the trigger with my index finger just like Mama taught me.

CHAPTER NINETEEN

DEVILS AND DUST

I T WASN'T MY intention to turn the airplane hangar into a pinball machine. But when I aimed at the ground and pulled the trigger, a candelabra and its seven candles went flying. Shot glasses tumbled in a spray of alcohol and flames. Maybe Mama's plinking lessons should've included the dangers of a ricochet bullet when shooting a concrete floor.

The pandemonium couldn't have created a better diversion if I'd planned it. When I fired a shot at my empty chair, Daisy dove to cover Papa's body with her own, perhaps worried that he'd be my next target. The feminal with the pink, spiky hair smothered a napkin fire with her bare hands. And before I could send another shot in their direction, the blond feminal shoved Levin and his ponytail under the table with enough force to make him cry out.

I was afraid to turn my back on the Violets. They didn't

move to shield their masters. Instead, their gray eyes seemed to calculate the most efficient way to rip the gun out of my hands, or perhaps, the most efficient way to rip my arms out of their sockets.

Levin's feminal edged around his empty chair. Even though I'd just fired a bullet in her general direction, the corners of her mouth curled and she winked a pale, blue eye at me. What was it with these blonds and their nonstop winking? I didn't consider her a threat until she took another step in my direction.

Aaron gave me the Ladysmith as protection against dangerous men. I had no idea if it could stop a dangerous feminal. She put one black pump in front of the other, slow and steady as if testing a tightrope. A bullet might slow her down, maybe short-circuit a few wires, but I didn't know where to find the bullseye on her artificial body. She matched every step I took toward the door, daring me to shoot her.

I aimed at the cleavage between her impossibly firm breasts. "Go back to your seat, sister. I don't want to hurt you."

She sprang.

And even with a finger wrapped around the trigger, my reflexes were no match for her speed. Momentum slammed the two of us against the metal door. The back of my head took the hardest blow. Pain radiated around my skull and settled in the space behind my eyes.

I grunted. My hips pushed against her black pantsuit and the creature inside it. Her frame felt like an intricate web of steel beams, trapping the Ladysmith between us.

The gun's curved hammer dug into my skin and I

couldn't turn it, couldn't point the muzzle in her direction. The rock mountains of her silicone breasts were immovable. And then… those mountains moved.

As fast as her weight had pinned me to the door, that weight disappeared. The smothering pressure against my chest didn't just subside. It was torn up and away, her knee clipping my arm as she fell backward. I bobbled the gun. The handle slid through my sweaty grasp and kept falling.

Rose lunged. And like a frog catching a fly, she snatched the barrel out of the air. I appreciated her quick retrieval of my weapon, but it was her other hand that grabbed my attention. Between her fingers, severed wires dangled from the roots of a blond ponytail. The black ribbon was still wrapped around the strands… and tied in a bow.

Levin's feminal twitched where she'd landed face-up on the floor. Her mouth spasmed in a series of odd tics. When Rose stepped over her body, the blond winked.

"Come on," I said. "We gotta go."

There was no time to debate the pros and cons of taking Rose with me. I opened the door and we hurried from the air-conditioned dining room into the hot kitchen of a Texas afternoon. Behind us, chair legs screeched across the concrete. Men shouted in so many accents and dialects, it sounded as if I'd kicked over the Tower of Babel.

"Give me back the gun," I said and slammed the door behind us.

"No. I must not allow you to harm yourself."

"I wasn't going to…" Holy hell, I wanted to shake her shoulders until her perfect, white teeth rattled. "We don't have time for this. Give me the gun and hold this door closed. Don't let anyone out until I'm gone."

Wasting precious seconds, she flung the mangled ponytail into the gravel and wiped at the new tears rolling down her cheeks.

"Rose, I promise," I said, giving her my most earnest, wide-eyed expression. "I will not hurt myself."

She wrapped two fingers around the doorknob, casual, as if she were in no hurry to leave the party. I didn't see much effort on her part until the pounding started on the other side. The handle jiggled but didn't turn.

"I need to shoot Papa's truck tires." I extended my hand toward the gun. "So he can't catch me and drag me back here. You saw how vicious those feminals were."

"Very well," she said. "But if you display irresponsible behavior—"

I didn't wait to hear the rest of her sermon. As soon as the gun's walnut grip touched my palm, I ran with it toward Papa's truck. The cylinder held four more rounds. Wasting all of them didn't make sense if he only had one spare in the back. I fired at the two tires on the driver's side, pulling the trigger against the rubber at close range.

My plan was to escape on foot, or to be more precise, on a pair of dusty, white sandals. All I needed was for Rose to give me a head start. And yes, I hatched this plan under great duress… running from a pack of men who vowed to keep me "with child" for the next thirty years. I will accept the blame for our sloppy getaway.

Pilots watched us from their cockpits. Papa said they

were armed. And when I murdered two tires in cold blood, I'm sure they reached for their weapons.

Someone intelligent inside the hangar had the bright idea to exit out the back door. Men in tuxedos and their overprotective feminals stormed around the side of the building… just a few pitchforks shy of being an angry mob. A bullet winged the gravel in front of my toes. Fragments of dirt and rock peppered the skin on my legs, making tiny cuts that stung once my shock wore off.

"Don't shoot her." Papa's scream came from behind the pack. "Tell your feminals to stand down."

I thought they'd obey, but Rose didn't wait around to find out. With one arm across my shoulders and the other behind my knees, she scooped me up.

"What are you doing? Put me—"

When her legs started pumping at full speed, my mouth snapped shut. I needed a getaway vehicle, and although she didn't have a speedometer, her pace would've given a greyhound a run for its money… the dog or the bus line.

The route she ran wasn't straight. As we zigged and zagged through the parking lot, she squeezed my ribs so tight I swore I heard cracking. The lump on the back of my head ached. And every time her foot hit the ground, my ankles banged together. I groaned between clenched teeth as our getaway became a rough ride.

The echo of gunfire continued even after we jumped the ditch and crossed the main road. A shot hit her right shoulder. I heard the bullet whiz toward my ear and felt her body jerk with the impact. It didn't exit on the other side—didn't slow her down. But when another struck lower, she stumbled and we pitched toward the grass under her stiletto heels.

I braced for our bone-snapping crash to the ground. It never came. Her head lifted. And like a gymnast after a one-footed landing, her body regained its balance. We were less than fifty yards from a grove of trees and the cover it could give us.

Even as Rose put more distance between us and the hangar, I couldn't shake the feeling of being hunted. A nagging unease became an outright certainty. The rhythmic crunch of dry weeds snapping under heavy feet was behind us, getting louder. Our speed dropped as one side of her body weakened, and instead of running with long, smooth strides, she leapt with her right leg and hopped with the left.

The creature on our heels was too fast to be a human. No matter which direction we ran, it followed. Rose crashed into a thick row of elbow bushes. They were a wall of round, green leaves and clusters of dark blue fruit. Lashing at our arms and faces, the branches punished us for trespassing.

I wanted to scream for more speed, even if the vegetation cut my skin to ribbons, but Rose stopped. In a small, circular clearing, she opened the cage of her arms and put me on my feet.

"Please remain here," she said. "Do not run. It would serve no purpose."

The largest tree was a maple but even its trunk was too skinny to provide cover. Daisy dressed me that morning to grab attention, not hide from it. With the bright roses on my skirt, only a florist shop could've provided the perfect camouflage. I wiped my palms on the satin fabric of my purse, leaving behind streaks of dusty sweat. Too bad the poor thing wasn't large enough to hold a box of ammo. This would've been a good time to reload.

I didn't need Rose's feminal hearing to track the footsteps coming toward us. They were slower now. Stalking. Flashes of Violet's red catsuit bobbed down the trail we'd just cleared for her. When she growled, we both turned to meet her head-on.

I counted the frayed bullet holes on the back of Rose's gown. Instead of the two puncture marks I expected to see, there were five, with one shot embedded in her shoulder, one in her left hip, and three shots below her waist. With that much damage, she should've been nothing but a pile of broken parts.

Violet's gray eyes swept the clearing and locked on my position. Without hesitation, she closed the gap between us, a revolver leading the way. Her sneer was gone. She was all business… a feminal with a job to do and a plane to catch. If she'd been the only shooter chasing us, I figured her gun held one more round in its chamber.

"Rose, give me the girl," Violet said. "Mirari must go back to Cyprus with my master. She must not be allowed to escape."

"You cannot have her." Rose sniffled. "Cannot."

"It is Andreas who wishes to have her. Your loyalty to the child is commendable. Rest assured, I will not kill her, merely immobilize her with a bullet to the knee or ankle. My master said she can choose."

"Nooo." Rose's moan raised the hair on the back of my neck. The sound was grief edged with a war cry. If this she-cat saw her opponent's tears and assumed they made her weak, she wouldn't be mistaken for long.

Violet lifted the gun. But instead of moving into the shooting stance Mama taught me, she tossed her hair and cocked her hip. She was programmed to strike a seductive pose, even in a fight. True to her word, she didn't point the weapon at my head or my heart. The muzzle was aimed lower with the straps of my sandals in its sights.

Before I could run or even flinch, Rose dove toward the revolver and took the bullet that would've crippled me. The shot was deafening at close range. As the two of them tumbled to the ground, her white gown curled around Violet's red leather, creating a writhing candy cane. She slammed her right knee into Violet's torso, repeated blows that dented whatever metal formed her ribcage.

The she-cat tossed the empty gun. She grabbed Rose's face with both hands and squeezed. Her painted nails dug in like ten, bloody daggers. Planting her boots in the dirt, she rolled in a burst of power and her leather tail whipped through the air.

Rose arched her back to throw off the weight, but her arms didn't move. Couldn't move. They were outstretched on the ground like paralyzed angel wings.

Violet must have detected the weakness in her prey. With an open-mouthed growl, her fingers roamed. She buried her thumbs into Rose's open eyes, pressing with so much force that tear fluid gushed between them like a geyser. Something metal snapped with a loud "pop" as her green irises disappeared into their sockets.

Rose never told me if she could experience pain. But as I watched, I put myself on the ground in her place. I felt the searing heat of torn muscles and fibers, as if this devil cat was blinding me inch by inch with her thumbs.

I must have screamed something, but I can't remember what came out of my mouth. My throat was raw as I pulled back the gun's hammer. Maybe I yelled words in English or Spanish or my mother's native Nahuatl language. Maybe I shrieked nothing but guttural sounds of rage.

A leaf drifted from a branch above Rose's head and landed next to her ear. Isn't it strange what a person can remember—the details that affix to an event like a sock with static cling? The maple's vibrant reds and golds paid homage to her autumn-colored hair as she thrashed on the ground.

Violet didn't turn when I came up behind her. Perhaps I was nothing more than a pesky insect she would swat down after destroying Rose. But I'd learned a few things from Violet. A bullet to the legs, shoulders, or even the chest wouldn't completely disable a feminal. I had one shot to take her down before she turned her wrath on me.

Violet's elbows were locked. Her thumbs were buried inside Rose's face up to the second knuckle. And her ebony hair parted on the back of her neck, framing the Martinez Motion name like black theater curtains. I crouched, lifted the oval patch, and fired into her charging port.

If I'd wanted her body to shake like she was being electrocuted, and I admit I kinda did, my wish wasn't granted. The bullet severed a nest of thin, steel rods, and copper wires. I could see daylight through the hole I blasted in her throat.

Without a single cry, her elbows bent, her chin fell to her chest, and her body collapsed.

I poked her with muzzle of my gun, ready to leap back if she made the slightest twitch. Violet was as still and lifeless as a toy without batteries. I yanked her by the tail. She didn't budge.

Grabbing fistfuls of red leather, I rocked her body back and forth until she rolled to the ground. Her dead weight sprawled next to Rose. My feet wanted to kick her, but she wouldn't have felt a thing and I would've broken a few toes.

"Rose, can you hear me?"

She sat up. But when I wrapped myself around her, she didn't hug me back. I buried my nose in her hair and inhaled a few seconds of comfort. After everything, she still smelled like roses.

"Are you okay?" It was a foolish question. She was far from okay. A better question would have been, "Does any part of you still work?"

"I am detecting multiple system failures," she said. "Would you like a full diagnostic report? I can begin with the sensors on the tips of my fingers. I am no longer receiving data—"

"No, um, I mean, that's alright. You can save those details for Aaron."

It's not that I didn't care about the mutilation she'd suffered. I cared too much. Anger stung my nose and made it hard to swallow. When I couldn't stall any longer, I held her at arm's length and looked into her eyes. They were gone. The remains of her black pupils and green irises were pushed under layers of thin, gray metal and the ragged edges of what looked like broken gears.

Yet again, I wished for a pair of sunglasses. The two gaping holes looked raw. Sunglasses would've given her some protection from the wind. I tugged at one of the bullet holes near the hem of her gown.

"I'm tearing a strip of fabric," I said. "I'll wrap it over your eyes, you know, like a blindfold to keep the dust out."

I didn't add the final bit of truth. If I had to look into her damaged face much longer, I'd fire another bullet into the she-cat. I put my gun back in my purse, zipping away the temptation.

"Can you walk?"

"You must leave me here, Lavender."

With the top half of her beautiful face wrapped in white fabric, Rose looked like a hostage. Her arms hung limp at her sides. I shook my head but she couldn't see me.

"Let's get you standing," I said and moved behind her. "I'll grab you around the middle. Just push up with your right leg. Ready? One, two, three…"

I groaned with the effort. The muscles in my arms and legs burned as they struggled to lift her even a foot off the ground. I was fighting a battle with gravity while simultaneously fighting a war with her.

"You're not trying," I said, heaving again. "Good Lord, how much do you weigh?"

"Without clothes, I weigh 263 pounds and five ounces."

"I'm not going anywhere without you." I slumped over her back. She had a stubborn streak but mine was wider.

"Okay, fine. We'll sit here like two chickens waiting to be plucked. When those men catch us and toss our tails into the frying pan, it'll be all your fault. They heard the gunshot. They'll be here any minute.

"And my skirt is in the dirt." I added the last jab without mercy, poking at the strand of code inside her that craved cleanliness. "I bet these stains will never come out. Not even with baking soda."

Rose stood… and not with a weak, wobbly effort. She lifted my body off the ground along with her own. It was too early to gloat. We had a long way to go and I had to keep her moving—for her sake and for mine.

"Don't worry," I said. "I'll be your eyes. We'll get you to Aaron and he'll fix you up… good as new."

As we stumbled through the trees, I didn't talk. Her ears were our alarm system. I had a vague idea where we were, but the sun was no help. When I guided us around one tree to the right, I went around the next tree on the left. It wasn't a Girl Scout approved strategy for wilderness survival, but they weren't giving out too many merit badges these days.

I plastered myself to Rose's hip, using an arm around her waist as a steering wheel. Even without a diagnostic report, I could tally her injuries. She had no use of her arms or hands and only one fully functioning leg. She could speak and hear but her laser-based sensors were trashed. I didn't want to think about internal bleeding or whatever kind of fluid might be leaking under her skin.

Violet was responsible for the damage to Rose's body. She was a product of her violent programing… pure and simple. But was she the only one to blame? The feline feminal should've been stalking Andreas on an island somewhere, not chasing me through the hill country of Texas with orders to drag me to the altar.

"Papa didn't organize all of this in one week," I said, more to myself than to Rose. "Interviewing those men must've taken him some time."

"Seventy-three days," Rose said. "Dr. Vega began the interviews on Saturday, July 21 at 9:06 a.m."

"How?" I stumbled and squeezed her tighter. "How do you know?"

"I served Dr. Vega a plate of buttered toast and a cup of coffee with no sugar," she said. "The telephone rang twenty-three times."

"What about Aaron?"

"He preferred a teaspoon of sugar in his coffee and strawberry jam on his toast."

"Hang on. Aaron was there during the phone calls. Is that what you're saying?"

"He volunteered to run a background check on each man," Rose said. "This pleased Dr. Vega very much."

"Yes, I'm sure it did. Papa likes information." My voice was as robotic as a first-generation feminal.

Rose kept talking. Every new detail chipped away at the numbness around my heart. I could feel the dam breaking. And when she said "they agreed it would be best," a flood of pain demolished every attempt to justify Aaron's participation. I staggered as the truth of his betrayal battered me from every angle.

Aaron allowed a squadron of jets to land inside his father's kith. Without one word of warning or even a good-bye, he expected me to marry a stranger today. He thought the newlyweds would fly off into the sunset. He believed "it would be best."

"I am your first wedding gift," Rose said. "You are my new master."

CHAPTER TWENTY

SWALLOWED UP

Rose heard the hum of their engines before I did.

"We need to find cover." She nudged me with her good leg when I didn't move. "I believe the men have organized a search party."

"What are you talking about? The road is at least a mile behind us."

"They are coming from the sky."

When I looked up, there was nothing over our heads… not even a cloud. That didn't stop me from believing her. "Okay, fine," I said and sighed. "Let's get going. I'll save my nervous breakdown for later."

My requirements for a suitable hiding place were simple. No squatting on a cactus or in poison ivy. I was game for anyplace else that blocked my brightly colored dress and her brightly colored hair.

For the next hour, the drone of a low-flying planes slowed our pace. Rose heard them each time. And before the search party circled above our heads, we dove into the nearest bush for cover. Mosquitos buzzed around my face but left her alone. I guess those blood suckers preferred salty, human skin. They ate me alive.

Our escape wasn't a death march. It's true, we both looked like death but a "march" implies that I knew where we were, or at the very least, where we were going. When we passed the same clump of Texas sage for the third time, my heart sank.

"I think we're walking in circles," I said.

"Perhaps your strategy is wise. The planes are no longer overhead. I can hear their engines, but they are searching farther away now."

"Those men are seriously overestimating our hiking skills. I have no idea which direction to go."

"Pileated woodpeckers prefer rotting wood."

"What?"

"Pileated woodpeckers prefer rotting wood," she said, pausing between each word.

"Is that code for something? Because I don't get it."

"I am not speaking in code. A dead tree is the bird's favorite hunting ground."

"Wonderful. Thank you, Rose." I pulled on her gown— my signal that I needed to remove another pebble from my sandal. "If I see Woody Woodpecker out here, I'll tell him where to find all of the good restaurants."

"Listen for the quick, drumming sound he makes with

his beak. And pass on the right side of his tree this time instead of the left side. I believe that will turn our circular path into a straight line."

It was irritating to get navigation advice from a blind feminal. And it was humbling when I saw the dead tree and was forced to follow her directions. Less than thirty yards later, we passed our first sign of civilization.

A board read "Hope is an anchor for the soul." It was low to the ground and horizontal, like the old Burma Shave signs with white letters painted on a red slab of wood. I wanted to spit on those words but every drop of saliva in my mouth was too precious to waste.

I'd had hope when I woke up that morning. Like a naive fool, I ate my breakfast and studied the men's names in order to please Papa. So much can change in a day… so many things can break.

"Well Rose, the only thing I can do now is count my blessings." I ticked them off on my fingers. "I'm not on a jet flying to Minsk or Cyprus with one of those despots. I have one friend left in the entire world. That's you, by the way. And… I have one bullet left in my gun.

"One is the magic number," I said. "Zero bullets would make my quick suicide more difficult and two bullets would be greedy. If your arms still worked, you could bury me six feet under but I guess a girl can't have everything."

"You must not die," she said. "Aaron will be quite upset—"

"Believe me, honey. I'm nothing to him but a giant pain in the ass. Aaron will be relieved when I'm gone."

There wasn't much I could still control in this world…

not where I'd live or how I'd spend my days, not even my body or if I wanted to create a human life someday. Death wasn't half as scary as the slavery those men were selling, even when the cages they offered me were 14-karat gold.

As we limped up a rocky incline, I imagined how I'd like to go. Maybe I could drive the Jeep to Mount Bonnell and put "Bohemian Rhapsody" in the tape player. Freddie Mercury's voice would be the last one I'd hear before pulling the trigger. But it would be Mama's spirit that would hold me when my heart stopped beating. With a tender hand, she'd guide me to the great beyond one more time.

I snorted. Even that plan had too much hope sprinkled through it. If I was serious about dying, why didn't I unzip my purse, pull out the gun, and end my life before someone could stop me? The only "why not?" I had left was Rose.

She was the reason I put one dusty foot in front of the other. If I'd abandoned her, scavengers would've picked over her body and stripped her bare. I remembered the men who found me asleep on the quilt. I remembered their plans to sell me for parts and the way they reeked of urine and damp decay. I remembered the way they touched me.

I had to get her to Aaron's house while her legs still moved, before her battery ran down, and without getting caught. And do all of this with no vehicle and no idea where we were. No problem.

Aaron called me a dragon once, laughing at the heat in my eyes when I was angry. What would he see on my face now? My soul felt like the charred remains of a campfire… spent, cold, and black. Without a word or even a backward glance, he extinguished a lifetime of friendship and the promise of something even sweeter. I never wanted to be one of those women who needed a man to be happy, and yet, his betrayal hurt even more than Papa's high-handed bullshit.

My father couldn't help it. He had centuries of patriarchal blood flowing through his veins. If I needed a man to put food on the table and keep the wolves at bay, Papa was going to find him. I wasn't the first young woman to disagree with her father's choice for a husband, or in my case, a table full of choices. And yeah, that part was still a nasty piece of manipulation.

It was Aaron who broke my heart. My vengeful attitude was immature, but I didn't give a damn. I wanted him to be as miserable as me. I wanted him to think about the man I'd marry and wonder if my new husband was richer, hotter, and a better kisser. I wanted to torture Aaron until he begged for mercy.

I kicked pebbles and smashed Mexican buckeyes under my feet, getting more bitter with every mile. It was impossible to move silently so I stopped caring. My thoughts wandered and I'm not proud of the morbid places they went.

I fantasized at least a dozen ways to punish Aaron. My favorite was using the Ladysmith he'd given me for protection. I'd pull the trigger on his front porch. When he found my blood rolling down his white, stucco walls, would he appreciate the irony?

"Let him clean up the mess," I said and Rose didn't ask for more details.

The trail in front of us widened and a second sign read

"Even the winds and waves obey Him." Someone misjudged the size of the letters. The first four words were too large, forcing the artist to paint the final three at an angle to squeeze them on the board.

I spotted "He leads me beside still waters" in an overgrown ditch and "Making fishers of men" propped inside a rowboat that might've been orange when I was a little girl.

"An engine is running nearby," Rose said.

"Is it a plane?"

"No, it is a truck or perhaps a bus." Without seeing the path or how it descended through the trees, she turned her head in the direction we needed to go. "Approximately 273 yards away."

"Approximately, huh? Your approximations are quite specific."

We slowed our already turtle-like pace as we approached a clearing. I steered us into the shadows, trying to stay hidden as long as possible. The air was cooler under the canopy of the oak trees, and through their leaves, I counted at least seven log cabins in various stages of ruin. Only the largest cabin had a roof without holes.

Every porch faced a ring of long wooden benches. In the center, an empty flagpole stood at attention. Fresh footprints made circles around it in the dirt. If this place was deserted, it hadn't been for long.

A white school bus idled on the edge of the compound. Under the row of windows, the word "Camp" was stenciled in blue paint. A cloud of exhaust swirled around four bald tires and no one sat behind the wheel.

"This looks too good to be true." I lowered my voice to a whisper. "It's a bus, practically begging us to take her for a spin. Can you hear anyone talking?"

"No, I cannot. But I hear music."

"Let's get closer. I want to—"

A squeal split the air. I searched the trees, but the noise was too electronic to be a flock of birds. Behind us, a rusted speaker was mounted between two sturdy limbs.

The feedback stopped. But before I could decide whether to turn back or keep pushing forward, the crackle of a turntable and a thumping piano riff swelled around us. A woman crooned *"this joyous day"* with a voice so low and rich it settled between my shoulder blades like a warm hand. A beat later, a choir echoed her every word.

I scanned the camp, looking for any sign of movement, and found nothing but two more speakers mounted in the trees. The music seemed to grow into a living thing as more people joined in and began to clap. *"Lord, in death's shadow, I will not fear. No, no, no. You walk with me. Yes, you do. This joyous day."*

My curiosity crescendoed with the music. Was this song for us? Or were we gate-crashing some sort of church service? While the final note still hung in the air, my questions were answered.

"Welcome to the Lake Travis Bible Camp," said a man. His words were muffled yet booming, as if he were eating the microphone instead of speaking into it. "I am Reverend Wendell Parks and my grandson's name is Curtis. All of this was his idea. I guess you could say he's been waiting for you."

"This is too weird," I said. "I don't like it—"

"Fear not," the man said and wheezed out a chuckle. "That sounds downright Biblical, doesn't it? If you ladies are too chicken to come any closer, stay where you're at. But give my grandson your attention. Curtis has some artwork he wants to show you."

I tugged on Rose's gown, but she wasn't ready to go. Instead of following me, she took two more steps toward the camp. I stumbled along with her.

"You have no eyes," I said. "I'm sorry to be mean, but this isn't the best time to become an art enthusiast. And my gun won't be accurate from here."

The boy I assumed was Curtis bounded down the steps of the bus. He had to be at least twelve years old, like everyone else on the planet, but his face looked younger. Most of his height came from a pair of long, dark legs that extended past his cut-off shorts and into a pair of leather sandals. The yellow tank top he wore was several sizes too large as if he planned to "grow into it" someday. His head was shaved close around the ears with hair springing from the top of his scalp in hundreds of black, corkscrew curls. Clutched in both hands, he held a tablet of paper as wide as his shoulders.

I crouched in a pitiful attempt at concealment. He looked straight at me as he lowered himself to the ground. When he waved, I waved back despite myself.

He flipped open the tablet. And after a long pause, he raised it above his head. His hands shook, maybe from the weight of the sketch pad, but I wondered if he was nervous. In the center of the page, he'd drawn a face. Other than the pink lips, every other feature was the color of charcoal. The person had no hair and was sleeping during a blizzard or a dandruff storm. I wasn't sure which.

When Curtis lifted the next page, I squinted as I studied the details. He'd drawn a girl in jeans and a black t-shirt. She was standing just outside the opening of a cave with dark braids curving over her shoulders. She held a wooden staff shaped just like the one Rose had carved for me.

I shook my head. There had to be a logical way to explain this. Maybe I was suffering from heatstroke and my eyes were playing tricks on me. "Come on," I said. "Let's get a little closer."

"Are you in danger?"

"No, I don't think so. Not yet."

Faster now, Curtis raised his pictures into the air. Each one was a memory highjacked from my mind. The drawings were colorful, with the feeling of movement I remembered from comic books mixed with the exaggerated features of a caricature.

As we hobbled toward Curtis, Rose and I looked like the losers of a three-legged race. I didn't try to shield the gun in my hand, but my show of force was just that, a show. In order to shoot it, I needed a clear head, and my field of vision was closing in, blurring around the edges. My pulse was loud in my ears, and between each throb, I heard the familiar, woozy whisper. It begged my knees to buckle and let the world go dark.

He waited before turning to the next page, like he knew I needed a minute to catch my breath. He lifted a picture of Mama's quilt. It was spread under a magnolia tree, and through a tunnel of vertigo, I saw the girl he'd drawn. She was taking a nap on the quilt with long, wild curls covering her face.

In the next picture, I was wearing a purple gown. The kid made my neckline higher than Rose did with her needle and thread. He also put a smile on my lips. I wondered if this was how my mouth looked after Aaron kissed me. I mourned the loss of the girl in that picture... she seemed happy.

Curtis and I were a few feet apart now. "Have—have we met?" I asked, gasping as I tried to focus on his face. "You look familiar."

His only answer was to flip the page. On this one, Rose and I were seated next to a flagpole. A gun rested in my lap. And instead of green eyes, a white blindfold was wrapped around Rose's head. Creepy but accurate. If this page was meant to be a gentle suggestion to sit down, we accepted his invitation.

Every drawing so far had been like the pages of a photo album. I'd lived these moments. I wanted this child to show me the future. Without uttering a word, he'd made me a believer in whatever kind of magic he possessed. Now it was time for the good stuff.

He took me to the next sheet. A man was driving a bus down a highway. He was bald with a silky white beard against his dark cheeks. Several rows back, my face looked out one of the windows. I leaned in to get a closer look. Rose couldn't see the drawing, of course, but her back stiffened.

"I hear footsteps," she said.

The preacher's voice barked from inside the cabin. "Just coming out for some fresh air." He no longer needed the assistance of a microphone and speakers.

A shadow in the doorway took on the hunched shape of an elderly man. He shuffled down the wooden steps wearing a gray suit, and even in the afternoon heat, his dress shirt was buttoned up with a black tie hanging straight down from the starched collar. Curtis had sketched his grandfather's face, showing all its lines and wrinkles with accuracy. The Reverend Wendell Parks was the spitting image of his picture.

"The boy made me look old," he said, staring at the sketchpad. "My beard isn't that white, is it?"

I was too distracted by his canteen to answer the question. It swung from his arm by a thick, leather strap. A solitary drop of water ran down its side and landed in the dirt. I tried to swallow but didn't have enough saliva to pull it off.

"Never mind." He waved an impatient hand. "Are you ladies ready to go?"

I lowered my gun... more confused now than afraid. "Go where?"

"How the devil should I know? Curtis didn't dream that part." The sigh he gave me was exaggerated, like I'd disappointed him somehow. "Give her a lift. That's all the boy saw in his sleep. And we don't have enough gas to waste on a joy ride so you better figure it out."

"Um, could I have a glass of water?"

"We don't have water to waste, either," he said.

"Please, I don't need much. Rose and I have been walking—"

"No." He glared at her injured face without sympathy. "And before you ask, we don't have a charging station, either. So if your batteries run down, the two of you are going to stay that way. Feminals are an abomination—a path to sin and depravity."

My eyes didn't turn red. But as I leapt to my feet, I felt the dragon's heat stirring in my gut. I wasn't going to stand here and let this man insult my Rose… no matter how thirsty I was.

"What kind of preacher are you? You oughta be ashamed of yourself." I waved the barrel of my Ladysmith like an angry finger, breaking Mama's number one rule about gun safety. "Didn't you read the story of the Good Samaritan? Maybe you should memorize it next time because your hospitality, well frankly, it stinks."

His mouth opened like I was about to get an earful, but instead of words, he puffed out nothing but air. As he studied the ground in front of my feet, he shook his head. Was he feeling remorse? But no, his gaze lingered too long. I looked down and saw the lines of dried blood streaking my legs.

"Give her a drink of water, Pop," Curtis said. I couldn't remember the last time I'd heard the voice of a child. The high, breathy sound was like a bird's song… his voice as much of a miracle to me as his drawings. "I told you she'd be a real girl."

CHAPTER TWENTY-ONE

BOOK OF DREAMS

Reverend Parks stood between me and the bus. He held a torn scrap of paper at arm's length, like the map I'd drawn had a bad odor. What did he expect? I didn't have his grandson's artistic talent. Along with the street names I could remember, my instructions included a few landmarks between here and Aaron's house, but nothing was drawn to scale.

He tilted the map toward the light. "Your boyfriend lives in the Colorado River?"

"Aaron is not my boyfriend," I said, as if my love life was the most outrageous part of his confusion. "Don't worry. I'll know the road to his place when I see it."

"You better." And with that, he grabbed the empty canteen out of my hands and disappeared into the bus.

I climbed onboard with one hand on Rose's back. "There are four steps," I said. "Go slow." If she'd lost her balance, Curtis and I would've tumbled behind her like a row of dominoes.

The preacher sat behind the wheel. On the dashboard, a crude machine gun swiveled from a tripod. I was curious if it was a prop from an old gangster movie but I didn't have the guts to ask—positive my question would've offended him. The bus had no windshield. Whether it'd been shot away or removed on purpose, I couldn't guess.

He watched Rose stumble on the hem of her dress and offered no assistance. "Pick a seat with a weapon" was his only advice as we struggled up the steps.

"I have a revolver," I said.

Shaking his head, he lifted his eyes upward… either inspecting the roof of the bus or the heavens beyond it. I seemed to be a constant source of irritation for this man. "You'll need a real gun. Somethin' the vultures can see from the road. Give your robot a weapon, too."

I shook my head right back at him. "Her arms don't work and she's blind."

"I noticed. You buy her that way on purpose?"

"I didn't buy her at all. Rose is, um, sort of a gift. And she's hurt because of me…" My voice cracked. If he didn't have fuel to waste, this wasn't the time to pour out a confession about who was to blame for her injuries. That list was a long one.

He reached inside his suit coat and pulled out a pair of mirrored sunglasses. "Here, put these over her eyes," he said, his tone softer now. "And prop a shotgun in her lap. The muzzle needs to poke out the window."

I sat Rose on the bench closest to the door. As I removed her blindfold and smoothed back her hair, a wave of tenderness made my breath catch. The preacher's shades were oversized on her delicate face but the lenses hid the severed gears under her skin.

"We need to go," Curtis said over my shoulder. "Sit somewhere behind Pop."

There was no picking. As I walked down the aisle, the bus lurched forward and tossed me onto the nearest seat. Curtis didn't bring his sketch pad, or I would've counted the windows to see if I'd fallen in the exact location he'd predicted.

Reverend Parks gave the bus more gas. "Grab the Mossberg," he said, the roar of the diesel engine muffling his command.

Curtis lifted a shotgun from the bench behind me. "This is the lightest one we've got. Pop taught me how to shoot it on my seventh birthday... he put a bow on the stock and everything. You ever fire a pump action?"

Instead of a bike or a pair of roller skates, the preacher had given Curtis a way to protect himself. I couldn't fault him for that. When every strange man could be a harem hunter, maybe arming a child and teaching him how to use it was a loving thing.

"No, I've never fired one," I said. "It looks complicated."

"After you pull the trigger, slide this part on the bottom toward you. That releases the used cartridge. The new one locks in when you push it back out. You'll get six chances to scare the vultures before you gotta reload."

"Men and not birds, right?"

"Oh yeah, right," Curtis said. "Vultures are the road gangs around here. Anything on wheels can be traded for drugs… even this ancient rust bucket. Pop says when they highjack a vehicle, they don't take hostages and they don't leave witnesses."

"Is the gun loaded now?"

"Yep. And we removed the safety so she's ready to go."

"Don't let anyone near our tires, especially when I slow down at the intersections." The preacher's white beard bobbed in the rearview mirror as he yelled. "Use the front sight to line up your target and lean into the shots."

Curtis took the row across the aisle from me. Instead of sitting, he hovered above the seat with his sandals planted on the floor and his shoulders pressed against the backrest. That position wasn't the most comfortable way to travel but it gave him more height. I followed his lead and rested the muzzle of the Mossberg outside of my open window.

"I bet they'll see our guns and leave us alone," I said. "We'll scare them straight."

"Pop is praying for that."

"And what about you? Are you praying for a fight?"

"The fight is comin' either way."

This was my first trip in a vehicle without the Martinez name emblazoned on its sides. I was free from the power and influence of Billy. But as I counted the weapons on the seats around me, I could see the price tag for this freedom. Was the cranky driver behind the wheel okay with the cost? He must've known he could lose his life, or even worse, the life of his grandson.

"Why are you doing this? Rose and I could've kept walking."

"You'll be captured if you stay near the camp. The men with the airplanes are searching on foot now," he said.

"But how do you know?"

"I saw them—"

"In a dream," I said, finishing his sentence.

"Yes."

"The last sketch you showed me was this one, you know, with all of us on the bus. What's on the next page?"

"It's blank," he said.

"Your dreams stopped with this bus ride?"

The shake of his head was almost imperceptible.

"So your dreams continued," I said. "Why didn't you keeping drawing them?"

"Pop knew you'd want to see the future. I'm supposed to tell you that Jesus gives us today and that tomorrow is none of our business." His voice faded as he shrugged. "Sorry."

"Oh. Um, okay." I turned my head away… a momentary retreat while I planned my next question. I didn't care what the preacher said. This conversation with his grandson wasn't over.

The bus slowed at the first intersection. I inhaled a mouthful of hot dust, a parting gift from the rough camp road as we turned onto the pavement. The preacher called out "Hudson Bend" like a train conductor announcing the next station.

"Keep a sharp eye out now," he said.

I scanned the oncoming lane and the ditch beyond it.

As we picked up speed, my hair flew back and rode on each gust. Low, flat houses hid behind the trees, showing us a flash of a roof or an overgrown yard here and there. A beagle ran toward the bus with a mournful bay but gave up the chase before he reached the end of his driveway.

I jumped at every sound. All the hours of target practice with Aaron jumbled together in a messy patchwork of dos and don'ts—fragments of firearm safety stitched together with homespun advice on how to stay alive.

"If you're not shooting, you should be loading," he'd said outside the cave. "If you're not loading, you should be moving. If you're not moving, you're dead."

It was dangerous to let his voice echo in my head. I imagined kissing his lips until they were swollen. I imagined punching them until they were puffy and bleeding, but he'd had enough of that in his life. My runaway thoughts about passionate reunions felt like the cravings of a man on death row... as bittersweet as a final meal.

What if Aaron wasn't home? And if he was, why did I believe he would help me? He might haul me kicking and screaming back to the airport. If this day had taught me anything, it was that Papa had his loyalty. Not me.

I could tally the pros and cons of my next move without a chart or a weighted point system. No matter how much it hurt, the smart plan was to drop Rose in his front yard, turn the bus around, and get far away from Aaron Martinez. The stupid plan was to kick his door down and demand an explanation for the arranged marriage, the men at the airport, his betrayal... all of it.

"And you won't be stupid," I whispered.

The muscles in my arms ached with tension. To relieve the cramp in my trigger hand, I reached for the box of ammo on my seat, practicing the movement until it felt automatic. So far, the road was deserted. I wanted to sit down, lower the shotgun, and give my eyes a rest from the gritty wind. Perhaps the old man was paranoid, seeing vultures around every corner when there were none, but I doubted it.

Across the aisle, Curtis was coiled like a spring. I trusted him... perhaps more than any other human on the planet. If this kid predicted an alien invasion, I'd wrap my head in aluminum foil and wait for the spaceships to land.

"So what's your story? Are you psychic? Do you have other magical powers?" When the floodgates of my curiosity opened again, I couldn't control the flow. "Or maybe you're like a prophet from the Bible. Daniel and Joseph had dreams, you know. They were messages from God. Were you scared? Did you think you were going crazy?"

"Pop thought I was crazy," he said. "And then he wondered if I was possessed by the devil."

"Yeah, I bet. What else have you predicted with your dreams?"

"Nothin' really. Just you."

My eyes should've stayed on the road, but I had to see his face, had to look for hints of dishonesty or evasion. "When did your dreams start?"

"April," he said. "I only know cause Pop thought a riddle about a frozen girl was a dumb April Fools' Day joke." He snorted a laugh that was pure little boy, the contrast between its bright notes and the dark rifle he held made me shiver.

"Did you keep the sketch pad by your bed?"

"I did at first but my dreams of you were different. I could draw what I remembered before breakfast or after dinner. Either way, the details stayed sharp."

"You knew I was coming today," I said. It wasn't a question.

"I looked for signs that—"

He paused, not interrupted by a noise but by the lack of one. Our speed was dropping. The roar of the diesel engine was now the idle of a vehicle coasting without gas. I leaned out the window as far as I dared. Without the rush of wind, strands of my hair fell in heavy clumps. I pushed the curls away from my face and searched for familiar curves in the road.

"Not yet." I cupped my hands around my mouth so the old man could hear my instructions. "Our next turn will be on the left but not for a few more miles."

I expected him to give me a nod, a wave, or with his temperament, at least a growl. Only the shoulder of his suit coat was visible in the wide rearview mirror. As the bus rolled to a stop, I was more irritated than panicked until a guttural laugh floated in from the road.

"Go get 'em, boys!" The war cry came from the direction of our back bumper.

"Vultures," Curtis said, too calm. He lifted his weapon. When he pulled the trigger, the sharp burst was the only exclamation point he needed.

I pressed the butt of the Mossberg against my shoulder. Sweeping the muzzle from left to right, I hunted for a target but the view from my side of the bus was peaceful. No one was hiding in the ditches. No one was creeping toward our tires.

With two quick pops, windows on both sides of the bus exploded. I ducked as fragments rained down. Shards bounced around our feet and tinkled like wind chimes.

"Drive!" My single-word cry must have reached the ears of the men outside. They responded with a flurry of shots.

"I believe Reverend Parks has been injured," Rose said. There were tears in her voice even though her eyes couldn't produce them.

I slid to the ground as Curtis aimed at something behind us. "I'm going up to your grandpa," I said. "Watch the back-door. They might try a rear attack."

The floor of the bus was littered with glass. It was oddly festive, as if we'd detonated a disco ball. My legs were already bloody. I would've lost another pint if I'd crawled through the mess. Keeping my head below the windows, I waddled down the aisle with my shotgun. The silver purse still hung from my wrist, swaying with every step.

Rose must've tracked my painful progress toward the front of the bus. The rifle remained propped up in her lap, and even though the tip of the muzzle hadn't moved, the window she faced was nothing but a jagged opening. I touched her leg. When she turned, fragments of glass were embedded in clusters along her cheekbone and down her neck. One wicked sliver, larger than the rest, jutted out from the center of her forehead.

"Now come on Rose, that's gotta hurt." I yanked the sharp, perfect triangle from her skin. "Thank goodness you don't bleed."

"I believe our driver is unconscious. His breathing is shallow," she said.

Reverend Parks still sat behind the wheel. From my low angle, he seemed to be studying a row of dials and switches… as if he could flip a few and we'd start moving again. I dropped the Mossberg on the bench next to Rose.

"More men are approaching," she said. "They are running toward us."

I tensed, ready to hit the floor if the gunfire started again. But instead of bullets, a handful of gravel sailed through the open windshield. They struck the machine gun and it spun on its tripod like a merry-go-round.

There was no time to examine the preacher's injuries or take his place behind the wheel. I crawled toward the accelerator, put both hands on the pedal, and pushed it to the floor. The engine roared. I expected a corresponding leap forward but that didn't happen.

Our tires began a slow roll, like the bus was suddenly all bark and no bite. The hesitation felt eternal, but it was just long enough for another fistful of rocks to pummel my back. When the bus grew tired of teasing its prey, we surged forward and hit something with a sick thud.

"Move… move… move." I hissed the word without knowing who or what was in our way. My eyes were below the dashboard. The only road I could see was through the two, thin panels on the door. I'd yet to spot a single vulture but I was kneeling in their mess. The rocks under my knees didn't cut like glass but their sting brought tears to my eyes. When I grabbed the wheel with one hand, I felt the bus lurch to the left.

"Curtis, come steer this thing." The sharp blasts from his weapon continued as I overcorrected and we weaved to the right, spraying gravel on the shoulder of the road.

I didn't hear him come up the aisle, but I couldn't miss the metallic "tat, tat, tat, tat" of the weapon mounted above my head. The old machine gun was clearly more than a movie prop and Curtis fired the antique without hesitation. It had a strange smell, like smoke and nail polish remover. I covered my ears, a reflex to the deafening noise around me, and the bus slowed. We swayed like an ocean liner in a hurricane.

"It's okay. I've got the wheel," he said. "Give it some gas."

I pressed the accelerator but with more restraint this time, stopping halfway to the floor. "Tell me when it's safe to slow down. We need to trade places."

"I can drive."

"But I know where we're going."

"So do I," he said. "Get ready to hit the brakes in a few minutes."

"Have you driven before?"

"Kinda. I'm not tall enough to reach the pedals but Pop lets me practice with the steering wheel."

I fidgeted in the confined space, desperate to take the weight off my knees. With my right shoulder pressed against the dashboard, I could reach the accelerator. It gave me a gruesome view. Drops of blood fell from the tip of the preacher's nose. They formed a thin, crimson stream and splashed from the control panel onto his dress pants.

"I don't think your grandpa got hit by a bullet."

"There's a brick in his lap," he said. "That's what clobbered him."

"Head wounds bleed a lot. When you clean 'em up, they can be just a scratch. Don't worry, Aaron will know what to do. He gets hit in the face all the time." With Billy as his father, it was a sad fact.

"Get ready to press the brakes. I see the next road."

"Are there a bunch of metal towers in the distance? The ranch has 'em all over the place... especially near the big house," I said. "But we won't get too close to the guards."

I felt rather than saw our slow turn off Hudson Bend. It was a strange sensation to drive this way. What came naturally to my feet required concentration for my hands.

"How fast are we going?" I asked.

"Eleven miles an hour. Got another turn coming."

Our speed was slow enough that we didn't need the brakes as he turned the wheel. I felt each bump under my legs when we reached Aaron's long, gravel driveway. Without being told, I pressed down on the accelerator, taking the bus up to a whopping sixteen or seventeen miles per hour.

"There's a silver van in front of the house," he said.

"Any trucks?"

"Nope, only the van. I'm gonna pull up next to it."

"Just don't hit anything."

As I applied the brakes, Curtis struggled to find neutral

or park or whatever gear would stop the bus. "Pop says the transmission is cantankerous."

"Stay here," I said and lifted my hands off the pedal. The bus gave a final lurch. "I'll go get Aaron. We'll need his help to move your grandpa. Be right back."

I'm sure I ran toward the front porch even though I can't recall a single detail. Maybe I practiced what I wanted to say. Maybe I smoothed my hair. I remember walking into the house without an invitation. I remember the clicking sound of my sandals on the terracotta floor. And I remember finding Aaron sprawled in front of the coffee table… lifeless.

His mouth hung open. His chest didn't move. I counted out the seconds, losing track and starting again, and still he didn't breathe. I covered my eyes and then cheated, peeking between my fingers like this was a slasher film where drunk kids are chased through the woods by a psychopath and, of course, the hot guy gets stabbed or hung from the rafters or fried with a tattered electrical cord. But none of it was real. The same hot guy would be interviewed the next day on Good Morning America about his next film project.

"No." That one word emptied my lungs.

Every inch of my skin felt bruised. My heart ached but it was the blistering pain behind my eyes that made me stumble. I pitched forward. And when I hit the tile floor, it was hard underneath me and impossibly cold.

On my hands and knees, I wove through crumpled beer cans, a t-shirt, and one white sock. I didn't see the bottle of whiskey until I knocked it over. The half empty container fell on its side and spun, the brown liquid pouring out in an uneven circle. The mouth of the bottle pointed at Aaron when it finished its rotation. If this had been a party game, everyone would've watched as I kissed him.

I crawled through the puddle. And stopping just an inch from his outstretched body, I bent over his face. The tips of my hair brushed his ears and his cheeks. One wild curl wrapped around his mouth.

"Aaron." I didn't realize I'd said his name out loud until his eyes opened. I screamed. It must've been deafening because his eyes opened wider.

"Oh, hey Mira—" He coughed, gagging on something that sounded wet. "Want somethin' to drink?"

CHAPTER TWENTY-TWO

LIVING PROOF

"**Y**OU'RE DRUNK." I spat the words. My relief wasn't enough to dull the edges of my anger. Now that I knew he was alive, I wanted to kill him.

"You betcha." Aaron peered up at me through bleary eyes. With both hands, he patted the tile around him like a man who'd misplaced his wallet. "It's a shit-faced kinda day."

"I knocked over the whiskey if that's what you're looking for. The bottle is empty."

His head hovered a few inches off the ground, held there, and gave up. The back of his skull hit the tile with a thump. It should've hurt but he seemed beyond pain, at least for now.

"Beer's in the fridge," he said and pointed in the wrong direction.

He didn't look like a guy who could drink this much liquor and enjoy it. But what did I know? All I had was a gut feeling that surviving in this crappy world could change a man. Maybe he'd become a boozy chip off the old block.

I considered dumping a bucket of cold water on his head, to sober him up and pay him back for the hellish day I'd had, but the alcohol would still be in his bloodstream. A wet drunk was still a drunk.

"Come outside with me. There's a man who is injured," I said. "His name is Reverend Parks. He needs a doctor, but, um, not my papa."

"Did you shoot him?"

"No. I didn't—"

"Shotgun wedding. It ain't right." His tongue sounded numb, each word bumping and slurring into the next. "Preacher had it comin' if you ask me."

"There was no wedding. Listen to me, a road gang hit Reverend Parks with a brick."

"Who the hell is Reverend Parks?"

"You don't know him but his head is bleeding and he needs help. Please, Aaron."

I wrapped my fingers around his wrists and pulled. His shoulders lifted off the floor. His chest followed but his head lolled back as if the weight was too much for his neck to support. When he squinted up at me, I could almost see the room spinning in his amber eyes.

"Damn baby, slow down." He winced. "Think I'm gonna puke."

"No, you're okay. Take deep breaths."

"Tastin' it."

I backed away. "Just nod if you have a first aid kit in the house. Can you do that?"

He pitched forward. I translated his bowed head as a nod rather than what it probably was, his body preparing to vomit. I had seconds to get the information I needed.

"Is it in the kitchen? Or in your bathroom?"

He groaned.

Pushing my luck, I nudged his ankle with my foot. "Aaron, where is your first aid kit?"

"Bath—"

"Got it," I said and left him where he sat, relieved to escape before he got sick. Don't get me wrong, I was glad he was alive, but every former schoolkid knows puke is contagious. Retching into a shared trashcan wasn't my idea of a romantic afternoon.

I found nothing but a half-empty tube of toothpaste in the hall bathroom. Under the sink in his master bath, the words "First Aid" glowed white in the center of a red, metal case. I grabbed it by the handle, added a stack of folded washcloths to my supplies, and ran back into the living room.

Other than rolling onto his side, Aaron hadn't moved. I suspected there was a disgusting puddle behind his back but no way was I going to look. His face was sweaty. His eyes were closed and something chunky pasted down his hair on one side. He clutched the empty bottle against his stomach as if the whisky might take the hint and return to where it'd come from.

I paused long enough to watch his chest rise and fall. No doubt, he felt like death but I was confident he'd survive. It was the preacher who needed medical care.

When I rushed through the front door, I should've noticed the bumper of a third vehicle. It was clearly visible from the steps. But I was exhausted, and if I'm being honest, my heart was back on the living room floor.

Was Aaron drunk because of me? Was he drowning his sorrows because the woman he loved was marrying another man?

"Stop it. This isn't the chorus of a country song," I said and rolled my eyes. The first aid kit banged against my leg with every step. I was about as quiet as a toy monkey playing the cymbals.

"That you, Aaron?" a voice bellowed.

My head snapped up. The rest of my body went rigid.

"Billy's been lookin' for your ass all day."

The pitch was lower than a normal human… more like the thundering bass unique to giants with beanstalks. He was too big to hide, and yet, I couldn't find the man who matched the voice. One sandaled foot was solid under me. The other hovered above the ground, ready to pivot in the opposite direction the instant I saw his bald head.

I'd met this man but there was no comfort in that familiarity. Fear inched down my spine like the tip of a cold blade. I crept toward the driveway, the opposite direction any sane person would go, and pressed my back against the side of the bus.

I felt Dwayne before I saw his face. He was inside the bus, and as he stomped up the center aisle, the rusted chassis groaned under his weight. I sidestepped toward the emergency door. My pulse spiked as he passed by the window above my head and I swear I could smell his armpits.

"Master, look what I found," said a higher voice. "He was hiding under Rose's seat."

I grimaced. Of course, Iris was with him and serving her man with the same sweet, childlike enthusiasm. And while I despised the callous way he abused her, I wished she was still half blind. She'd found Curtis with her repaired laser sensors.

"The boy should fetch a good price," Dwayne said. "Tie him up with the old man."

"Perhaps ropes will not be needed for the gentleman. He is sleeping," she said.

"I don't give a damn if he's dead. Tie him up, anyway. This bus is armed to the teeth."

I lowered the washcloths onto the ground. And inch by tiny inch, I dropped the first aid kit into the soft nest without rattling the supplies inside. My hands needed to be free, with nothing between my fingers and the gun.

I opened the cylinder on the Ladysmith revolver and counted my way through the bad news inside. I had one bullet left. It was the shot I'd saved for myself but I didn't mind sharing a death sentence with Dwayne.

Slow and silent, I edged around the rear bumper of the bus. The muzzle of my gun turned the corner an instant before the rest of me. I locked eyes with Curtis.

He didn't seem surprised to see me. He sat in the bed of Dwayne's truck with the tailgate up. Both of his shoulders were pushed back at an unnatural angle. Iris crouched next to his feet. With a giggle, she wrapped a rope around his legs, like she was playing a game with Curtis instead of taking him hostage.

I pantomimed coughing. He gave me the slightest nod. And drawing in a long breath, he barked and gasped as if he were having an asthma attack. His performance was over-the-top, but it allowed me to pull back the hammer on the Ladysmith and creep closer without being heard.

"Better sell that kid off before he kicks the bucket. He ain't sounding too healthy," Dwayne said.

Ready or not, I stepped out into the open with both hands on the butt of the gun.

Iris spun toward me just as an enormous pair of black, combat boots cleared the final step of the bus and landed in the gravel with a crunch.

I had two potential threats in my sights. Iris believed she was my bathroom buddy and perhaps the furthest thing from an enemy. Dwayne was certainly the bigger target, the equivalent of hitting the broad side of a barn, but he was carrying Reverend Parks.

He'd slung the elderly man's limp body over his shoulder. The preacher's legs dangled down and blocked the easy shot at Dwayne's gut. I aimed at the vast space above the giant's eyes… the place where hair once grew.

"Oh master, look. Lavender is here." Iris clapped her hands. "What a lovely surprise."

"Hello Iris." I assumed she was smiling her gapped-tooth grin at me, but I didn't dare take my eyes off her master.

"Go get Aaron. Billy wants to talk to him," Dwayne said. His gaze settled on my chest and didn't go any higher. "Oh, and haul that broken Rose off the bus. She's been ridden hard and put up wet."

When I didn't respond, the muscles in his jaw twitched. A feminal's primary job was to look desirable and obey orders. My modest dress must've been a crime in his eyes… the ultimate turnoff. He ignored the gun in my hands and didn't reach for his own weapon. Instead, he tugged on the preacher's belt, readjusting the weight on his shoulder like the older man was nothing but a knapsack.

"Put Reverend Parks on the ground," I said. "Real easy. And tell Iris to let the boy go."

My hands were steady as I moved to stand in his path. Nine times out of ten, I could've hit the center of a target as large as his skull. But this wasn't a tin can on a fence post. If my aim had been off, just the slightest bit too low, the bullet could've struck the preacher's back instead of Dwayne's forehead. I had to get closer.

"I don't know what the hell is wrong with your programming. I don't care," he said, looking me in the eyes now. "But you better put that girlie gun away or I'll shove it down your throat sideways."

"Not if I kill you first."

With the volume of a pissed off bull, he inhaled and exhaled. Both of his nostrils flared. Maybe I was the first feminal to ever challenge him. No doubt, I was waving a red cape in front of his horns and daring him to charge me.

"You want 'em so bad? Here, take him."

Dwayne didn't drop his arms and let gravity pull the unconscious Reverend Parks to the ground. Bending his knees, the giant launched the man into the air with both hands. His body arched and hit the ground in front of me with a sick, bone-crushing thud.

Panic wrapped itself around my ribs like a vise. Bile crawled up my throat and stayed there. I'd taunted a violent man. And sprawled out lifeless at my feet, the preacher was suffering the consequences of my reckless decision.

A cloud of dust rained down on his gray suit, coating his arms and legs and sticking to the blood on his face. He didn't moan. He didn't move. One hand seemed to reach for his grandson with joints swollen from arthritis.

"Pop?" From the back of the truck, that pitiful, one-word question was worse than a thousand accusations. "Oh God, Pop."

The boy's cry mutated into a howling wail that was inconsolable. He thrashed against the ropes that held him. And when his feet broke free, Curtis screamed and stomped the tailgate with repeated blows. The "bang, bang, bang" was a steady, aching heartbeat that echoed between the truck and the bus.

I was drowning in horror. That's the only explanation I've got. I should've shot that giant in the middle of his fat forehead right then... without hesitation. But with every breath, I was swallowing the child's cries and suffocating under his grief.

I crouched next to Reverend Parks. All I wanted was to find a pulse or hear him breathing... anything to stop his grandson's screams. I reached out. My fingers made the briefest contact with his neck before a meaty hand descended from the sky and the left side of my face exploded.

The pain was blinding. Lava hot, it radiated through my

skull and found secret places to hide within the roots of my hair and deep inside my teeth. I curled into a ball on my knees. And with each moan, I rocked back and forth in front of this blazing altar. It stole my other senses. Even my fear of another blow wasn't enough to pull me from its clutches. I don't know how long I held my face, how loud I whimpered when even breathing hurt like the devil.

Taste came back first. Dirt mixed with the copper saliva in my mouth to form a vile, gritty paste. His palm had been open when he hit me or I would've been spitting teeth. My nose ran like a faucet. And when the ringing in my ears faded, I heard a noise I didn't understand. It was a human sound, near me but not coming from within me. The gasps were high-pitched and wet, like someone whistling and gargling mouthwash at the same time.

I tried to open my eyes. The left one was swollen. Puffy skin blocked everything but a thin sliver of light. I squinted through my right eye as a pair of black pumps teetered toward me. Following the line of her legs, past a miniskirt and halter top, I reached the blond head towering over me. Below her unblinking gaze, scarlet teeth swam in and out of focus. Strong hands lifted me off the ground.

"Do not be alarmed." Iris cradled me against her chest, swaying back and forth like a mother comforting a fussy baby. "Your master can fix the damage to your skin. My friend Lavender will be as good as new. Would you like me to carry you?"

"You're hurt. There's blood dripping off your chin," I said.

Did Dwayne hit her in the face after he hit me? But

no, that couldn't explain her injuries. The stains around her mouth and the river of red streaks on her throat felt wrong… felt too human. Feminals didn't have veins. They couldn't bleed.

"Where's Dwayne?"

"My master is taking a nap with the elderly gentleman. See?" Iris bent at the waist to give me a closer look.

Dwayne was on the ground. His considerable height was stretched out less than three feet from Reverend Parks but the giant wasn't sleeping. His mouth was open. His eyes bulged and blinked at the sky above him. Blood pulsed from a jagged hole near the base of his neck like a fountain.

Big squirt, little squirt, big squirt, little squirt.

"What happened to him? I don't understand—"

"Iris was a naughty girl. That's what happened," said a voice inside the bus. The tone was thicker than Aaron's. It was barbed with something sharp, something that poked through the humor of his words. "I think somebody messed with her programming. Naughty… naughty."

I flailed to escape her arms and the man behind that voice. It wasn't much of a fight. Her hands were unyielding as she carried me like a pagan sacrifice, like a virgin to be tossed into a fiery pit. The ache in my cheek sunk its claws in deeper.

"No, Iris." My hiss rose in volume as I dug my fingernails into her cold skin. "Take me and Curtis to the house."

"Mr. Martinez will help us find your missing eye. He is a nice man," Iris said.

Her "nice man" was the one person Papa feared most. And Iris was hauling me, kicking if not screaming, toward the one moment Papa dreaded most. He'd drugged his daughter to avoid this—recruited husbands to avoid this.

My terror was a strange animal. Trapped in the prison of her feminal arms, I couldn't "fight or flight." As Iris bowed in front of her creator, fragments of an old nursery rhyme teased me with, *"How old is she, Billy Boy, Billy Boy, How old is she, charming Billy? She is sixty times eleven, twenty-eight and forty- seven, She's a young thing and cannot leave her mother."*

Billy sat on the stairs of the bus. His long legs were wrapped in denim and crossed at the ankles. The tips of his brown, leather boots poked out of the door, just another guy warming his toes in the autumn sunshine. Nothing diluted the picture of a man at peace other than the assault rifle across on his lap.

"Lavender lost her left eye. I will find it, Mr. Martinez," Iris said, her programming reaching new heights in earnestness. "You can count on me. I will not be naughty any more today."

He removed his cowboy hat and examined me with piercing, dark eyes—the way an art critic might appraise a rare painting. I'm sure I was a sight… dirty, bruised, and sticky with snot. But was I the real thing or a well-engineered forgery? He seemed transfixed by the cuts on my legs and the puffy skin on my cheekbone.

I refused to fill the silence with nervous chatter. Instead, I examined Billy right back. His hair was full with more silver strands than black. His body was trim but his face looked bloated. Spider veins branched in all directions. And when he opened his mouth, his teeth were stained as brown as the bottom of a coffee cup.

"Honey, you ain't the only naughty one here," he said. With one hand on the stock, he aimed the gun at Iris. She didn't flinch. She didn't try to avoid whatever punishment he thought she deserved.

"I think Dr. Vega has a few naughty secrets, too." He rotated the gun toward me.

"So there's no need to go lookin' for a runaway eyeball." The muzzle flipped back to Iris. Like the sweeping movement of a metronome, Billy used his rifle to tick off each fact with precision.

"When the swelling goes down, her eye will be right where God placed it," he said. "Ain't that right, Mirari?"

He pointed the rifle at me. And this time, the weapon was aimed at my heart.

PART THREE

One Day Later

CHAPTER TWENTY-THREE
THE PRICE YOU PAY

ON MY FIRST day at the ranch, I put on the clothes of a dead girl. I inhaled the fabric, searching for a hint of her floral perfume. All I could smell was the acrid odor of mothballs.

As teenagers, Lili had been shorter than me. The hem of her jeans stopped several inches above my ankles. Her Born to Run t-shirt didn't cover my stomach when I lifted my arms. I wore it anyway, wrapping the memories of that concert around me like a suit of armor.

For my sixteenth birthday, we'd celebrated with third row seats for Bruce Springsteen and the E Street Band. The tickets were a gift from Lili. And even with a new driver's license burning a hole in my pocket, we weren't allowed to go alone. Papa insisted on being our chauffeur.

The magic happened about halfway through the show.

As the Boss pounded out the electric guitar introduction to "She's the One," he looked right at Lili as the lights came up, like he was playing for her and her alone. She stood mesmerized, too awestruck to even squeal, and bought this t-shirt on our way out the door.

"To remember this night forever," she'd said.

During the drive home, I teased her about becoming a groupie and traveling with the band. "Maybe you could be his girlfriend."

"He's not married. He's older than me but women mature faster than men, right? Do you think he'd like me?"

Papa burst her bubble. "Don't let your father hear you talk like that. He'll lock you up and throw away the key," he said and we laughed, like Papa was kidding, like there was no way Billy would imprison someone in his own home.

It wasn't funny anymore.

On my second day at the ranch, I asked to be moved to Lili's old bedroom. The Daisy who delivered my breakfast denied my request with a click of her tongue. After dinner, I asked to see Billy face-to-face, promising to give Mr. Martinez "very important information."

"My master has an appointment scheduled with you on his calendar," she said. "He asks for your patience until that date."

"What date?"

"He did not say."

Her mouth seemed programmed to fall into a stern line. She wore a yellow pantsuit that matched the flowers in her coiled braids. The bright color didn't improve her dour, no-nonsense personality. Compared to this feminal, Papa's Daisy was the class clown, practically the life of the party.

On day seven, I begged to go outside. "Just for a few minutes so I can see the sun. I need the vitamin D."

"My master provides you with well-balanced meals including spinach, fish, cheese, and eggs," Daisy said. "Those foods are rich in vitamin D."

On another day, and God help me I have no idea which one, I demanded a calendar, a clock, and some books to read. "If he doesn't give them to me, I'm going on a hunger strike," I said. "All I do is stare at these walls. I don't know if it's day or night, Monday or Friday, in here. He needs to let me go."

My requests were no longer phrased as a question. Daisy processed my words with an arched eyebrow, and I suspect, a recording of every demand. But when she carried in my breakfast tray the next morning, a bundle of paper was tucked under her arm.

"My master says he will strap you down and feed you intravenously if you attempt a hunger strike. However, he gave his consent for one magazine and a pocket calendar. I have circled today's date," she said. "An electric clock is forbidden. You could hang yourself with the cord. A battery powered clock is also forbidden. You could eat the batteries."

"For crying out loud, I'm not gonna chomp down on a pair of Duracells. I don't go anywhere. I don't see anyone but you. What is the point of all this?"

She handed me the stack of glossy paper. John Travolta smiled up at me from the faded cover of an old Teen Beat magazine. I set it aside and focused on the calendar. There was a crayon wedged between the pages. A box with October fifteenth was circled in red.

"If you scribble on the walls or the furniture, my master will confiscate the magazine, the calendar and, of course, the crayon."

"I'm not a preschooler," I said and dismissed her with the wave of a hand.

When I'd played in this basement as a kid, it was an unfinished space—a cement box where we could whoop and holler during storms and not bother the adults upstairs. Now this box was hiding the world from me, as if I were the natural disaster. The solid, oak door was always locked. The queen-sized bed and the attached bathroom meant I never had to leave.

Daisy brought me each meal like clockwork, as reliable as the Timex I wasn't allowed to have. She checked my blood pressure, requested urine samples I refused to give, applied antibiotic cream to the hundreds of tiny cuts on my skin, supervised every bedtime shower, dried my skin with fluffy towels, and draped a fresh nightgown over my head. I made a circle in the calendar every night before I fell asleep… my only anchor to reality.

On day eleven, she asked if I preferred a "pad or tampon?" I wasn't shocked. Papa's Daisy had been just as intrusive, and I'd lost my shyness back in the cave. Her basket of supplies beat shoving wads of toilet paper into my underwear.

"How old are these suckers? It's not like there's big money in manufacturing feminine hygiene products anymore."

"I could find no expiration date," she said. "Because the

packaging is intact, I believe they are safe for you to use. Would you like my assistance?"

"That's a super sweet offer but I think I can manage." My grin was brittle, more a baring of my teeth than a smile.

"Very well," she said and made a note on her clipboard.

"What are you writing down?"

"I am recording today's date."

"Why?"

"This is the first day of your menstrual cycle," she said.

"Yeah, but why write it down?" A bubble of unease expanded inside my stomach, threatening to burst into an all-out panic. I could think of several reasons why Billy would request this information and none of them were comforting.

"My master was quite specific," she said. "He wishes to know when your menstrual cycle begins and ends. This data will be essential for your meeting with him."

"May I see your clipboard? I would like to pass along a message to Mr. Martinez."

She tilted her head. Her eyes narrowed as if she was running a complex math equation behind her laser-based distance sensors.

"You can babysit me the entire time so I don't stab myself with the ink pen or get a vicious paper cut. I'll behave." I raised my hands in the air like a hostage, which of course, I was.

"Very well," she said, surprising me with her consent.

Next to her neat block lettering with today's date, I scribbled my short note. I considered starting it with "Dear Bully" rather than "Dear Billy" but that seemed childish. Instead, I wrote "I was your daughter's best friend." When I returned the clipboard, Daisy said nothing.

A human would've read my words and perhaps felt the sting of emotion behind them. A human might have tossed the paper into a trashcan and never delivered it to Billy… afraid that he'd kill the messenger. Daisy was programmed to be a literal creature. I believe she carried my note to her master. But did the memories of his dead daughter soften him or add more calluses to his already scarred heart?

After several days of silence, I gave up on receiving a note back and concentrated on staying sane. My daily routine was mind-numbing. Each morning after breakfast, I walked the perimeter of my bedroom, measuring it with small steps and giant leaps.

When the swelling on my face went down, I counted the white, square tiles on the bathroom floor with both eyes open. I read and re-read my one magazine until I had huge portions of the articles memorized. And even though I hoped John Travolta was still alive, the celebrity gossip and full-page advertisements on how to shrink my pores were meaningless.

I did half-hearted pushups with my hands and knees sinking into the thick carpet. I did jumping jacks and jogged in place until sweat ran down the center of my back. All of this activity still left me with more than twenty-two hours to fill.

I'd hated sit-ups in high school, but I was bored enough to add them to my exercise routine. I climbed into the middle of the bed and counted them off. The headboard slammed against the wall each time my head hit the pillow, leaving dents in the beige paint. I didn't care. With a steady rhythm, I touched my toes and flung myself backward.

"Psst… Mirari."

My name floated down from the ceiling—each syllable so soft I thought I'd imagined it. I strained to hear the sound again.

"Are you there? It's me," the voice said, the tone too high to be Papa or Aaron.

I sprang from the bed in a heap of twisted sheets. And spinning in a circle, I hunted for any corner where a person or a feminal could be hiding. The closet had no doors. The bathroom had no doors but I checked behind the shower curtain just in case. The bathtub was empty. As I was searching under the bed, a scraping noise, like a mouse chewing a hole, brought me back to me feet.

"I'm on the other side of the wall," the voice said, louder now and somewhere above my head. "Talk into the opening where the cold air comes out."

Standing on the mattress, I put my face next to the metal vent. "Curtis? Is that you?"

"It's me."

"Can you open my door? Take if off by the hinges if you have to." I was too excited to keep my voice down.

"Only if you can open my door first."

"You're locked in?"

"Yep," he said. "It's boring in here but the food is good."

I slammed my fist into the wall with a single, muffled thud. I wanted to scream and cry and pound the barrier between us until my arms gave out. Instead, I huffed a bitter laugh. "Oh yeah, Billy isn't starving us… at least not yet."

"The Daisy brings me a tray. Sometimes I get cookies and once I got a big slice of pecan pie. But she makes me brush my teeth after breakfast and before I go to sleep. I told her the toothpaste is too spicy."

"Have you been in this basement since, um, we were on the bus?" I almost said "since the day Dwayne killed your grandpa" but I caught myself.

"Aaron let me crash on his couch for a few weeks. His refrigerator didn't have much in it. We ate a lot of cereal but he let me watch TV, drive his van around the yard, pretty much do whatever I wanted."

"Was he drunk the entire time?"

"Nah, he sobered up real quick after you left. Barfed a few times though."

"I bet."

"He drove me back to the camp," he said and took several long beats before going on. "We buried Pop's body by the flagpole. It's a good spot, you know, in the center of the circle."

"I—" My voice cracked with emotion. I swallowed but the lump at the back of my mouth refused to move. It was stubborn… as if it had something important to say. "I'm sorry about your grandpa. He would still be alive if I'd never walked into your camp."

"When Pop climbed on the bus with you, he knew what would happen."

"He knew because of your dreams. Is that right?"

"I couldn't draw the giant standing over him. I tried but it hurt too much. So instead of showing him a picture, I told him about the road gang, and the brick, and how his head would bleed, and how the giant would throw his body into the air." He exhaled. The release of pent-up air was loud enough for me to hear on the other side of the wall. "Pop wouldn't listen."

"He didn't believe he would die?"

"He made jokes about David and Goliath, and how the giant always loses, but Pop knew he would die. We argued about it. He wouldn't give me the keys to the bus no matter how many times I begged. He said he'd made his peace with the Lord. And every morning, he put on his best suit so he'd be ready to meet you."

"Why, Curtis?" Tears rolled down my face and I let them fall. "Why would your grandfather die just to give me a ride? He didn't know me. He didn't even think I was a human until he saw the scratches on my legs."

"Pop was a preacher without a church," he said.

I waited for more but Curtis let the silence stretch between us. "Um, okay, but I still don't get it."

"When you met him, you saw nothing but a grumpy, old man."

"Well, I wouldn't say it like that." Curtis was right but it felt disrespectful to criticize this boy's grandfather, especially so soon after the man's horrible death.

"Before I was born, Pop packed 'em in every Sunday. The ladies would faint in the heat because the pews were so crowded. He said one of the local TV stations wanted to broadcast his sermons but nobody was brave enough to put a black preacher on the air.

"After all the women were gone, his church fell apart. Men didn't believe in anything anymore. Pop said he felt like Moses. Lost in the wilderness, you know? He prayed to find it before he died."

"Find what?"

"The sign… the one thing that would prove Jesus still loves us. He thought my dreams were the sign. And once he saw your face, Pop said he'd be okay with whatever came next. Even his own death."

"Giving me a lift was a dumb reason for your grandfather die." My words hissed through the vent like a whip searching for tender flesh. I didn't want to hurt this kid's feelings, but I couldn't let him believe a lie. The preacher had sacrificed his life for nothing.

"I know it feels that way. But maybe—"

"But maybe nothing. Look at us. What good came from our bus ride? Aaron was a total bust. He was too drunk to do anything but puke on the floor and watch from the window as his father hauled me away. And despite Papa's twisted scheme to marry me off, Billy has me now. If this is God's plan, you're right. I don't get it."

"Aaron is helping you," he said.

"How?"

"He tied me up and got Billy to bring me here."

I squeezed my eyes shut and rubbed them until tiny bursts of light erupted under the lids. I counted to ten. I rolled my shoulders before I opened my mouth, just like I'd watched Papa do my whole life.

"You volunteered to be locked down here? And Aaron, who is supposed to be a grown man, participated. Is that what you're telling me?"

"Aaron knew you'd be mad."

"Mad about sending a child into a war zone? Mad that he's too afraid of his father to come here himself?"

"Billy won't let anyone in the house now, not even his own kid," he said. "Aaron tried, I swear. He even bribed the guards with a bunch of Roses."

"Flowers or robots?"

"The robot girls with the red hair. And that part worked."

I sighed. "Of course, it did."

"So while the men were, um, busy with their Roses, Aaron came up the driveway and parked behind the house. Everything looked good until he ran head-first into a Violet on the back porch. She almost killed him."

"Or so he says."

"No, I saw it. I hunkered down inside his van and watched the entire fight. She had Aaron by the throat. The safe word didn't stop her cause she was choking him so hard he couldn't talk. He got the hatch open on the back of her neck. After pulling a bunch of wires, she twitched like she was having a seizure and fell over."

The next logical question was "is he alright?" My lips parted, formed the first word, and stopped. I was terrified to hear the answer. What was wrong with me? I was furious when I thought Aaron was a coward and scared out of my mind when he wasn't.

"He had bruises and a sore throat. His voice sounded funny for few days. Other than that, he says he's good. Don't worry," Curtis said with an intuition beyond his years.

"None of this explains why you are here."

"Oh, I'm not done. Aaron called the ranch a few days ago, real angry, and told his dad to come get me. He lied and said that I'd attacked him in the middle of the night. Laid it on real thick about how violent I was. He asked Billy how much I might be worth to a harem hunter. I could tell his dad didn't believe him at first. But Aaron went on, talking about the cost of my surgeries and how much profit they could make.

"Billy picked me up the next morning," Curtis said. "When he saw the bruises around Aaron's neck, he laughed and said I needed my nuts cut off… that it'd teach me not to mess with the Martinez family."

"Only the father is allowed to bruise his son," I said. "You're lucky he didn't kill you on the spot."

"That's what Aaron was afraid of. I had to show him my pictures of the ranch before he'd believe me about the dreams. I drew the kitchen, the hall, the stairs down to the basement. Everything had to look right before he'd call his dad." Curtis lowered his voice to a whisper. "You need to play along with Billy's plan. You know, just pretend you're good with it."

"What kind of plan? If he thinks he can force me—"

"It's the only way you can escape and you gotta escape. You gotta find her."

I almost missed those two little words. He'd said "find her" as if it were an afterthought, like an "oh by the way, you have a sister" postscript at the end of a letter. I could feel myself falling and grabbed the headboard to stay on my feet.

"Mirari?"

"Yes—um—I'm here. Just trying to…" My breathing was too shallow. My heartbeat was too rapid and the wall against my face felt hot. "Holy crap, Curtis. Are you sure?"

A key rattled in the door. If Daisy had the same bionic hearing as Rose, Curtis and I were already busted. I needed two seconds. That was it… just two precious seconds to ask one final question.

"How will I escape?"

"Inside a blue Jeep."

CHAPTER TWENTY-FOUR

INTO THE FIRE

JUMPED ON THE bed like an over-caffeinated child at a sleep over. "Come in," I called and waved at the open door. "I'm just getting some exercise."

The top of my head brushed the ceiling with every bounce. The springs in the mattress squeaked in protest. I panted, more from fear than physical activity. If the bed had caved in around my feet, Daisy would've confiscated my furniture and made me sleep on the floor.

"This form of exercise is unacceptable. Get down at once." Her right eyebrow lifted higher than I'd ever seen it, arching more than an inch above the left one. "My master will be displeased if you harm yourself on the day of your meeting."

Two Irises stood in the hallway behind her. One clutched a black and white polka dot suitcase and the other held a matching garment bag. Both wore pantsuits in shades of orange and lime green. Clustered together, their outfits were as cheerful as a bowl of rainbow sherbet, but their expressions were anything but sweet. All three looked ready to haul me to the woodshed.

"It's about time. Take me to your master," I said, loud enough for Curtis to hear me through the vent. With a final bounce, I curled into a ball and dropped onto the mattress.

"I cannot present you looking like this. Your hair is frizzy, your shirt is wrinkled, and your skin is wet with perspiration." The head Daisy gestured the rest of her crew into the room. "We must make you more presentable. Shower, hair, cosmetics, perfume, clothes, and shoes… in that exact order."

"I've known Billy, um, Mr. Martinez since I was a little girl. Why go to all this trouble? I just want to have a conversation with the man."

"His orders must be obeyed."

"Yeah, but—"

"We can inject you with a tranquilizer or you can cooperate."

"Fine," I said and rolled my eyes.

If I'd been too willing to be their dress-up doll, my compliance would've been suspicious. I had to grumble a little before giving into their demands and keep my eyes open for a way out. Curtis didn't say anything about his escape from the ranch, but I wasn't going anywhere without him. We were going to "find her" together or die trying.

The torture began when one of the Irises threw open my shower curtain. Half blinded by the soap running down my face, I shrieked and lashed out with a wet arm. She grabbed it. Without asking my permission, she applied a gritty paste to my elbow.

"We must exfoliate your dead cells," she said as she scrubbed. "Turn please."

"Can feminals get wet or am I about to be electrocuted?"

"I can be submerged in water for two hours before my seals are compromised. Turn please."

An hour into the shaving, tweezing, and waxing, I sat on the toilet as they dried the strands I had left. Daisy brandished a flat iron. As she adjusted its dials, the stench of acrid heat filled the room.

"This will smooth out your curls," she said. "We will work section by section."

I waved my hands to fend her off, knocking a can of hairspray and a fat, round brush into the sink. "Stay away from me with that thing. Do you hear me? I've gone along with all this beauty shop garbage but you are not straightening my hair."

"Your consent is irrelevant."

"Just try to straighten my hair without it. If you hold me down, I'll leave this bathroom with burn marks all over my face. Will that please your master?"

Behind her eyes, Daisy scrolled through an index of options, weighing her next move as if I were a piece on a chessboard. She was programmed to be both arrogant and analytical—engineered to overcome obstacles. She seemed to have tenacity in every line of her code.

My stubborn streak was more organic. I'd been born with my mama's curly hair and her determination to persevere. I wasn't going to lose either one in this bathroom.

Daisy squeezed the flat iron until its metal shell creaked with the abuse. Would she blow a gasket as she calculated a way to defeat me? Could I make smoke pour out of her ears? Her assistants stood at attention with their hands clasped in front of them. They seemed to await her final decision with endless patience.

"Very well," she said. "Begin her makeup. We will twist her hair up with pins after she is dressed."

The feminals I'd met so far either spoke the truth or didn't speak at all—a vast improvement over the human tongue. As the minutes ticked by and the iron cooled, I relaxed as they smeared junk on my face. Six hands worked around me in perfect synchronicity. To her credit, Daisy didn't glare or pout or stab me with a mascara wand in retaliation.

I was prepared for round two of our battle as she reached for the garment bag. No matter what Curtis said about "going along with the plan" in order to escape, I wasn't wearing some skimpy harem costume. I crossed my arms over my chest.

The artificial light over the bathroom sink was so cold it looked blue. But when it touched the gold cloth tucked inside the garment bag, the room exploded in warmth, like Daisy was unzipping a piece of the sun. The gown was magnificent. Bands of delicate, luminescent crystals radiated from the base of its V-shaped neckline in all directions.

I should've despised the gown on principle. It reflected the warped femininity all around me. It stood for every decision I was no longer allowed to make and every man who wanted to control me. I reached for the hanger, holding the fabric against my body.

"Does the style meet with your approval?" Daisy's mouth curled up at the edges. "We designed each detail with you in mind."

"Zip me into it. Let's find out."

With a silky hiss, the hem floated down my legs and pooled on the floor. Tiny crystals seemed to hug every curve. A web of beads formed a cape of sorts that fastened behind my neck and draped over my shoulders, attaching to golden cuffs around my wrists. It provided no warmth for my bare arms. But when I moved, the walls around me sparkled.

"You look like a queen," she said.

"Oh, I don't know about that."

"This is a gown worthy of Nefertiti. I have information about her life in my database, including an image file of her statue in the Neues Museum. She was a queen in ancient Egypt. Her name meant 'the beautiful one has come' and she had many daughters. You shall be the same. My master said this will be your destiny."

And with those words, Daisy won. She got her revenge on me without lifting a hand and she didn't even know it. Her pretty speech was a bucket of ice water over my head… a plunge in a frozen river. My chest tightened. My heart skipped several beats and then raced to catch up.

"That's insane. I am no fertility goddess."

"Please be seated," she said. "We will put your hair up."

"Listen, I've got nothing against babies. They're cute when they aren't screaming or puking or pooping down their legs."

She lifted a clear box of pins from the suitcase.

"I know I'm the first woman you've ever met," I said. "So, um, I understand your ignorance on this subject. Yes, women had babies before the pathogen, giving birth to both girls and boys. And yes, it was a wonderful thing. A miracle, really. But some women never had children, not even one, and lived long, rich lives. It isn't fair to say they didn't fulfill their destiny or—"

"Sit please," she said again.

"I don't need to become a baby factory to have a destiny."

"Mirari, sit down."

"And who cares what Billy thinks? Like my destiny is any of his business—"

Daisy put a hand on my shoulder. Two rigid fingertips pressed down, finding a nerve I didn't know I had, and I howled. My knees buckled. Her assistants caught me at the elbows and smoothed my gown as I collapsed.

"Damn, that hurt," I said, rubbing my neck. "I would've sat down if you'd asked."

Her only response was another arched eyebrow.

Why was I arguing with a gaggle of feminals about women's rights? It was a waste of energy… a distraction. I stared straight ahead as they wove my curls into something that felt elaborate on the top of my head. My mouth stayed shut, even when the occasional bobby pin scraped my scalp and the hairspray made it hard to breathe.

Daisy lifted my ankle. With so much oil on my skin, the high-heeled pumps slipped on my feet without resistance. I tilted them from side to side, admiring the shape and the way the gold fabric rivaled the sparkle in my gown.

"I'm gonna look like a solar flare. Well, Billy can either take me or leave me. Let's hope it's option B," I said and stood, three inches taller now.

The Iris in the green pantsuit sprayed a final cloud of perfume into the air as they led me from the room. For the first time in weeks, I could see windows and the world beyond it. The cloudless blue sky should've given me hope. But our parade through the empty house felt like a walk through a graveyard—the "clack, clack, clack" of our heels like the rattle of dry bones. I hesitated in the kitchen, confused when we didn't continue toward the front of the house and Billy's office.

Daisy opened the backdoor. "This way," she said. "Hurry now."

I'd seen the mall parking lot the week before Christmas. I remembered the asphalt jungle at the Texas State Fair. Sedans and station wagons would jockey for a space closer to the front gate. But this jumble of vehicles in Billy's driveway had no order... no rhyme or reason. They'd been left at odd angles on the pavement, in the grass, and even in the flower beds, like the drivers abandoned the wheel while their tires were still rolling. If Mama's blue Jeep was out here, it was just another shiny hood in a sea of trucks and vans.

The silence bothered me the most.

No one sat with the motor running and the radio on. No small clusters of men leaned against their bumpers to guzzle beer, tell dirty jokes, or complain about the high cost of gasoline. And yet, there must have been a party somewhere because nothing other than alcohol or drugs could explain the mess in this driveway.

We slowed in front of a long, stucco barn with a red roof. Back when Lili was alive, it'd housed a riding arena with bleacher seats on one side and a line of stalls on the other. We raced our spotted ponies up and down that ring until they'd had enough, baring their teeth and nipping at us. I still had a faint scar on my right leg in the shape of a bite mark.

A guard stepped around the corner of the barn. Without thinking, I reached for the sticker on the back of my neck. It wasn't there. My days of pretending to be anything other than a human female were over. As we approached, he tipped his cowboy hat in our direction.

"Afternoon, ladies," he said.

The man wore the same gray uniform as the border patrols. He was tall with more height in his torso than in his bowed legs. A blond mustache curved around his mouth like a bushy set of parentheses. His eyes were unreadable behind his sunglasses. I had no problem reading the identical lumps on his hips. His jacket didn't conceal the firepower strapped underneath it. If anything, the jacket seemed to emphasize the hard edges of his weapons.

I gripped the front of my gown in both fists. With or without a sticker on my neck, my feminal act wouldn't have fooled anyone. My hands shook. My eyes were open too wide. And despite the perfume, I smelled like sweat and fear.

A sign nailed to the building read, "No guns or unauthorized feminals in the arena." The guard opened the door for us, allowing Daisy and her Irises to enter. They weren't mine to command, but I was relieved they were on the approved list. I didn't want to meet Billy alone.

Inside the barn, voices boomed like an approaching thunderstorm. We'd found the party. The men couldn't see me, not yet, but I was the reason they were here. Nothing else made sense. A piercing laugh rose above the din and my body seized as if I'd been hit by lightning. The Iris in the orange pantsuit slammed into my back. I stumbled and only her quick hands kept me from hitting the ground.

"What's going on? You told me this was a meeting with Billy."

"It is," Daisy said. "My master is waiting for you. Come along."

As she led me down the hall, I inhaled as much oxygen as my tight gown would allow. The odor of horse flesh and hay was strong. Skylights illuminated the ring in front of us. A red carpet ran down the center of the floor and ended at a raised platform. Buried under flowers and red-white-and-blue ribbons, Billy's impromptu stage could've doubled as a Fourth of July parade float. A line of wooden horse stalls behind it were decorated to match.

We stopped inches away from the arena. Daisy turned and ushered me into an office with windows overlooking the stands. Her assistants didn't follow. One of them shut the door behind me with a menacing click.

I frowned.

The men seated at the table frowned back, as if I'd walked into the wrong meeting by mistake. When I fidgeted, the sequins on my gown threw pinpoints of light on the walls, the filing cabinets, and over their faces. Both of these guys knew me and yet both of them seemed confused. Their lips gaped open like a pair of largemouth bass. It was Billy who spoke first.

"Well now, Mirari. Ain't you as pretty as a picture? Just lovely. Daisy tells me your bruises have healed." When he smiled, the dirty stains on his teeth were gone. His new dentures were a brilliant white and looked sharper… more piranha now. "And Iris will be pleased we found your missing eye. She's limping around here somewhere."

The cowboy hat resting next to his elbow was an exact match to the one worn by his guards. But instead of a gray suit, Billy wore a black tuxedo. When I didn't acknowledge him, his gaze roamed from the top of my head to the tips of my shoes. He cleared his throat, checked the time, and adjusted the cuffs of his jacket. The man seemed as nervous as a groom on his wedding day.

"I must admit, your body defrosted nicely," he said.

"Yes sir… without a hint of freezer burn."

"And you still have your mother's saucy mouth. That must be a comfort to your father."

His insult landed like a slap but I didn't let it show. I would not fall to my knees in front of this man. I would not beg for mercy. Turning my gaze toward the arena, I changed the subject.

"Are you hosting a livestock auction? Early morning might've been cooler," I said. "Lili's ponies never liked the heat. It made them irritable. But I'm sure your Arabian horses are better trained and never forget who's in charge."

"In fact, these men are here to…"

A weight slammed against the wall. After another thump,

someone began yelling. The words were thick and unintelligible. A more sober voice hurled back a string of obscenities, questioning the first man's parentage in explicit detail. He got raucous laughs.

"Dammit," Billy said. "Hang on."

He stood. And muttering more obscenities, he stomped toward the window. When he beat the glass with his fists, the repeated blows made the frame shake. The crowd went silent.

While Billy's back was turned, the other man at table lifted his chin. Brown eyes, the same color as mine, searched my face. His attire was less formal than Billy's. He wore a white dress shirt with a Martinez Motion logo on the chest and no jacket. The dark circles above his cheekbones were just a few shades lighter than his black dress pants.

"Hello, Mirari," he said.

"How are you, Papa?"

"Better now that I can see you. The last several weeks have been—" He swallowed something that must've been large and painful. He winced. "The last several weeks have been long."

"I'm glad you survived the mob at the airport. Those guys and their feminals were, uh, kinda ticked off." I shrugged. "But here you are. Safe in the bosom of the Martinez family once again."

At the mention of his name, Billy turned and gave us a paternal smile. "I'm glad your family feels safe here. Me and the doc, we've been friends for a long time, haven't we?"

"Since both our girls were in pigtails." Papa's mouth tightened but his tone remained low.

"Forgive my manners," Billy said. "Mirari, please be seated. Can we get you something to drink? Daisy, pour our honored guest a glass of water. As she said, the day is heating up and she must be thirsty."

I lowered myself into a chair with the strangest sensation of déjà vu. With the gown, the heels, and the men critiquing my appearance, a voice in my head said, "sit up straight and be charming." This entire day was too much like the beauty pageants Lili dragged me into. Watching me with critical eyes, the judges scored my poise and the dimensions of my childbearing hips.

"Mr. Martinez—"

"Please call me Billy," he said and returned to his seat.

I inclined my head. "Billy, there are a lot of men out there waiting for something. Can you tell me what that something is?"

"They're waiting to meet you, darlin'." He waved a hand toward the crowd. "It's been a long time since they've seen a woman. As you can tell by their excitement, the boys are anxious to make your acquaintance."

"That's it? They just want to meet me? So I'll smile, blow a few kisses into the stands, and Papa will drive me home."

"Not exactly. Your first guess was closer to the truth."

My eyes swept over his tuxedo. "Is this, I mean, are they here for a wedding?"

"Are you proposing?" Billy smiled again and this time it reached his eyes. "No, my dear. You can put those romantic ideas away. This is an auction and those are my customers."

I didn't ask "what are you selling?" because the answer

was obvious. Billy didn't dress me up like Miss Queen of the Planet for nothing. "I'm the animal they want to buy."

"It's crude to put it that way but…"

"And you'll auction me off like, like what? Some prized broodmare?"

"You underestimate me. Unlike your papa, I would never send you away."

"I don't understand."

"I'm not selling you. I'm selling what's inside you."

Papa's head dropped into his hands. Whatever was coming, he couldn't look at me. He couldn't face it. Was this his punishment for betraying Billy? Because he didn't share a valuable resource with his almighty kith leader, was he forced to watch as his daughter went to the highest bidder? Now wasn't the time to start a fight, and yet, the stink of Billy's plan smelled familiar. Both of these men wanted to take my choices away.

Stalling for time, I reached for my water glass. Cool liquid sloshed over the rim. I raised it to my mouth, but my lips were too numb to hold a single drop. Daisy took the glass before I spilled everything in my lap.

"I don't claim to be a scientist like Dr. Vega," Billy said. "I'm just a rancher who made a few bucks putting a cow and a bull in the same pen and letting mother nature do her thing. My herd grew one calf at a time. I reckon that was fine, the way God intended. But honey, that birthrate ain't gonna work for humans no more."

"I'm sorry, Billy. What animal am I supposed to be now? A horse or a cow?" I flattened my hands on the table in front of me, using the hard surface like an anchor to stay upright in my chair.

"You are a woman, a woman who was born with a million eggs inside her body, give or take a few. And according to your papa, you've got about 250,000 eggs left. He'll freeze them in his tanks. Not all of them will be viable, of course, but these men will pay for the right to fertilize one egg…"

"Oh God, you think I'm a chicken," I said and snorted. The sound was so animal-like that it tickled. Before I could cover my mouth, a shrill giggle escaped. It bounced around the glass cage… too high, too unhinged even in my own ears. The room seemed to tilt as another bubble of laughter pushed against my ribs.

Perhaps my reaction to his plan was different than he expected. His face contorted, morphing from shock to rage in jerky tics. Above the collar of his tuxedo jacket, splotches of heat darkened his neck.

My control broke like a high fever. I doubled over, crying and laughing from the same lips. My forehead thumped the table as I sang, "Eggs. For. Sale." When I snorted, the muscles in my stomach cramped. My tears and snot formed a growing puddle on the shiny wood and the pins in my hair went flying.

I was getting zero points for poise. Heck, even the title of Miss Congeniality was slipping away. The judges were too quiet. I knew from experience they were writing notes like "polish your interview answers" and "control your emotions" and "try not to laugh so much." They'd finish with something positive like "keep reaching for the stars." Whatever that meant.

I gave the table one final thump with my forehead… a drop from about six inches. When it landed, two hard fingers pressed into the base of my neck. A bolt of pain flashed white hot behind my eyelids. I writhed and slid toward the floor as everything went black.

CHAPTER TWENTY-FIVE

ALL THAT HEAVEN WILL ALLOW

THE MATTRESS SUCKED. It was rock hard, grinding into my back without mercy. I struggled to remember where I was. Muffled voices ebbed and flowed around me, not in the room but close by. Someone pried my eyes open. I heard the click of a pen light a moment before the thing blinded me.

"Her pupils are constricting," Papa said.

"Is that good?" Billy asked.

"Yes, it means your Daisy didn't give my daughter a concussion when she hit the floor."

"Hang on now. This ain't Daisy's fault. If the girl has brain damage, it's from banging her head on this table. And I reckon she lost a few ice cubes in your freezer. Ever think about that?"

My tongue felt swollen. It stuck to the roof of my mouth as I croaked, "I'm thirsty."

They scurried to help me up. Billy put an arm around my shoulders and Papa tugged on my arms. Before he released me, he pressed something long and metal into my palm.

I was slow to catch on. But thanks to Curtis, I didn't open my fist or ask, "Gosh Papa, what did you give me?" The key felt big in my hand and too large to conceal for long. Closing my eyes, I could almost see the Jeep's logo with its five-point star stamped at the top.

Billy patted my knee. "Daisy, get Mirari some water. Or maybe she'd like something stronger?"

"Water is fine," Papa said.

Daisy held the glass to my mouth as I took small sips… but there was no sympathy in her eyes. Perhaps she was angry because my curls had escaped her updo. She'd spent more than an hour creating her Nefertiti and I'd destroyed the goddess in five minutes.

"See that, Doc? She's good as new," Billy said.

"Mirari is in no condition to go out there. Give her another day."

"Are you deaf? Don't you hear that crowd? Those boys will riot if we don't deliver what we promised… hang us both from the nearest tree. And the networks booked satellite time, which ain't easy to get these days. She's going out there."

"There's no need to rush into this—"

"Daisy, escort Dr. Vega into the arena. And bring back a hairbrush and something to fix the girl's face. Make her presentable again. Shouldn't be too hard," Billy said and tucked a runaway curl behind my ear. I shivered when the back of his hand grazed my cheek.

Beyond the window, the men cheered as Papa found his seat. He gave them a half-hearted wave. A camera crew hustled to get the best shot and someone swiveled a microphone into his face.

Billy watched through the glass like a visitor at the zoo. "They worship Dr. Vega almost as much as they worship you," he said. "Because of his ingenuity twelve years ago, mankind ain't dead yet. He's been telling the world about your miraculous survival. Newspaper articles. Television interviews. Tours of the cryogenic plant."

"Sounds like a giant commercial for your egg sale."

"What's the old saying? All publicity is good publicity? Your papa supplied the advertising and you'll supply the product."

"Good Lord, this is twisted." I wasn't laughing now. My voice sounded tired and Billy heard it, too. When he turned to face me, his eyes were almost compassionate.

"No, my dear. This is business. The opening bid to purchase one of your eggs will be five gold bars. We call 'em good delivery bars. Each one must be 400 ounces of gold at 99 percent purity. And no refunds. If for some reason an egg can't be fertilized, that's too bad. These men are buying a chance. Not a promise."

"Who's going to carry all these babies for nine months?"

"We'll have tanks for that. Feminals will monitor the development of each fetus. The technology needs a few tweaks, but the doctors are chomping at the bit to get started. If we can develop artificial women, how hard can it be to grow real ones?"

"The next generation will all be girls," I said, a statement rather than a question.

"Yes, ma'am. That's in the contract with the bill of sale. The sex chromosomes of each child must be XX. If you'll pardon my frankness, the sperm will be sorted. The boys in the lab call it preimplantation genetic testing. We'll only use the sperm that'll give us females."

"Why didn't you do all of this twelve years ago? Women were dying. No one thought about freezing their eggs or trying to clone them?"

"We had working cryobanks. Those operations needed electricity and liquid nitrogen to keep the eggs frozen. That was no big deal in 1976, right? But after the pathogen, our entire power grid collapsed. Even if a cryobank could keep a generator from being stolen, there was no fuel to run it. We had a shitstorm of problems."

He went on talking, lecturing me about the girl who was captured on North Inachi Island and how she was "a horribly mismanaged global asset." Her discovery gave him the idea to harvest human eggs if another female was ever found.

My mind wandered. It was a luxury I could afford because of the key in my hand. Without it, every word pouring from Billy's mouth would've been the stuff of nightmares.

"If necessary, males can be born after a few generations," he said.

"What happens 150 years from now when I'm everyone's

great, great, great grandmother? Babies will have scales instead of skin and webbed feet and horns."

"Don't believe everything you read in comic books." He grinned. "Now, that's not to say genetic diversity isn't important. We gotta think ahead. That's why each man can only purchase one egg. That's it. And no continent will be allowed to have more than 25 percent of the total eggs harvested. With those rules in place, we believe your grandbabies will be just fine."

"You've masterminded quite the plan," I said. "Just like an evil villain in those comic books I shouldn't be reading."

"I'm no saint, that's for damn sure, but I ain't the devil you think I am. I'm doing you a favor."

"By stealing my fertility?"

"By giving you freedom. As long as those eggs are in your body, you'll be hunted like a rabbit."

"Cow, horse, chicken, and now a rabbit."

His eyes narrowed, like I might bang my head on the table at the mere mention of another farm animal. "You'll have the best surgical team my money can buy. And they'll give you good drugs. When you wake up, you won't remember a thing," he said. "No stitches. No scars."

"You mean no scars on the outside. What about on the inside?"

"Hell, if you need a shrink, I can hire one." He nodded, as if this idea was growing on him. "Might be a good idea. It'd be a pity if you had another fit and gave yourself brain damage."

"Unbelievable… like I'm the one who needs a psychiatrist."

Daisy pushed into the office with her polka dot suit-case leading the way. "Master, I am ready to begin. We will start by addressing the black smudges on her cheeks and the red bump above her eyebrows. A cucumber can reduce the swelling."

"I'll leave you ladies to it." As he closed the door, he gave Daisy a final order. "Keep your fingers off the girl's carotid artery."

She did as she was told but with all of the authority of the second-in-command. I was her lowly soldier, assigned to vegetable duty. My job was to hold the cucumber slice against my forehead while she wiped my face and applied a new layer of makeup. It felt thicker this time, like she'd mixed it with plaster.

After Billy left, I thought of all the questions I should've asked. I directed them at Daisy instead. "There are television shows dedicated to finding living, human females. Is that correct?"

"Yes," she said.

"And sometimes, a person comes forward and claims to be a woman. Is that also correct?"

"Yes."

"How do they confirm or deny these claims?"

"A doctor does an examination."

"An examination performed on camera?"

"Yes," she said. "They claim it improves the television ratings."

"The men in the arena were told that I'm a woman. But won't they want proof?" The trembling started in my throat and spread until my whole body shook with fear. Curtis told me I'd escape but said nothing about getting out of here with my dignity. "Will… will they expect to see, um, to see me?"

"You must sit still. It is difficult to apply cosmetics with accuracy on a moving target."

"Daisy, will they look under my gown with a camera?"

"The video file provided the proof," she said.

"What are you talking about?"

"An engineer downloaded the recordings. Turn your head to the right, please."

"Wait, hang on," I said, brushing away her eyebrow pencil. "Are these recordings of me?"

"A Rose taped every detail of your recovery, beginning from the moment you regained consciousness inside the cave. KZZI-TV distributed an edited version to every media market in the world. We must assume this recording provided enough proof."

"How can we assume that?"

"My master filled the 250,000 spots for this auction in less than one day. Men are bidding by phone through a telethon system run by the networks," she said as she emptied a can of hairspray on my curls.

"Dear God," I whispered.

So much of my time in the cave was a blur but I remembered enough to cringe. When she wasn't on her charger, Rose had been by my side. She bathed me and carried me around with my butt hanging out of a hospital gown. She heard me cuss and cry and ask if Aaron loved her. She killed three men to save me. Did the video include their death scenes? That clip would be gruesome… R rated at the very least.

"You've marinated me enough." I dodged the eyelash curler she held. "Stick an apple in my mouth, light the coals, and throw me on the fire."

She clicked her tongue. "No one is going to roast your body."

"This waiting around is torture."

"Very well. I will get your crown," Daisy said.

"A crown? Come on, you can't be serious."

"The queen shall wear a crown when she is presented to her subjects. This is her destiny."

"We should talk about destiny sometime," I said and slid off the table. "Mine isn't as ironclad as you might think."

She opened a dented filing cabinet against the wall. It was a drab place to store the jeweled creation she lifted from the bottom drawer. With my dress and shoes, I guessed the crown would be gold. And perhaps gold was the precious metal holding all the gems in place. I couldn't tell. Tiny diamond chips covered every inch, and in the middle, an enormous red stone demanded attention.

"In a cooler climate, the base would be lined in Russian sable," Daisy said. "My master was concerned your perspiration might give the fur an unpleasant odor. The 8-carat ruby centerpiece is Burmese in origin and prized for its clarity and color."

Small combs protruded from the bottom. She pushed those into my repaired updo. Once upon a time, I'd worn Lili's tiaras for fun, strutting around her bedroom and waving like a pageant princess. Those were almost weightless compared to the crown Daisy put on my head. She wiggled the tallest peak. Between the combs and the hairspray, it sat firm.

"Are you ready?" Without waiting for my answer, she opened the door.

The hall wasn't empty. A man's back blocked our way, and when he turned, I was face-to-face with my twin. Maybe he smiled. I'm sure he smiled but I was too stunned to pay any attention.

His gold suit had as many crystals as my dress. He wore a rhinestone cowboy hat instead of a crown and his boots had a tall heel, giving him the extra inches he needed to reach my height. The long microphone he held was the only part of him that didn't sparkle.

"Ma'am," he said, removing his hat. In contrast to my dark curls, his hair was white and fell on his forehead in snowy drifts. "My name is Rutherford T. Burton. You may call me Uncle Ruthie. It's the nickname my loyal viewers gave me years ago. I host a syndicated talk show on KZZI-TV and I'll be your escort for today's festivities."

"We'll look like matching salt and pepper shakers."

"Just as you say, Mirari." His laugh was a rumble from someplace deep in his chest. "Oh, please forgive my manners. May I call you Mirari?"

"Yes sir, you may. I'm afraid I don't understand all of this fuss. It's a bit overwhelming," I said, copying his polite manner of speaking.

"I imagine that is true. Please take my arm and we shall navigate the spotlight together. By the end of the day, I believe we will be great friends." He squeezed my fingers and the key tucked inside them.

After the way the crowd greeted Papa, I expected a warm reception. I wasn't prepared for the surge of bodies that rushed at us. They jumped the low wall that separated the stands from the livestock ring. Billy's guards scrambled to form a barrier around me. With the butt of their rifles, they jabbed flabby stomachs and tender kneecaps. It hurt to watch.

The television crew caught the chaos of our entrance. Multiple cameras swept the arena. A man lowered a pole with a boom mic over the rowdiest section. They shrank back as if he'd threatened them.

When he spun the mic toward me, I understood their reaction. The man's face was horribly disfigured. Unlike my escort, he was dressed to avoid attention and wore a black turtleneck despite the heat. Burned skin pulled at one side of his face. Under his KZZI-TV cap, pink ridges of flesh ran over his cheekbones and along his chin.

Uncle Ruthie didn't miss a beat. He lifted his microphone and commanded control. "Gentleman, we must welcome our queen with southern hospitality. Take your seats. It's time to begin."

With his arm linked through mine, we stepped onto the red carpet. I couldn't find Papa in the crowd and maybe that was for the best. Whatever emotion he was feeling wouldn't help me now. I refused to smile as a trio of cameramen followed our progress.

The first one walked backward, panning between Uncle

Ruthie and me. He was bald, and colorful tattoos around his neck looked like a shirt collar. Another cameraman came in for a close-up and focused on the heels that peeked out from beneath my gown. With his kinky, orange hair, he could've found work as a rodeo clown. The final man brought up the rear with an ass-cam shot. I fought the urge to swing my hips at him.

Ahead of us, Billy waited but not patiently. He paced the width of the stage. To anyone watching from home, he was a man determined to save the human race… a freakin' humanitarian.

Uncle Ruthie bounded up a wooden staircase. Once he reached the platform, he offered me his hand. I took it but didn't lift my skirts. I was afraid I'd drop the key. My shoe caught on the hem of my gown and I stumbled on the first step.

"Allow me to assist you," said a hoarse voice behind me.

His grip under my elbow was firm as I climbed. When I turned to thank him, a scarred face stared into mine. I'm ashamed of the way I pulled back from his touch. It was from shock, not horror, but he didn't know that. This man had been kind and I'd been ugly in return.

"Thank you," I whispered.

His eyes didn't condemn me. In fact, warm flecks of copper sparkled with humor. His mouth lifted in a crooked grin I'd seen a thousand times before. The movement caused the surface of his skin to slide. On the tip of his nose, a clump of pink goo dangled by a thread and yet his face had never looked more handsome.

"Don't bump your crown on my boom pole," he said. "It's a long one."

I shook my head. Only Aaron would crack a dirty joke with cameras everywhere. Did he believe this disguise was foolproof? Billy was close enough to see the flesh dripping off his son's jaw. My fingers ached to brush away the mangled mess on his face, but I had to turn away.

Daisy's gown was the star of the show as I walked across the stage. Rows of sequins glittered in the spotlight and I was thankful for the diversion. My body felt more rigid than royal. Despite Lili's pep talks, I'd never been beauty pageant material. No one ever "oohed and aahed" when my name was called. I'd won this contest by default... my prize for being the last girl standing.

"Gentlemen, it's time to meet a young lady who needs no introduction." Uncle Ruthie lifted my fingers and kissed the air above them. "We've seen her amazing recovery from the cryogenic chamber. We held our breath when she opened her eyes. We laughed when she laughed. And when she stepped out of that cave on her own two feet, we cheered. Men of the world, I give you Queen Mirari Vega."

The arena erupted in a clamor of stomping boots and wolf whistles. Their admiration wasn't as genteel as Uncle Ruthie's. He stepped closer to me, his sequins joining with mine to create a curtain of reflective light.

"It is an honor to finally meet you," he said. "Since hearing about your survival, I've been dying to learn more, if you'll pardon the expression. What was it like to be frozen? Did your soul leave your body for twelve years?" He tilted the skinny microphone in my direction… the cue for me to start talking.

For months, no one had bothered to asked. No one seemed to care. And now, in front of millions of people, this veteran television reporter hit me with the mother of all questions.

"I think, um, I think my soul was happy. I wasn't cold even though my body was -320 degrees. But—but that doesn't mean I was hot." I stammered to explain. "Not like fire and brimstone hot. Wherever I was, I didn't want to leave."

Uncle Ruthie chuckled with his deep rumble. "We're so very glad you did, my dear. On behalf of everyone watching right now, we welcome you back with open arms—"

"Sometimes I wonder if I'm still dead." I pulled the microphone toward me. "Like I wonder if my body is in the cave but my soul is here. Maybe this place is my eternity—my punishment for climbing into Papa's suicide machine.

"You look like men but perhaps you're really demons who chase me and drug me and assault me and kidnap me. And today, you'll buy little pieces of me. My body is being harvested." I repeated the word, punching every syllable. "Har-vest-ed. Sounds pretty hellish, doesn't it Uncle Ruthie?"

When I released the microphone, I was as wide-eyed and surprised by my words as he was. Where had that come from? I didn't blink… didn't breathe. If the viewers wanted to see what I looked like frozen, I was giving them a good impersonation.

"Uh, yes. Yes, indeed. You've certainly had a trying time," he said. "I couldn't imagine being the only man on a planet filled with women. I'd never get any sleep." He wiggled his eyebrows for the camera and the crowd laughed at his antics. "Can you tell us more about your adventures?"

"A Violet chased me through the woods with a loaded gun. That was quite an adventure. Or perhaps you'd like to hear about the homicidal giant who smacked me across the face after killing an elderly preacher."

Uncle Ruthie didn't take the bait. "After watching the recordings, I believe you enjoyed the company of a certain young man," he said. "Are there any juicy details you can give us?"

I shook my head but it felt more like a spastic twitch. "I don't, um, I don't know what you mean."

"Surely you haven't forgotten about your childhood friend, Aaron Martinez. There was romance after your sleepover together, and according to the video, you made the first move."

"I kissed him. That's it."

Billy cleared his throat behind us. "This is an auction, not an afternoon soap opera. Move on."

"Our curiosity is only natural," Uncle Ruthie said and gave the camera a 100-watt smile. "We want to know more about our queen."

"She a fertile woman looking for 250,000 fertile men. That's all you need to know."

"If this is an auction, the buyers need to see the merchandise."

"You're looking right at her," Billy growled. "What more do you want?"

"I've been in the news business for a lot of years. I know how easy it is to alter a video tape. And after Rose's heavy-handed editing, we saw very little of the queen's body. This auction could be nothing more than an elaborate get-rich-quick scheme. The buyers need proof before one ounce of gold changes hands."

With a steady pressure against my back, Uncle Ruthie pushed me toward the edge of the stage. Every pretense of being a southern gentleman was gone as he fired-up the crowd. "What do you say, men? Should we look under her pretty skirts? See what she's hiding? Let's do it right here, right now, live on KZZI-TV."

One man in the rowdy section stood and cried, "Proof—Proof—Proof!" His buddies joined in with raised fists. Their chant grew hotter in intensity and spread like a wild-fire. Everyone was on their feet. Everyone was screaming, "Proof—Proof—Proof—Proof!"

I tightened my fingers around the key. Its metal tip pushed back, finding a space to burrow between the muscles and tendons in my hand. I squeezed until the pain rivaled the roar of the crowd.

The guards were on high alert. The business end of their rifles were aimed and ready to fire. Along the front of the stage, the rodeo clown crept closer. He swiveled the video camera, looking for the best shot.

My horrified expression was always an option. Who doesn't enjoy watching a frigid queen melt down? And yet, there was a fight brewing next to me with two powerful men facing off. Billy was the perfect picture of fury. He stood nose-to-nose with Uncle Ruthie, showering the shorter man with spit as he cursed.

I didn't pay attention to the first yank. But when the clown pinched my skirt between two stubby fingers, I felt his hot breath against my ankles. He lifted the hem into the air with a real flair for building anticipation. His knees were bent, perhaps to improve the angle of his shot, and his lens followed a path up my bare thighs.

I didn't think about the advice Curtis gave me to play along. I didn't think about Papa or Billy or Uncle Ruthie. I didn't think at all. With the pointed toe of one golden shoe, I kicked the clown in the teeth. The wet crack wasn't loud enough to be heard in the stands but maybe the viewers got an earful.

I wanted him to land on his butt under a pile of video equipment. That didn't happen, at least not immediately. He spun to the side. His legs wobbled. And with his eyes squeezed shut, he didn't know the exact location of his camera until he tripped over it.

My attack on the clown didn't go unnoticed. Like some sort of grand unveiling, the crowd had watched as he exposed my legs. They saw my kick. And when he toppled, their chant died with a final "oof." The place went silent.

I couldn't look away from the blood bubbling up from the clown's mouth. From where I stood, it looked like melted lipstick—the crimson clashing with his orange hair. A fat drop ran into his ear.

Around the arena, the collective shock didn't last long. With one kick, I'd provoked a building full of demons. How could I be surprised when all hell broke loose?

CHAPTER TWENTY-SIX

THE RISING

IF VIOLENCE SELLS, we were giving KZZI-TV its highest ratings ever.

"Get her" was the crowd's new battle cry and it emptied the stands. The men called me names that were too obscene for daytime television. With fists swinging, they poured into the ring. They punched the guards, each other, and any stray camera that got too close to the fight.

I ducked when the proverbial shit hit the fan—even though I was the one who threw the turd into the spinning blades… so to speak. I stepped away from the front of the stage. Billy pulled me back even further, positioning himself between me and the riot.

Whatever else he was guilty of, he didn't want a camera going up my skirt. A live gynecological exam would've given his buyers the proof they wanted and a sick thrill at the same time. Maybe Billy was feeling benevolent because of my friendship with his daughter or maybe Papa begged him for mercy, father to father. I was afraid to ask… afraid he'd change his mind.

A guard in the middle of the mob fired a shot above his head. It blasted through the skylight and glass rained down like ice. Instead of quieting the men, the threat enraged them. They surged forward and a line of bodies fell as the guards opened fire.

"Time to go, my dear," Uncle Ruthie said, his deep voice cutting through the din. I heard every word but I wasn't the only one.

Billy spun to face us. "My security team has this under control. They'll crack a few more skulls and we'll get this auction rolling. Mirari ain't goin' nowhere." He grabbed my left wrist, his fingers within an inch of the key and my promised getaway.

"If those men reach the stage, they'll tear her apart," Uncle Ruthie said and seized my other wrist.

In an instant, I became the rope in their macho tug-of-war. Billy pulled with both hands. Uncle Ruthie tossed his microphone and did the same. My arms were stretched wide with the tendons in my elbows taking the brunt of each jerk. When the strands of my cape snapped, hundreds of crystal beads bounced around our shoes.

"Stop it!" My scream was swallowed in the pandemonium. I planted my legs and twisted back and forth. "You're the idiots tearing me apart."

From the floor below us, a boom mic whizzed through

the air. The metal pole hit Billy's jaw with a thwack. The furry tip of the microphone continued its arc, flying off the end of the long handle. The blow was well-placed. When his head snapped to the side, he lost both his cowboy hat and his grip on my arm.

I fell into Uncle Ruthie. Behind me, the whoosh of the boom mic came around for a second swing. The sound was different this time, more meaty, as if the pole made contact with Billy's throat rather than his jaw. When he fell, the platform shook under my feet.

Uncle Ruthie turned me toward the stairs. "Watch your step. These damn beads are slippery."

"I—I don't understand. You're letting me go?"

"My apologies for being so rough," he said. "We had to create a diversion and trust that Aaron's men could control the bedlam. Hurry now. He's waiting for you."

Billy was flopped on his side. Other than the red mark slashing his cheek, the man looked peaceful, like a child taking a nap after lunch. I could've stepped around him… that's what a dignified queen would have done. But his eyes were closed and his right hand was open. He was offering me his greatest weapon. It was a gift I had to accept.

Bending my knees, I jumped as high as my gown would let me. One shoe landed in the center of his palm and I felt something snap under my three-inch heel. I brought my foot down again, squashing his knuckles and pinching the skin between his fingers.

His moan gave me the tiniest taste of satisfaction. I wanted more. I wanted to cry, "That's for every time you punched your son, you blackhearted monster." I wanted to jump again and again and again until his hand was a mangled stump, but Billy's son was watching me. And this was his fight. Not mine.

Aaron didn't help me down the steps. Instead, he dropped the boom pole and lifted me from the top of the platform. His grip was tight around my waist as he lowered me to the ground. And with his face just inches from mine, I got a closer look at his disguise. There wasn't much of it left. Only a few wads of pink flesh clung to his chin.

"How fast can you move in those bone crushers?"

"I'll keep up," I said. "Will the guards shoot us?"

He grinned. "They say they're loyal to me. We're about to find out."

We couldn't leave the arena the same way I'd entered it. Bodies littered the doorway. Some of the men were out cold while others were bloody and still swinging. With our heads down, we raced toward the long line of horse stalls. They were blessedly empty. Even Billy's well-mannered Arabians would've been in a frenzy with all of the gunfire around us.

The cameraman with the neck tattoo leaned against a fence as he recorded our escape. I was prepared to climb into the closest stall, with or without a television audience, but this guy had a better plan. He tugged on a rope and a gate rolled to one side. The gap was wide enough for us to squeeze through.

"Hold 'em back as long as you can… but don't die trying," Aaron said to the cameraman. "This ain't the Alamo."

I matched Aaron's pace as we ran. It wasn't pretty. I was

sweating underneath my crown, and with every step, the tiny combs bit into my scalp. My knees ached. My breathing was ragged. And my long skirt dragged wood chips, flower petals, and clods of manure along for the ride. Our trail was a giant sign reading, "They went that way."

Ahead of us, a man emerged from one of the stalls. He positioned himself between us and the open barn doors. His face was in shadows. A ray of sunlight shone through his bowed legs. When he raised his weapon, his arms were graceful, like the practiced movements of a deadly ballerina.

Aaron didn't slow our speed. Instead, his stride lengthened as the man took aim and pulled the trigger. Something heavy hit the dirt behind us. Without looking back, we charged straight toward the shooter.

"Get 'im in the chest?" Aaron asked.

"Between the eyes." The blond's mustache curved into a broad smile. He blew air across the muzzle before handing it over.

"Showoff," Aaron said and took the weapon.

The guard gave me a tip of his cowboy hat. "Nice to see you again, ma'am. My name is Ron. We've got a caravan ready to escort you."

"Escort—me—where?" I asked, panting between the words.

I inhaled and sucked in the scent of roses. That smell was my only warning before powerful hands grabbed me. I yelped, twisted, but couldn't break away. It felt as if a forklift was lifting me off my feet.

Rose held me in the cage of her arms. Her green eyes

scanned every detail of my appearance...from the dirty hem of my dress to the top of my crown. She could see. And she was holding me on two sturdy legs.

"A simple handshake or hug would've been fine, Rose," I said. "There's no need to maul me."

"A bump is marring your skin. Did someone harm you?"

I touched the spot where I'd banged the table. "I'm fine. But hey, what's your story? You were a pile of broken parts the last time I saw you."

"My repairs were successful," she simply said.

"Yeah, no kidding. You look great." Emotion made my words feel thick. "I can't believe I'm about to say this, but I've missed you. At least, a little. The Daisies here are a bunch of bullies."

"I will never leave you again, master." Her lips trembled before a single, piercing wail broke free. Saltless tears rolled down her cheeks. They dripped on my face, my neck, my chest... a person could drown under the flood of her devotion.

"I even miss your crying fits," I said and wiped her tears from my eyes.

"Perhaps I should address you as 'your highness' or 'your majesty.' Please tell me which you prefer."

"I don't prefer either one. This queen crap was nothing but an advertising ploy for the auction—"

A blast inside the barn interrupted our reunion. In the shelter of Rose's arms, I couldn't see who was firing or from what direction. My instinct was to hide. Her instinct was to bolt. Without waiting for a direct command, she took off toward the open pasture, and this time, I didn't groan when my ankles banged together.

Aaron sprinted next to us, losing his ball cap somewhere behind him. He had speed in his long limbs but fell behind as Rose plunged through taller clumps of prairie grass. And with an arsenal of weapons around his waist, Ron's bowed legs didn't stand a chance in this foot race.

He huffed and puffed and yelled, "Take her to the vans. I'll catch up."

"Stop," I said. When Rose didn't slow, I raised my voice. "I order you to quit running. Now."

She hit the brakes, and without a word of protest, dropped me to the ground. I almost laughed with the heady authority of being her master. No doubt she disagreed with my command and yet she obeyed me. How far could I push her? By the end of the day, I was sure I'd have my answer.

We stood side by side as Aaron and Ron closed the gap. I felt her body shudder. She was crying again but with the volume turned down. "Poor Rose. I know you're worried but I swear I'm not suicidal," I said as I patted her back. I stopped short of telling her that I'd be okay. She'd never lied to me. I couldn't lie to her.

As his run slowed to a jog, Aaron gave me a quick once-over. "Are you hurt?" He rushed on without taking a breath. "We gotta keep going. The vans are in the creek bed. We'll stay off the roads until just north of Highway 71."

"Where's Curtis?"

"What?"

"Where—is—Curtis?" I asked, slower and louder this time. "I'm not leaving this ranch without him."

Aaron looked at Ron. "Did you get him?"

Ron pulled a handkerchief from his back pocket. As he wiped the sweat off his neck, he mumbled a vague, "The kid's around here somewhere."

I made a show of searching the pasture in every direction. "Somewhere… like Curtis is waiting by the vans? Or somewhere… like Curtis is still locked in Billy's basement?"

"He's fine," Ron said. "My guys will take care of him. No need to worry your pretty head about it."

I poked his chest. It was like ramming into a tree trunk. My finger throbbed but I did it again. "Don't give me that 'pretty head' garbage. With harem hunters around every corner, the child is not fine. We're taking Curtis with us because no one is getting sold today. Do you hear me? No one."

Ron turned toward Aaron, maybe hoping for some kind of back-up, but found none. He sighed. "Ma'am, I appreciate your feelings. But it's not safe for you to be here."

I lifted my arms. "Rose, pick me up. I need a ride to the house."

"Hang on," Aaron said. "We can't run in there half-cocked. We'll get Curtis out but we need a strategy."

His eyes locked with mine… level and sincere and gorgeous. My heart begged me to trust him, but he'd always been good at poker. Was he bluffing or telling me the truth?

"Okay," I said. "I'm listening."

"I'll go in alone. The rest of you will wait outside."

"Absolutely not."

"I'll be armed," he said. "And the head Daisy knows me. I'll talk my way past her. I'll find Curtis. Give me ten minutes… but not one minute longer. If I don't make it out, you must follow Ron to the creek bed. Do you promise, Mirari? You gotta promise me."

The threat of losing Aaron made me sway, dizzy with the ache of it. In order to save one life, I was risking the death of another. My throat tightened. I didn't trust my voice, so I nodded instead.

"Good." He exhaled. "Find the KZZI satellite truck and tell Uncle Ruthie the new and improved plan. He'll hide you, and if the crowd breaks loose, everyone will assume you're long gone. They won't think to search the truck. I'll get Curtis free and we'll meet you there."

Aaron was half right about his plan. It was certainly new. But from the moment we approached the rear of the house, nothing about it felt improved. Instead of a kiss, he pulled me into a bear hug. And instead of romantic words, he growled "ten minutes" into my ear.

"Alright already," I said and wiggled out of his arms. "I'll wait for ten minutes and then leave your sorry butt behind."

"Where's your watch?"

I held up my wrists. "Just bruises."

"I've got a watch. We'll start the countdown once you're out of sight," Ron said.

Aaron released the magazine inside his pistol, reloaded, and pushed it back into place. Every step was precise. And if we were shooting tin cans, his skill with a firearm would've been fun to watch, but this looked too much like preparing for a battle.

"If you bump into a Violet, shoot her in the back of the neck…" My voice faded as I added, "if you can."

"If you bump into Billy, shoot him anywhere you want." He gave me a final grin and climbed the steps into the house. The door wasn't locked. Who needs a deadbolt when a homicidal feminal is on duty? He slipped inside without a sound.

Ron jabbed a thumb in the direction of the barn. "Ready? We need to find the satellite truck."

"Hang on. I promised Aaron I'd leave after ten minutes. I didn't say anything about Rose. She's staying here."

"Oh no, master. I must go with you. I must protect you," she said. Her eyes blazed with an emotion programmed to resemble outrage. It was impressive.

"Do you still have those bionic ears?"

"I can detect both low and high frequency pitches. My auditory range goes well above 200,000 hertz, superior to most bats. In fact…"

I held up a hand to stop her lecture. "You can tell me all about it later. Your job now is to stand next to the back door. Kick it down if you hear fighting, especially the growl of a she-cat. Do you understand me?"

"Master, please."

"Ron will protect me. He has a gun."

"I have three," he said. "All of 'em loaded."

"Did you hear that, Rose?" I asked, teasing her and her superior auditory range. "He has three guns and he's going to share one with me. Right, Ron?"

"Uh, sure. I guess." He didn't look convinced.

"Get Aaron and Curtis out alive," I said. "Oh, and if you're going to bawl, keep it quiet."

She complied with a final whimper—her face more miserable than I'd ever seen it. Once she was in position, Ron and I crept away from the house. I gestured for a gun and he put a monster of a weapon in the palm of my hand. It made my Ladysmith feel like a toy.

"I wanted a pistol. Not a cannon."

He chuckled. "She's the lightest one I got."

Our search for the news truck was short. It sat in front of the sale barn like an oversized ambulance. KZZI-TV was painted on its side in primary colors and an enormous satellite dish was mounted on the roof. Ron pointed at it, as if he'd made a huge discovery, and I rolled my eyes.

We were less than one hundred yards from the truck, but a jumble of vehicles surrounded it on all four sides. I ducked behind a brown van with lace curtains in its windows. He followed me as I edged between a pair of compact cars. And when I brushed against an old pick-up truck, it left rust marks on my arm. I was too preoccupied to care. Because beyond its tailgate, the headlights of a blue Jeep Renegade looked me in the eyes.

I gasped.

Ron unholstered both of his remaining guns. "What? What's wrong?"

"Change of plans."

"Another one?"

"This is my Jeep," I said and held up the key. "Well, technically, it's my mama's Jeep but she'd want me to have it."

"Aaron told us to hide in the satellite truck."

"Come on… how can a truck that big maneuver through all this mess? We'll be stuck here for hours. And if the mob sees Aaron running from the house, they'll follow him and swarm the truck and bust out the windows and grab me by the hair and drag me through the jagged glass and—"

"Good Lord, woman. Enough." He grimaced and the pointed tips of his mustache wiggled. "I agree with you. This Jeep will get us to the creek faster. Give me the key."

"I'm driving."

"You can't drive."

"Of course, I can drive. Think about it. Who has more experience with weapons?"

"I reckon I do."

"Exactly, so you should ride shotgun." I gave him back the cannon. "Get in and buckle up. We'll meet Aaron and Curtis at the backdoor."

My confidence was an act. It had been more than twelve years since I'd driven this Jeep and my hands were wet as I turned the key. The engine died four times before I got us rolling.

To Ron's credit, he didn't say a word as we crept along in first gear. The blue denim seats were warm underneath us, and with the top down, we could see in every direction. I was determined not to dent the vehicles around us. But as I navigated between the gaps, I tapped a few bumpers along the way.

Ron remained calm until we heard a door slam. It came from the direction of the sale barn, booming like a gunshot and sounding just as dangerous. "We got trouble," he said. "My guys ain't holding them in."

"How long has Aaron been in the house?"

He glanced at his watch. "Coming up on seven minutes.

"He must have Curtis by now. Let's—"

A howl pierced the air. It came at us from all directions, soaring above our heads and rising up from the dirt under our tires. My mouth snapped shut.

"Aaaa… Aaaa… Aaron. Where ya hidin' boy?" The words were garbled but sounded more debilitated than drunk. A taunting laugh became a cough. "You and the girl think yer big 'nough to whup me? I don't need her alive to harvest those eggs. Nooo, sir."

"There he is." Ron pointed out his side window. "He's coming around that brown van."

We caught glimpses of Billy as he stumbled through the parking lot. His body was hunched. His right hand was con-torted and tucked against his chest. In his left hand, he waved an enormous revolver in the air. It looped above his cowboy hat like a lasso.

I slid down in my seat. Ron moved in the opposite direc-tion. He was nearly standing as he tracked Billy with the barrel of the cannon. "That man is weaving like a son of a bitch," he said under his breath. "What's wrong with him?"

"My guess would be a splitting headache, a bruised wind-pipe, and a broken hand."

"Stay on his tail. If I get a clean shot, I'll give him a real headache."

"Got it," I said.

"You can close your eyes when I shoot him. It won't be pretty. But—"

"Just kill him." Those words should've hurt my mouth. They should've stabbed my tongue and cut my lips. But instead, I breathed them out like a sigh. "Don't worry about me. Take him down however you can."

"It's really our only option," he said. "We don't have jails anymore."

"You're joking."

"No ma'am. Nobody's gonna feed and house a criminal anymore."

"What, um, what happens to him?"

"For the petty stuff, he'll get flayed with a cow whip. But if he pisses off the kith leader, he'll get the death penalty. Usually a hanging. It's cheap and easy."

I had more questions but no time to ask them. Billy required all of my attention. We chased him at a whopping three miles per hour. He staggered and lurched, disappearing behind a vehicle, doubling back, and popping up where I least expected.

Ron cursed when his prey eluded him again. "This damn cat and mouse game isn't working." He tapped his watch. "We're at nine minutes. Let's get back to the house."

I avoided the crowded driveway and went off-roading through the grass. The engine roared as I accelerated. Adrenaline pumped through my veins, giving me a heavy foot.

Aaron was going to be shocked to see me driving the Jeep, but Curtis wouldn't be surprised at all. He'd dreamed of my escape. And I figured Rose would scold me for not sticking with the plan.

"If all three of them climb in the backseat, it will be a tight squeeze," I said. "But it's better than walking—"

I didn't slow as we turned the corner of the house. I didn't check if the coast was clear before racing into the backyard. I didn't think the hunter could become the hunted so quickly.

Billy was waiting.

His head was tilted at an odd angle, like the weight of his cowboy hat was too much to hold. The left side of his face was red and swollen. He glared at me with his one good eye… straight down the barrel of a gun.

I swear I was his intended victim, but the heavy weapon shook as he tried to steady it. This wasn't his dominant hand. And as Billy pulled the trigger, the muzzle twitched.

A bullet punched a quarter-sized hole in my windshield. Ron jerked. His startled grunt mixed with the smell of gun powder and something else… something burning. As he fell headfirst into the dashboard, the Jeep's engine sputtered and died.

CHAPTER TWENTY-SEVEN

CHIMES OF FREEDOM

I GREW UP IN a house with one television and two parents who believed in a free press. Like it or not, I got a daily dose of the evening news. Tornados, car crashes, bar fights… it didn't matter. Survivors would look into the camera and say "it's all a blur" or "everything happened too fast."

After Ron collapsed, I wasn't so lucky. The next three minutes clicked by with the precision of a marching band and the drum inside my chest didn't miss a beat. When a second bullet clipped the air freshener, the pine tree twirled like a top.

"Okay. We're—we're okay but we gotta get down." I pushed Ron toward the floorboard, yelling when he wouldn't move fast enough. "Can you unbuckle your seatbelt? Stop… let me do it. Watch out for the roll bar."

Ron wedged himself between his seat and the dashboard.

He moaned when I pressed against his shoulder. And no matter how hard I shoved, he couldn't go any lower. The cannon was missing, maybe trapped under his legs, but the top of his head was in clear view if Billy wanted to put a hole in it.

A third crack and metallic "ping" pulled my hair from the roots. I reached up, expecting to feel bone fragments or gooey bits of brain. My fingers were empty… no bullet wound and no crown. All that remained was one broken comb. Daisy would've been proud. It took a gunshot to break her hairspray's hold.

"They should print that on the can. Right, Ron?" I snorted a laugh. It felt as uncontrollable and unwelcome as a wet fart.

"Wha—what?" His breathing was ragged now.

"Never mind," I said and snorted again.

After all of those years in the freezer, I was definitely "missing a few ice cubes." Billy had been right. My windshield looked like Swiss cheese, my scalp burned, and my bodyguard was bleeding. And despite all that, or because of all that, I had to cover my mouth to stop the next wave of giggles. Our shooter was angry enough without hearing my manic laughter.

"I didn't raise no coward, but now look at ya." Billy's voice rose into a bellow. "Hiding behind those skirts like a sniveling baby while I kill your girlfriend."

"I'm right here. Come and get me… Daddy." Bitterness dripped from the name.

I counted to five before peeking above the steering wheel.

Billy's one good eye wasn't focused on me. With his back to the Jeep, he shuffled toward the house. The revolver bobbed in his left hand. He was about thirty yards from the door and the feminal who guarded it.

Rose watched him, too. Her arms and legs were spread wide, pinning Aaron and Curtis against the house like a cage. She wasn't large enough to protect every inch of their bodies. The curve of a shoulder, the tip of an elbow, the edge of a hip were all visible behind her. When Billy lifted his revolver, she roared in fury and took a step back. Her heavy frame smashed them against the stucco wall without mercy.

My feminal was obedient. In her enthusiasm to follow my command and keep them alive, she made it impossible for Aaron to raise his own weapon. I could've ordered her to stand down. Rose wasn't a perfect shield. But without her, they would've been completely exposed. I opened my mouth, sucked in a breath, and waited too long to speak.

Billy fired. The boom echoed off the wall and was answered by a smothered cry. I couldn't tell who made the sound—couldn't tell if it came from terror or pain.

Spots danced on the edge of my vision. The air rushed from my lungs and I swayed, darkness threatening to pull me under. With a vicious snap, I bit the inside of my cheek. Blood oozed from a cluster of stinging cuts. Tears burned my eyes but the fog inside my brain lifted.

I started the Jeep.

If the revolver was fully loaded when Billy left the livestock barn, he had two bullets remaining… two more chances to hurt someone I loved. Was he doing the same math? I couldn't let him get close enough to shoot at point-blank range. Even with his left hand, he wouldn't miss.

I floored the accelerator.

He didn't turn around. And if he heard an engine revving behind him, he never showed it. He lumbered toward the house like a man with all the time in the world. As the Jeep ate the distance between us, I shifted into second gear. The motor screamed. I screamed. But nothing could distract the father from reaching his son. He lifted the gun, pulled back the hammer, and took aim.

I hit Billy at thirty-two miles per hour.

Before the moment of impact, I would've said that my speed was slow, like the Jeep might dislocate a knee or bruise his back. I was wrong. My front bumper tossed him into the air. For the second time in one day, his cowboy hat went flying. The top of his skull struck the windshield. It left a bigger hole in the glass than his bullets. Before I could duck, Billy continued his somersault over my head and beyond the tailgate.

I stomped on the brake.

The tires bit into the grass, but couldn't get traction. I jerked the steering wheel to the right. It was a miscalculation... a horrible mistake that was now coming at me fast. The Jeep was on a path to sideswipe the house, crushing all three of them against the wall, and still Rose held them pinned with her body.

She lunged the instant before I hit her. With outstretched arms, she reached for the Jeep like it needed a hug. Her hands were slim. Her wrists were narrow. It defied logic that a creature who looked so delicate could stop a moving vehicle, but my door crumpled under her fingers.

The Jeep rocked, tilted onto two wheels, and landed on its side. My seatbelt held firm, but Ron wasn't wearing one. Momentum slammed him against the roll bar. Through his window, I saw nothing but grass.

There was no sound as we hung there. The world paused, like it'd seen enough and needed a coffee break. I wondered if God and Mama hovered above us, debating the future of this vehicle and the people inside it. Knowing Mama, she was giving him an earful.

My foot remained on the brake… which was silly. We were beyond its help now. I bit down on another wave of giggles.

With or without divine guidance, it was Rose who decided our fate. I felt her grab the chassis somewhere under my feet. She gave it a tug. The Jeep squealed in protest but held together as she lowered us to the ground.

My trembling didn't start until we were upright. But once all four wheels touched down, I shivered so hard that my teeth chattered. I reached for Ron's limp hand and let my mind float above the yard and the house and the people who came running. The silence didn't last for long. Voices called out, everyone yelling instructions at the same time.

Curtis raced toward Ron's door. Rose tore my dented one off by its hinges. And with more force than necessary, Aaron unbuckled my seatbelt and lifted me out of the Jeep.

"Are you okay? Where's—where's Billy? Did you get his gun?" My questions were rapid fire.

"It's alright. We're alright." Sweat rolled down the side of Aaron's neck and he winced as he held my full weight. He didn't look alright.

"You're hurt," I said and touched his cheek.

The crooked grin he gave me was more of a grimace. "That damned Rose. When she flattened us, my ribs cracked. I don't think they're broken, or at least, not very broken."

"She flattened you and you flattened me," Curtis said. "I was about to pass out."

"We're alive, so no whining."

The child didn't argue. But as he examined Ron, his frowned deepened, making him look more like his grandpa. He tore a strip from the bottom of his t-shirt and pressed it against the man's shoulder.

"Is Ron going to—" I wanted Curtis to look into the future but I was afraid what he'd see. "Is Ron still bleeding?"

"A doctor will be here soon. He'll help—"

"A man is approaching on foot," Rose called out on cue.

Papa sprinted around the corner of the house. When he saw me, color rushed back into his face. His smile faltered as he surveyed the scene, and instead of coming to my side, he moved toward something behind the Jeep.

"What's Papa looking at? Is it Billy?"

"I think so," was all Aaron said.

As we watched, his arms tightened around me… as if my papa was a new threat. But that didn't make sense. The two of them were a team. The two of them plotted my arranged marriage to a stranger without giving me a clue.

"I know what you're doing," I said.

"And what's that?"

"Holding me back… like I'm gonna faint at the sight of blood or a broken bone."

"I'm holding you because I like the way you feel," he said. And even when Papa joined us, giving the younger man a pointed look that should've made him squirm, he didn't let go.

"Do you mind if I check my daughter's pulse?" Papa asked, reaching for my wrist.

"Fine by me," Aaron said. "But she's staying here."

I pointed to the Jeep. "Don't worry about me. Go to Ron. He's the one who needs help."

Within seconds, Dr. Vega was shouting orders to a pair of Irises like a medic on the battlefield. "Put some pressure on this gunshot wound and get him inside the house. The bullet went through his shoulder so there's an exit wound on his back.

"And cover Billy's body," he said, almost like an afterthought. "Use a sheet or a table cloth… whatever you can find."

The claws of something cold and sharp found its way under my hair. It pricked my scalp and etched a path down the back of my neck. In that instant, I understood what I'd done. Billy wasn't injured. Billy was dead… because of me.

I pushed against Aaron's arms, struggling to break free. "Put me down."

"You don't need to look," Aaron said.

"Put—me—down."

He stiffened. Did he think I'd run to Billy's side if he

let me go? That I'd cry over Billy's mangled corpse and have nightmares for the rest of my life?

Tears stung my eyes. They were for the son and not his father. As Aaron lowered me to the ground, my knees wobbled. I stumbled and grabbed his shirt, pulling him into a hug in order to stay on my feet.

When I tightened my hold, he hissed, "Ooh, easy there. Somebody's been working out."

"Oh God, I'm so sorry."

"About my ribs? They've taken a beating before," he said. "They'll heal."

"Not just sorry your ribs. I ran over your dad right in front of you. It's a terrible thing. And, and, I'm sorry you had to see that but I'm not sorry I did it—" I hiccupped and let the tears fall. "I would kill him again."

Aaron inhaled… deep and then deeper. It had to hurt. I felt his chest move under my hands. He opened his mouth to speak but I rushed on.

"It's my fault Ron is hurt. I messed up everything and drove us straight into the path of Billy's gun."

"Mirari—"

"And it's my fault Rose pinned you against the house. She takes everything too far. I ordered her to keep the two of you alive, and look, she almost crushed you in the process."

"Yeah, I wondered about that," he said.

"I'll understand if you can't forgive me."

"Forgive you?" He stepped back, locking his gaze with mine. I don't know what he saw there but it made him smile… sweet and sad at the same time. He kissed the next tear that rolled down my cheek. "How about this? I'll forgive you for saving my life if you'll forgive me for trying to save your life with a stupid scheme to marry you off."

My eyes narrowed. "That was pretty stupid."

"And painful," he said. "And you deserve an explanation."

"So let's hear it."

"We've gotta go, Mirari. This place is a war zone. I promise we'll sit down as soon as—"

"No, I need your explanation now. Maybe not all of it, but if we get shot in the next five minutes, I don't want to die thinking…" I stopped and shook my head, choking out the painful words in a whisper. "Thinking you wanted me gone."

"I inherited a special brand of stupidity from my mom," he said. "That's the reason."

Of all the excuses I expected to hear, and I was ready for some lame ones, this wasn't it. "I always thought Mrs. Martinez was a bright lady."

"My mom was bright. And once upon a time, I believed she was brave—a real 'stand by your man' kind of wife. Billy was obsessed with her," he said. "Most of the time, she could charm the beast.

"But when he was really pissed or really drunk, she'd hide Lili and me under the stairs. Mom said it was our clubhouse. She stocked it with the Three Cs… coke, candy bars, and comic books. Like the clubhouse was a fun place to go. Like once we were inside, we wouldn't hear him beating her."

My heart broke for him… again. I didn't think there were any pieces left to shatter. I could've filled the silence with another "I'm so sorry." Instead, he held my weight and

I held his. We couldn't stay in this cocoon for long, but while everyone hustled around us, every second I had was his.

"After Mom died, I took her job." His voice was hoarse now. "I couldn't charm Billy out of being angry, but I could take the beatings. I protected Lili. And when the time came, it felt right to protect you. Hide you. I even gave you candy bars… how messed up is that?"

"You were a victim of abuse."

"Sure, okay, I was victim when I was a kid. But I can tell you the exact day when Billy looked at me with fear in his eyes. We were lifting hay bales and I was stronger than him. He knew I could fight back if he pushed me too far. He hired Dwayne the same week."

"Did you ever hit Billy?"

"Never," he simply said.

"Maybe your self-control is a type of bravery."

"Mom and I weren't brave. We were arrogant. She should've left him. I should've left him. We both had this warped sense of duty, like Billy was a religion and we were martyrs for the cause. Our bruises were badges of honor… our suffering was proof of our devotion." He puffed out a ragged breath. "If you love someone, it's gotta hurt. That's what Mom taught me. And God, how I suffered for you."

"What are you talking about? I saw that little party you threw for yourself," I said, searching his face for a lie. "You were happy to send me away."

"No, what you saw was a man who was gut-wrenchingly unhappy. I thought you agreed to marry one of those guys. Your dad said he'd show you their pictures, let you read their bios, and get your consent. That was the plan. When he said the airport was a go, it hurt like hell but love's gotta hurt, right? I swear, Mirari, if I'd known it was an ambush—"

"When did you figure out all this stuff about your warped sense of duty?"

"You know the answer to that. Tell me you do." His amber eyes filled with tears and he didn't blink them away. "When Billy grabbed you at my house, I snapped. I would've killed him on the spot, but I was too drunk to open the front door.

"Curtis found me. He poured coffee down my throat and let me howl. At some point during the night, he hid the keys to my van. Now that was brave," he said and frowned. "The kid told me I couldn't drive while I was puking so what difference did it make. I sobered up the next day. We made a plan to get you back… we made several of 'em. Today was Plan D. The first three were a bust because I underestimated—"

As he told his story, feminals scurried around us. Rose tossed my mangled door into the backseat of the Jeep. Two Irises spread a plaid blanket on the grass, like happy twins preparing for a family picnic, and lifted Billy off the ground. The cloth covered everything except the man's swollen hand. It dangled down, swaying as they carried him toward the house. Their unblinking stares and vacant smiles made the removal of his body even more macabre.

I couldn't let Aaron see his dad like this. No kid should see his dad like this.

"You said you've never hit Billy… but that's not true," I said, distracting him with the first thing I could think of.

"When I was in trouble back there, you whacked him with a metal pole. Twice. And in front of a worldwide audience. So don't tell me you're not brave cause I'm not buying it."

"I'm a controlling ass who wanted to protect you. And now I'm a reformed ass, hoping for a second chance. Do you buy that?"

"Hmm, I'm not sure." I paused, considering my next words and if he was ready to hear them. "I love you the way you are. I don't want to reform you… maybe just harness you a little."

"Sounds kinky."

I felt a wave of heat that wasn't embarrassment. The yard was empty now. His mouth was inches from mine but I had to keep going. The next few moments would tell me everything.

"I'm done running," I said in a rush. "I don't want to live that way… always looking over my shoulder. Always afraid. I know you've got a caravan ready to spirit me off to God knows where."

"An island in the Gulf of Mexico. It's deserted—accessible only by boat. We can be there before sundown."

"No, Aaron." I clutched the front of his shirt in both fists, like he might run away if I didn't hold on tight enough. "No more hiding. No more clubhouses under the stairs."

He flinched. But instead of quick comeback or a flat refusal, he met my eyes. It gave me enough hope to go on.

"I'm a woman. Big deal. Billions of women have come before me. And maybe I've got sixty years before I die or maybe I've got sixty minutes. How does that make me different than anyone else?"

"You're not an anyone," he said. "You're an only one."

"I don't believe that and Curtis doesn't, either. There's another girl in his dreams."

"He's going through puberty. Of course, there's a girl in his dreams."

"Yeah, sure, Curtis is twelve-year-old boy. But he's more than that. He's like a prophet or an oracle or something. I believe what he says."

"It's a crime to harbor an undocumented woman. Did you know that? After all these years, Billy still orders door-to-door sweeps. All of the kiths do. We don't knock first or get a search warrant. If a man is caught with a woman, he's shot on sight. And no one—"

"And no one is surprised," I said. "Why not take a human life while searching for a human life?"

He ignored my sarcasm. "I went on my first sweep about eight years ago. I tapped on walls, crawled through basements, and found nothing but rats and a few armadillos. Believe me, harboring a woman is a crime that can't be committed."

"The numbers don't make sense, Aaron. How can an entire planet of women disappear?"

"You'd have to ask a dinosaur."

I sighed, blowing out my frustration before it became anger. "Okay, fine. How about a friendly wager? Give me one year and I bet I'll find another woman. Curtis says she's out there."

"And you're gonna, what? Go searching on your own?"

"I promised Rose I wasn't suicidal. She'll go with me and Curtis, too, if he's willing. And, um, I want you to come with us. We're gonna need your help."

"My help and the protection of every loyal man I can round up. Traveling beyond this kith is dangerous. You've seen that. And we're not going anywhere if I can't keep you safe."

"I don't need your permission. That's not what this is about. I'm going… and I'm inviting you to join me."

He frowned. "And maybe I'll accept your invitation. If we can negotiate a peace treaty that actually sticks, and if our neighbors don't start a kith war, then—"

"So you're saying yes?"

"I'm saying maybe… and only because Curtis says she's out there. But if I help you search, what's in this friendly wager for me?"

"I will give up the hunt on day 366. We'll go live on your island. I'll wear a coconut bikini top and a grass skirt, even though it'll be itchy as the devil—"

"Billy was a threat to your safety, but he wasn't the only one. You understand that, right?" Aaron ran a hand through his hair. The dark waves stood up and formed its own crown. "Another kith leader will take his place."

"That's what I'm hoping for." In my heels, it was easy to reach his lips. I brushed them with mine, coaxing away his frown. "I've heard there's a new kith leader with big plans to reunite Texas. I've heard he could be its next president. And…" I said as I gently pulled him against me. "I've heard he's pretty hot."

He groaned. "You're not playing fair."

"Nope."

His fingers tickled as they circled my hips and met at the base of my spine. The weight anchored me against his body.

Crystal beads teased faded denim. Soft curves teased hard angles. As his touch skimmed lower, it was my turn to groan.

"Marry me," he said against my cheek. "Not because your papa is forcing you or because you need a sperm donor. Marry me because you love me. Marry me because I loved you when the world had billions of women and I love you now. You've always been my only one."

"Mmm… an interesting side bet." I grinned a wicked smile he couldn't see. His proposal was flattering and would've had my full attention if he wasn't so damn touchable.

Using my teeth and my tongue, I went exploring. The stubble along his jawline was rough against my mouth. I clawed at the collar of his shirt and felt his pulse thrum against my lips. Kissing my way up, I nuzzled his ear and the sensitive skin behind it.

"So what do you say, Queen Mirari Vega?" He shuddered when my kisses became tiny bites. "Will you marry me?"

"Nope," I said again. "But I'll be your Vice President."

THE TIE THAT BINDS

Two Hours Later

JOSE KISTO CLIMBED the ladder again. This was his fourth trip onto the roof in as many hours. He was relaxed as he moved, scaling the old clapboard like a cat and avoiding the soft spots where the rafters were rotten. When the winds were calm, his TV antenna could've pick up KDJO out of Phoenix with a crystal-clear picture. Today wasn't one of those days.

"We've got the only snow in the Sonoran Desert." He had to shout to be heard over the generator. "Too bad it's on our TV."

"Ha, ha," his kid called through an open window.

Jose rotated the antenna with light taps. The difference between a strong signal and snow could be less than an inch. "How is it now?"

"Fuzzy."

Tap. Tap. "How about now?" he asked.

"Still fuzzy."

Tap. "Now?"

"Wait. Maybe… um… yes. We've got a picture."

"Is it rolling?"

"No, the vertical hold is holding."

"Got it," he yelled. "I'm comin' down."

He backed away from the antenna with his hands in the air, afraid to bump it or even breathe on it. Metal rods jutted in every direction from a central pole anchored to the chimney. It looked like an ugly clothesline to him, but the dealer at the warehouse called it "the Cadillac of remote viewing."

"Look at this beauty here," the man had said, standing the thing up to its full height. "She's tall enough to receive alien broadcasts from Mars."

Jose didn't believe him, but he bought the antenna anyway and hauled it down Highway 347 under the cover of darkness. This was the newest piece of equipment he owned. Heck, this was the newest piece of equipment for miles around.

In a ghost town, that was nothing to brag about.

Buzzard City had never been as prosperous as Goldfield or Jerome… their closest ghost town neighbors. Only one structure remained standing, and he was climbing on its roof. Back when the mine ran two shifts, this building housed a general store. The sign over the front porch was faded, difficult to read as the sun went down and impossible to read at night.

Buzzard City had no lights. No electricity. No nothin' and he was fine with that.

"Hurry, Dad. You're gonna miss Uncle Ruthie."

"I could hear his blasted voice from the roof," he said as he walked through the door.

The volume knob broke years ago. Between the TV's spotty reception and its deafening noise, he didn't watch it much. That was fine, too. The news was depressing. But today was a special occasion… today the TV would run until the generator died.

He imagined what this gray picture would look like on a color television. The warehouse kept a few of them under lock and key. "For special customers," the salesman had said as he flipped one on. "These tubes are 38 percent brighter than any others on the market. It'd be the perfect thing for your new antenna. I can quote you a price."

"No, thanks. My set shows me everything I need to see."

And sure, he couldn't tell the color of Uncle Ruthie's suit, but he could tell it was shiny. He sipped from a canteen as he watched the black and white screen. The water was warm, but he'd never complain. They had a deep, clean well in the backyard—a daily miracle in the middle of a desert.

"If the TV signal holds for at least five minutes, I'll join you on the couch," he said and wiped his mouth. "Where's he at now?"

"He said 1100 Congress Avenue… wherever that is."

"You think he's got the queen? She really hightailed it out of that barn."

"I wouldn't have run away. I would've demanded piles of gold and become their ruler—"

Uncle Ruthie interrupted them. "Men of the world, thank you for joining us on this historic evening. We are broadcasting live from the steps of the former Texas State Capitol building. And with us is Queen Mirari Vega."

Someone jostled him from behind. "Back up," Uncle Ruthie said and threw an elbow. "Give her some room."

A line of men in matching suits parted and Mirari stepped forward. When the spotlight hit her gown, circular flares danced across the TV screen. Jose squinted until a second camera went live. This one had a wide angle, showing her face and a sandstone pillar that arched above her.

"Look Dad, she's not wearing her crown."

"Maybe it was giving her a headache," he said.

Uncle Ruthie put an arm around her shoulders before he continued. "Please remember, this isn't a press conference. The queen will not answer questions. She wishes to make a statement and that is all. Remain quiet until the end." With a slight bow, he gave her the long, skinny microphone and moved out of the shot.

She clutched a piece of paper in her hand but didn't read from it. The mic trembled against her mouth. Jose leaned forward to listen, expecting her voice to be as shaky as the rest of her.

"Uncle Ruthie welcomed the men of the world. I am here to welcome the women of the world." Tears glittered in young woman's eyes, but her words were strong. "I am not your queen. I'm a survivor... just like you. Your hiding place is different than mine. Your story is different than mine and yet our next chapter will be the same. We will step out of the shadows. We will lift our heads and be counted.

"I beg you to keep the faith. There is so much work to be done, but with the friends standing next to me, the Republic of Texas will rise again." She looked off camera, giving someone a wide smile before she continued. "This land will welcome any woman who needs a home and a chance to live free and unafraid. Please pray for that day to come quickly. And may God bless you, my sweet sister, until we meet face-to-face."

Jose lunged for the television. He smacked the power button like a mosquito and couldn't look away as the face on the screen dissolved into a single, glowing dot. The generator continued to rattle outside, burning fuel he shouldn't waste, but he was too thunderstruck to turn around.

He was furious with the roof, the antenna, the TV—and he was furious with himself. He was the fool who let hope into his house, practically inviting that damn monster to sit on his couch. Hope could give a girl courage. Hope could whisper dangerous ideas in her ear and promise a future that died in the past. He'd given up everything to protect her. And now...

"I've never been to Texas," his daughter said. "Is it a long drive, Dad?"

AUTHOR'S NOTE

I hope you enjoyed Freezing Reign. The idea for this book began at my high school cafeteria table. Over a nutritious meal of cheese puffs and diet soda, we debated the pros and cons of being the only woman left on the planet. It was a discussion that captured my imagination.

By the end of lunch, my "Oh yeah, millions of guys would want me" became "Oh no, millions of guys would want me."

If you paid more attention in Anatomy class than I did, please forgive the liberties I took with the female body. I wrapped science around my little finger in order to tell this story. On the subject of estrogen, medical studies report that women are less likely to develop acute septic shock than men. Research also shows that estrogen can inhibit the spread of viruses. So yes, girl power starts at the cellular level.

I welcome your feedback and value your reviews. Please visit goffreads.com for the latest information on the release of Acid Reign… the next story in this series. Until then, stay well and God bless.

ACKNOWLEDGEMENTS:

Thank you to the wonderful team who made this book happen including Terri Valentine at Writers Digest, Copy Editor Chris Barcellona, Proofreader Lindsay Bagnall, Damonza for the beautiful cover and layout, and the army of beta readers who have me honest feedback. I appreciate each one of you.

And finally, thank you to Bruce Springsteen and the E Street Band. I couldn't write a love letter to the past without celebrating its music. Your song titles set the tone for each chapter with perfect pitch.